ChangelingPress.com

Bear/Grimm Duet

A Dixie Reapers Bad Boys Romance

Harley Wylde

Bear/Grimm Duet

A Dixie Reapers Bad Boys Romance

Harley Wylde

ISBN: 978-1-60521-867-0

Publisher:
Changeling Press LLC
315 N. Centre St.
Martinsburg, WV 25404
ChangelingPress.com

Printed in the U.S.A.

Editor: Crystal Esau
Cover Artist: Bryan Keller

The individual stories in this anthology have been previously released in E-Book format.

Table of Contents

Bear (Hades Abyss MC 9)
A Dixie Reapers Bad Boys Romance
Harley Wylde

Faith -- I fell for Spade when I was only sixteen. He got me pregnant and moved me into a house with him. Then I saw his true colors. He beat me. Made me lose my baby. It's been eighteen years and I'm still trapped, until I find the courage to take my girls and run. I didn't count on finding another biker. This one seems different. He's kinder. Gentler. And I think he may be just what we need.

Bear -- No sooner do I tell my Pres I want to retire from the position of Sergeant-at-Arms than I catch a teenage girl shoplifting. I followed her. Banged on the motel door, ready to tell the parents they'd f**ked up. Then a cute little pixie opened the door, and I knew I was a goner. Now they're living in my house, I've given them my name, and I'll do whatever it takes to keep them safe. Even take out another club.

Prologue

Faith

The smell woke me before anything else. Stale cigarettes, beer, and cheap perfume. It seemed Spade had enough of the clubhouse and had come home. Lucky me. I didn't dare move, or give him any hint he'd woken me. I heard him stumble around and bump into things, then the thump of his boots hitting the floor. By the time he'd undressed and fallen into bed, tension filled every muscle in my body, and I was ready to bolt if necessary.

Within minutes of him falling into bed, I heard the first snore. I breathed a sigh of relief and forced myself to relax. It seemed he'd had too much to drink. As much as I hated him driving here intoxicated, I was also grateful he'd passed out. It meant I didn't have to deal with his bullshit.

If I'd known he was part of a motorcycle club called the Raging Demons, I'd have never gone on that first date. Instead, he'd lured me in with his charm and good looks. I'd paid the price for so long. One stupid mistake led to years of abuse and suffering at his hands. I hated him. Not just him. His entire club. They were all cheating assholes who took out their anger on whatever person was handy. Didn't matter if that ended up being their girlfriend, kid, or an innocent bystander. They made me sick.

And I'd been stuck with him for years.

At sixteen, I'd thought I knew everything. People warned me away from Spade, and I hadn't listened. They'd called him an outlaw. A bad seed. Said he ran with a rough crowd. It had thrilled me that an older guy liked me. Until I discovered he'd knocked me up. He'd forced me to drop out of high school, saying he'd take care of us. While he'd made sure I had food to eat, a car to drive, and a roof over my head, it hadn't been worth the hefty price.

No more. At thirty-four, I'd found my courage. Or maybe I'd finally just had enough of Spade and the Raging Demons. I'd planned to run tonight. The fact he'd come home wrecked my plans. I'd have to suffer through his presence a little while longer. He'd likely go back to the clubhouse tomorrow, or maybe the day after. Once I knew he was gone and not coming right back, I'd make my move. I'd been setting aside some cash. Had a bag stuffed with fake IDs, the keys to an old car, and clothes for me and the kids. Everything we'd need to start over, far from here.

I'd felt so stupid. I wasn't even the one who'd come up with this plan. No, that honor went to my courageous daughter, Piper. She might only be sixteen, but she had a strength I'd never possessed. She'd done her research and found a way for us to leave. A woman she knew at the hospital, one who had treated our wounds one too many times not to become suspicious, had helped with the identification, stash of money, and the car.

If I'd been smart, I'd have left long before I had children. No, I'd have never dated him to begin with. When I told him about our first baby, he'd seemed happy. I'd dropped out, moved into this house with him, and then the abuse started. He'd sent me tumbling down the stairs one night, and I'd lost our baby. If that hadn't happened, Piper would have had an older brother. Looking back, I wondered if Spade had done it on purpose. He wouldn't have liked having another man in the house, even if it was his son.

After Piper, I'd had another miscarriage, also a

boy. Her sister, Cordelia, wasn't born for several more years. Even still, at twelve, she understood far more than she should have. I'd had another miscarriage after Cordy. Another boy. The doctor said I shouldn't have more children and cautioned me against getting pregnant again. I'd gotten on birth control pills, except I'd gotten sick and had to take antibiotics.

It figured Spade would want sex during that time. The pills had been rendered useless, and I'd gotten pregnant again. The child in my belly now would be another casualty of Spade's jealousy and anger if I didn't escape. I didn't know for certain if I'd carry the baby to term, but I refused to let the wretched man hurt another of our children. Even though I was only fourteen weeks pregnant, the doctor felt certain during the ultrasound my baby was a boy. I'd known then I needed to leave. The moment Spade realized I was pregnant with another boy, it would all be over. I couldn't let him kill another of our children.

I mentally went over everything I'd gathered, and how we'd get to the car stashed in a parking lot a mile away. I didn't have a destination in mind. I just knew I needed to get as far from Spade and the Raging Demons as I possibly could. Whatever it took, I'd keep my children safe. I refused to lose another one, especially since the doctor said this would likely be my last. If this baby didn't make it, I wouldn't have the chance to have another.

Just a little more time… soon, we'd be free from this hell, and we'd never look back.

The door opened slowly, and I peered into the hallway. Piper pressed her finger to her lips as she glared at her dad snoring next to me. She crept into the room, silent as a mouse, and kneeled beside the bed.

"Cordy is sick," she whispered. "She has a fever.

A bad one."

I nodded. Maybe we could make a run for it after all. As much as I didn't want to use my daughter's illness as a means of escape, it couldn't be helped. If I stayed until she recovered, we might lose our chance to get away for quite a while. Not to mention, it meant I'd risk Spade figuring out the baby was a boy. The doctor had printed a picture from the ultrasound, and while I'd hidden it, Spade always had a knack for finding things. It amazed me he hadn't discovered my little stash so far. If he had, I'd likely be dead by now. He wasn't the type of man to let someone walk out on him.

"I'll write your dad a note and we'll take her to the hospital," I whispered back, then winked at her, so she'd know it was time to leave and not come back. She gave me a nod, her jaw tightening. I saw the resolve on her face and knew she was ready to get out of here.

I eased off the bed. Once I stood, I paused. Spade stopped snoring. I stared at him, my heart racing, and realized he was staring me down.

"Where the fuck you going?" he asked, his words slurring.

"Cordelia is running a high fever. I need to take her to the ER. Get some rest. You know those doctors take forever. We'll likely be gone a few hours."

He grunted. "Better have breakfast on the table in the morning."

I nodded. "I will. Promise. Just need to get her some medicine so she'll sleep and get better. You know if I don't, she'll cry and keep you up all night."

"Fine." He rolled over and almost immediately started snoring again.

I didn't dare take any extra time. I changed as

quickly as I could, grabbed what we needed, and hustled the girls into the car. I'd originally planned to leave it at the house, but I couldn't now. I didn't dare chance him coming out when he didn't hear the engine turn over. Instead, I'd stash it within walking distance of the parking garage, then we'd switch to the other vehicle.

It wasn't until the neighborhood was a speck in the distance I finally loosened my white-knuckled grip on the steering wheel. I glanced at Piper and saw her scanning our surroundings.

"We'll ditch the car in a minute and walk to the other one. I know your sister needs medical attention, but we'll have to stop along the way. Preferably in the next state and using our new IDs. I'm just not sure we have enough cash to cover an ER visit." I worried at my bottom lip. "Maybe one of those emergency clinics? We can find one along the way."

"Cordy will be fine, Mom. You know she'd rather get the hell away from that asshole, no matter what it takes."

I nodded. Yeah, I knew. We all felt the same way, and now our dreams were coming true. I wouldn't rest until we had lots of miles between us and the Raging Demons. Only then would I allow myself the hope we could have a new start. I'd at least stop at a pharmacy for some over-the-counter pain reliever and fever reducer. It might help keep her comfortable until I could get her to a doctor.

"We've got this, Mom," Piper said.

"I know." I reached over and took her hand. "You've been so brave and resourceful. If it weren't for you, we wouldn't be able to escape. I'm sorry I've been such a horrible mom. I should have never stayed with him, but if I didn't, then I wouldn't have you, Cordelia, or your little brother. And I adore all of you."

"We love you too, Mom. Just get us out of here."

We parked the car and made our way to the one the nurse had purchased and stashed in the parking garage. By the time the sun was rising over the horizon, I was barely awake and knew we needed to stop for a while. I bypassed any large cities and pulled off when I saw a sign advertising a small town. It looked like they had a few places to eat, two gas stations, and one motel. I didn't think Spade would try to find us here if he even figured out which direction we went. We'd made it out of state at the very least, so I felt marginally better about stopping for a bit.

For that matter, he might wake up, realize we were gone, and go celebrate the fact he no longer had a bunch of women costing him money.

I could hope at any rate.

Then again, he'd always threatened to kill me if I left him. He didn't love me. Barely tolerated the girls. I didn't know why he made us stay unless it made him feel powerful. Or perhaps he didn't want to lose his favorite punching bag. I'd never know, because I wouldn't see that man again. I'd run as far as I had to, as long as he couldn't find us.

Chapter One

Bear

I stared at my phone and the message I'd just sent to Fox, my club's President. Aside from Spider, our previous President, I was the oldest living member in my chapter of the Hades Abyss MC, and I was feeling every one of my sixty-eight years. My bones creaked more often than not. My brown hair had gone silver. While I still kept in shape, I couldn't maintain the definition I had in my younger days. Which meant it was time…

Need a new SAA. Time for me to retire.

He'd read the message two minutes ago. I still hadn't received a reply or a phone call. I'd thought I would get at least one of those, if not both. That told me one of two things. He was either ignoring me in the hopes I'd forget about retiring, or he was just too damn busy to deal with it right now. Now that he had a family, he didn't always drop what he was doing to answer the phone. And that was fine. Raven and their daughter, Harlow, deserved every bit of attention he could give them.

I put my helmet on the seat of my bike and went into the corner market. I'd given up cigarettes and beer, but there was one thing they'd have to pry from my cold dead fingers -- jerky! I didn't indulge as often as I used to, but I still got a taste for it once or twice a month. Today happened to be one of those days.

The bell over the door jingled as I stepped into the cool interior. Scanning the area, I clocked a teen girl two aisles over, an older man at the back, and a young couple at the register. Making my way down the center aisle, I checked out the jerky options and grabbed a package.

The teen girl shifted from foot to foot and kept casting glances around the store. The clerk hadn't noticed anything was wrong. Yet. I hoped she didn't do something stupid. Then again, teens were notorious for making bad choices. Looked like this one wouldn't be any different. The second she thought no one was watching, she shoved a few things under her shirt and made a beeline for the front door. She actually made it into the parking lot, and I shook my head.

"Just what I fucking need," I muttered. I held up the package of jerky for the clerk to see and tossed some money onto the counter. More than enough to cover the price. "Keep the change."

I went after the girl, keeping her in my sights. As much as I wanted to get on my bike to follow her, the Harley Davidson Freewheel wasn't exactly a quiet bike. And yeah, I'd gotten a damn trike. The club had given me shit about it when I traded in my Street King, but I was getting too damn old for this shit. The trike put less strain on me, and I still got to ride with my club.

The girl left the parking lot and headed down the sidewalk. The longer I followed, the more I wished I'd taken my bike. When she went into a room at the local motel, I decided to give her a minute or two, then see if her parents knew she'd been shoplifting. Although, this place was a goddamn dump. There was a good chance she'd been following orders. Most people here were either drug addicts or prostitutes.

I knocked on the door and heard a hesitant, "Who is it?"

"Need to talk to the parents of the girl who just went into this room."

I heard a *thunk* and a deep sigh. I wondered if the person on the other side had just banged their head on the door. The rattle of the chain let me know someone was about to open the door. I backed up a step so I wouldn't scare whoever was on the other side. A petite woman with a gently rounded stomach opened the door. Dark circles under her eyes told me she hadn't slept in a while. Not well, at any rate.

"Ma'am." I gave her a nod. She blinked at me, then her gaze dropped to my cut. Her face paled, and she swayed. Figured she'd have that reaction. People either loved us or we scared the shit out of them. I held up a hand. "Easy. I'm not here to hurt you."

"We don't want any trouble," she said, her fingers tightening on the door.

"The girl who just entered this room stole some stuff from a store down the street. I wanted to make sure her parents were aware of the situation."

The woman closed her eyes and her shoulders slumped. "Piper, did you steal something? Is he telling the truth?"

Holy. Shit. *This* woman was her mother? No fucking way. Older sister, maybe, but mom? The girl in question appeared behind her mom, and as I looked into the room, I saw another girl on the bed. Sweat coated her little face, and her cheeks were pink. Fever?

"Everything all right, ma'am?" I asked. "The three of you in trouble of some kind?"

The teen, Piper, narrowed her eyes at me. "We're fine. The last thing we need is another biker in our lives."

My eyebrows shot up. Interesting. *Another biker.* I had so many questions and not enough answers. In fact, they hadn't willingly told me a damn thing yet. Everything I'd learned had merely been from observation.

"Did you steal something?" her mom asked,

sounding exhausted.

"Cordy needs soup. The kind we can microwave. You said our money would be gone after tomorrow." Piper folded her arms. "If we're about to be living out of the car, I wanted to make sure she had something to eat first."

Motherfucker. I couldn't walk away and leave these girls in a dire situation. My club would kick my ass if I did. Hell, I'd kick my own ass.

"I know we're strangers, but I'd like to help. My name is Bear and I'm part of the Hades Abyss MC here in town. We're kind of known for helping women and children in need. You can ask around if you'd like."

"In need." Piper rolled her eyes. "That's one way of putting it. So you expect us to believe you'd help us out of the goodness of your heart? Nothing in this life is free."

Seemed like the girls had a bad experience with another club. Or maybe… I eyed the pregnant one again. "Your man around?"

I hadn't thought it was possible, but she paled even more. Yep. That cinched it. Whatever trouble these three had found, it had to do with a biker. I fucking hated the assholes who gave the rest of us a bad name.

"No, he's not," Piper said, inching closer. "Why? You going to call him? Tell him where we are? Because we're not going back! I won't let him kill another of my brothers, or beat the hell out of my mom ever again!"

The girl was screaming by the time she'd finished, and the mother looked like she wanted to run as far as she could. I pulled out my phone and called Fox. At least the fucker answered this time.

"I don't want to hear about retirement," Fox mumbled.

"Not callin' for that. There's a woman and her two daughters who need some help. Need permission to bring them back with me."

"Fine, but I don't have a place to put them right now. So if you bring them here, they're bunking with you." Fox hung up before I got a chance to respond.

"The younger one is sick?" I asked.

"Yes," the mother answered, glancing at her daughter on the bed. "I thought I'd have enough money to get her to the doctor, but the motel is going to eat up all our funds. I'm sorry Piper shoplifted. As soon as I figure out our finances, I promise to pay the store back for the soup she took."

"No need. I'll pay them when I go back for my bike. Right now, I need you to load up into your car and drive me back to my bike. Then you're going to follow me to the compound."

"Why would we do that?" Piper asked. "What if you're just trying to lure us there to be used as club whores?"

I blinked and stared at her for a moment. "One, I won't lie and say we don't have those because we do. Two, I don't ever want to hear you talk about them again. It's not a topic meant for someone your age. Those women are there of their own free will. No one forces them to show up. So don't go talkin' about things you don't understand."

"Mom, we can't trust him," Piper said. "We can't trust any of them. What if they're like Dad?"

So their daddy *was* the biker they were running from. Just what kind of shithead had the little woman hooked up with? And why the hell had she stayed with him for so long? Unless…

"You his old lady?" I asked.

Her eyes went wide, and she shook her head.

"No. We were never married, and he kept us away from his club."

"Which club?" I asked.

"Raging Demons." She licked her lips. "My ex-boyfriend's name is Spade. And my daughter is right. He hurt me, killed my babies before they could be born, and we won't go back to him. I refuse."

I forced myself not to tense up. Raging Demons? How the hell had this little thing gotten involved with them? Thankfully, they didn't have a chapter in the state of Missouri. Seemed this crew had been on the run long enough to at least cross the state line. Didn't mean the fucker wouldn't come looking for them.

"Honey, I'm not going to make you go back. But I do want you and the girls to get in your car, take me to my bike, and we're going to figure out your situation. You can't stay here. Not if you're about to run out of money. And that little one needs medical attention."

"You'll take her to the doctor?" Piper asked.

"Even better. I'll have him to come to us. I'm sure Dr. Briar can be persuaded to make a house call."

"We should go, Mom," Piper said. "Cordy needs medicine."

Seemed like it hadn't taken much to change her tune. She'd been ready to fight to keep me away from her family. Something told me she was a good kid. If they hadn't been desperate, I didn't think she'd have stolen the soup.

The mom stared at me. "My name is Faith. My daughters are Piper and Cordelia, and if you're willing to help us, then I'll trust you. For now."

I couldn't help but smile. The woman knew when to let someone help her, but she wasn't going into this completely blind either. For now, she'd see what happened. If I put so much as a toe out of line, I had a feeling I'd see her inner mama bear come roaring out. I'd take them home and get them settled. The girls could share a room, and the mom could take my bed. I'd sleep on the couch until I could clear out the other bedrooms and get some more beds. It wasn't like I ever had company.

I'd be willing to bet they all needed food and sleep.

I didn't know much about the Raging Demons, except they had a horrible reputation. I hoped someone in the club would be able to tell me more. Whoever this Spade was, I needed to make sure he never got his hands on this family again. They'd suffered enough. What the hell kind of man killed his own children and beat his pregnant girlfriend? A coward, bully, and all-around dickhead who needed his ass kicked. That's who.

If that motherfucker ever showed his face in this town, I'd make sure he drew his last breath. These girls didn't need to live their lives looking over their shoulders. I wanted them to find peace. To be happy.

Shit. Something told me I'd just fallen prey to the same curse that took down Spider, Rocket, Slider, and Fox. A damsel in distress. My club's fucking kryptonite.

I was so fucking screwed right now.

* * *

Faith

We dropped the biker off at the store, and I watched as he went inside. My cheeks burned when I'd recalled saying something about paying for the soup Piper stole. My debt to him would grow with every passing day, but I couldn't say no to the chance for Cordy to see a doctor.

He came back out and got on his bike. We followed behind him to the Hades Abyss compound. While I didn't know if we should trust him, I didn't see what other choice we had. Little Cordelia needed medical attention and time to rest, and I was out of money. The motel might be falling apart, but they'd still charged me over one hundred per night. I hadn't had much to begin with. Between the gas to reach this town, and our first night here, half my money had been gone.

I hadn't been able to get Cordelia to a clinic, as everyone I called wanted payment up front. I could understand. They didn't want to provide treatment without knowing they'd get paid. It made sense, even if it meant my little girl had to suffer. I could have gone to the ER, but I knew that the bill would be even higher. Not to mention, I didn't like the idea of leaving a paper trail for Spade to follow.

As much as I wanted to scold Piper for stealing the soup, it had brought Bear to our door, and we needed him right now. I didn't like the idea of owing him anything, and I wasn't sure I could trust a biker. I just didn't have any other options right now.

"I'm sorry I stole stuff," Piper muttered.

"Just don't do it again, all right?"

"You really think he's any different from Dad?"

I nodded. Even though he'd scared me at first, the more I'd looked at him, I realized he wasn't anything like my ex. I'd seen kindness and concern in his eyes. He hadn't raised his voice even once, and when he'd helped me to the car, his touch had been gentler than Spade's ever had. I couldn't guess his age, but I knew he was a lot older than me. His hair and beard were completely silver.

At the same time, I knew he could also be faking it. There was a slight chance he was acting nice so he could lure us in. I'd try to stay on my guard. Fatigue pulled at me, and I didn't know how much longer I'd remain upright. I hadn't had more than an hour or two of sleep before Spade came home, then we'd been on the run. The two nights we'd stayed at the motel, I'd slept with one eye open after seeing the sort of people who stayed there. I'd even noticed a drug deal going down in broad daylight.

We pulled through the gates behind Bear, and he rode down the winding road. We were quite a way from the clubhouse, which I appreciated once he stopped. I tried to hide my surprise when he parked in front of a rather ordinary-looking house. Gray brick with dark red shutters and a matching door. It didn't seem to fit the tough-looking biker at all. The house was... cute. He even had some shrubs out front that gave the place a homey feel.

Bear came over to the car and opened the back door, lifting Cordelia into his arms. He carried her as if she weighed nothing at all, even though I knew her to be quite heavy. Piper and I followed him. When he pushed open the door and stepped into the house, my breath caught. I'd never lived in a place as nice as this one, and I envied him just then.

Exposed beams ran across the ceiling of the living room. The hardwood floors were clean and well-kept. Even his furniture looked like it cost more than any place I'd ever lived. Piper shut the door behind us, and I saw the awe in her eyes. I wasn't the only one impressed.

"There's only two bedrooms set up right now," Bear said. "The girls can have the spare room. You can have my bed."

Piper sputtered behind me. "You expect her to sleep with you in exchange for your help? I should have known better! You're just like the others."

Bear stopped mid-step and looked at her over his shoulder. He arched an eyebrow. "I don't recall saying I'd be in the bed with her. I think you and I need to have a talk. The lack of respect you show your elders is appalling."

Piper's cheeks flushed, and so did mine. As her mother, I should have stopped her before she got carried away. She'd gotten so used to saying what she wanted whenever her dad wasn't around. I hoped she didn't pay the price for it. At least he hadn't kicked us out right then and there. I wouldn't have blamed him.

Bear went into a bedroom on the right and eased Cordelia down onto the bed. He took a quilt out of the closet and settled it over her. Tears pricked my eyes when I realized my daughter's father had never done such a thing for her. Who was this man? Did he really not expect anything in return? I hadn't realized men like him existed in this world, especially one who was a biker.

"Should we call the doctor now?" I asked.

"I did it already."

My brow furrowed. "When? I haven't seen you use the phone."

A slight smile curved his lips. "Bluetooth. I'm old, but I'm not a fossil. Called on the way here."

I placed my hand over my mouth to stifle the snort of my laughter. Sure, he was an older guy, but I'd have never accused him of living when the dinosaurs roamed the earth. He was too sexy for that.

Why did I think he was sexy? My eyes widened, and I pressed my lips together. I couldn't recall when I'd last found a man attractive. Probably Spade, before

I'd gotten pregnant. Once I'd seen his true colors, I'd found him to be downright hideous. Not once had I felt a spark for anyone else. Until now.

"We should get our stuff from the car if we're staying here," Piper said. "What about the motel? We didn't check out."

"I'll have someone handle it," Bear said.

"So, what are we supposed to do now?" Piper asked.

Bear pointed to the living room. "You go sit. We're going to have a chat about your attitude, the shoplifting, and set a few ground rules."

I leaned down to kiss Cordelia on the forehead, then followed Piper from the room. When Bear placed his hand on my lower back to guide me over to the couch, my heart skipped a beat. Why did his touch make me feel weird? Butterflies swooped around in my stomach, and my hands trembled. Not once had Spade ever made me feel like this. No one had, for that matter.

I sank onto the couch and Piper took the spot next to me. Bear folded his arms and stood in front of us, staring down at my daughter. She fidgeted, and I fought back the urge to defend her. She'd been a good girl, and I knew she'd only taken the soup because she'd been worried about her sister. I'd failed as their mom, more than once. What if the clerk caught her? She could have gone to jail, or maybe things would have gone horribly wrong and she'd ended up dead.

"While you're living here, there will be rules," Bear said.

"What kind of rules?" Piper asked, tipping her chin up at a stubborn angle.

"First, respect your elders. Me, your mother, and anyone else here more than a few years older than you."

Piper leaned back against the cushions. "Fine. I can do that."

"Second, stay away from the clubhouse unless I've mentioned it's a family day. If there's a party going on, I don't want you anywhere near the place. Got it?"

She snorted. "Don't worry. I respect myself too much to become a club whore."

He pointed a finger at her. "And that right there is rule number three. You watch your mouth. You're not an adult yet, so don't go around actin' like one."

"Got it," she said, her posture relaxing even more.

I'd expected her to balk, but Piper surprised me. If anything, I thought she almost liked the man giving her orders. Had she craved more discipline from me all this time? Maybe I'd treated her too much like a grown-up the last year or two. I'd relied on her heavily, when she should have had time to hang out with friends and be a kid.

Great. Now I felt like the worst mother on the planet.

"I appreciate you helping us," I said, standing. "Piper normally wouldn't do something like shoplift. She's a good girl. They both are, and I'm not just saying that because I'm their mom."

Bear's gaze softened as he looked at me. "When you opened the door, I figured you were her older sister. Don't look old enough to be a mom to those two."

My cheeks burned. "I was eighteen when I had Piper."

"And she was sixteen when my dad knocked her up the first time." Piper narrowed her eyes at Bear again. I had a feeling those two were going to butt heads often, or my protective girl was going to get us all kicked out of here. "Asshole found out she was having a boy and threw her down a flight of stairs."

"I'll let your language slide that time, because I'd have to agree… any man who'd do something like that is an asshole." Bear came closer, and I flinched when he reached up to tuck my hair behind my ear. Then I felt bad. He didn't deserve that reaction. "Sweetheart, it's clear you've been through hell. You and your girls. You stay as long as you need to, and I'll help however I can. You'll be safe here."

"If you really want to help, you can make sure my dad can't ever get his hands on us again." Piper stood. "I'm going back to the room with Cordy."

I cleared my throat after she left and shifted on my feet. My daughter kept putting me in an awkward position with this man, and we'd just met him. "Piper had to grow up fast. We never knew when Spade would stop by, or how long he'd stay. He provided the house for us, and money for food. She learned early on, he wasn't good for much else. I don't remember him hugging her, tucking her into bed, or doing anything a father should do."

"You stayed out of fear," he said.

I nodded. "Until now. I found out this baby is a boy. Spade killed every one of our sons before they were born. I couldn't live through that again, especially since the doctor said this will probably be my last pregnancy. He'd recommended I not have more kids after the last miscarriage."

"Birth control failed?"

I didn't know how he'd guessed. I liked that he didn't assume I'd gotten pregnant on purpose, despite what the doctor said. People had accused me, more than once, of getting pregnant so many times so I could get a check from the government. Except I didn't get a dime from Uncle Sam. If Spade's money couldn't pay for what we needed, we went without. I made sure the girls had food and clean clothes. Everything else sorted itself out. Since Spade did come home from time to time, he made sure we had cable and Internet. The only nice thing he'd done for Piper was give her a laptop he'd gotten on sale last Christmas.

"I got sick. The antibiotics made the pill useless. It was one of the times Spade decided to come home, and I found out four weeks later I was pregnant."

"I meant what I said to your daughter. I want you to have my room. You're pregnant and need a decent night's sleep. You won't get that sleepin' on the couch." He moved in even closer, and I breathed in his spicy scent. Whatever cologne he wore, I wanted to close my eyes and lose myself in it. "You're safe now, Faith. I won't let your ex get his hands on any of you."

"Thank you." I wondered if he knew exactly how much all this meant to me. To us. I couldn't remember the last time I'd felt like I didn't need to sleep with one eye open. Probably before I moved in with Spade. As much as I didn't want to kick the man out of his bed, I was grateful for a place to sleep. One where I could really rest and not worry about the girls.

I'd find a way to pay him back. Whatever it took.

"Piper's right about one thing. We need to make sure your ex doesn't come for you. Is there any way he could track you here?" Bear asked.

"I don't think so. I didn't bring my cell phone with me. Piper's never had one. The car isn't even in my name. A nurse paid cash for it and let me have it as a way to escape from Spade."

"No other electronics?" he asked. I hesitated a

moment. I honestly didn't know if Piper had brought her laptop or not. It was about the only thing of value she had, so it was possible she'd grabbed it. "You're not sure. What could he use to track you?"

"My daughter has a laptop, but I don't know if she packed it. Piper got it for Christmas last year."

"I'll ask her. Then I'm going to get you a phone, and don't argue. It's not safe for you to run around while you're pregnant and not have a way to reach out to anyone if you run into trouble."

"Thank you, Bear. I can't tell how much all this means to me."

He hesitated a moment, a strange look crossing his face. "Call me Charlie."

"Charlie?" I asked.

"It's my name. Well, technically it's Charles. When the rest of the club is around, I'm Bear. But here at home? You can call me Charlie."

My cheeks warmed again. "All right. Charlie."

Spade had never told me his real name. He'd refused to sign the birth certificates for our daughters. How sad was it I'd lived with a man for eighteen years and never known his real name? What the hell was wrong with me?

Chapter Two

Bear

Why the hell had I given her my real name? I shook my head. I knew better. Then again, I hadn't asked anyone to call me that in decades. Hell, I'd probably been her age or younger the last time I used my real name.

I'd gotten Piper's laptop from her and carried it over to Surge's house. He'd made sure Spade wouldn't be able to use it to find the girls, then gave it back to me. I hadn't wanted to keep it from Piper any longer than necessary, although Surge had muttered something about it being a cheap piece of crap. I refrained from running out to buy a new one for Piper, even though it was tempting.

I didn't think Faith would accept an expensive phone, so I added her to my phone plan and picked one of the free options. It was probably still nicer than what she expected. I had the tech guy set it up, then I added in my number, as well as the other club officers and a few of the old ladies. Something told me they'd be stopping by once they learned about Faith and the girls.

The doc's car was in the driveway when I got back, and I felt the tension ease from my shoulders. I had no doubt he'd get the youngest one back on her feet, and little Faith would be able to sleep better. She might be tiny, and it was clear Spade had beaten her down, but I still saw that mama bear glint in her eyes when it came to her girls.

The house seemed a little too quiet when I went inside. I set Piper's laptop down, as well as Faith's new phone. A low murmur of voices drew me down the hallway and I stopped in the guest room doorway. Dr.

Briar had his arms folded and a stern look on his face as he spoke with Faith. The slump of her shoulders had me fisting my hands and wanting to rush to her side. Whatever he said, it didn't seem like he had good news.

"What's going on?" I asked, entering the room.

Piper shot a glare at the doctor. "He's blaming Mom for Cordelia's condition. Basically called her an unfit mother. He has no idea what we've been through!"

I placed my hands on Faith's shoulders and drew her back against me. The fact she let me told me enough. His words had hurt her, and I had a feeling she'd have crumpled if she weren't trying to be brave for her kids. Why the fuck was Briar being such an asshole?

"I'd have to agree with Piper. It's not like you to be so judgmental, Dr. Briar. I wouldn't have called you if I'd thought you'd react this way."

"The girl is malnourished. She clearly hasn't been getting healthy meals, or enough food. Her fever is 103.4, and she needed medical attention long before now. She's dehydrated on top of everything else."

I kissed Faith's temple before reaching for Dr. Briar. I fisted his lab coat in my hand and yanked him from the room, dragging him to the front of the house. When I opened the front door, I tossed him out, and followed. The sweet woman inside didn't need this bullshit!

"Bear, what the hell?" Dr. Briar straightened his coat.

"That woman and those girls have suffered for years at the hands of another club. She ran before her ex-boyfriend could put his hands on her again and kill another of their children. The choices she made were necessary, whether you want to see it that way or not. Then you accuse her of being a bad parent? Do you have any idea how close you are right now to me knockin' your damn teeth down your throat?"

Dr. Briar lifted a placating hand. "All I can do is treat what I see and observe. And that young girl should have seen a doctor a long time ago."

"Fuck you! Get the hell out of here and don't even think of coming back to this compound. We'll find another doctor." I took a step. Then another, drawing closer as the rage built inside me. "You dare enter *my* home and insult that sweet woman?"

I heard a whistle and glanced over at the house next door. Fox, Spider, and Hornet stood in the yard. The President glowered at Dr. Briar, and I knew he'd back me up.

"Dr. Briar, if you value your life, I suggest you do as he says and leave. Otherwise, I won't stop him when he starts swinging." Fox came over, leaving Hornet and Spider behind. We watched as the doc got into his car and sped toward the front of the compound. The Pres clapped me on the back. "So... introduce me to your new family."

"Who said I was claimin' them?" I asked. Fox stared me down. Unblinking. It always unnerved the fuck out of me when he did that shit. It was unnatural. "A biker hurt Faith. I think he abused the kids too."

"Not up for the challenge?" Fox asked.

"Don't want to traumatize them more than they already are," I said.

"I'll hold off for now, but I think they're yours, Bear. Never seen you so angry on behalf of a woman before. That combined with the fact you brought them home? Yeah, those girls are yours, whether you're ready to admit it or not." Fox smirked.

"Would that keep Mom safe?" I spun at the sound of Piper's voice and saw her a few feet away. "What he said about you claiming my mother… would it mean she'd be safe from my dad and his club?"

Fox cleared his throat when I didn't respond right away. I knew he wanted me to say yes. Truthfully, it would give her an added layer of protection. The girls too, especially if I had Surge work his mojo and make them mine legally -- illegally? Whatever. Anyone who went looking would think the files were legit. That's all that mattered.

"That's a conversation I'd need to have with your mother first, then you girls."

"Who's he?" Piper asked, jerking her chin toward Fox. I bit my lip so I wouldn't laugh. The move reminded me too much of just about every damn brother here. Yeah, a biker raised her. No getting around that. I just hoped she hadn't picked up all of her dad's bad habits as well.

"My name's Fox, and I'm the President of the Hades Abyss. The two men behind me are Spider and Hornet. Spider was the President before me, but he retired to spend more time with his family. And you are?"

"Piper." She lifted her chin, cast me a quick glance, then focused on Fox again before pointing at me. "And I'm his daughter."

And on that note, she left me slack-jawed as she turned and went back into the house. Fox nearly busted a gut, laughing so hard he doubled over. When he straightened, he wiped tears from his eyes.

"You're going to have your hands full with that one. Looks to me like you have a family, Papa Bear."

"Shut it, Pres. You go spoutin' that bullshit, and then everyone will start callin' me that."

"I'll get your woman a property cut. No sense taking this one to Church. Seems your kid has spoken." Fox snickered again. "I have a feeling things are about to get interesting around here."

"Did you just jinx the club?" I asked.

He sobered. "No. But if you're concerned about their sperm donor, I'll have Surge look into him and his club. Maybe we'll call in the other hackers too. We won't leave any stone unturned, and we'll make sure your girls are safe."

"Thanks, Pres."

Spider came over, a grin on his face. "Heard all that. Can't wait to meet them, officially. For now, how about I have a doctor come by?"

"You're sending Dread over, aren't you?" I asked.

"I am." Spider smiled. "No worries. He won't scare them. I'm sure that's why you didn't call him to begin with."

I shook my head and went inside. Faith stood in the hallway, her brow furrowed. I wondered if Piper had come in and told her about my discussion with Fox. This wasn't the way I'd wanted to handle this. I'd planned to build trust with her, keep her safe, eliminate the threat to her and the girls… and then I'd have asked her to stay with me permanently. It seemed Piper had other ideas.

"Piper just told Cordelia their dad would make sure Spade never hurt us again. I'm more than a little confused right now."

I pinched the bridge of my nose, then motioned for her to sit on the couch. "We need to talk."

Then I spent the next fifteen minutes telling her what happened outside and giving her the new phone. She hadn't said a word, and I worried what it might mean. The Pres seemed set on her being mine. If she asked to leave, I'd let her. Then my club would look at me like I was a fucking idiot who couldn't hold on to his woman. But so be it. I'd always put Faith and the girls first.

"What does it mean to be yours?" she asked softly.

"You'd be my old lady. Do the Raging Demons have any?"

"I don't really know," she said. "Spade kept me away from the club. I know we weren't exclusive. At least, not on his part. If I'd have been with anyone else, he'd likely have killed me, but I know he slept with the women at the clubhouse. Most nights, he didn't bother coming home. When he did, he smelled like cheap perfume and cigarettes. More often than not, he'd have lipstick smeared on him somewhere, or around his..."

She stopped mid-sentence, her cheeks flushing, and I filled in the rest. Ring around the cock. I snorted. Classy. I wondered if he'd done it on purpose. Was it another way for him to tear down Faith? Make her feel useless and unworthy of his attention? I wanted to beat the shit out of the asshole.

"Around here, it means you'd be mine. I'd be faithful to you and expect the same in return. It's like a marriage, but without all the paperwork. It also means you couldn't leave. In this club, when a man claims a woman, it's forever. No divorce or changin' your mind later. I'm afraid my President took that choice from you."

"Because of what Piper said?" she asked.

"Partly." I rubbed the back of my neck. "You're the first woman I've brought to this house. The fact I have you and the girls here is rather tellin' to my club. Not to mention I let you use my real name."

"That's something only an old lady would do?" she asked.

"Or a wife, but yeah."

Her cheeks warmed again, and she glanced away. "Does that mean we'll be sharing your bed after all?"

I reached and gripped her chin lightly, turning her to face me again. "If you want time to get to know me better, just say the word. I'll sleep on the couch and let you have the bed as originally planned."

"I'm... I'm not sure what I want," she said.

A knock sounded at the door, and I went to let Dread in. I introduced him to Faith, then held her hand as he checked on Cordelia. I felt a slight tremor in her hand, and knew it made her nervous to have another biker in the house. She'd learn to trust us. Our conversation would have to continue later. Right now, we had more important things going on. Like making sure our little girl would be okay.

Fuck me. Our little girl.

I'd analyze the way I felt later, but my heart warmed, and I wanted to smile at the mere thought of these girls being mine. I'd have to thank Piper for being so brash. It seemed she'd done me a huge favor by telling the Pres I was her daddy. Now I'd have what I really wanted -- a family. *My* family.

* * *

Faith

The club's doctor, Dread, wrote a prescription for Cordelia, and Piper took the car to pick it up at the local pharmacy. Bear called ahead and told them to put it on his account and he'd pay the next time he was in. I couldn't begin to describe the relief I felt over Cordy getting the care she'd needed. Thankfully, it was just an infection making the rounds. Some antibiotics and she'd be good as new. Until her fever broke, Dread said to keep giving her Ibuprofen, or to switch between that and Tylenol.

For dinner, we'd had pizza delivered, and I'd managed to get some chicken broth into Cordy. Now I lay in Bear's bed, staring at the ceiling. It had been one hell of a day, and exhaustion pulled at me. So why was I awake? Because I felt guilty. The man said he'd claimed us, after my daughter told his club President Bear was her father, and I'd asked him to sleep on the couch. I felt awful about it.

A quick glance at the bedside clock showed it was nearly midnight. Piper went to bed hours ago, and Cordy slept peacefully. I'd come in here three hours ago, intent on going to sleep. And here I lay, wide awake.

I knew what I needed to do.

I threw off the blankets and padded down the hallway. The living room remained silent. I crept over to the couch and peered down at Bear. His eyes were closed, and his chest rose and fell in deep, even breaths. Had he managed to fall asleep out here?

"Stop staring," he said softly. "Go to bed, Faith."

"You're awake?"

He opened his eyes. "Yes. The question is, why are you?"

I glanced away before holding his gaze again. "Um. The bed is really big."

"California King. I'm not exactly short. Needed the extra length."

"I think you, me, and both girls would fit in there with room to spare. My point is… we can share the bed."

"Told Piper I wouldn't touch you unless you

were ready."

I gasped, and my cheeks burned. "I didn't say I was ready now! Why can't we sleep in the same bed without sex being involved?"

"So you're inviting me to sleep in the same bed," he said. "No touching."

"Right."

"Fine. But if Piper has a fit in the morning, make sure she knows I'm in there by your invitation. I don't want to start off on the wrong foot with the girls."

"She likes you too much for that," I said. Bear stood and followed me down the hall, back to the bedroom. I lay down in the bed, pulling the covers over me, and shut my eyes. The other side of the mattress dipped when he got in, and I felt my body relax.

Why did I suddenly feel safer with him so close? We were strangers, and after my experience with Spade, I should have given any bikers a wide berth. Yet this one seemed different. I hoped I was right, because it seemed as if I was his. Forever. I still couldn't quite wrap my brain around what it meant to be his old lady.

Oh, God! I'd told him I couldn't have more kids. What if he decided he wanted one of his own?

"Woman, what the hell are you worrying about over there?" Bear mumbled.

"Nothing." He grunted, then rolled so he was facing me. I could tell he didn't believe me, and knew I'd need to say something. "I have two daughters and a son on the way. This is my last baby because of everything I suffered at Spade's hands. What if you want children of your own?"

He sighed and reached for me, tugging me closer. I went willingly and let him hold me. I had to admit, I loved the feel of his arms around me. For an older man, he'd kept in shape. He had more muscle than Spade ever had, and yet, his touch remained gentle. I didn't fear for my life like I had several times with Spade.

"These kids aren't just yours anymore. They're mine. And when this little one is born, I'm having my name put on the birth certificate. No one will ever question whether or not I'm the father of our children."

"But the girls..."

"Did Spade claim them?" he asked. "Is he listed as their dad?"

"No. I don't even know Spade's real name. He never told me in the eighteen years we were together. I thought it was just part of him being a biker until you shared your name with me."

"Then I'll ask Surge to hack into the vital records for your home state and add me to the birth certificates on both girls. They'll have my name. New social security cards too, and a driver's license for Piper." He hugged me closer. "And while I'm at it, I'll tell him to marry us. All four of you will have my last name. No one will ever take you from me. Understood?"

Tears pricked my eyes. "Yes, Charlie."

He kissed my forehead. "Good girl. Now get some sleep. I left the door partially open, so we'd hear the girls. I'll get up if Cordelia needs anything. Since Piper is with her, she shouldn't be too scared the first time she opens her eyes. You need to rest."

"As for me wanting kids of my own... the girls and this little one are a blessing. I can't have children. No one knows about it. The doctors say there's no way to know if my exposure to Agent Orange in the military could have caused it. The VA has a list of illnesses they consider common for those exposed during the Vietnam and Korean wars, but infertility isn't on the list."

"But you weren't infertile before the military?" I asked.

"Don't really know. Never came up."

"I'm not sure I want to know why it came up later." I had no reason to feel jealous. He'd had a life before meeting me. For that matter, I'd only been alive about half as long as him.

"Got drunk and careless. Thought for sure I'd ended up getting the woman pregnant. When nothing came of it, I thought I'd dodged a bullet. Until I did the same damn thing a year later. Decided to get checked by the doctor. Found out I'm shooting blanks."

"I'm so sorry." I snuggled into him. "I love my girls and this baby. I can't imagine living my life without children."

"And I'm going to love them too. I'll make sure they have everything they need, and I'll guide them the best I can. I won't promise to never fuck up, but I can admit when I'm wrong."

"You've already done more for them than Spade ever has. He paid the rent and left us money for food. What he never gave them was love and attention. That's what they need most."

His hold on me tightened again. "I can promise they'll be loved, Faith."

"I know you said we need to go to sleep, but I'm not tired anymore."

"All right. How about a hot cup of tea? We can sit in the kitchen for a little while."

"Decaf?" I asked.

"I'm sure I have some. Not really a tea drinker myself, but I keep it on hand in case any of the women stop by. I keep ginger or peppermint for the pregnant ones. It seems to help with their morning sickness. I probably have some that's caffeine free as well."

"Will I get to meet them soon?" I asked. I couldn't remember the last time I had friends. Spade had made sure I didn't have anyone who could help me. I hadn't questioned it until he'd started beating me. Then I'd realized he'd kept me isolated on purpose.

"I'm sure the President's old lady, Raven, will set somethin' up soon. Most of the men here are still single, but there's a handful of old ladies you can meet, and quite a few kids."

"Any close to the ages of the girls?" I asked.

"Piper is the oldest. Two are slightly older than Cordelia, and there's a boy her age. I'm afraid Piper will have to make friends at school. Speakin' of which, we'll get them both enrolled once Cordelia is back on her feet. No sense rushin' things."

He put on the kettle, and I sat at the table. I hadn't even thought about their school records. What if their schools called the house? I didn't know what Spade would tell them. Was he even looking for us?

"You're frownin' again," he said.

"Just wondering if my ex is searching for me and the girls. He'll either be incredibly angry I left him, or he'll be relieved and won't care that we ran off."

Bear grunted. "Guy like that? He'll need to look so he can save face. His club will give him shit for three girls runnin' out on him."

He made a good point. I didn't think I'd left a trail, but what if I was wrong? Piper had her laptop. I hadn't realized it at the time. Bear took it to someone, and supposedly, there wasn't a way for Spade to find us through it. Had he been able to before then?

Bear set a steaming cup of tea in front of me.

"Decaf, like you asked for."

I blew across the surface before taking a small sip. Lemon burst across my tongue, and I greedily swallowed more.

"What can you tell me about Piper and Cordelia?" he asked. "Anythin' in particular they both like?"

"We never had the money for extracurricular stuff at school. Even though public school is technically free, all that stuff costs more. Cheer. Dance. Sports teams. Even the clubs have fees."

"What do they like doin' at home?" he asked.

"Piper usually helps me around the house. She didn't have a lot of friends, so she didn't go to many places on her own. Cordelia likes to read and do puzzles. Give her a stack of puzzle books and she's a happy girl."

"I'll remember that. Did she bring any with her?"

I shrugged. "Not sure. Piper packed their things. I had a small bag ready with two changes of clothes each, cash, and the keys to the car we drove here. I tried to keep it simple."

"All right. After we've gotten some sleep, I'll show you around town and we can pick up some things. You and the girls will need more clothes and shoes, and we can get anythin' else they may want or need. Like puzzle books."

"You don't have to spoil them," I said.

He smiled faintly. "Yeah. I kinda do. Think all of you need a bit of spoilin'."

I had a feeling I was going to lose every argument tomorrow. Whatever he thought he should buy for us would end up coming home, whether I liked it or not. As much as I wanted to be angry about it, I couldn't. He was right. The girls deserved so much more than I'd ever been able to give them. If Bear wanted to do that for them, I couldn't say no.

Within reason.

Chapter Three

Bear

The more I got to know Faith, the more I liked her. I knew there would be people who questioned why she'd stayed with Spade for so long. If they paid attention, they'd see the fear in her eyes every time he came up in conversation. Piper might have a lot of fire in her, but her mother seemed to have a gentle soul, and that bastard had done his best to break her.

In all honesty, when I'd followed Piper to the motel, I'd planned to tell the parents she'd shoplifted and be on my way. Until Faith opened the door. She'd been so small and delicate. Every protective urge inside me rose to the surface. Even now, I couldn't fathom anyone wanting to hurt her. I'd yet to hear her raise her voice or lash out.

I respected her. Wanted to care for her.

Which meant I was currently in an odd predicament.

I'd claimed her and the girls in front of Fox and Spider, which meant Faith was mine. But I'd also told her she could have time to adjust to this new life and get to know me before we became intimate. And yet, my dick was hard as a fucking rock, and sweet little Faith lay sprawled across me. If she woke and discovered my cock was trying to escape from my sweatpants, I'd likely scare the hell out of her. At the same time, if I tried to move her, with her current position, she'd end up touching the tent in my pants.

Looked like I was fucked either way.

I ran my hand down her arm, marveling at how soft she felt. The slight swell of her belly pressed against me. I couldn't remember a time I'd ever felt this content. She mumbled something in her sleep and snuggled closer.

Down the hall, I heard a door creak open. Reaching for the covers, I yanked the blanket over us in hopes of hiding my condition. Last thing I needed was Piper losing her mind when she saw me sporting wood with her mom in my arms. Hell, I didn't need my daughter seeing me like that period.

"Mom?" Piper whispered as she got closer.

"She's asleep," I said, keeping my voice low. "What do you need?"

"Cordelia is awake and hungry. She said she feels better." Piper stepped into the room but didn't come any closer. "I can fix something for us to eat."

I glanced at Faith and felt torn. I wanted to go take care of the girls, but I didn't want to leave her either. Piper seemed to understand my predicament and smiled.

"What do you find so amusing?"

"I can't remember ever seeing her sleep so peacefully. Even when Spade wasn't around, I think she slept with one eye open. She's never relaxed."

I hugged Faith. "She doesn't have to be so strong anymore. I'll help shoulder the responsibilities."

"You didn't think she was weak for staying with him?" Piper asked.

"No, and anyone who says that to her will have to deal with me. Men like Spade are a dime a dozen. They rip girls or women away from their support systems, beat them down, and leave them without self-esteem or a way to provide for themselves or their children."

Piper nodded. "All right. I'll leave Mom in your capable hands. I'm going to shut the door and take Cordy to the kitchen."

I arched an eyebrow and watched as she did

exactly as she said. I sure the fuck didn't miss the wink she gave me right before the door shut, either. Meddlesome little brat. I had a feeling I'd have my hands full with that one. Couldn't wait!

"It's too early," Faith mumbled.

"We don't have to get up yet," I said. "Piper is taking care of Cordelia. You haven't been resting enough."

"I don't think my daughter had rest in mind when she shut the door."

I snorted, then started laughing. I faced Faith and cupped her cheek. "You're not wrong. She even winked at me."

Faith groaned and buried her face against my chest. "She's never done something like that before. I guess you really do have her stamp of approval. That girl has been fearless all her life, except for where Spade was concerned. He scared all of us."

"My club is looking into him, and the Raging Demons. If he's going to come looking for you, we'll be prepared. For now, I just need all of you to relax, settle into your new lives, and make some friends. Let us handle everything else."

She shifted her hips and her gaze crashed with mine when she felt how hard I was. I watched and waited. No sense apologizing for a natural reaction to having my beautiful wife in my arms. Shit. Wife. I hadn't mentioned it to Surge yet or asked him about making me the girls' father. Something told me he might have already taken those steps on his own. He seemed to be following in Wire's footsteps and married people, whether they liked it or not.

"How long have you been in this particular state?" she asked.

"A while."

"And you didn't take advantage?"

"Faith, I promised you'd be safe with me, and you could set the pace. I'm not going back on my word. It's morning wood. Not like I'm going to die from it."

She bit her lip and glanced at the closed door before focusing on me again. "Cordelia hasn't met you yet, so I don't want the girls to hear us doing... *that*."

"Like I said, you set the pace, sweetheart. Just because I get hard doesn't mean I expect to have sex with you."

"With Spade, things weren't... pleasant. He didn't care if he hurt me. It didn't matter if I was ready or not. He'd pin me down and take what he wanted. Not at first. He was sweet until after he moved me into the house. He changed once he'd isolated me."

"What's your point, Faith?" I asked.

"I know it wouldn't be like that with you. You've treated me better than he ever did, and you care about the girls already. It doesn't stop me from wanting to be cautious. I'm scared I'll get my hopes up and find out everything was a lie. But I can't live like that, Charlie. I don't want to let Spade rule the rest of my life and decisions. It's not fair to you, me, or the girls." She took a breath and let it out slowly. "I guess what I'm getting at is that I want to have a real relationship with you. Thanks to Piper, you've already claimed us. You said it's forever, so it's not like I'm running out of here anytime soon. Besides, this place would be harder to escape than the house where we lived before. Spade didn't keep us near his club."

"Things don't add up when it comes to your ex, but that's a problem for another day."

"Take a shower with me?" she asked.

"You sure?"

Faith nodded. "Maybe not the most romantic setting for our first time together, but the water would drown out any sounds, so I won't worry about Cordelia hearing us."

I leaned in and brushed my lips against her forehead. "I'll go start the water so it can warm up."

I got out of bed and went into the bathroom, then flicked on the light. While the water in the shower warmed, I brushed my teeth and wondered if I was doing the right thing. Faith deserved more than this. A honeymoon, or at the very least, a nice dinner out somewhere. I'd said she could take the lead, but she'd surprised me with this move.

Faith came in behind me and her cheeks flushed as she glanced at the toilet. I stepped out to give her a moment to herself. When I heard the shower door shut, I went back in. She'd placed her clothes on the counter and stood under the spray. I watched and admired her for a moment before stripping out of my T-shirt and sweatpants, then I joined her.

Her eyes opened, and she gave me a soft smile.

"Not too late to change your mind," I said.

"I'm sure, Charlie."

I reached for the shampoo and cleaned her hair, massaging her scalp. Her eyes shut again, and she leaned against me. I rinsed the suds down the drain, then slowly washed her body. Her nipples hardened against my palms as I slid them over her breasts. As I washed the soap from her body, I let my hands linger anywhere that seemed sensitive.

Her eyes opened. They were darker as she watched me. Slipping my hand between her legs, I stroked her pussy and rubbed her clit. She gasped and her nails bit into my shoulders as she tried to hold herself up. I felt her thighs trembling and wondered if that stupid asshole had ever made sure she enjoyed his touch. She said he'd started taking what he wanted, but he hadn't been that way before. And yet… she acted like a woman who'd never experienced pleasure.

"This still okay?" I asked. She nodded. In the past, I might not have kept checking, but Faith had already suffered enough at a man's hands. I refused to be like Spade.

I backed her to the tiled wall and leaned in to kiss her. The moment my tongue touched her, her knees gave out. I held her tight, pinning her between my body and the wall. I couldn't remember the last time I'd enjoyed kissing a woman this much. I worked her clit as I ravaged her mouth and felt the moment she gave herself to me completely. Any remaining tension left her body, and she clung to me as if I were her lifeline.

Lifting her leg over my hip, I eased inside her. She cried out as I entered her fully, and I felt her tighten on my cock. I didn't think I'd last long. Hell, it had been so long since I'd been with a woman, I was surprised I hadn't come the second I'd gotten inside her. I tried to use long, deep strokes to draw out the pleasure for her. The moment she came, I gave up holding back.

I thrust into her hard. Fast. I pounded into her, not stopping until I flooded her pussy with my cum, and even then I kept fucking her. It wasn't until I felt myself growing soft that I stopped and pulled out. Faith panted, her cheeks flushed, and her eyes bright. The smile on her face made me want to kiss her again.

"Is that what it's supposed to be like?" she asked, and fuck if that didn't make me feel like a damn king. At the same time, I wanted to put my fist through Spade's face for treating her so poorly.

"No, honey. That's what it's like when it's just us. Not with anyone else." I gave in to temptation and kissed her. When we were both breathless, I pulled back. "Come on. I need to wash you again, then we'll go check on the girls and I'll feed you some breakfast."

"Charlie… if it takes Cordy a little while to warm up to you, please don't take it personally. Spade never wanted anything to do with her. She may not know how to react and might not trust you won't hurt us."

I placed a finger over her lips. "I know, Faith. It's all right. She can have as much time as she needs."

She reached between her legs, her eyes going wide, and I realized I'd taken her bare without having a conversation about it first. She was already pregnant, so that wasn't an issue, but I didn't know if Spade ever gave her an STD, and she hadn't asked me about my health either. I helped her wash up again, making sure I got it all this time.

"I'm clean, in case you were worried," I said.

"Me too. Spade hasn't touched me in over a month, and because of how much he frequents the clubhouse I've gotten tested regularly. Either I've been really lucky, or he always used protection with the girls at the Raging Demons."

"Good. I liked not having a barrier between us."

Her cheeks warmed and I kissed her again, unable to help myself. We finished our shower, put on some clothes, and went to find the girls. I'd won over Piper and Faith. However long it took, I'd earn Cordy's trust as well. My girls would never suffer again. Not for as long as I drew breath.

* * *

Faith

Piper offered to stay home with Cordy while

Bear and I ran some errands. I could tell she really wanted to go. If Cordelia hadn't been sick, I'd have suggested we all go. Even though her fever finally broke this morning, I knew it would be a few days before she was back on her feet. After breakfast, her eyelids had already drooped, and I shooed her off to bed.

It seemed besides the motorcycle, which Bear called a trike, he also had a truck. I'd felt relieved when I'd noticed it, since the thought of riding on the motorcycle had scared the crap out of me. With my car being a complete piece of crap, I didn't think he'd ever willingly drive it. It might have helped me escape from Spade, but it probably needed to be in a junkyard somewhere.

I hadn't ridden on Spade's bike since my first pregnancy. At sixteen, I'd thought he was cool, and I'd gotten a thrill out of riding behind him. Once he'd shown his true colors, he'd become reckless when I rode with him. After one too many near misses, I'd used the kids as an excuse to not go with him. It hadn't taken him long after that before he'd started spending more time at the clubhouse and away from home.

When Bear mentioned buying us each a new wardrobe, I'd thought we'd go to a thrift store. Instead, he stopped at the mall, and I nearly had heart failure thinking of how much it would cost. He held my hand as we went inside, and I had the insane urge to hide my face against him, like I wasn't good enough to be in this place. Even before my years with Spade, I'd never shopped at stores like these.

My parents had been far from rich. We'd lived in the trailer park, and while my clothes were clean, I'd never had new ones. Spade hadn't given me enough to buy new things either, but since it was a luxury I'd never experienced, I hadn't cared. It seemed when Bear said he wanted to spoil us, he meant it.

"We could have gone somewhere else," I said.

He stopped by the mall map and looked down at me. "Somethin' wrong with the mall? I thought all women loved to shop."

How did I explain to him I'd never shopped in a place like this before? I didn't want his pity. I already felt like I was so far beneath him. Bear was the type of man I'd thought I'd never have. It didn't matter if he was a biker. He'd been in the military, had a nice house, two vehicles, and a fully stocked kitchen. Maybe to some that didn't seem like a lot. For me, it was like being in the presence of royalty.

He cupped my cheek and pressed his forehead to mine. "Faith, I can't fix what's wrong if you don't talk to me. Why don't you want to be at the mall?"

"It's going to cost too much," I said.

He smiled a little and kissed me. "I have enough to buy my girls the things they need. Stop worryin', all right?"

I nodded and let him lead me to the first store. We started with things for Cordy. He found a shop specializing in clothes for little girls. I selected a package of panties, some socks, and three outfits. When I tried to head to the register, Bear grabbed the back of my shirt and pulled me back.

"This is plenty," I said.

"No, it's not. For one, she'll be startin' school soon as she's well. The kids will tease her mercilessly if she only has a few outfits. Then I'll have to go up there and start bustin' heads."

I gaped at him, then scanned the racks again. I selected two more outfits and tried to pay once more, only for him to stop me. By the time we finally checked out, Bear had added another five outfits, three sets of pajamas, hair clips, and two necklaces. As much as I wanted to protest, I couldn't. Not when I saw the look of pure joy on his face as he chose things for his new daughter.

Bear led me to the next store and paused outside long enough to send a text. Then we went into the department store, and I tried to ignore the price tags. We started in the juniors department to buy a few things for Piper. Bear picked out a pair of jeans and a shirt, while I selected a casual dress for her. When I tried to get more, he placed his hand over mine.

"We're only getting these two, some shoes, and maybe some jewelry. I plan to get her a gift card and let her come pick out her own things. Somethin' tells me she hasn't gotten to experience this before, since you haven't been shoppin' at the mall either."

"How did you... Never mind. You're right. She hasn't. None of us have."

He picked a necklace and bracelet, then stared at the earrings. "Are her ears pierced?"

"Yes. It was the present Spade gave her for her thirteenth birthday. He took her to Walmart and had them pierce her ears."

He picked out a pair of modest silver hoops and a pair of fake diamond earrings. They were the best fakes I'd ever seen, though, and I knew Piper would love them. After we had her shoes, we paid for her things and he added a three-hundred-dollar gift card. I knew it wouldn't stretch very far, but he said he wanted to wait and see what she picked out before he bought anything else.

I stared at the bags weighing him down and wondered if I could convince him to leave and take me somewhere else to shop. Before I could say anything, another man walked up, wearing a leather cut.

"Took you long enough," Bear grumbled, handing the bags to the guy.

"Sorry. Had to do something for Fox before I could head over. Where do you want these?"

"Take them to Spider's house and tell him I'll come pick them up on the way home. I don't want the girls getting nosy before we're there."

The man nodded, then glanced at me before quickly looking away. Bear sighed and waved a hand at the man. "Faith, this is Joe. He's one of our Prospects. Joe, this is my wife, Faith."

Joe gave me a quick smile. "Welcome to the Hades Abyss, ma'am."

He walked off, carrying all our things, then Bear guided me to the women's department. My cheeks burned as I selected bras and panties, but Bear insisted I needed at least five bras and twice as many panties. As I browsed the pajamas, I saw him eying a satin nightie with lace trim. I'd worn nothing like it before, and part of me wanted it. The more reserved side of me said it was impractical.

"If I buy this, will you wear it?" he asked.

"It won't fit for long. My stomach is only going to get bigger."

"But you'll fit in it again after the baby, right?"

I shrugged. "I should. It's hard to say. It's been twelve years since I last gave birth. Now that I'm older, my body may not drop the weight as easily as before. Then again, I have enough of a belly already. It may be loose after the baby gets here."

Bear held onto it. "I'll get it. Even if you only wear it another few weeks, I'll consider it money well spent."

"I know you want everyone to have a big

selection of clothes, but I shouldn't spend a lot right now, Charlie. I already need maternity clothes. Once the baby is born, I'll need to buy new things again. Since I can't have another baby after this one, I don't want to get expensive things."

"Fine. One nice maternity dress from here, and then I'll take you somewhere else. And don't argue. I'd like to take you somewhere respectable for dinner sometime soon."

"Respectable?"

He grunted. "A sit-down place with tablecloths and candlelight."

I gave in and picked out a dress and matching shoes. Then he insisted on tennis shoes and even a pair of sandals. Before we left the mall, we stopped in the bookstore and selected a few puzzle books for Cordy. I knew Piper loved magazines, so we got a few for her to flip through. Bear wouldn't leave until I'd selected at least two paperbacks. I'd never had a new book before and had to admit the thought of being the first person to read it really excited me.

"Last stop," he said, herding me into a jewelry store. I balked, but he refused to give in, tugging me to the counter.

"Good afternoon." The older woman behind the counter smiled. "Picking out something for your daughter?"

Bear looked at me, then the woman. I could tell from the gleam in her eyes that she found him sexy. He didn't even answer her question. Instead, he turned around and led me right back out into the mall.

"If you left because she called me your daughter, you know we'll probably hear that again sometime."

He grunted and hunted down another jewelry store. This time, the man behind the counter openly sneered at us. Bear walked out again. Since the mall didn't seem to have any other jewelry shops, I figured that was the end of it. I should have known better. On the way to the next store, he pulled over in front of a jewelry store on the main strip in town.

The man inside greeted us warmly and even asked if Bear needed something for his wife. I felt the tension in him ease as he led me to the wedding rings.

"We both need weddin' bands," he said.

His words startled me. "You're going to wear one too?"

"Of course, I am."

I didn't think Spade would have ever offered such a thing, even if we'd been married. Thankfully, we hadn't been. If Illinois were a common-law state, I'd have been in trouble.

"Nothing fancy," I said. "Please, Charlie. I just want a plain band without stones."

He growled and leaned down close to my ear. "That's twice today you've said my real name while we're out in public. At home, you can call me that. Around other people, I'm Bear."

"S-sorry." I backed up instinctively. If I'd screwed up around Spade, by now I'd have been on the floor. Was this when Bear would show his other side? I felt the blood drain from my face as I took another step back. He cursed and lunged for me. I cringed and threw my arms up to block the blows, but he wrapped his arms around me and held me close.

"Easy, Faith. I'm not him, all right? No matter how upset I get, I will *never* hit you. You're safe, honey." I felt tears slip down my cheeks and I clung to him. Even though I'd messed up, he was still comforting me. He looked over at the man behind the counter. "Find some bands she might like."

Bear wiped the tears from my cheeks and led me back to the jewelry counter. The man gave me a kindly smile as he set out a few rings on the black velvet displays. Bear picked up a silver band with rose gold flowers etched into it. He slipped it onto my finger, and it actually fit.

"Excellent choice," the man said. "That band is white gold with rose gold accents. It will give your wife a band without gemstones, and yet it's delicate and has stunning craftsmanship."

"We'll take it. I need somethin' sturdy for mine."

"Most men who work with their hands either select a rubber ring, which has to be ordered, or they select a carbon steel band."

"Do you have the steel ones?" he asked.

"I have a few." The man pulled them from another counter and set them out for Bear to check out. He picked up a plain silver-toned one and slid it on. It didn't fit, so he put it back and tried another. A solid black band ended up fitting, so he bought it.

He led me out to the truck and helped me buckle before taking my hand and kissing my fingers. "I'm sorry if I scared you in there. It was never my intention."

"Can we go home yet?"

He shook his head. "No. You still need clothes. One more stop, then we'll go back to the girls and show them what we got them today."

It took another hour before we pulled into the driveway at home. He went across the street and got our other things, then we carried everything inside. The girls were both on the couch watching a movie, and I saw their eyes light up.

"Who's ready for presents?" Bear asked.

"Me!" Cordelia gave him a shy smile.

He gathered her things first and carried them over to her, then kneeled down at her feet. The quiet way she watched him, and the tentative touches she gave the new items, made my heart warm. She hadn't accepted him in the same way Piper had, but I could tell Cordelia liked Bear.

"Thanks, Dad," Piper said, when she got her things.

"Can I…" Cordelia looked away.

"Can you what?" Bear asked.

"Can I call you Daddy?" she asked softly.

"I'd be honored," he said. "In fact, I'm going to ask a friend of mine to make sure the two of you are legally my daughters. Would you like that?"

Cordy nodded and threw her arms around his neck. I pressed my fingers to my lips and fought back tears. I'd thought it would take her longer to warm up to him, but it seemed as if she could sense the goodness inside him.

My girls finally had the one thing they'd always wanted… a father who cared about them.

Chapter Four

Bear

It took Cordelia another two days to get back on her feet, which gave Surge the time he needed to handle their previous school records, vital records, and anything else that needed to be changed. The girls were now officially Cordelia and Piper Dupont, and if anyone went digging, they'd see Faith and I were married. All I had left to deal with was getting the girls into school, finding something reliable for Piper to drive, and figuring out what the fuck was going on with Spade and the Raging Demons.

It had been quiet since my new family arrived. Too quiet for that matter. I knew there was no fucking way that man would let them walk out on him and not want to retaliate in some way. So why hadn't he made a move? Even if he hadn't found them yet, Surge would have noticed some movement, wouldn't he? I'd asked him to look into things. Virtually spy on the Raging Demons, and Spade in particular.

My phone chimed with a text and I checked it. *Church in ten.*

It would be my first time attending since claiming Faith and the girls. Since Fox hadn't given me a heads-up, I wasn't sure what to expect. Did he just want to make things official for my new family? Or was something else going on?

Cordelia and Piper were in the backyard, along with Zoe and Luka. I knew Piper probably wanted to meet people her age, but I was grateful Cordy would have some friends when she started school. Since it was Saturday, I wouldn't be able to enroll her for a few more days. Until then, I'd invited the kids to stop by whenever they wanted, in hopes she'd make some friends.

I found Faith in the kitchen, baking cookies. My mouth watered at the scent in the air, and I had a feeling she'd be fattening me up like Santa in no time. I might not be quite as fit as I once was, but I still kept in shape. Or I had.

I walked up behind her and placed my hands on her hips. Leaning in, I kissed the side of her neck. "You and the girls going to be okay for a little while?"

"Are you leaving?"

"Fox called Church. Not sure how long I'll be gone. I'd prefer it if you didn't leave the compound without telling me. It could be dangerous, and I don't want to risk losing any of you."

"I agree. We'll wait here."

"If it's an emergency, text my phone." I kissed her again and walked out. I took the bike over to the clubhouse, leaving the truck for Faith. Even if she didn't leave the compound, I didn't want to walk if she didn't have to. I knew the old ladies would be sending her invitations to various things in the near future.

A line of bikes sat outside the clubhouse, and I made my way inside. A few of the club girls were at a table in the back, each with a bottle of beer in front of them. Judging by the state of their undress, they'd been entertaining my brothers before I'd arrived. I headed to the back and pushed through the doors into Church. Most of my brothers were already around the table, except Marauder, Shooter, and Freak. I had a feeling they'd be here soon.

"Looks like you didn't give us all enough time to get here, Pres," I said as I took my seat. A few days ago, I'd wanted to give up this seat. Retire as the club's Sergeant-at-Arms. Now I needed my position to keep Faith and the girls safe.

"Didn't think we needed to wait. Joe will be joining us as well. He has information we need," Fox said. "I'll give everyone a few more minutes, then we'll start."

I leaned forward and caught Surge's attention. "Everything done?"

He gave me a thumbs-up before focusing on his laptop again. I didn't know what he was working on, but it likely had to do with this meeting. The fact Fox hadn't told me ahead of time made me a little ill at ease. Did it have to do with my family?

Joe came in, as did the three remaining members. Once everyone took a seat, Fox stood up.

"I think most of you know Bear has a family now. I didn't take it to a vote because of his daughter, Piper. Girl has brass balls." Fox smiled. "She claimed Bear as her daddy in front of both me and Spider, and since Bear's woman and daughters were tied to the Raging Demons, the girl knew what she was doing. They aren't flying blind."

"We had to rush here for that?" Iron asked.

"No. That's only a part of what we need to discuss. Although, the next matter does tie into it." Fox gave a nod to Joe.

The Prospect cleared his throat. "I came to Fox today because we have a problem. The Raging Demons aren't happy Faith and the girls ran. It made it worse that they ran to another club, or that's how the Demons are seeing it. They want to teach us a lesson."

"How do they plan to do that?" I asked. "And why the fuck wasn't I told before now? How the hell did they even find them?"

"We're working on that. I think there's a tracker somewhere in their belongings. Probably some place you wouldn't think to look," Surge said.

Fox placed a hand on my shoulder. "Easy, brother. I called Church the second I found out what they planned. No time to discuss it with anyone. Let Joe finish."

"Two of their club whores plan to infiltrate our clubhouse. While they're here, they're going to drug a girl, and make sure she's found in a compromising position with one of the brothers."

"How do you know all this?" Freak asked.

"The girl they want to drug is someone I know. They're holding something over her head, forcing her to agree to this. She came to me in secret so we wouldn't be blindsided. As to how they knew they could manipulate her, that's her business." Joe shoved his hands into his pockets. "I know it looks bad, but she's a sweet girl. She's trying to protect someone she cares about. They knew exactly how to get her compliance, which means they aren't stupid. They watched, plotted, and figured out how best to get their revenge."

"Who's the girl?" Marauder asked. "Why would anyone give a fuck if she were found in the clubhouse?"

"She has political connections. Well, not her, but her family. Her mother's cousin is none other than Judge Baskins. You may have noticed the campaign signs around town. He's planning to run for Governor. If the girl is found here, and it looks like we drugged her, then raped her…"

"Motherfucker," I muttered.

"So what are we going to do?" Hornet asked.

"We're going to let them into the clubhouse," Fox said. "Joe is going to watch for the girl. We'll let them plant her in one of the rooms. Then Joe is going to pretend to be drunk and stumble into the room. We'll give them a show. Make them think they've won."

"Why do I feel like this is going to go horribly wrong?" I asked. "And what the fuck do the Raging Demons get out of this?"

"Spade knows how Faith feels about his club. He wants her to second-guess her trust in us. Specifically in you. The girls wanted to bait you, but we all know that wouldn't work. Hell, you probably won't even be at the clubhouse. You aren't most nights anyway." Fox folded his arms over his chest. "To be safe, I want to make sure all men who are taken avoid the clubhouse the night this goes down. We don't have a date just yet, but we should know something soon."

"What do I tell Faith?" I asked.

"Don't let her leave the compound," Fox said.

"The girls are supposed to start school this week. It's not right to keep them home." I pinched the bridge of my nose. "I don't want to tell those sweet things they're on lockdown because of their shitty sperm donor. I know they'd understand, but I don't like it."

"Send them to school," Joe said. "I know. I'm overstepping but hear me out. There's a kid I've been mentoring. He's like a little brother to me, and he wants to prospect for the club. He's seventeen right now and a junior at the high school. If he keeps an eye on Piper, keeps her safe, then maybe you could agree to speak with him about prospecting? All he wants is the chance to talk to someone."

"Fine. I'll agree to talk to him but only if he helps Piper," Fox said. "He doesn't have to do anything stupid. If something doesn't look right, or Piper seems scared, all he has to do is notify one of us. We'll take it from there."

"I'll let him know," Joe said.

"And Cordy?" I asked. "She's only twelve. She'll

be at the middle school with Luka and Zoe."

"I have someone inside who already keeps an eye on our kids. I'll make sure they include Cordelia," Knox said. "She'll be safe once she's on school property. As long you can get her there in one piece, and back home, she should be fine."

"Any chatter about Faith?" I asked. Surge looked away. Hell, Fox wouldn't hold my gaze either, which meant they knew something and didn't want to tell me. "What?"

"Spade is holed up two towns over. One of the girls who comes here occasionally noticed his cut. Heard him running his mouth. When he started mouthing off about teaching us a lesson, she listened long enough to know she'd be in danger if he caught her. She got out of there and called us." Fox turned to face me, and I saw the heartbreak on his face. Shit. What the fuck had the asshole said?

"Just tell me."

"Once their plan with the girl works, and Faith is vulnerable, he's going to take her. He doesn't care as much about the girls. But Faith is another story. He said he's going to get rid of the baby in her belly." Fox audibly swallowed. "Then he's going to let his club teach her a lesson. Bear… they're going to…"

My heart slammed against my ribs. My imagination ran wild with all the things they could do to my sweet Faith. She'd already suffered horribly at Spade's hands. How could he hurt her more?

"They're going to rape her all night." Surge cleared his throat. "He specifically said the club would rape her to death."

I stood with a roar and slammed my fists into the table. The wood cracked, but I didn't give a fuck. My chest heaved with every breath, and I looked around, needing a way to vent my fury. I stormed out of Church, not giving a shit that we hadn't been dismissed. I stood on the porch and screamed my outrage to the sky. That sorry son of a bitch would pay. I'd gut him like a damn fish. Let him watch as his intestines spilled out. But not until after I'd tortured the shit out of him. He'd pay for every moment he made Faith suffer. I'd make him beg and plead for his life, but I'd grant him no mercy.

Spade might be a Raging Demon, but he'd just unleashed hell… and the devil was coming for him.

* * *

Faith

I knew something happened, but Bear wouldn't speak of it. He'd come home in a bad mood, even though he'd smiled and tried his best to set us at ease. It hadn't worked. I'd seen the darkness in his eyes, and knew he was ready to tear the world apart. I'd seen the same expression on Spade's face, except it had always been directed at me. Piper noticed as well. We shared a glance as Bear drank a beer and watched TV.

If I were still with Spade, I'd have walked on eggshells, and given him a wide berth. So far, Bear hadn't hurt us. In fact, he'd gone out of his way to do nice things for me and the girls.

Cordy went into the kitchen and came back with a plate holding two cookies. She carried it over to Bear and tugged on his jeans to get his attention.

"What is it, little one?" he asked, setting his beer aside.

"When I have a bad day, Mama always says a cookie will make it better. You look like you've had a bad day, Daddy." She handed him the plate, and I watched as the big, tough biker melted. He gave her a slight smile and lifted her onto his lap.

"Thank you, Cordelia. I should have known I couldn't hide anything from the three of you." Bear winked at me over her head. "The three of you must be very perceptive. I'm the luckiest man in the world to have two beautiful daughters, and the sweetest wife."

"What if our other daddy comes to get us?" Cordy asked, snuggling against him. "He's really mean. I don't want to go back with him."

"You won't. Not ever," Bear promised her. "Not only will I do anything I can to keep you three safe, but so will my club. The Hades Abyss isn't like the Raging Demons. We appreciate our women and children and will fight to the death to keep them from harm."

Cordy's eyes teared up and she sniffled. "But I don't want you to die, Daddy. We just found you!"

My heart nearly broke at those words, and I had to admit I felt the same. I moved closer as Bear hugged her tight. I placed my hand on his shoulder and leaned down to kiss his cheek. I didn't know how we'd gotten so lucky and found this incredible man. How the hell was he still single? I didn't understand why some woman hadn't tried to snap him up already. There were times he seemed too good to be true.

"Piper, why don't you take your little sister for a walk? Stay inside the compound and keep away from the clubhouse." Bear jerked his head toward the door. "Go on. Introduce yourselves to anyone you see."

"All right, Dad," Piper said. She helped Cordy off his lap and led her outside.

Once they were gone, Bear pulled me down and held me, much the way he'd just been doing with Cordelia. Something told me he'd sent the girls away so we could discuss whatever was bothering him.

"The Raging Demons are about to make a

move," he said, once we were alone. "I need you and the girls to be vigilant at all times. I've got them covered when they're at school, but I don't like the idea of you leaving the compound. From what we've heard, Spade isn't that interested in Piper and Cordelia. It's you he wants."

"Me? He hated me. Why would he care if I ran or not?" I asked.

"It made him look like a fool. He wants revenge and plans to hand you off to his club." Bear audibly swallowed and looked away. "I won't go into details, but it's not something you'll survive, Faith. Whatever happens, Spade can't kidnap you, or lure you away."

"I'd never go with him willingly."

"I know, but we're not dealing with people who care what you want. If they can't grab you outright, they may convince you to go willingly by threatening the girls. Can you tell me if they said they had Piper and Cordelia that you wouldn't hand yourself over to them in an effort to save your babies?"

I sagged against him. "No, I can't. But it would be the wrong thing to do, wouldn't it? If he had them, he wouldn't let them go just because I gave myself up."

"No, he wouldn't. The club has a plan. I need you to trust me, and my brothers. We'll keep the three of you safe." He placed a hand on my belly. "Four. The four of you."

"Were they upset you claimed me and the girls?" I asked.

"Not at all. I think Fox is still laughing over Piper declaring me as her father in front of him and Spider. Girl has guts. Maybe I'll teach her how to ride a motorcycle. Something lightweight. One of the old ladies at the Dixie Reapers can ride."

"She'd probably love that," I said. "I guess we

need to figure out how I'm getting the girls to school this coming week."

"I'm going to register them," Bear said. "As for getting to and from classes, Cordelia can ride with Luka and Zoe. I'm going to get rid of that junker you drove here and get Piper a decent vehicle. Something safe. Won't be brand-new, but it will be reliable."

"You've already spent so much on us," I protested.

"I'll check around. Maybe someone is ready to upgrade and has a small sedan Piper could drive. As for you, if you aren't comfortable driving my truck, we'll find something for you too."

"You didn't listen to me at all, did you?" I asked.

He smirked. "Nope."

"What do the other ladies drive?"

"Some drive SUVs, some have cars. One drives a truck. Just depends."

I sighed. "Fine. I don't think I'd be comfortable with something as large as your truck, but I'll need a car big enough for the girls and a baby seat."

"We don't have to rush out and get one right away. But I do want a car for Piper before she starts school this week. I'll have one of the Prospects follow her to and from school. Maybe one of my brothers too."

"Don't smother her. I know you want to protect her. I do too, but we need to talk to her about it. I know Piper. If she thinks we're going overboard, she'll balk."

He nodded. "Fair enough. We'll tell her you're in danger and she may be as well. She seems sensible enough to understand why she'd need bodyguards when she leaves the compound."

"She really is." I sighed. "I wish it wasn't the case. She should have had the chance to be a kid.

Instead, she grew up fast because I couldn't bring myself to leave Spade. I let fear rule me, until I saw how brave my daughter had become. If it weren't for her, I'd probably still be with Spade. Or he'd have killed me when he found out the baby I'm carrying is a boy."

"Don't plan anything for dinner. I'm going to ask everyone to gather at the clubhouse for a potluck. If you want to take something, make a dessert or some rolls. It's time for you and the girls to meet everyone. It's why I told Piper to introduce herself on their walk," he said. "They need to see she's not a pushover."

I snorted. "She certainly isn't. Are you sure you want them to meet Piper when we aren't around to hold her back? If anyone says something insulting, she'll probably put them on their butts."

"Good. Makes her a fitting daughter for the Sergeant-at-Arms. I may be getting too damn old for this job, but I want them to know my girl is tough. If they touch her, they not only have to deal with me, but they'll have to put up with her too."

"Was Spade the only thing bothering you?" I asked. "Nothing else? It seemed as if you had the weight of the world on your shoulders when you came home."

He reached up to cup my cheek and I leaned down to kiss him. The touch of his lips on mine was enough for my toes to curl, and all my cares to melt away. I drew back and ran my fingers through his beard. Bear's beard was far longer than Spade's. Thicker too. Then again, so was his cock. I smiled and kissed him once more.

"It's my job to worry, Faith. You've done enough the last eighteen years. Let someone else carry the load for a while."

"If you aren't careful, I'm going to fall hopelessly in love with you."

He touched his forehead to mine. "That's the idea, sweetheart."

I noticed he said nothing about loving me in return. I wondered if he'd ever been in love. Not once had he spoken of other women. At his age, it wasn't likely I was the first woman he'd taken an interest in. Had he dated before? Had a serious relationship? As much as I wanted to trust everything he said, part of me still held back a little. Life had taught me to be cautious.

He'd mentioned two pregnancy scares, when he'd told me how he discovered he couldn't have children. Were those women he'd cared about? Maybe even loved?

I'd lived without it all this time. At least with Bear, I didn't fear for my life or those of my children. I'd take what he offered, even if it meant I never had his heart. It would have to be enough.

Chapter Five

Bear

It had been easy enough to spread the word about the potluck, and the ladies were all excited to meet Faith and the girls. Even my brothers seemed curious about my family. Faith baked more cookies, as well as a peach pie. When she'd tried to do more, I'd put my foot down. This event was for her and the girls. The last thing I wanted was for her to work hard tonight.

I'd piled everyone into the truck and drove to the clubhouse. Faith held the pie in her lap and entrusted the cookies to the girls. By the time we arrived, it looked like everyone else was already present. The parking lot was overflowing.

"Remember, these people are your family now. No one in this club will hurt you," I said. "They wouldn't fucking dare."

"Because you'd hurt them back?" Cordy asked.

"Exactly. No one touches my girls and lives to talk about it." Faith elbowed me, and I realized I might have gone a little too far with that last bit. The girls both smiled though, so I figured it was all right. "Who did the two of you meet earlier?"

Piper crossed her arms and huffed, which told me plenty. Someone inside had pissed her off. I almost felt sorry for them.

"The Prospect called Joe, Hornet, Cotton, and Breaker," Piper said.

"I liked Breaker," Cordy said. "I don't know why Piper got so mad. He was only being nice."

Piper growled and I knew I'd have to find out what happened. Later. Clearly, she'd rubbed someone the wrong way, or vice versa. Even as my daughter, there were some people she didn't need to mouth off to. "Everyone out. And, Piper, be nice. You insult the wrong person, and even I can't save you."

"Fine." She threw open the door and got out, with Cordy following in her wake. They carried the cookies inside, leaving me and Faith alone in the truck.

"Who's Breaker?" she asked.

"He was a good kid. All grown up now and older than you by a few years. Risked his life to save Spider's woman, helped Rocket pull his head out of his ass and claim Violeta. If there's anyone here I trust with the girls, it would be Breaker." I reached for Faith's hand and gave it a squeeze. "You ready?"

She nodded. "As I'll ever be."

We went inside and I took the pie from Faith, handing it off to a Prospect. Carlos took it and carried it over to the tables of food. I held Faith's hand as I introduced her to everyone. I could see how overwhelmed she felt and gave a subtle look to the old ladies. I needed them to take her under their wing. Make her feel accepted.

I led her over to a table and kissed her temple. "I'll bring you a drink and a plate of food."

Raven and Luciana came over and sat beside my wife. I felt good leaving her with the two of them. Since Raven was the old lady of the current President, and Luciana was with Spider, they were both excellent sources of information for Faith. They'd answer all her questions and set her mind at ease. Something told me they'd both share their stories with her, so she'd know she wasn't the only one to suffer at a man's hands.

Fox clapped me on the back. "The girls seem to be doing well."

I looked around the room and spotted Cordy with Luka, Zoe, and Marianna. Piper stood nearby, watching over her little sister. It sucked she didn't have anyone here closer to her age. I saw Carlos carry a drink to her and wondered if I'd have to warn him away. He spoke to her a few minutes, then walked off.

"Easy, Papa Bear," Fox said. "No one is making a move on your daughter."

I flipped him off, and knew he was going to make that damn name stick. I'd be kicking asses for the next several months to keep that shit from spreading like wildfire. Fox chuckled, and the smirk on his face made me want to hit him. I held back, not wanting to upset his wife, or mine.

"Jackal and Scratch both have boys closer to Piper's age," Fox said.

"Are you tryin' to marry off my daughter already?"

"Just making a comment. Never know what might happen in the future. Wouldn't be a bad thing to have ties with another club. We're already tied to the Dixie Reapers through Sofia."

I narrowed my gaze at Fox. "You're not usin' my kids as a bargainin' chip to have a deeper connection with the other clubs. Fuck off, Pres."

"Worked for the Reapers and Devil's Fury. Could work for us too."

"Fine." I folded my arms and stared him down. "In fourteen years, use Harlow."

He scowled at me. Yeah, take that, motherfucker! Doesn't feel so great when it's *your* kid being offered up, does it? He stormed off, but I'd made my point. That was good enough for now. It wasn't that I opposed the thought of Piper being with a club I trusted. However, I wouldn't push her to do anything. If she met any of those boys and fell in love, that was different. She'd have my support. I wanted her to be happy. Same for Cordelia. When she was old enough, she could date. As long as I approved of the guy she wanted to see. Like Luka for instance.

I caught Faith's gaze and she flashed me a smile. She seemed more relaxed. In addition to Raven and Luciana, she now had Violeta, Vasha, and Colette at the table. They'd pulled chairs over and barely fit around the small round table. This was the best idea I'd had in a while. I could tell it was precisely what my family needed.

Joe came to me and leaned in close, lowering his voice so only I could hear him. "Got word from my friend. Those women are pushing the timeline. It's going to happen in the next few days. She's trying to stall them, so we have time to properly prepare."

"All right. Wait until the families head home, then tell Fox and the other officers."

"You got it, Bear. And congratulations on your family. Your wife and daughters are beautiful."

I glanced at him and noticed he seemed riveted on Piper. That girl would chew him up and spit him out. I didn't even have to warn him away. She'd take care of him on her own, of that I had no doubt. Unless she fell for him… I eyed him again, wondering if he might be her type. There was an age difference. Wouldn't matter in a few years, but right now? Yeah, I had a problem with it.

"Think of her as your sister," I said.

Joe startled. "Bear, I…"

I held up my hand. "Save it. I saw the look in your eyes. You like my girl, and when she's old enough, it will be up to her if she returns those feelings. For the next two years, she's off-limits. You can be her friend. Give her your support if she needs it or asks, but that's it. I find out you took things any further, and you and I will have an issue. Understood?"

"Got it." His cheeks turned pink. "But when she's eighteen, then…"

I laughed. "Then may God have mercy on your soul because that girl is going to tear you apart, unless you're lucky enough she loves you. You're also assumin' you'll still be here. If you don't have a patch, you aren't goin' after her."

"I can accept all of that," Joe said, a smile curving his lips as he stared at Piper again. "I know she's underage, but I've never met a sixteen-year-old like her before. She's strong. Bold. If someone hadn't told me her age, I'd have thought she was eighteen or nineteen at the very least."

"Piper is one in a million." I noticed the way she twitched whenever someone got too close. She didn't do that at home, which meant all these strangers had her on edge. "Take her a drink, Joe, and maybe one of her mom's cookies. Just don't blame me if you end up wearin' it."

He grabbed a soda and cookie, then approached Piper. She scowled at him for a few seconds before accepting the offerings. As she bit into the cookie, I watched the tension drain from her body. The girl wasn't dealing with all this as well as she pretended. I'd have to keep an eye on her. Yeah, she was strong and bold like he'd said, but she was fragile too. I didn't think anyone realized how easily she'd break.

Rocket stepped up beside me, sipping on a beer. "It seems our girls have become fast friends. Violeta wanted to invite Cordelia over to spend the night, but she didn't know if you'd approve."

"I'm fine with it, and her mom probably will be too. Now that she's met your wife, she won't be quite so jumpy about the girls being out of her sight. Piper on the other hand... she may have a fit over Cordelia not bein' home."

Rocket shrugged. "Let her come too. Hell, I'll ask Spider if Marianna can join them. They can all camp out in the living room and do girly shit all night."

"If you can get the girls to agree, it's fine by me. I'll talk to Faith and let her know what's up."

"Think Violeta already mentioned it," he said. "Luka isn't too happy about being left out. Wish we had a boy closer to his age. Poor little guy."

"Give him a few years and he'll be delighted to be surrounded by girls."

Rocket shook his head. "Poor Slider. He's not going to have it easy."

"Nope. Not even a little." I watched Marianna and the other kids. She was still a little slower than the rest, but with a lot of hard work, she'd come a long way. She took classes in the special education building at school, and I knew she got teased for it outside the compound. Everyone here loved her. "Spider and I aren't getting any younger. Never thought I'd be leavin' a family behind when it's my time to go. Think he worries about his daughter?"

"I know he does," Rocket said softly. "He wants her to experience everything the other girls will. Including falling in love. I've told him the right guy won't care that she had to take remedial classes and got held back. She's a sweetie and some guy will take notice one day."

"And if they don't?" I asked.

"Then everyone here will take care of her." Rocket shrugged. "Can't force someone to fall in love."

No, you couldn't. As I watched my family and the other kids, I realized something. Spider and I had taken a long time to find our special person, which meant our kids weren't as old as, say, Torch's or Venom's. Although, Torch's youngest was closer in age to our kids. Would I still be alive when my girls fell in love? Would Spider get a chance to approve of whomever fell for Marianna?

"Rocket, do me a favor," I said.

"Anything, Bear. Just name it."

"You're about fifteen years younger than me. If I'm not around when my girls get married, will you make sure they don't end up with some shithead who's goin' to hurt them?"

Rocket faced me fully. "What the fuck kind of question is that?"

"The realistic kind," I said. "I'm nearly seventy. I've lived a hard life, and I don't delude myself into thinkin' I'll be here another twenty years. Hell, I could end up with a bullet in me any day. We may have toned things down, but it's not like we run from danger."

"You're going to die in your bed, an old, feeble man, with your family surrounding you. Faith and those girls just found you. They need you, Bear. So whatever bug crawled up your ass to bring this shit up, you better deal with it. Don't let them hear you talking like this."

I nodded, knowing he was right. Getting old just sucked big-ass donkey balls.

* * *

Faith

When the women first came over, I felt a bit overwhelmed. I couldn't remember the last time I'd had friends, or had a woman to talk to at all. Spade kept me so isolated, I'd not had anyone in my life other than him and the girls. Now it seemed all that would change. I had no doubt Bear arranged for them to come meet me. I knew he'd set up this entire night. Just thinking about him, and how kind he was, warmed my heart.

"You doing okay?" Raven asked.

I nodded. "I think so. It's a lot to take in. Even though my ex was a biker, his club wasn't anything like this one."

"Fox saved me. I'd been raped. Abused. I'd learned not to trust anyone." Raven took a swallow of her drink. "I'd never met someone like him before. The moment I set eyes on him, I felt safe. Like if I could just stay by his side, everything would be okay."

I knew how she felt. Bear made me feel the same. Even though Piper trusted Bear, I could tell she didn't feel the same about the rest of the Hades Abyss. Not yet. I didn't blame her. Having this many men surround me, had me a bit on edge too.

"My father sent me here," Luciana said. "Told me to treat the men right and give them whatever they wanted. He'd been whoring me out for a while. I offered myself to Spider that first day. Stripped in his kitchen. I'll never forget the look on his face. It devastated him, realizing what I'd been through. These are good men here. Not an evil bone in their bodies."

"Surge and Aidan protected me," Colette said. "Aidan nearly lost his life because of me."

"I'm Luciana's sister." Violeta smiled. "I tried to seduce Rocket that first day. He ran from me, a look of horror on his face. I'd never had someone react that way before. He was so gentle with me. So caring. I fell for him almost instantly."

"My story is a bit different," Vasha said. "Surge saved me by bringing me here from Russia and gifted me to Slider. Even married us. I didn't realize until I arrived he didn't know anything about me, nor had he wanted me."

I gasped and reached out to place my hand over hers. "How awful! You must have been terrified. New country. No family here, I'm assuming."

Vasha nodded. "Correct. I ran, thinking he didn't want me. In the end, things worked out for the best. We love each other, and our children are a blessing. I love Luka and Anya. In fact, we'll be having a third child before too long."

I smiled. "Maybe our babies will grow up to be the best of friends."

Colette's cheeks turned pink. "I didn't want to say anything just yet, since it's still rather early, but we're pregnant too. Only seven weeks."

Raven looked around the room, spotted Fox, then quickly looked away. I wondered about her reaction, until she leaned in and whispered to me.

"I'm pregnant too, but I haven't told Fox yet. He's going to lock me away to keep me safe. I'm only four weeks, so I'm trying to hold off another month before I say anything. Will you keep my secret?" Raven asked.

I nodded. I didn't know why she'd confided in me of all people, but I vowed I'd keep her secret. It seemed we were all pregnant, except Violeta and Luciana. The look of longing on Luciana's face made me wonder if she couldn't have more children.

Violeta caught Rocket's eye and motioned him over. After whispering in his ear, he smiled and took her hand, helping her stand.

"Everyone, Violeta and I would like to make an announcement." Rocket waited until the room went quiet. "Spider, could you come over here with your wife?"

The older man stood behind Luciana and placed his hands on her shoulders. She reached up to cover one of his with her palm. Were they about to announce another pregnancy? No. That didn't seem right. Why would Spider and Luciana be involved, even if the two women were sisters?

"As most of the club knows, if not everyone, Luciana was unable to have more children. We all know how much the two adore Marianna, but the little one deserves a sibling or two." Rocket smiled widely. "Which is why, with Spider's permission, Violeta and I took a little trip recently. Luciana, sometime in the next week, you'll be welcoming a new member to your family."

She stood so abruptly, she slammed her chair back into Spider, making him grunt from the impact. "What? What are you talking about?"

"You've both done such a wonderful job with Marianna. Through all the ups and downs, doctor appointments, seeing specialists… that girl couldn't have had two better parents. Which is why Spider agreed to help a little boy who's in need."

She spun to face her husband. "You did? When? Why didn't you discuss this with me? We needed to prepare Marianna for something like this."

Spider lifted a hand to calm her down. "Honey, I already talked to Marianna. She's excited. I know I should have asked you, but I've seen the way you eye the women here when they have a baby. I know you wanted more children. I can't promise to be around in another ten or fifteen years. You may end up raising the kids on your own, but I think this little boy is meant to be ours."

My throat tightened and I blinked back tears. I

looked from Spider to Bear and wondered if he felt the same way. They were both older, having gone completely silver. Did he worry that he wouldn't be around to watch our youngest grow up? He winked at me, but I saw the sadness in his eyes and knew I'd guessed correctly. The thought of him not being by my side one day made me want to cry and scream at how unfair life was. I tried to focus on the two couples again.

"Corvin is sixteen," Spider said. "Rocket had some help finding him. He's currently undergoing medical care at a hospital in Texas. Corvin, along with three other children, were saved from a trafficking ring. They've all been abused in various ways, drugged, and some are scarred for life both physically and mentally. Corvin is one of those."

Rocket pulled out his phone and turned it so we could all see the teen boy on the screen. They'd shaved his head and his scalp was a mass of stitches and bruising. His eyes were swollen shut. More stitches were in his lip and in various places on his face. What the hell had that sweet baby been through?

"Once he's healed and released from the hospital, you can bring him home," Rocket said. "Wire found him, so he handled the paperwork. The other children have been claimed, or will be placed in psychiatric facilities where they can stay until their minds have healed. We made sure they weren't corrupt places, so no one will go through the same thing as Raven."

Piper inched closer, her eyes riveted to the screen. I wondered if she felt a kinship to him. While Spade had never hurt her that badly, he'd sent me to the hospital multiple times. Something told me she'd befriend Corvin whenever he came to live with Spider and Luciana.

"Sneaky fucker," Bear muttered.

Rocket grinned. "Sorry. I didn't think we'd be saying something this soon, but it seemed Violeta felt it was time."

"We were all talking about babies," Violeta said. "I saw the look in my sister's eyes and knew she needed to hear about Corvin now. I know he's not a baby, but he'll still be your son."

"And I love him already," Luciana said.

Just what the heck had Bear and Rocket been discussing earlier? The comment didn't make any sense to me, but Rocket had known immediately what Bear meant. It made my mind circle back to my earlier question… did Bear fear he wouldn't be around to see the kids grow up?

Well, the occasion turned somber rather quickly. I cleared my throat and smiled at my new friends. "I'm so happy for you, Luciana! And for everyone's who is expecting right now."

"The club is growing," Fox said, as he joined us.

More than he realized. Raven winked at me before smiling up at her husband. I wondered how Fox would take the news when he found out. Would he really lock her up in the house like she feared? Considering everything the women here had been through, I could understand why he'd be overprotective. I'd be willing to bet all the men were the same way.

"Is he going to be all right?" Piper asked, still staring at the picture.

Rocket's eyebrows rose and he smirked, but it was Spider who answered.

"The kid is a fighter. He'll pull through." Spider walked away from Luciana and approached Piper.

"He's going to need friends. Even when his hair grows back, he'll have scars from head to toe. He may never want to discuss what he's been through, and emotionally, it may take a long time for him to heal. If he ever does."

Piper nodded, her jaw hardening. "I'll be his friend."

I looked up at Bear and saw the calculating gleam in his eyes. It seemed he'd taken notice of her fascination with the boy as well. I had no doubt she'd befriend him. But knowing my daughter as well as I did, I thought she probably wanted more than that from Corvin.

Bear looked from Piper to the Prospect he'd called Joe. The man's expression shuttered as he stared at Piper, and I knew I was missing something. Bear came back and leaned down to kiss my cheek, whispering to me as he did. "I'll explain later."

"Everyone grab some dessert, get a drink, and have fun," Fox yelled. "This is a party. Act like it!"

The noise level increased again, and for a while, I could pretend my life wasn't in danger. I enjoyed the company of the women and got to know their men a little better. All the while, I kept an eye on my girls. Cordelia sat at a table with Luka, Marianna, and Zoe playing a board game. Piper stood nearby keeping watch, as if she were afraid her sister might vanish if she didn't stick close.

Every time someone approached, she flinched a little before smiling. All except one person. Joe would bring her things, and she'd take them. Not once did she shy away from him, which meant he'd gained her trust. How long before she felt the same about everyone else here?

Maybe she'd been so fascinated with Corvin

because she realized he might be as broken as she was. To the world, she came across as brash and fearless. I knew different. She'd come across as strong because she had no choice. Inside, she was just as scared as I was.

Did Bear realize how broken we really were? I hoped he knew what he'd gotten himself into. Because now that I'd experienced his touch, had his arms around me, and knew what it was to have a man care… I knew I'd never willingly walk away from him. He was stuck with me from now until forever.

Chapter Six

Bear

It surprised me how the girls voluntarily went somewhere else for the night. Although, I was happy the two were making friends. It was time for them to get the chance to be kids and not worry about the darkness in the world. I still needed to take care of Spade, and I would. It wouldn't be much longer before I gave them the good news their past would no longer come back to hurt them.

I ran a bath for Faith and helped her into the warm water. One of the old ladies informed me hot baths were a no-no while she was pregnant. Raven had even been kind enough to bring a few things she thought Faith might enjoy, like bath bubbles and massage oil.

I leaned over the tub to kiss her and started to walk out, until she stopped me.

"What did you mean you'd tell me later? About Piper."

I sat on the toilet lid beside the tub. "Joe likes Piper, but he knows she's too young. He agreed to watch over her and bide his time until she's eighteen. I told him if she didn't return his feelings, that was the end of it, and made sure he knew he had to earn a patch before he asked her out."

She worried at her bottom lip, and I wondered if she was thinking about Corvin. I'd noticed the look on Piper's face when she saw the picture. Even though the two of them hadn't met yet, she felt a connection to him. Probably due to the abuse they'd both suffered.

"Joe won't cross any lines and won't hurt our girl," I said. "Honestly, it makes me feel better that he's goin' to keep an eye on her."

"Does this have to do with the age thing?" she asked, skimming her hand over the water and not looking my way.

I'd known this would come up. When I'd claimed her, I'd told her I was a lot older than her. It wasn't fair to saddle her with someone like me. I took risks for my club. Some of those meant I could come home in a body bag instead of on my own two legs.

"I'm sixty-eight, Faith. On top of that, I'm the Sergeant-at-Arms for this club. It means I put myself at risk before I ask anyone else to step up. I've been shot. Stabbed. Nearly blown up a few times. Anytime I go out on a job, it means I could die. Even if I were to retire from my position tomorrow, there's still my health to consider."

She cut her eyes over at me. "Then we eat healthy. No more sodas in the house. Cut down on salt and sugar. And I want you to go in for a checkup."

My lips twitched as I fought back a smile. "All right. I can do that. Let's not go overboard on the food and drinks just yet. I'll schedule an appointment and we'll go from there."

"Fine." She looked at me and reached over to take my hand. I didn't even care that she was getting my jeans wet. "I didn't find you to lose you right away. Take care of your health and do your best to come home to us every time you go on a job. Deal?"

"I can do that." I lifted her hand and kissed it. "Finish your bath, then I'll work on relaxin' you more. We have the house to ourselves. I think we should enjoy it."

Her cheeks turned pink, which I fucking loved. I went to the bedroom and got things ready. I smoothed a towel over the sheets, set out the massage oil, and even lit a scented candle. I had no damn clue where it came from. I didn't remember buying it, and yet it was here.

I heard the water draining a few minutes later and went to help Faith. I didn't like the idea of her getting in and out of the tub by herself. If she slipped, she could hurt herself or the baby. I wrapped her in a fluffy towel and helped dry her off. Then I lifted her into my arms and carried her to the bed.

"You know, for an old man, you're awfully strong."

"Watch it. I might turn you over my knee and spank you." Her cheeks turned a deep red and I wondered if she liked the idea. I hadn't really been into that sort of thing, but it didn't mean I wasn't willing to give it a try. "Can you lie on your stomach?"

She nodded. I unwrapped the towel from her and watched as she stretched out. I took off my cut and placed it on the dresser before stripping down to my underwear. I straddled her thighs and poured some oil into my hand. Rubbing my palms together, I warmed the liquid before I smoothed it over her back.

I dug into her muscles without going so deep I'd hurt her. She moaned and I felt her slowly relax into the mattress. Starting at her neck and shoulders, I worked my way down to her waist before starting over. I backed up so I could reach more of her and slid my hands over her ass cheeks. Her breath caught as I kneaded the muscles. Sliding my hands down farther, I worked her thighs, letting my fingers slip between and slide up toward her pussy. I lightly brushed her curls with my fingers and felt how wet she was.

I kept rubbing her thighs, then her calves before working my way back up. She parted her legs, and I couldn't hold back. I worked her hard little clit, not stopping until she'd come. The soft cry that left her made my cock hard as steel.

"Bear, I need you," she murmured. Faith lifted her head to look at me over her shoulder. "Please."

I stood long enough to remove my underwear, then covered her body with mine. I slid my cock along her folds before pressing inside her. Placing my hand over hers, I laced our fingers together and braced my weight with the other one. With slow, deep thrusts, I savored the feel of her.

"So wet, and hot." I brushed my lips against her ear. "You feel incredible."

"Don't stop! I'm so close."

"Couldn't if I wanted to." Sweat slicked my skin as I fought for control. I maintained my pace until I felt her pussy tighten on me. She let out a whimper that turned into a keening sound. The heat of her release hit my cock, and it unleashed something inside me. I took her harder. Faster. As her pussy clenched on me again, I came, pumping into her until every drop of cum had been wrung from my balls.

I tried to catch my breath as I pulled out and collapsed on the bed next to her. Faith immediately cuddled into me, and I held her close, kissing the top of her head.

"Sorry that didn't last longer," I said. "Been a long time since I was with a woman. Guess I don't have the stamina I once did."

"Charlie, did you hear me complain?"

"No. Doesn't mean I don't feel like you deserve better."

She pressed her lips to mine. "There's no one *better* than you. So hush and just hold me."

"Sassy woman!"

"I didn't used to be." She sighed. "Spade beat it all out of me. I guess I'm slowly finding myself again."

"You be as sassy as you want. I like it." I slid my hand down to her ass and gave it a squeeze. "Want to come again?"

She lifted her head. "What? But you said…"

"Doesn't mean I have to. Roll onto your back and spread your legs."

She did as I said, and I leaned down to suck her nipple into my mouth. The hard peaks were so sensitive she nearly came right away. I rubbed her clit while I licked and sucked the hard tips of her breasts. She came again, soaking the towel, but I didn't stop. I wouldn't be satisfied until I'd made her orgasm so many times all she wanted to do was sleep for a while. I didn't think anyone had ever given her that. She'd seemed surprised when I'd made her come our first time together.

"That's it, beautiful. Come for me. Scream as loud as you want."

By the time she'd come four more times, she pleaded for a break. I kissed her. Held her close and savored this time we had together. Soon we wouldn't just have the girls, but a little boy too. It would be harder to find time like this to have with each other.

"You're an amazin' woman, Faith. I can't tell you how glad I am that you're mine."

She pressed a kiss to the center of my chest. "You're the best thing that ever happened to me, Charlie. There's nowhere I'd rather be than right here with you."

"I hope the girls will be happy here. I'll do whatever I can to make this family work."

"Charlie, just be yourself. I can tell the girls already love you. They're happier than I've ever seen them, and that's thanks to you."

"We have some hard times coming." I didn't

want to keep anything from her, unless I had to. "Spade will make his move soon. I'll do whatever is necessary to protect our family. I need you to trust me and do as I say. Can the three of you do that?"

"We can, and we will."

"He won't be a problem for much longer. I promise this will be in our past soon enough." I kissed her and hoped we'd all make it through this unscathed. I knew the Raging Demons wouldn't play fair. Just because we'd been tipped off about their plan, it didn't mean there wouldn't be complications. Whatever happened, I'd keep my girls safe, and our unborn baby too.

My little family had quickly become everything to me. I smoothed Faith's hair and wished I could say the words I held inside. *I love you.* But I knew it was too soon, and I didn't want to scare her off. I'd tell her when the time was right.

* * *

Faith

Bear wasn't home, and Cordelia had gone across the street to play with Marianna. Which left Piper home with me. She sat at the kitchen table, twisting her glass of lemonade in a circle, and staring into space. It was the most vulnerable I'd seen her in a while.

"Want to talk about it?" I asked.

She shrugged a shoulder. "Not much to say. We get a fresh start, but I have a feeling my asshole sperm donor is going to wreck it."

"What makes you say that?" I asked, wondering if someone had said something they shouldn't have. While we'd told the girls to be vigilant, we hadn't given them details.

"I saw them," she muttered. "The Raging

Demons. Two were outside the fence, watching. I know they saw me, but all they did was stare. They're here, Mom. You know it means Spade is here too, and he's going to be after us. You specifically. I don't think he realizes Cordelia and I exist most of the time."

"The club is aware they're in the area. Bear and the others are doing their best to keep us safe. We have to trust them, sweetheart. We can't hold everyone at arm's length forever. The men here are good. They aren't like Spade."

She leaned back in her chair. "I know. Bear is the best thing that's ever happened to us. It's why I'm glad he's claimed you. I didn't give him much of a choice, but that still could have blown up in my face. Instead, he rolled with it."

"I know it's lonely since you're the oldest," I said. "Corvin will be here before too long. Hopefully, the two of you will get along well. And when you start school this week, you'll make new friends."

"It's the middle of the year. No, not even that. It's nearly the end of the school year. Making friends won't be easy."

"Your dad is getting a car for you. Maybe you could get a part-time job in town to get some extra spending money."

Piper nodded. "That would be a way to kill some time when I'm not in class. As much as I love Cordelia, the kids here are closer to her age. Mom, I'm not the normal sixteen-year-old. I've seen too much, experienced things they can't imagine. How many of them had to run in the middle of the night to escape their sperm donor and his biker gang? And yeah, I know it's called a club, but let's be real… the Raging Demons are a gang. They're nothing but thugs."

She wasn't wrong. The Raging Demons were

nothing like the Hades Abyss. It was the difference between night and day. Bear might say his club didn't always walk on the right side of the law, but they were all good men. I could tell. None of them were evil. Spade's club couldn't say the same.

Not one man here would think of raping a woman, and yet Spade threatened that and more. He'd already done that to me many times. The more I thought about it, the more I realized I hadn't always agreed to have sex with him. I hadn't realized at the time it was rape, since we were together. Now that I'd had time to think, and to see how other men treated their women, I knew different.

"I'll send Bear a message to let him know what you saw. Where were you?" I asked.

"It wasn't far from Luka's house. I went for a walk to stretch my legs, and I'm still trying to figure out who lives in which homes."

I pulled out my phone and sent the text to Bear. I knew he was in Church, but hopefully he'd find the information useful. There was a chance he already knew. However, in case he didn't, I wanted to keep him informed. He might not fear Spade, but I did. I knew how evil the man could be, had experienced it firsthand.

"At least Cordy only went as far as Spider's house," I said. If she'd gone farther into the compound, I might have worried the Raging Demons would find a way inside and snatch her, if for no other reason than to get to me. Spade knew I'd do anything for my girls. Bear had been right to be concerned I'd offer myself up in exchange for either of them.

"Want me to go keep an eye on her?" Piper asked.

"No, honey. Spider used to be the President of

the club. I'm sure his house is just as safe as this one, if not more so. I think Fox lives nearby too. It's time we trust the Hades Abyss to do what they said and keep us safe. We can't say they're better than the Raging Demons, then keep doubting them."

She nodded. "You're right, but it's not easy. After not being able to rely on anyone other than ourselves for so long, it's hard to trust in someone else. I'm trying, though."

I ran my hand over her hair. "I know. Bear knows it too. You put on a brave face. It might fool everyone else, but I've seen the look in your eyes, watched the way you flinch whenever someone gets too close. You're still scared, and it will take time for that fear to fade."

I wanted her to be a kid. She was nearly grown, and she'd already spent most of her life trying to protect me and Cordy. It wasn't fair. When did Piper get a chance to do things other teen girls did? Go on dates, hang out with friends, get a job… worry about school. She'd done none of that. As far as I knew, she'd never kissed a boy. Part of me worried she'd never let someone get that close to her. It didn't matter how she'd reacted to Corvin's picture, or that Joe seemed interested. If she kept everyone at arm's length, she'd never experience the good parts of life.

"Promise me you'll try, Piper. Give everyone here a chance, and the kids at school too. Don't judge everyone you meet by what you've experienced so far. Our lives are about to be so very different from before. They already are! Bear is a hundred times better than any man I've ever met. The others here seem to be the same. I don't want Spade to win. If you let him taint your view of the other people in the world, then you lose, Piper. Do you understand?"

She nodded. "I promise I'll try to give everyone a chance. But I don't know about dating. Let's start with me making some friends."

"That's a very smart decision."

"Do you think anyone here will get hurt because of Spade?" she asked. "What if we're responsible for getting someone hurt? Or worse, killed…"

I placed a hand on her shoulder. "We can't think like that. Bear seems pretty fierce, and so do the others. From what the other old ladies said, they've each brought trouble with them. This club isn't going to run from danger. Bear and I discussed it yesterday while you and Cordy were gone. He worries he won't come home one day, that he'll get shot or stabbed. It's happened before, even though he survived. We can't live our lives worrying about what tomorrow will bring. The only thing we can do is live for today and hope we get tomorrow too."

Piper smiled faintly. "Were you always this wise?"

"I don't know. Spade beat me down so much, for so long, I lost myself along the way. I'm slowly remembering who I was before I met him and discovering new sides to myself. I was your age when I met him, and he controlled my life. There hasn't been time for me to grow up and experience much. You're not the only one trying to figure out this new world we're in. But I try to make decisions I think would make Bear proud of me."

A throat cleared behind me. "Sweetheart, I'm always proud of you. All of you."

I turned and saw him standing in the doorway. Blood dripped down his arms and I gasped before rushing to his side. "What happened?"

"Got into a scuffle with a few Raging Demons.

Didn't see Spade among them, but one got in a lucky shot."

"And the others?" Piper asked, standing to come closer.

She saw the blood and hurried to the drawer by the sink, pulled out a clean towel, and wet it for me. I took it from her and cleaned the wound, wincing at the ragged skin. Whoever cut him, it had gone deep enough he'd need stitches.

"Most are dead. Fox wanted to keep one alive for questioning. I need the two of you to stay here, or over at Spider's, until all this is handled. Understand? They shouldn't be able to get into the compound, but I don't like taking unnecessary risks. Not with my family." Piper threw her arms around him and hugged him hard enough he grunted before patting her back. "I'm hard to kill, even if I don't look it."

"Is someone going to come look at your arm?" I asked.

"Dread. He should be here in a minute. Had to go get his kit."

I led Bear over to the table. He sat and propped his arm up. I dabbed at the wound, not liking how much it still bled. "Piper, I need another towel. A dry one."

"The kitchen is out. I'll grab one." She hurried down the hall and returned a moment later with a hand towel. I pressed it to Bear's wound and hoped it would slow the bleeding before Dread arrived. If this was going to be part of my life now, I needed to take some first aid classes. I didn't like feeling useless while he bled all over the place.

"That look… what did you just think about?" he asked.

"I want to learn how to treat your wounds when

you come home like this. Or at least be able to patch you up well enough until Dread can get to you. I don't like knowing you're in pain, or seeing you bleed so much. I feel helpless and useless."

He reached up and cupped my cheek. "Sweetheart, you're far from useless. As to the helpless part… you're doing just fine. Not much more you can do unless you know how to put in stitches."

I shook my head. "I can't, but maybe I should learn."

"All right. We'll talk to Dread. Maybe he'll let you shadow him when he patches any of us up. Teach you a few things. Just some basic skills. If it's something you enjoy, maybe you can go back to school for a nursing degree."

I gaped at him. "Are you serious? I didn't even finish high school!"

"Then work on your GED first. I'll help. But only if that's something you want to do. Don't feel like you need to prove anything to me or anyone else. If you pursue your education, I want you to do it for yourself."

"It's not a bad idea, Mom." Piper sat in one of the other seats. "I know you've always hated not having a high school diploma. Even if you didn't go further than a GED, it might make you feel better about yourself."

"We can discuss it later." I heard a knock at the door and rushed off to let Dread into the house. While he stitched Bear's wound, I sat and watched, wondering if Bear was right. Could I get my GED, get a nursing degree, and help this club? They were putting their lives at risk to keep me and the girls safe. I wanted a way to give back.

It made me wonder how the other old ladies contributed to the club or the town. I had a feeling none of them sat around doing nothing all day. It hadn't come up in our conversation at the clubhouse last night. Once this issue with Spade went away, I'd have to talk to each of them. Maybe it would help me figure out my place here. I needed something to focus on other than Bear and the children.

For the first time in eighteen years, I could do something for myself. I had the chance to better my life and the lives of those around me. And it's something I wanted to do more than anything.

Chapter Seven

Bear

I knew Faith had questions. So far, she'd kept silent. Dread patched me up and went to check on the others. After he left, Piper went to Spider's house to sit with Marianna and Cordy. Even though we were alone, I wasn't in any shape to do much but enjoy a movie with my woman. I'd let her pick and a rom com played on the big TV. I'd taken a seat on the couch, and Faith cuddled against my side. The one that didn't have stitches in my arm.

I glanced at the bandage and wished I'd made those fuckers hurt more.

Once I'd received Faith's text, Fox had called a halt to Church so we could check it out. As the Sergeant-at-Arms, I'd led the attack. Hornet, Iron, and Fangs had gone with me. We'd found four men skulking around the fence line, clearly trying to find a way inside. I knew it would cost a fuck ton, but I think we needed to seriously consider electrifying the damn fence. At the very least, we needed cameras and someone to monitor them at all times.

Like Fox had said… the club was growing. We had more kids and babies on the way. Even if we weren't into the same shit as before, our past could come back to bite us in the ass at any time. Not to mention we all seemed to fall for women who had trouble nipping at their heels.

We'd gone through the front gate, not hiding the fact we were leaving on foot. Iron had gone to the left with me, and I'd sent the other two to the right. Iron and I found the men, then called the others to us. I hadn't wanted to wait, though. We'd snuck up behind them. I could have ended them quickly, but I'd held back. I'd wanted them to suffer the way Faith had.

Iron stabbed one of them in the side immediately, then slit the bastard's throat while he was on the ground. As he launched himself at another one, I'd cuffed the one in front of me on the side of the head. It stunned him long enough I could go after the last one. I'd landed blow after blow. Rage had engulfed me, and I'd forgotten about the first man. He'd shaken off his stupor and cut my arm.

Everything after that was a bit of a blur. Iron had made sure I didn't kill the last one standing, but we'd beaten the others until they had no fight left in them. We'd soaked the ground with their blood, and I didn't fucking regret it one bit. Those assholes deserved that and so much more.

Faith sighed, and I glanced down to see she'd focused her attention on me.

"What?" I asked.

"I've been talking to you, but you were a million miles away. Thinking about Spade and his men?"

I nodded. No sense lying to her. Didn't mean I'd give her a play-by-play of what happened earlier, but I needed her aware of what was going on. Enough that she'd keep herself safe at any rate.

"The fact they were here and tryin' to get inside means they aren't sure their other plan will work. I don't know if they're aware their sacrificial lamb has a tie to this club, or if they just don't trust their whores. I'm hopin' it's the second option. I don't like the thought of that girl being in any more danger than she already is. It took guts for her to warn us."

"Why did she?" Faith asked.

"She knows Joe. It's just a coincidence she has ties to the Hades Abyss. If Spade was aware of it, I think he'd have chosen someone else. They have somethin' they're holding over her head. Forcin' her compliance. We'll do everythin' we can to keep her safe."

"You think they're going to make another move soon?"

"If it were me, I'd stop and reassess. Not sure what's goin' through their minds right now. They have to know their men are dead, and one is missin'. Could mean they'll change their plans entirely. Or they could trust he won't talk and move forward."

"Why did you specify the girls and I have to stay here or at Spider's house?" she asked.

"Motion detectors," I admitted. "I have some set up around the perimeter at both houses. I get an alert if it's anything bigger than a raccoon. Not right up by the house. Closer to the property line. So you and the girls can go out without tripping them. They're well hidden, so no one will notice them."

"Why do I get the feeling after this you're going to increase the security at the house?"

I smiled. "Because you're learning. I'm going to have an alarm system installed, including camera feeds at each external door and all the windows. Not where anyone would watch us being intimate, but I want to make sure no one can enter this house without me knowing about it."

"I don't have an issue with that. Might not want to tell the girls. Or this little one," she said, putting a hand over her belly. "That way if they get bold and try to sneak out later, we can catch them."

"Don't think Piper will be sneakin' anywhere. She's too bold to slip out a window." I shifted and pulled a set of keys from my pocket. "Her new car is at the clubhouse. The people delivered it right before Church. Didn't want to bleed all over it, so I left it there for now."

"What did you get her?" she asked, reaching for the keys.

"Nothin' big. It's a Ford Focus. One owner car. Well maintained. It's three years old so the warranty should extend to us for another two years."

"Sounds expensive." Her nose wrinkled. "I thought you weren't going to go crazy when you picked out a car for her."

"Spent a little more than I'd planned, but there's a reason for it. The car belonged to a girl three towns over. Kid had a brain tumor. Died a few weeks ago. She only got a chance to drive the car a handful of time, so it has less than three hundred miles on it. Mom didn't want to look at it anymore." I looked at the keys in Faith's hand. "The town is far enough away, no one at Piper's school should tie the car to that girl. She won't get shit over havin' the vehicle. It's why I didn't look at things closer to home. Didn't want to get a leftover from one of her classmates. I know kids can be cruel as fuck."

Tears slipped down Faith's cheeks. "That's so awful! I can't imagine how heartbroken the mom must be right now."

"Yeah. She didn't even want to look at it when I sent someone to check it out. Askin' price was only five grand, which was way too low. Once I heard the reason, I had Carlos offer her a fair price for it. She wouldn't accept it when she heard a sixteen-year-old girl would get it, but I did get her to take nine thousand. In this economy, with gas prices bein' sky high, she could have easily gotten double that."

"You need to tell Piper the story behind the car. Maybe not the price, but everything else. She'll appreciate it that much more, and if I know my daughter, she'll try to do something for the woman." Faith leaned her head against my shoulder. "Thank you. Not only for doing something so nice for our child, but for trying to help that mom too."

"Don't make me out to be a saint, Faith. I've done bad things in my life."

"The world isn't painted in black and white, Charlie. Everything is shades of gray if people looked at things honestly. You're a good man, and nothing you say will ever change my opinion."

I kissed the top of her head and held her close. Whatever I'd done to deserve a woman like Faith, I hoped I never crossed a line so bad she saw me as a monster. I hadn't kept it from her when we killed those men today. Hadn't told her the entire story, and she didn't need to know it. But even realizing I'd taken a life, she still sat here in my arms, letting me love her. And anytime I'd killed someone, it had been necessary. It wasn't like I'd go out and shoot some innocent person.

"I'll never be able to thank you enough, Charlie. The day you saw Piper shoplifting, you could have alerted the clerk, or called the police. Instead, you followed her, made sure I knew what she'd been up to, and tried to give her another shot. Not everyone would do something like that. They'd have thought she was a bad kid, or on her way to a life of crime. Instead, you looked beyond the act itself and tried to think of why she might do something like that."

"Like I said. I'm not a saint, Faith. We've all done things we wish we could go back and change. Havin' her arrested wouldn't have solved anything. Bein' in Juvenile Detention might have hardened her more. Made her less likely to lead a productive life later. More than twenty-five percent of kid offenders will end up committin' another crime within a year of bein' released."

"Do I even want to know why you have that information?" she asked.

"Probably not."

She didn't need to know it's because I'd checked on the ones released who had nowhere to go, wondering if they'd be a good fit for the club. Not the violent ones. But kids like Piper who got picked up for theft were another matter. As long as they weren't stealing shit for fun and had a reason, it meant they could have a good life here with the Hades Abyss, or with other clubs like ours.

Knowing my sweet Faith, she'd put me even higher on a pedestal than it seemed she already had. That was the last thing I needed. The higher you were, the harder you'd fall.

* * *

Faith

I could tell something was happening tonight. Bear kept glancing at his phone, as if he expected a call or text. The girls felt the tension and kept shifting in their seats. I'd made meatloaf and mashed potatoes for dinner, even though it didn't adhere to the diet I'd mentioned earlier. Since I'd never paid attention to that sort of thing before, I'd need to research some recipes before the next shopping trip.

I set the table and got glasses of lemonade for everyone. When I took the meatloaf out of the oven, Bear came to get it from me. I set a trivet down so the hot pan wouldn't scorch the wood and he placed the food in the center. Then he brought over the mashed potatoes.

Cordy stared at him with wide eyes. Bear paused

and watched her, his brow furrowing as if he couldn't figure out why she looked at him that way.

"What is it?" he asked. "Do I have somethin' in my beard?"

She shook her head. "You helped Mama with dinner."

He looked from Cordelia to me, then back again. "She's pregnant and shouldn't carry heavy things."

I refrained from pointing out four pounds of ground beef hadn't been too heavy. Mostly because I'd enjoyed him taking care of me. My cheeks warmed as I thought about our night without the kids. I wondered if I gave him a massage if it would end the same way.

Bear smirked at me, clearly knowing where my mind had wandered. He cut the meatloaf and set a slice on each of the girls' plates as well as mine, before adding three to his. When I stared at the plate, he growled softly.

"Watch it, woman. Don't ever try to take the meatloaf away from me. I'm old. Not dead."

"Which is the part I'm hoping to avoid. We'll start eating healthy in the next few days, so enjoy all the salt you can while it lasts. I'm throwing it out after the next grocery trip."

Piper's jaw dropped. "What? Why are we giving up salt?"

"Because it's not good for your heart. Don't you want your dad to be around a long time?"

She snapped her mouth shut and straightened in her chair. "Right. No salt in the future. You shouldn't eat greasy things either. Or drink soda and beer."

Bear glared at me before staring down our oldest. She didn't cower, though. Nope, our daughter held his gaze and lifted her chin slightly.

"Girl, you even think of touchin' my beer, and

you'll be grounded until you're forty."

"If you don't stop drinking it, you won't be alive long enough to see that threat through," she said, making me choke on my lemonade. "I didn't get such an awesome dad only to lose him because he's too stubborn to give up things that are bad for him."

I watched as Bear's eyes lit up, his lips twitched, then he cleared his throat and scowled at her. "I think I'm old enough to decide what I should and shouldn't consume."

"Good. Then you know beer is bad for you, so I'll make sure I take what's left in the fridge and give it to someone else." Piper took a bite of her food and ignored Bear. If she'd been looking, she'd have noticed he coughed to cover a laugh. She was something else.

"Don't ever change, Piper," he said.

"Didn't plan on it," she said before taking another bite.

Bear winked at me and dug into his food. Cordelia watched everything with interest but didn't join in the conversation. Still, I could tell she was at ease around Bear, and seemed happier than I'd ever seen her before. Both my girls loved it here, and so did I. We'd finally found a home.

Even though we'd lived in the same rental all their lives, Spade made sure we didn't have friends. If the girls started getting close to someone at school, something bad would happen to their families, and the kids would distance themselves from Cordelia and Piper. Same for me. The one time I'd tried to start a friendship with a neighbor, Spade scared them off and made sure the woman never spoke to me again.

I liked the women at the Hades Abyss, and Bear wasn't holding me back. If anything, he encouraged me to try new things, meet more people, and figure out who I was. It made me fall for him even more. I already knew I loved him. How could I not? I just hadn't had the guts to say the words. Things were too new between us, and I worried my heart would break when he didn't say it back to me.

For now, I'd be content with things the way they were. When I felt like I contributed more to our relationship than I took from it, maybe I'd have the confidence to confess my feelings. Bear needed someone strong to stand beside him. Right now, I didn't feel worthy of the position, but one day soon I'd be able to look at my reflection and not see a broken woman. I was well on the way to healing.

We finished our food, and the girls cleared the table and loaded the dishwasher while Bear and I went to the living room. He started the TV and selected a movie all of us might enjoy. Even though he'd claimed his favorite chair, he'd pulled me down onto his lap and held me close.

"I almost feel sorry for whichever boy has the guts to ask out our daughter," he said. "She's a force to be reckoned with."

"She is." I ran my fingers through his beard. I'd discovered it was something I enjoyed doing. "She's more fragile than anyone realizes, though, despite her tough exterior. I'm not sure I'm ready for her to have her heart broken. Spade did that enough already."

"No one's going to hurt our girl. If they do, they'll answer to me." He kissed my temple. "All of you take such good care of me. Worryin' about my health. Wantin' to patch me up. Never realized what I was missin' all these years. I'd wanted a family, but experiencin' it is somethin' different."

"Of course, we worry about you. Do you have any idea how much you mean to us? And it's not because you saved us. Well, not entirely. That is a part of it, but mostly it's because of how amazing you are. You're exactly what we needed. The missing piece to our family."

He wrapped his arms around me and held me. I snuggled against him, breathing in his scent, and wishing the moment could last forever. I had a feeling, sooner or later, he'd be called out tonight. Whatever had him constantly checking his phone would lure him from the house, and it most likely had to do with Spade and the Raging Demons.

"Promise me if anything happens tonight, you'll be careful. I can't lose you, Charlie."

"You won't. I'll come home to you. Whatever it takes, I'll always come back."

I lifted my head to look him in the eye. "You told me recently you could return in a body bag, so forgive me if I want to make sure you mean you'll walk into this house on your own two legs and not as a zombie."

He snorted. "Stop watchin' reruns of *iZombie* and oglin' Major Lilywhite."

"I didn't do any such thing!" My cheeks burned, belying my words. I had to admit the guy was cute, but I much preferred the silver fox holding me right now. Besides, I liked the fictional character. It didn't mean I wanted to run off with the actor who played him.

"Sure, you didn't." He smiled and leaned in to kiss me. His lips were warm and soft, and I found myself melting against him.

The girls finished in the kitchen and joined us. Bear started the movie, and we settled in to enjoy a night as a family. Before too long, we'd have a new addition. I hadn't had time to think of names. I wondered what Bear would want to call him.

Bear's phone buzzed and he checked it. His eyes

darkened and his jaw tightened. I knew before he said a word that he'd be leaving. I struggled to stand, and he helped me, then held onto my hand a little longer.

"You need to leave, don't you?" I asked.

"Yeah, I do. The three of you stay here. Keep the doors and windows locked. No one leave."

"Spade? Is he… did the Raging Demons get into the compound?" I asked.

"I can't give you details. As far as I know, he's not inside the gates. I'm not takin' any chances, though. The four of you mean too much to me. Keep yourselves safe and I'll be back as soon as I can."

Piper stood. "Wait! If someone gets in, we're sitting ducks. We need a weapon."

"You know how to shoot?"

She shook her head. "No one ever taught me, but it can't be that hard. Just point and pull the trigger, right?"

He folded his arms and rocked back on his heels. "Arming you with a gun before going over how to properly hold and fire one, as well as the safety rules, wouldn't be very responsible of me. But I can give you a knife. It means you'd have to get in close to hurt them, but it's better than nothin'. Startin' tomorrow, I'll teach you about guns and make sure you know how to defend yourself."

Cordelia came up beside Piper. "I want to learn too, Daddy."

"All right. Wait here and I'll get one of my knives, then I need to leave. Just remember what I said." He walked out and returned a few minutes later with a pocketknife. He showed Piper how to open and close it, gave me a kiss, then rushed out the door. I made sure to twist the lock, then double-checked the windows and back door, before sitting down with the girls.

"Come home safe, Charlie," I murmured, staring at the closed front door. I could handle a lot of things, but if I lost him, it would devastate me.

Chapter Eight

Bear

I stepped out onto the porch and heard the lock click. Before I made it down to my bike, the door flew open and Cordelia raced out toward me. She threw her arms around my waist and hugged me tight.

"Promise you're coming back?" she asked.

"You have my word." I reached down and picked her up. She might be twelve, but she was so slight I barely noticed her weight. Like her mother, she was a tiny thing. She clung to me, and I saw the tears in her eyes. "Hey, you're my brave girl, right?"

"Yes, Daddy." She buried her face against my neck, and I rubbed her back. Piper wasn't much bigger than her mother, but that girl was like a powder keg. If someone lit a match, she'd go off and likely take out an entire city block with her explosion. Cordelia seemed quieter like her mom.

"Can you do me a favor? I have a really important job for you while I'm gone." She lifted her head to hold my gaze. "Piper is going to try and keep all of you safe. If someone manages to get into the house, I need you to help your mom get to the master bathroom. Close yourselves in, you hear me?"

"I will! I can do it."

"I know you can." I smiled and kissed her cheek. "Get back inside and lock the door again. If you can get Piper to go to the bathroom too, I'd prefer all of you be in there. Whatever it takes, all of you stay alive until I can get to you."

"All right, Daddy."

I set her down and she ran back into the house and slammed the door. I listened for the lock again before I got onto my bike and rode over to the clubhouse. While it wasn't likely Spade would try to enter the compound and break into the house, I couldn't discount it entirely. Right now, I had to go deal with the shitstorm at the clubhouse.

How the hell did things get so fucked-up? We'd known their plan. Prepared for it. And yet, it went sideways when those women decided it was time to strike.

I parked at the end of the long line of bikes and went inside. My brothers had two women pinned to the sticky floor, both cussing and screaming. I went past them and down the hall. Pushing open the third bedroom door, I took in the scene.

A cute little thing seemed to be passed out in the bed. Someone had gone to the trouble to cover her. Probably the brother currently holding his head in his hands. Joe was supposed to fall into the trap, make it seem like he'd taken the bait. So how the fuck did Cotton end up in this room?

"Want to tell me what happened?" I asked.

His head jerked up and he winced, shutting his eyes a moment. "I think someone drugged my beer. I remember needing the bathroom. Next thing I know, I woke up in here. Naked."

"And the girl?" I asked.

"Same. But..." His cheeks turned pink. "I don't remember having sex with her. You'd think I'd know if we'd been intimate, right?"

"What makes you think you were?"

He cleared his throat. "My cock was wet and she, um... she has cum on the inside of her thighs and on her..."

His face flamed so red I worried he might burst into flames. It wasn't like Cotton to be so bashful. I noticed he kept cutting his gaze toward the girl and quickly looking away. She wasn't a kid, but she did appear to be quite a bit younger than Cotton. I knew he was in his early forties. If I had to guess, I'd put the girl in her early to mid-twenties. I'd thought Joe said she was younger.

"Where's Joe?"

Cotton shook his head. "No idea. But it's worse, Bear. There's some blood. I think she was a virgin."

Shit. I tipped my head back and wondered how the hell we were going to fix this. I needed to talk to the bitches who set everything up. Figure out what the hell was going on. Most importantly, I needed to get this cleaned up before anyone came looking for the girl in the bed. If they'd set this up in order to trap our club and put us in a bad light, then I needed to make sure they couldn't find the evidence they needed.

I stepped into the hall and yelled for Dread. I heard the thump of his boots on the wood floor, and he appeared with his medical bag in his hand.

"Take blood from both of them. Find out what they were drugged with and help me find a way to spin this so a pile of shit doesn't land on our doorstep."

Dread nodded. "On it."

"Once you're done, someone get the both of them to Cotton's house. Ask one of the old ladies to be on standby in case the girl freaks out. Anyone seen Joe? She's supposedly his friend."

"About that." Dread winced. "Um, she's not Joe's friend. We think she's a last-minute replacement. Joe got word that his friend was in a car accident. It's why he's not here. He went to check on her."

"I bet she did something to tip them off. Not intentionally. They've been watching us awfully close. She probably showed her hand, and they realized she knew someone here, which means her accident might have been intentional. If they had a contingency plan in place, they would have implemented it the moment they saw Joe go running to that other girl." I sighed. "Great. Now we don't know what the fuck is going on, or who this girl is. I don't like this shit."

I left Cotton and the girl in Dread's capable hands and went back to the main room to question the other two women. We'd known this was coming. Thought we'd planned accordingly. Hell, we hadn't known what the two whores looked like, and it wasn't like the same women showed up at our gates every night, but still… we'd royally fucked up this time.

I'd question them. Find out what the fuck was going on and handle it accordingly. Iron lifted one, and Freak grabbed the other. We hauled them outside behind the clubhouse. It was risky, but if the Raging Demons were watching, I wanted them to know these bitches were caught. I didn't think it would be easy to get information from them. Didn't mean I wouldn't do my best to scare the fuck out of them.

"Make them kneel," I said, facing the two with my arms folded.

My brothers shoved the women to their knees. I looked from one to the other, trying to find the weaker link. Deciding the blonde looked more scared than angry, I decided to start with her.

"We already know the Raging Demons sent you. I need to know their plan. Why did they send that girl here? How did you get her to cooperate?" The blonde trembled. The darker haired one glared at me. Leaning down, I got in the blonde's face. She flinched and looked away. "Better start talking. Otherwise, I'll find ways to *make* you talk."

She whimpered and held my gaze. "Don't hurt me. They forced me to help."

"Shut up!" The dark-haired one snarled at the blonde and snapped her teeth at her like a rabid dog. "They'll kill you if you talk!"

I smirked at the darker one. "Who said I won't kill you if you don't?"

"I can't," the blonde said. "You don't understand. They have my little boy."

Interesting. So she wasn't one of their club whores? Or maybe she was, but they'd used the kid as leverage. Seemed she wasn't loyal to the Raging Demons. The she-bitch next to her, however, seemed to be one hundred percent in their corner.

"We'll get your kid from them and keep him safe," I said. "If you cooperate with us, and tell us everything you know, we'll relocate the both of you to wherever you'd like to go."

"You won't." Tears slipped down her cheeks. Looked like she'd been around the other club long enough to have been interrogated before, or witnessed one. "It's all my fault."

"Girl, you're talking in circles and giving me a fucking headache. Spit it out."

She looked away and fidgeted. The way she scanned the area tipped me off. She was stalling. The innocent act had been a way of luring us in, treating her nicer than the other one. They wanted to soften us up, distract us with a woman in trouble. And it had fucking worked!

I yelled out for Hornet. He charged around the corner. "What's up, Bear?"

"Go to my house. Check on my family. Something tells me none of this was an actual plan to ruin the club. It was a distraction, and we fell for it."

"What? Me? You don't want to…" He shut up at the look I gave him. Did I prefer to be the one checking on my wife and kids? Yes. But as the Sergeant-at-Arms, I had a job to do. Not to mention, I didn't want to give the Raging Demons the satisfaction of me racing over there. If they had anyone else watching, it would tell them Faith was important to me.

Hornet took off and I heard his bike start a moment later. I hunkered down in front of the blonde and noticed the darker-haired one smirking at me. Yeah, they'd laid a trap and I'd walked right into it.

"You even have a kid?" I asked.

She nodded. "It belongs to one of the Raging Demons. If I do what they say, I get to keep my son."

"And your friend here?" I asked.

"She likes their attention. She's just as twisted as the lot of them. I didn't mean to get involved with them. Someone invited me to a party. It wasn't until I got there, I realized I was the entertainment. They drugged me and raped me. My son is the result of that night. Since then, they've kept tabs on me. If I don't do what they say, when they say, they threaten my son's life."

"Such a stupid whore," the other woman said, spitting at the blonde. "You think your boy will be safe after this? He won't. And neither will you."

"Lock the two of them up. Have Surge look into the blonde's story. If there's a boy in trouble, we'll find a way to save him. As to the other one, I doubt she'll be alive much longer. That one seems to be rotten to the core. We can either handle it ourselves or let the Raging Demons think she talked. If we release her after making them doubt her loyalty, she won't last long."

The dark-haired woman paled, and I knew I was right. She might be supportive of them, but she was just another hole to fuck. None of them would think twice of ending her life.

"You got it, Bear."

The fire flickered to life again in the dark-haired one's eyes, and it sent a chill down my spine. "You're too late anyway. By now, Spade has what he wants. That cheating whore is going to pay for what she's done. When he's finished with her, she'll wish she was dead."

Iron and Freak dragged the women away. As much as I wanted to race to my house to see if what the bitch said was true, I needed to take care of the mess here first. If they had Faith, I'd stop at nothing to get her back. I only hoped she could hold on until I got there. For now, I needed to act calm and cool. I couldn't let anyone see how shaken I was.

I went back into the clubhouse to try and figure out what the hell was going on. I'd had every intention of sticking around until we got the tox screen back on Cotton and the nameless girl, as well as information on who the hell she was. That is until Hornet came bursting through the doors with an unconscious Piper in his arms, blood dripping off her fingertips.

The moment I saw my daughter in such bad shape, I was no longer acting as the club's Sergeant-at-Arms. I became her father first and foremost and knew whoever had hurt her would pay with their life. Calm and cool? Not any-fucking-more.

"Where's Faith and Cordelia?" I asked as Hornet carried Piper over to the bar and set her on top. I took her hand, not liking how cold it felt, or the pallor of her skin.

"Gone." Hornet held my gaze. "Someone not only broke into your house, they tried to kill Piper and busted in the bathroom door. We found Cordelia's shoe in the front yard, but no sign of her or Faith. They took them."

"Get Fox and Rocket. If Dread is finished with Cotton and the girl, bring him too."

I tried to remain composed. Inside, it felt like a demon had been released. I seethed with fury. Wanted to bathe the world in blood. When I caught Spade and the Raging Demons, I'd tear them apart with my bare hands. Nothing would be left when I finished with them.

No one takes my wife and daughter, or hurts anyone in my family, without paying the ultimate price. As soon as I knew Piper would be okay, I'd hunt them down.

Hold on, Faith and Cordy. I'm coming for you.

* * *

Faith

My heart slammed against my ribs. I could only hope Piper would be all right. I'd never forget the sight of her lying on the floor bleeding. Spade tore through the bathroom door, splintering the wood. He'd grabbed me by my hair and dragged me out. One of his club members had picked up Cordelia, who screamed and thrashed, trying to break free.

Tears streaked my cheeks, but I tried to hold it together. I'd noticed Piper was still breathing, which meant she had time if someone found her soon enough. Whatever had sent Bear away from us, I had a feeling Spade and the Raging Demons had planned it. He'd only been gone fifteen minutes before Spade made his move.

"You shouldn't have run, Faith."

"I couldn't let you kill another baby." I glared at Spade. "The doctor said after this one, I can't have more children. I refused to sit back and let you destroy our child."

He smirked. "So it's a boy, then."

"Please, Spade. Just let us go! You don't want any of us. Think of the freedom! No one to take care of. No financial responsibilities outside your club. My running away was as much a favor to you as it was to me."

He lashed out, his hand cracking across my cheek so hard it knocked my head sideways and my face throbbed. "There was your first mistake, Faith. You dared to *think*. You were supposed to be silent and obey. That's all I needed from you."

"You don't love me. You don't care about any of us! Why did you keep us?"

"Because I *did* need you, Faith. Having you under my thumb gave me a thrill. Everyone who met you and our little brats felt sorry for you. They wanted to help you. To save you from me and my club." He grinned. "I put every one of them in their place, made sure they knew if they helped you escape, I'd do unspeakable things to all of you."

"You're a monster," I said, lifting my chin. "I'm glad I ran. It allowed me to meet a *real* man. You're pathetic, Spade. You control people through fear and pain, but Bear will always have the one thing you can never have."

He snarled and leaned in closer. "And what's that?"

"Respect."

He fisted his hand, and I flinched when he moved. He slammed his knuckles into my face once. Twice. On the third blow, my ears rang and my vision blurred. I tried to focus and saw little Cordy slipping out of the room. *Good girl*!

Spade's club not only dragged us from our home, but they'd tossed us into the back of a van. While they'd been occupied, I'd leaned in to whisper to Cordelia. She was our only hope.

"I'm going to distract them. When I do, you need to run. Don't stop until you find your way back to the Hades Abyss. Pay attention to your surroundings. You'll have to tell him where to find me."

Cordelia nodded and leaned into me. "Promise, Mama."

"Be brave. As long as I know you and Piper aren't with the Raging Demons, I'll be able to hold onto hope."

I hadn't told her my one and only goal had been saving her. I knew Spade would do exactly as he'd threatened. Not only would he make sure I lost the baby, he'd let his club do whatever they wanted to me. By morning, I'd most likely be dead. I hoped Bear would take care of the girls. Keep them safe. Help them grow up to be strong women.

A tear slipped down my cheek. Spade grinned, clearly thinking it was because of the pain of him hitting me, but it wasn't. No, it was because I knew I'd never see Bear or my children again. I didn't see a way for me to get out of this alive. Why hadn't I told him how much I loved him? Now I'd never get the chance.

I was weak. Pathetic. I'd not only let Spade capture me and our youngest, but I'd stayed with him far longer than I should have. I'd let fear rule me, and now I'd pay the price. I'd been so stupid at sixteen, falling for Spade and all his lies. As much as I'd suffered at his hands, I couldn't regret everything. If I hadn't been with him, I wouldn't have Piper or Cordelia. They'd been the light of my life, and I could never wish them away.

"Spade, the little bitch is gone," one of his brothers said.

"Doesn't matter. She won't survive long in this

neighborhood. We have what we came for." He reached out to smooth my hair back from my face. I glared at him, wishing I could tear his hand off. "So let's get to it, shall we? Someone bring the syringe to me."

Wait, what? What the hell did he plan to give me? I tensed, wondering if he'd drug me before letting his club have me. No, that would be a kindness. So that meant… he planned to get rid of my baby.

"Boss, I think…"

Spade lashed out, smashing his fist into the man's face. Why did they call him *boss*? I didn't see any patches on his cut denoting him as an officer. I'd never met anyone from his club before. He'd kept us separate from them. The few times they'd stopped by the house, he hadn't let them inside.

"I get that you're pissed, but this isn't the answer, Spade. I think you're starting to believe all the lies you've told," said another man. I saw the patch on his cut said *Thumper*.

"What lies?" I asked, before I could stop myself. The guy called Thumper winced.

"I didn't start out as a criminal," Spade said. He'd surprised me. Not only his words, but the fact he was going to tell me what Thumper meant. Of course, in movies that always meant the person was going to die. I wouldn't be a threat to him once he'd finished with me. "When I met you, I'd been part of the Raging Demons for about two and a half years. I had to do whatever they said so my cover wouldn't be blown. They noticed the way I looked at you and gave me an order. Lure you in. Use you. Chain you to me any way I could. I didn't have a choice but to listen."

"What?" My brow furrowed. "You aren't making any sense. The way you looked at me?"

Thumper came closer. "We were never supposed to be part of this club. We were deep undercover. But the Raging Demons were suspicious of us. Spade decided to start checking out underage girls, appear less law-abiding. It worked. So he asked you out. It got us deeper into the club, but then everything went to shit. Our superiors discovered Spade here had not only been dating you but had gotten you pregnant. You were underage, and he was quite a bit older than you."

My head was starting to hurt from information overload. I couldn't make sense of any of it. Why had they tried to get into the Raging Demons? Superiors… Undercover. Had they been cops? Or federal agents? Either way, how had Spade not gone to jail after they learned he'd gotten me pregnant?

"Did you know I had a younger brother who looked just like me?" Spade asked. "He was the original Spade. He came home one night and OD'd. That's when my boss had the brilliant idea of putting me in my brother's place. Even though I was five years older than him, we could have been twins. Even the Raging Demons didn't notice. A few times they seemed to question if I was still the same man, but I'd gotten the same ink as my little brother, studied him and the club. I was able to step into his shoes without issue."

"Then Spade pulled me in, along with another undercover agent. The goal was to take down the Raging Demons. Instead, things went so far, we lost our jobs and had no choice but to start living the lives we'd made with the Raging Demons. Since we didn't report Spade immediately, or try to stop him, we were also held accountable." Thumper folded his arms. The tenseness in his jaw, and the darkening of his eyes told me he didn't like the life he'd been handed. "Except this one went too far."

I looked at Spade and saw the rage in his eyes, as well as a good dose of insanity. Was all of this true? It seemed like too much. It had to be a story they were fabricating as a way to lower my guard, right? This sort of thing only happened in movies, didn't it?

"What's in the syringe?" I asked.

"Drugs," Spade said. "It seems Thumper still has a conscience. So I'm going to dope you up before the fun begins. I only planned to use the girls as a way to control you, until you died. Then I was going to sell them."

Bile rose in my throat. "How could you have ever been a decent man? You'd sell your own children? You're going to drug me and let your club rape me? You're a monster, Spade, and that didn't happen overnight. I think you were always evil."

He smiled. "You're right. Thumper here is basically a good guy. Same for our old buddy, Ratchet. They didn't like the things they had to do in order to infiltrate the Raging Demons. Me? I got off on it."

"So why are you listening to them now?" I asked. Maybe if I stalled him long enough, Cordelia would get to Bear. I didn't think it was likely, but I could hope. Or maybe I could find a way to appeal to Thumper. He didn't look like he wanted to be part of this.

"If they don't prove themselves tonight, the club will kill them. They've been drawing too much attention to themselves with those pesky consciences. Since I brought them in, it means I'll be punished as well. A little drug to knock you out, and the boys will be able to perform just fine."

No, that was too easy. I watched Spade and the other two. That's when I realized Spade only wanted to save himself. He needed them to get through this little test with the club so no one would hurt him or try to kick him out of the Raging Demons. Once the test was over, he'd see Thumper and Ratchet as a complication. A loose end.

"You're going to kill them, aren't you?" I asked. "When all this is over, you'll stab them in the back."

Thumper eyed Spade, and I knew he'd realized the same thing. He lifted his gaze to Rachet's and before I realized what was happening, they both dove for Spade. The men threw punches and kicked at Spade. The brawl destroyed the room we were in, and I wondered why no one had called the police. Then I remembered Spade saying we were in a bad area. I hoped like hell Cordelia had gotten away safely.

I inched my way to the corner, hoping to stay out of their way. The door was too far. I'd never make it. I pressed tighter to the wall and crept farther away from the men. I'd nearly made it to the hall when a loud *bang* startled me. I saw Spade standing with a gun in his hand, and Thumper lay on the ground. Blood soaked the carpet under him, and his sightless eyes stared up at the ceiling. Before I could utter a sound, he swung the weapon toward Ratchet and pulled the trigger twice more. The other man fell, and I knew my only chance for escaping was now gone.

Spade tucked the gun into his holster. "Now. The distractions are gone, and we can have some fun. How about it, Faith? Let's get reacquainted. Show me everything you've learned while you've been with the other club."

I fisted my hands at my sides and realized I had one last chance to get out of this. Play along, give him what he wanted, then run like hell the second he dropped his guard.

"Fine. Where's the bedroom?"

Spade smirked. "Knew you'd be a good girl. Down the hall. We'll spend some quality time together, then I'll take you home. My brothers can't wait to have a taste."

I'd die first. Before I let any of them touch me, I'd take my own life. I'd be dying either way. Might as well go out on my terms.

Please forgive me, Bear. I wasn't strong enough.

Chapter Nine

Bear

Dread managed to patch up Piper and gave her fluids through an IV. I didn't want to take her home until I'd had time to wipe out any traces of what happened. Spider offered to let her stay at his house. Besides, I had to go after Faith. There was no telling where she was. On the off chance the girls were taken, I'd put a tracker in their shoes. Except they'd left Piper behind, and the shoe Cordy lost was the one with the tracking device.

I'd put one in Faith's purse and could track the phone I gave her. Neither item had left with her. I had Surge checking footage from the cameras around town, hoping we'd see something. He'd caught them loading Faith into an unmarked van, then tossing Cordelia in behind her. No plates. A complete dead end. The camera feed didn't extend far enough for us to see which way they'd gone. It could take a while for him to locate the van again.

"Anythin' on Cotton and the girl?" I asked.

Fox leaned against my living room wall. "Her name is Roe Wagner. She's twenty-two. Goes to church every Sunday, volunteers around town, and helps anyone who is in need. Girl is a fucking angel. I have no idea how they got her here, but it's clear why they chose her."

"Saint Roe…" I shook my head. "They wanted the town to crucify us once everyone heard what happened. How's Cotton handlin' this?"

"Good, all things considered."

Surge entered the house without knocking. "I didn't find the van, but I found something better. Let's go."

I made sure I had my keys and walked out with Fox on my heels. The two of us, along with Rocket and Yankee got on our bikes and followed him out of the compound and through the streets of town. When we entered the worst part of town, a knot of worry settled in my gut. He'd have told me if Faith wasn't alive anymore, right? Or if she'd been hurt… He wouldn't let me walk into that blindly.

Surge pulled over and jerked his chin toward the front of a convenience store. And that's when I saw her. Little Cordy, with only one shoe on, huddled in the shadows. My heart gave a kick and I got off the bike, striding toward her. The moment she saw me, tears ran down her cheeks and she ran for me. I scooped her into my arms and held her close.

"I've got you. Everything's goin' to be all right."

She held on tight and shook her head. "Mama is in trouble."

"I know. We're going to get her. But you're safe now, Cordelia. I'll have Rocket take you back with him. All right? You hold onto him tight, and he'll ride slow. Let Dread check you out when you get back to the compound, and I'll be right behind you with your mom."

Some of the tension drained from her slight body. "I don't know how far I ran. She told me to escape and pay attention to landmarks. I saw a place with neon lights that made it look like ladies were dancing on the sign. A store that sells alcohol, and… and… A church! It looked really run down."

I knew where she meant. That narrowed down the neighborhood. Now I just needed to know exactly where Faith was. "Can you tell me which buildin' she's in?"

"House. It… it was blue, I think. The porch

sagged and I thought I'd fall through the boards when I ran. It smelled bad too."

"I'll find it."

Surge took her hand. "Cordy, can you tell me what direction you came from? When you saw the dancing ladies, were they on your right or left?"

"Left," she said.

"Did you turn any corners before getting there?"

She nodded. "One. I only saw houses right there and it was about a block later I saw the church."

"Last question, then you can go. When you turned the corner, were you on the same side of the street as the church or across from it?"

"Across."

"Good girl." Surge ruffled her hair. "We're going to go get your mom. You've been a lot of help, Cordelia."

I set her down and Rocket came to take her hand. He led her over to his bike, then got on, not moving until she'd climbed on behind him and had a death grip on his waist. I watched them ride off before facing Surge again.

"You know where she's talkin' about?" I asked. "I've got an idea of the general vicinity, but not that particular street and house."

"Yeah. The street anyway. Finding the exact house? Let's just hope the van is there."

I let Surge lead the way. By the time we reached the street, I was ready to beat the hell out of someone. I'd make an example of everyone who hurt Faith and my girls. They'd dared to enter my home and take them. I also knew after this, I'd retire whether Fox liked it or not. If I couldn't keep my own wife and kids safe, I wasn't fit to be the Sergeant-at-Arms.

Surge slowed when he saw the blue house and

the van he'd spotted on the camera footage. We stopped at the curb, and the hair on my nape stood up. No one inside came to check out the noise of our bikes. I didn't think that was a good sign. We should have asked Cordelia how many there were.

"Surge, how many put my girls into the van?" I asked.

"Two, plus the driver. No idea if they met up with more after that, though."

I nodded. Pulling the 9mm I'd holstered at my side, I approached the house and went up onto the porch. As Cordy said, it felt like I'd fall through the rotten boards. The door didn't appear to be latched and I nudged it with my toe. My eyebrows went up when I saw the body just inside the door. Blood soaked the floor. I entered and spotted a second one. Did that mean only Spade was left?

I knelt and felt for a pulse, even though the guy was clearly not getting back up. His skin hadn't cooled yet, so he hadn't been dead for too long. Same for the second one. Thumper and Ratchet were on their cuts.

I heard yelling from the back of the house and went deeper into the house. Fox and Surge were right behind me, watching my six. As we neared what I assumed were the bedrooms, I heard the words Spade spewed, and I tightened my hold on my gun. As badly as I wanted to put a bullet in his head and end it, I needed more than that. I wanted to make him suffer. To beg for his life.

I kicked in the door and what I saw made a red haze settle over my vision. I pulled the trigger and the fucker fell to the floor. Faith scrambled off the bed and ran for us. Instead of catching her, I stepped to the side and let her crash into Fox. I approached Spade and kicked the asshole in the ribs.

"You get off on rapin' another man's woman?" I asked.

"She's just a stupid whore." He spat blood on the floor. Looked like I'd hit something vital. Didn't give me as much time as I'd have liked. Without medical attention, he'd bleed out. "Not like I haven't fucked her before. Brat in her belly is mine."

"Wrong answer." I holstered my gun and pulled the brass knuckles from my pocket. I slammed my fist into his face, then kicked him again so he rolled to his back. I noticed his pants were unfastened, but it didn't look like he'd gotten further than that. If he had, I'd have cut off his pathetic little dick.

I used his head as a punching bag until he spit out teeth and appeared to be seconds from blacking out. Yanking him off the floor, I landed a blow to his kidneys twice, then pulled back my arm and put every ounce of power I had into the next hit, right in the middle of his spine. The metal of the brass knuckles hit bone, and I heard the *crack* right before he screamed and crumpled to the floor.

"Bear." I looked over at Surge, chest heaving, and still wanting this fucker's blood. "Your woman and girls need you. Finish up."

I hit both his knees multiple times, broke his hands and every fucking finger. When I finally stopped, I made sure he didn't have a way to contact anyone, and I left him lying in his own piss and blood.

"Want me to shoot him?" Surge asked.

"No. I want him to suffer until he's drawn his last breath. He'll be dead within the hour. Just make sure no one finds him. Once he's gone, bury all three of them."

Surge nodded. "You got it."

I rinsed my hands and the brass knuckles. I

slipped them back into my pocket before I went out to Faith and Fox. He held her close, and I realized he'd given her his shirt. As much as I hated seeing her in another man's clothes, it was better than her flashing her breasts to the world. Since Spade managed to tear her shirt and bra, she'd have been exposed.

"Thanks, Brother. I got it from here." I lifted Faith in my arms and kissed her softly. "Come on, sweetheart. Time to go home."

She curled into me. "I was afraid I'd never see you again."

"Told you I'd keep you safe. I fuckin' failed, but there was no way I wouldn't come for you, Faith. I'm glad you were strong enough to hold on until I got here, and it was smart as hell to send Cordelia out of here to go find help. She's the reason we got to you as quickly as we did."

"Good. I'm glad she's all right. Take me home, Bear. I need a shower."

"Not goin' home. Not yet. Need to straighten the place up still and get a new bathroom door and front door. Have to replace the floorin' too. Might as well paint the walls."

"Piper?" she lifted her head. "Is she…"

"Dread patched her up. She'll be okay."

"Bring her to my house," Fox said. "I'll ask Raven to get clothes for Faith and the girls. They can clean up while you figure out where everyone is going to stay. Sounds like a good time for a vacation. Take the family out of town for a week."

"This isn't over," I said. "You think they won't come for us now that we've taken out some of their men?"

"I don't think they will," Faith said. "I'll explain later. Right now, I really want to get clean."

I kissed her again and helped her onto my bike. Had Spade acted on his own? Was it possible his club hadn't given a shit either way about Faith and the girls? Even though the fucker would be dead soon enough, I still had more questions than answers. I didn't like feeling that we had unfinished business with the Raging Demons.

Later. Right now, I needed to take care of Faith. She and the girls were more important than anything else right now.

* * *

Faith

Dread treated me and the girls, and once Piper could be moved, they brought her to Fox's house. We'd overtaken their living room, but Raven didn't seem to mind. She fussed over the girls.

"So you're telling us Spade and the two dead men at the house were all undercover agents?" Fox asked. "Like local police or higher up?"

"Right. At least, that's what the one called Thumper said. From the way he spoke, I think maybe DEA? Since they were investigating the Raging Demons, that would make more sense. Then Spade went too far, and whoever they were affiliated with cut ties with them. I guess they blamed Thumper and Ratchet for not reporting Spade or stopping him. They were officially outlaws then, and part of the Raging Demons for real."

I leaned against Bear's side, and he had his arm around my shoulder. He hadn't let me out of his sight since he'd brought me back to the compound. I wondered how long before I'd be allowed to even use the bathroom on my own. He'd helped me shower and dress, which had been nice. I wasn't sure my legs would have held me. Spade had shaken me more than I'd liked. I hadn't been gone from his house all that long, and yet the pain he'd inflicted felt as shocking as it had the first time he'd raised his fist to me.

"Make a list of what you want done to the house, and I'll make sure it's handled," Fox said.

"Where are we going to stay right now?" Cordelia asked.

"The Pres said we need to take a vacation," Bear said. "Where do you want to go?"

"Can Piper travel?" I asked.

"Not today, but we'll have Dread check her again tomorrow. If she's stable enough for a car ride, we'll take the truck and hit the road." Bear motioned for Cordelia to come closer. "Name a few places you've always wanted to see, or things you've wanted to do."

"I've never been to a zoo," she said. "They look fun, but I don't think Piper can do that right now."

Piper opened her eyes and looked at us. "I can rest somewhere while the three of you go to the zoo. Just FaceTime me or something so I can be there too without having to walk around."

I looked at the bandage on her shoulder and the ones on her leg. She hadn't given me any details, but it seemed someone shot her in the shoulder, then used her own knife to slice up her leg. Deep enough, she'd needed stitches in each wound. Because of the location of the cuts, she wouldn't be walking very far for a while. Not until she'd healed a bit. I'd only gleaned that much from Dread when Piper hadn't been paying attention. My brave girl was doing her best to hide her condition from me.

"Piper, we should go to the zoo as a family," I said.

"Right, and we will be. Even if I'm only there

virtually, I'll still be part of it. I don't want Cordelia to miss out on anything else, especially because of me. I'll be okay, Mom. Just make sure I have something to eat and drink."

"Are you a pet?" Bear asked, smiling a little. "What if we rented a wheelchair at the zoo? Think you could go, then?"

"Maybe."

"I'll go pull a list of the three closest zoos, and the other family attractions around each," Raven said. "Want me to check on hotels in those areas too?"

"That would be great," Bear said.

"What happened when the men entered the house?" Fox asked. "How did you get hurt, Piper?"

"She wouldn't come into the bathroom with us," Cordelia said.

"Stubborn girl," Bear muttered. What had he thought would happen when he armed her? She wanted to be tough, invincible… but she wasn't. "Once you're healed, I'm going to teach you how to use a firearm, and how to fight with a knife. Wouldn't hurt for Cordelia to learn too."

"Not me?" I asked.

"Not while you're pregnant." He glanced at my belly. "The baby all right? I'd feel better if you got checked out at the hospital, or at least had an ultrasound."

"The baby is moving around, so he's fine." He put his hand over my belly. I didn't know if he'd be able to feel it or not. I felt little flutters here and there, so I knew the baby had made it through the ordeal. I probably had another month or two before Bear would be able to feel it. Spade had never cared, and it had been too long since Cordelia was a baby for me to remember much about the pregnancy milestones.

"If the girls don't mind camping out in the living room, all of you can stay here. The adults get the spare room, and the kids get the couch and a sleeping bag." Fox rubbed his hands together. "This could be fun. Harlow is only four, but it can be her first official sleepover. She may want to camp out with Cordy and Piper."

"If Piper wants the couch, I could sleep on the floor in Harlow's room," Cordy said. "I don't mind."

"Then it's settled. I'll order something for dinner, make sure we have popcorn for the girls to munch on during a movie, and the adults can move to the kitchen to strategize this impromptu vacation."

Raven came back with several sheets of printed paper in her hands. "I heard that. I'll go put on some coffee. Faith, do you prefer tea? I could boil some water for you."

"Thank you, Raven. I'll come help."

Bear tightened his hold on me. "No, you'll sit and rest. You look like you went a few rounds with Mike Tyson. You've started to bruise already. By tomorrow, part of your face will be black and purple."

"With Piper all banged up too, people are going to stare," I said.

"We'll just say the two of you were in an accident. Easier to explain than what really happened."

"I'm still figuring out what happened," I muttered. How could have Spade have led an entirely different life, and I'd never known about it? For that matter, how did that monster ever become part of law enforcement?

"Pres, need to have a chat with you," Bear said, standing up. "Faith, go sit with Raven in the kitchen. I'll be there in a minute."

"No, you'll go there now. I don't accept your

resignation," Fox said. "Didn't take it the other times you tried to step down either."

"I fuckin' failed!" Bear growled and folded his arms over his chest. "My wife and kids could have died."

"And through it all, you took care of the club, then went after them. I saw you stay at the clubhouse, get things sorted, and then go look for your family. I also know what it cost you to do that. In the future, just tell me you're leaving and get the fuck out of there. I'd have understood, and so would your brothers. But your wife and daughters might not be so forgiving that they came in second to this club."

I stood on shaky legs and held onto Bear's bicep. "I do understand. To some extent. What would have happened if you left the clubhouse and came for us the second you realized something was wrong?"

"I'd have been the one to find Piper, would have taken her out of the damn house and called Dread to tend to her, and then I'd have been spinning my wheels trying to figure out what the hell happened to you and Cordelia," he said.

"And by staying, did you learn anything useful?" I asked.

"Sort of. Found out it was Spade for certain who had you. The two whores talked a little, but not as much as I've have liked. Then Surge checked any camera footage he could find around town and the compound, trying to figure out the best way to track you. It's how he found Cordelia."

"So you'd have needed to stay at the compound regardless until you had more information," I said. "Sounds to me like you did the right thing. Whoever you sent to the house didn't get there before we'd been taken. You couldn't have done anything different by going yourself."

"Dad, we don't blame you for what happened," Piper said.

"Well, I blame myself."

I tugged on his arm and led him to the kitchen. He pulled out a chair and sat, then brought me down onto his lap. I leaned back against him and wondered how I'd get through to him. Spade had watched and waited. He not only had the experience behind him of being an outlaw biker, but he'd been in law enforcement too. Bear might have had military experience, but he hadn't counted on Spade's secret background. He'd gone into a fight without all the facts, and I thought he'd handled things rather well.

Raven handed the papers to Bear, and we looked over the options. Once we'd selected a destination, he left with Fox to discuss the particulars. I caught the President's gaze on his way out, and he gave me a nod. I knew he'd have a talk with Bear and try to get the tough guy to go easy on himself. He'd done what he'd thought was best. I couldn't blame him for it, not when it's what he'd been trained to do.

It looked like I'd have a week to work on him. Hopefully, by the time we came back, he'd be ready to step back into his role as the Sergeant-at-Arms for the club, and he'd have forgiven himself.

Life was too short for regrets.

Chapter Ten

Bear

After we learned more about Spade, Thumper, and Ratchet, I'd asked Surge to dig into their backgrounds a bit more. The last thing the club needed was the damn Feds nosing around the Hades Abyss. If they were tracking those men, and knew they'd come here, there could be problems. I knew Fox already spoke with the Raging Demons' President and settled the issue with their club. Finding out all three men were once undercover agents had gone a long way to smoothing things over. In fact, they'd said we did them a favor.

I pushed Piper's wheelchair as we made our way through the St. Louis Zoo. Cordelia bounced with excitement and made a huge deal out of every exhibit. I found it cute as fuck, and I could tell Faith did too. I pushed Piper up to the railing so she could watch the elephants. One stood in the water and kept using his trunk to spray water everywhere.

Piper lifted the little digital camera I'd bought her this morning and snapped a picture. Turning her chair, I motioned for Cordelia and Faith to come closer.

"Let me see the camera, Piper. Need a shot of my three girls in front of the elephants."

A woman with four kids slowly approached. "I couldn't help but overhear. Would you like me to take a picture of the four of you? I know how hard it is to get a shot of the entire family."

I gave her the camera and went to stand behind Faith. The woman snapped the photo and gave the camera back to Piper.

"Thank you," I called out to her. She smiled and waved before herding her kids in the other direction.

"What animal do you want to see next?" Faith asked.

"Bears!" Cordelia clapped her hands. "I hope they have a lot of them."

"Piper? What animal are you most looking forward to seeing?" I asked.

"I like bears too, but..."

"But what?" I asked.

"I'd like to see the hippos and I heard there's an aquarium." She glanced at Cordelia. "But the bears sound fun. Why don't see those first?"

Faith looked at the map. "We're in the River's Edge right now. Looks like hippos are here, but so are Andean and Malayan Sun bears. I don't see why we can't visit both before moving to another area."

"Any food on there?" I asked, my stomach growling loudly.

"We could see whichever bear is just ahead, then backtrack to the cheetahs. Food isn't too far from there, then we can see the other exhibits before we exit this area." Faith folded the map and tucked it back into the pocket of her dress. "Does that work for everyone?"

"Fine, but you need to feed *this* bear," I grumbled.

Piper snickered. "All right, Papa Bear, but it clearly says not to feed the animals."

"Watch it." I playfully tugged her hair before pushing her chair again. Because of her shoulder wound, I didn't want her trying to wheel herself around, and Faith didn't need to strain herself. Besides, I enjoyed helping our oldest in her time of need.

Since I hadn't known whether the other places we'd visit would have a wheelchair we could rent, I'd purchased one. I'd gone to two local pharmacies, Walmart, and finally found one at the hardware store, of all places. It wasn't spectacular, and I'd bought an extra cushion for it, but it would do for now. And the club would have access to one if we needed it again in the future.

By the time we made it to the food, I was ready to eat everything on the menu. Then I saw my wife's face. She frowned as she stared at the selection, and I knew she was thinking of all the grease and fat. I'd already told her I wasn't going to eat healthy while we were on vacation, but I had a feeling I'd be paying for it later. Every cheeseburger I consumed probably meant I had to eat a salad when we got home. If my brothers knew my current thoughts, they'd laugh their asses off. But honestly, I liked having someone worry about me.

"Everyone get whatever you want. We won't eat again until after we leave the zoo. We'll stop somewhere for dinner on the way to the hotel."

"No, we'll go shower and change before we eat anywhere," Faith said. "I'm not going to sit down somewhere smelling like we rubbed ourselves all over the smelly animals."

Cordy rolled her eyes. "Like anyone is going to say something in front of Daddy. You could probably throw up on someone's shoes, and they'd take one look at him before apologizing for being in your way."

I covered my mouth so I wouldn't laugh. That girl was something else. She'd really opened up and come out of her shell since being kidnapped with her mom. I'd told Faith that our youngest had grown up a lot that day. Running for help had been good for her, even if it had scared her shitless.

We got our food and sat at a nearby table. I helped Piper stand and sit on one of the benches so she could take a break from being in the wheelchair. Once I had her settled, I made sure everyone had what they needed, then dug into my food.

"We should probably rest in the mornin', then check out some other places around lunch or just after," I said. "I think we're going to be pretty wiped out after walkin' around this place all day."

Faith reached up to touch her face, and I knew she was checking her makeup. One of the old ladies had told her about some stuff to cover her bruises. I had to admit, it worked really well. I'd have been fine without her hiding her wounds, but I knew she felt self-conscious about it, and worried someone would think I beat her.

"It's fine," I told her, reaching over to pull her hand down.

By the time we finished, and I had Piper back in her wheelchair, I had to admit I was ready to call it a day. Not my girls, though. Nope, if anything, Cordy seemed to have twice as much as energy as before. I kept an eye on Faith and Piper, not wanting either of them to overdo it today. The moment they seemed exhausted, I'd call a halt to the zoo visit. It wasn't like we couldn't come back some other time.

Piper took pictures of every animal we saw, including some of our family. We found a few other people willing to take pictures of all four of us, and by the time we left, even Cordelia looked tired.

"Did everyone have a good time?" I asked as we loaded into the truck.

"Yes!" Cordy smiled widely. "It was the best day ever! I can't wait to see what we do tomorrow and the day after."

Thanks to the renovations on the house, we'd be in St. Louis for at least another three days. Fox said to stay longer if that's what we wanted to do, and I rather liked having this time with my girls and not worrying about club business. At the same time, I wouldn't mind sleeping in my own bed again sometime soon.

"Since your mom doesn't want to smell like the zoo, we'll go to the hotel so we can shower and change. Then we'll decide where we'd like to eat. I think after dinner, we need to call it a night. You girls can stay in your room and watch TV if you aren't ready for bed."

Faith leaned into me to whisper. "Not very subtle."

I lightly swatted her ass. "Don't care."

Since this was our first family vacation, I'd splurged a little and gotten a two-bedroom suite. We even had a small living area and a mini kitchen. Mostly, I'd wanted to have some alone time with Faith. If we'd had to share the same room with the girls, I knew I'd have blue balls before we went back home. Not that Faith and I were having sex every day. Still, it was nice to be intimate with my wife when we were both up for it. Hell, even just holding her at night, and being able to talk to her without the girls overhearing was enjoyable.

In fact, we'd had such a pleasant time, I wanted to do this at least once a year. Maybe not come back to St. Louis for the next trip, but there were plenty of places within driving distance. I wanted my little family to experience all the wonderful things they'd missed out on. For that matter, I hadn't done fun shit like this either. All my traveling had been either for the military or club business. Having time to relax and enjoy my family was something I planned to do as often as possible.

* * *

Faith

We'd only been home from St. Louis for two days when Bear said the entire family needed to head to the clubhouse. He'd explained before there would be family days. It still felt odd going to the same building where the men screwed random women. As a mother, I wasn't sure how I felt about my children entering the place.

Bear put his arm around me before we went inside and tugged me against his side. "What's botherin' you?"

"This is where all the parties are, right? With random women, alcohol, possibly even drugs or at least cigarette smoke."

"Well, yeah, but none of that will be goin' on tonight. It's family only. Prospects scrubbed the place down." Bear eyed the building. "Why does all that matter right now?"

"You're asking our teenage daughters to enter a place where men have sex with strangers, get intoxicated, and who knows what else goes on in there. It doesn't seem wrong to you?" I asked.

Raven and Fox came up beside us, and I saw her looking at the building with a disgruntled expression. "I never thought about it before, but she's right. Should we take our daughters into a place where women are treated like whores? We're basically saying the place needs to be cleansed before it's okay for them to enter, but it's perfectly fine for y'all to treat women like something to be used when your kids aren't around."

"You two are about to open up a can of worms you don't want to touch," Bear said. "I get where you're comin' from, but what do you suggest? Put up an entirely different building just for family days? Tell the single guys they can't cut loose at their own compound anymore?"

"Looks like I'm calling Church tomorrow," Fox said. "For tonight, come inside and hang out with the club."

Bear held me back when the others entered. I wondered if he was angry over what I'd said. At least if he was going to get upset with me, he made sure not to do it in front of anyone. We hadn't had a fight yet. I knew it wasn't realistic to think we'd never disagree about anything.

"Faith, you and the girls went in there just fine when you met the other families. What changed?"

"I heard about Roe." I turned so I was facing him. "I know she's not a child, but she's someone's daughter. It made me wonder how I'd feel if something like that happened to Piper or Cordelia when they were older. If your club wasn't known for being with any woman who walks through their doors, would Roe have gotten hurt like that? The Raging Demons wouldn't have been able to use her against the club."

Bear nodded. "You're right, in some ways. Yes, our lifestyle here gave them an opening, and they used it, hurting an innocent girl in the process. For that, I'm truly sorry. She didn't deserve that, and poor Cotton feels like shit about the entire thing. But we aren't law-abiding men, Faith, and the single guys have every right to party and screw whoever they want. No woman here is forced. They walk through the doors on their own."

"And Roe?" I asked.

"Why don't we go inside, and you can ask her yourself?" Bear nudged me toward the door. "She's here."

I looked behind us to tell Piper and Cordelia we were going inside, only to realize we were alone. I hadn't realized they'd gone in with everyone else earlier. I let Bear guide me into the building, and he took me straight to a table in the back, where a young woman sat. One I hadn't met before. *This must be Roe.*

"Roe, this is my wife, Faith. She's been worried about you," Bear said, pulling out a chair for me.

I sat and Raven came to join us. It wasn't long before our men brought drinks and a plate of food, and I noticed Cotton did the same for Roe, a blush staining his cheeks. Interesting. I wondered what happened between the two of them while I'd been on vacation. Roe flashed him a smile and said thank you before focusing her attention on us again.

"You have questions. Everyone has." Roe folded her hands in her lap. "First, I should tell you a little about myself. My name is Roe Wagner, and I'm an orphan. I never knew my parents. According to the state, someone abandoned me at a hospital the day I was born."

I placed my hand over my heart, pain piercing me at the thought of never knowing where she'd come from. I knew her parents must have had a reason for leaving her there. At least, I hoped they hadn't done it simply because they were selfish. While I couldn't imagine dropping my kids off somewhere and walking away, I knew there were moms out there who did so in order to give their children better lives.

"I've never found out who my parents were, or why they left me. I bounced around the foster system for a while. When I was eleven, a retired teacher adopted me. She was older, but she gave me a good home. Taught me to think of others and give back to the community. I loved her." Roe smiled, but I saw the sadness in her eyes. "She passed away when I was nineteen. Left everything to me, which wasn't much, but it's allowed me to live without stressing over where I'd live."

"She sounds like a wonderful person," I said.

Roe nodded. "She was."

"How did you get tangled up with the Raging Demons?" Raven asked.

"Two women approached me. Claimed to know who my father was." Roe took a sip of her drink. "The women said my father was part of this club. He'd gotten someone pregnant, and the woman had died giving birth to me."

I shared a look with Raven. "I don't know about all the men in this club, but if it had been Bear, he'd have never let go of his child."

Raven pressed her lips together. "It's not just him. So, Roe, if you really are the child of someone here, they didn't know about you. I can promise you that much. Did those women say who it was?"

"No. But they gave me my mother's name, which is something I hadn't had before. I looked into it before deciding to come here. Her name was Mary Mathis. While I couldn't dig deep enough to figure out who she'd been seeing, several people who'd known her confirmed she'd been pregnant and had been seeing someone at this club."

"How did they get that information? And why?" I asked.

"I didn't think to question them about it," she admitted.

Raven stood and glanced around the room, then waved Surge over. His brow furrowed as he approached. "Something wrong?"

"Did you know about why Roe came here?" she asked. "Don't tell me you couldn't figure out who her dad is, not with your skills. So who is it? Have you told them yet?"

Surge cleared his throat and stared down at his boots. "It's complicated. When I started digging, I realized Roe's father has more than one kid, and he isn't aware of either of them. I haven't known how to handle it."

"Did you tell Fox?" Raven asked, then gasped. "Wait, is it my Fox? Is he her dad?"

Surge shook his head. "No, it's not an officer. And neither is her half-brother."

"Oh, crap!" My eyes widened. "Are you telling me her dad's other kid is part of this club, and neither of them know about it?"

"Right. Now you see why I haven't said anything yet." Surge rubbed the back of his neck. "And when he finds out Roe is his daughter, I worry about what he'll do to Cotton. It wasn't Cotton's fault since he was drugged too, but…"

I motioned for Bear to come back over to me. He knelt beside my chair and took my hand. "You all right now?"

"I'm fine, but we have a problem. Do you know the name Mary Mathis?" I laced our fingers together. I knew it wouldn't have been Bear, since he couldn't have children. "Was she dating someone at this club twenty-two years ago?"

Bear went completely still. "Are you telling me Mary Mathis is Roe's mom?"

I nodded. "Surge said it gets worse. Whoever the dad is, one of your club brothers is also his kid, and neither of them is aware of it. Do you know who it is?"

"Marauder dated a much younger woman back then. Name was Mary. Sweet girl. He didn't bring her to the clubhouse more than twice because he could tell it made her uncomfortable. They dated for a few months, then one day, I never heard any more about her." Bear stood and pointed at Surge. "And you knew and didn't say anything?"

Surge held up his hands. "Bear, I didn't know how to tell him! Not only about Roe, but also…"

"Who?" Bear demanded.

"Iron," Surge muttered. "Roe's half-brother is Iron. They're both Marauder's kids."

A chair fell, slamming into the floor so loud it made the entire place go quiet. Surge turned and paled when he saw a large man glaring at him from the next table, fists clenched. I looked around the room and spotted Iron. He stared at the floor and stood so still I couldn't even tell if he was still breathing. Had we spoken louder than we'd realized? It seemed he'd heard us.

"I think the cat is out of the bag," I said.

"I have a son and daughter?" Marauder asked. "And you didn't fucking tell me?"

"I didn't know how!" Surge backed up a step. "I wasn't keeping it from you on purpose. Neither of your kids knew either."

I leaned into Bear so I could whisper to him. "How old is Iron?"

"Thirties. Marauder would have been in his twenties when he fathered him, which meant he either hadn't been patched yet, or was a new member of the club. I had no idea who Iron's mother is," Bear said.

"My mother was a piece of shit who didn't care if I ate as long as she got her next fix," Iron said. "If I had to guess, she was probably a club whore. She went by Bunny."

Marauder nodded his head. "Yeah, I remember her. Didn't know she'd gotten pregnant. Same for Roe's mother. Neither of them ever said a word to me.

I'd have never let them keep my kids from me."

Roe stood and slowly approached Marauder. "Then all of this was worth it. If it means I finally get to meet my dad, and get a brother too, I'd do it all over again."

Marauder pulled her into his arms and hugged her tight, then held his hand out to Iron. The other man stared at Marauder and Roe before walking out of the clubhouse. It looked like he wasn't quite as thrilled over finding out he had family. I hoped, for Roe's sake, he would come around.

"You like causin' trouble, don't you?" Bear whispered.

"It's not my fault!" I leaned back in my seat. "It's Surge's fault for keeping it a secret."

Raven stood. "Faith brought up a good point before she came inside tonight. She asked why we had family nights in the same building where our single members party. I think we just learned that Iron was conceived in this building, and I'm not sure how he's going to feel about this structure for a while. I know if it were me, I wouldn't want to step foot inside here. I propose we build something new for family nights."

I released Bear's hand and got up. "I second that!"

"Third," Colette said.

"Fourth." Violeta smoothed her hair back. "I've never liked what happens in this building, not after all I suffered before coming here. I know Luciana doesn't care for it either. We want a new building, one that hasn't been tainted."

"Pres, you going to let the old ladies run wild like this?" Shooter asked. "Since when do they make the rules?"

"As a father whose daughter was drugged and

raped in this very building, I agree with the women," Marauder said.

Cotton staggered back a step, all the blood draining from his face. I knew Marauder's words had hit him hard. Even though I hadn't spent time with him, if I'd learned anything it was the men here were honorable. I didn't think rape was something any of them would ever be guilty of.

"Cotton was a victim too," Roe said. "Please don't ever say that again… Dad."

"I think this family night is over," Fox said. "Church in the morning. Be here by nine o'clock. We have a lot to discuss."

"Any kids who want to hang out longer can come to our house," Spider said. "They can take over the living room and kitchen for another hour or two. Play games, watch movies. Whatever they want."

Everyone filed out of the building, and I saw Piper and Cordelia heading off with Marianna. I hadn't meant to start a revolution, but maybe it was time for some things to change. I only hoped Bear wasn't furious with me for opening my mouth tonight.

* * *

Bear

Several of my brothers already had a beer in their hands. I'd opted for coffee. While I'd been a little upset with Faith for stirring shit up last night, she'd only voiced her opinion, and it happened the other old ladies agreed. The night was meant to be a celebration. Fox had her property cut, and I'd wanted to give it to her at the party. Then everything went to hell.

Marauder took a seat, looking like he'd last slept a century ago. I noticed Cotton kept glancing at him, then quickly looking away. It made me wonder if the two had exchanged words after everyone left. Iron wouldn't look at anyone. Apparently, he was still sore over finding out who his dad was. Or maybe the way he'd found out was the most upsetting. The old ladies shouldn't have pushed as much as they had. I didn't know how Fox was going to react, especially since one of them had been his.

"I think we're all here," Fox said. "First, I'd like to apologize to Iron and Marauder. They shouldn't have found out about their relationship like that. Second, I already informed Surge I'm docking his cut on future jobs by five percent for the next three months. He should have come to me the moment he found a connection between Marauder, Iron, and Roe."

"And the women?" Shooter asked.

"Raven shouldn't have spoken up the way she did last night. However, it seems all the old ladies feel the same way about the clubhouse and the activities here. We all know the women enter those doors of their own free will. Even Roe came because she wanted to. What happened to her is another matter entirely."

Cotton cleared his throat and stood up. "I'd like to offer my own apology. Dread ran some tests and it showed both Roe and I had been drugged, however, I'm still the one who robbed her of her innocence. I'm sorry, Marauder, if I've offended you or your family. Roe is a sweet girl. I've offered to claim her, but she said no."

"You asked her before coming to me?" Marauder glowered at him.

"She's the one I wronged," Cotton said. "And it's her life. I won't force her to remain with me. She stayed at my house those first few days before returning to her own home. I invited her to family night, in the hopes of showing her we weren't so bad. Then it blew up in my face."

"The club will make reparations to Roe," Fox said. "She's welcome to attend family events anytime she wishes. After all, she's both the daughter and the sister of patched members of this club."

"She doesn't blame any of us for what happened," Cotton said. "We've talked quite a bit since she woke up at my house after the incident. I've never met anyone like her. She's like an angel."

"Back to the old ladies," Fox said. "They brought up a good point. There's a lot that happens at the clubhouse, things I don't want my daughter involved in. No matter how much the place is cleaned before family events, we could miss something."

"Yeah, like a used condom," Rocket said. "One of the kids found one last night. I didn't bring it up then, but I trashed it and made them wash their hands thoroughly."

"So the idea of having a separate building for family events isn't bad. I think it's time we make some changes to the compound. Bear has a family now, with a third kid on the way. Several of us have at least one child, if not more. I know we've made a few changes in the past, but it's time for more. The area near the pond would be good for the new building. We could include a deck that overlooked the water. Maybe put some fish in there in case anyone wants to catch them." Fox looked around the table. "Any objections?"

"So the clubhouse would be strictly for Church, club parties, and the Prospects?" Shooter asked.

"Yes." Fox held up his hand. "Everyone in favor, raise your hand."

The vote was unanimous. We discussed the logistics for a few minutes before Fox steered the conversation in a different direction.

"Roe got hurt because we allow anyone eighteen and up to enter the compound for parties. Well, any women. We do have some regulars, but there's a few new faces every night. That needs to stop. We can't risk anyone else getting hurt."

"What do you suggest?" I asked.

"Ask the regulars if they're willing to sign something. A non-disclosure agreement of sorts. Whatever happens at the clubhouse, stays at the clubhouse. If they're caught lying to a brother, or trying to manipulate the club, they'll be dealt with. But in addition to that, I want at least five or six women available. The same ones every night."

I ran my hand down my beard and thought it over a moment. I understood what he was trying to accomplish, but I didn't think it would work quite the way he'd planned.

"What about four or five who live outside the compound but come here on the nights they're up for a party. We can still have them sign something, and make it clear they're the only ones allowed to enter until they decide they're done and want to move on. But I propose we also find two or three girls to live at the clubhouse." I noticed several brothers sat up straighter. I had their attention for sure. "They could keep the place clean, entertain the single brothers, and they'd be here any time of day someone needed to blow off steam. In exchange, they get a roof over their heads, free food and drinks, and maybe a little spending money."

Rocket leaned back in his chair. "The only women I can think of would be those who are struggling and need those things. Wouldn't we be taking advantage of them?"

"They'd be here voluntarily. And if they want to

learn some skills to better their lives later, then we make those arrangements for them. Help them get their GED if they didn't graduate. Let them take some online classes for some sort of certification."

"I know someone who would take that offer without hesitation," Knox said. "If this is something we're doing, I'll ask her about it. I can vouch for her. She's a good kid. Only twenty, but she's had a hard life."

"Everyone in favor?" Fox asked. Every hand went up again.

"I was going to present Faith with her cut last night, but that didn't work out. I know we didn't take it to a vote. Since she instigated some of the issues last night, I want to make sure every brother here is all right with her getting her property cut. She's my wife either way, so she's not going anywhere."

"But she wouldn't have the respect of being an old lady like the others," Rocket said. "Are you sure?"

"As the Sergeant-at-Arms, I can't look the other way when my woman causes trouble. If her punishment is that the club won't accept her as my old lady, then so be it." I just hoped like hell I could explain it to Faith without breaking her heart. But I also needed to make sure I respected my brothers, and I felt like they needed this.

"All in favor of Faith being Bear's old lady, raise your hand," Fox said.

All but Shooter's hand went up.

"Since only one is opposed, I don't see an issue with her being your old lady," Rocket said. "What about you, Pres?"

"I say the motion passes." Fox stood. "Let's take a break. I have a few more things to discuss, like jobs that have come up, but we can do that in an hour."

Everyone left, except the officers. Fox crossed his arms and stared at me.

"What?" I asked.

"You took a big gamble at the end there."

"I did, but it was necessary. If the club didn't feel like Faith deserved the property cut, I'd have honored their wishes. And now that I know only Shooter has an issue with her, I can keep an eye on him."

"Sneaky bastard," Knox muttered.

"Go see your wife and kids," Fox said. "And give her the damn cut already!"

I stood and made my way outside. It looked like I had my orders. I took the cut out of my saddle bag and stared at it a moment. Seeing Faith wear this would fill me with pride, and probably make me twice as possessive of her. I only wished I had way to add a layer of protection to my girls.

I'd talk to Fox about it. Maybe we could at least get them a T-shirt or something.

I rode my bike home and when I pulled into the driveway, Faith came out onto the porch to greet me. I carried the cut over to her and slipped it over her shoulders.

"You're officially mine in the eyes of the club. You need to wear your property cut whenever you leave the house."

She ran her hands down it. "Like the one Raven had on? And the other women?"

I nodded. "Except yours says *Property of Bear*."

"Can you tell me anything about what you discussed today?"

"Nope. You'll find out things when the other women do. And some stuff you'll never hear about. That's how it will always be, Faith. Can you handle that?"

"I can." She reached up to cup my cheek. "I trust you, Charlie. And… I love you."

I pulled her to me. "Say that again."

"I love you. I've known it for a while now. It was my one regret when Spade took me. I'd never confessed my feelings to you, then I got too scared you'd not feel the same way. So I kept silent when you found me." She went up on her tiptoes and kissed me. "But I'm not hiding it anymore. I love you, and I want everyone to know."

"Love you too. Even when you're being a pain in my ass."

"If the two of you are finished, can we eat lunch?" Piper yelled from inside the house. "Preferably before I lose my appetite."

"Shut it! I'll kiss your mom whenever I want, and you'll deal with it. Don't like it? Don't watch."

Faith giggled and hugged me tight. "Thank you, Charlie. For loving me, the girls, and just for everything. I'm so glad you followed Piper that day. Meeting you was the best thing that ever happened to us."

"No, sweetheart. The three of you are the best thing to ever happen to *me*. I was lonely as hell before you came here. Now I have the family I never thought I'd have."

Cordelia popped her head outside. "Can we eat? Please? I'm going to die of starvation."

"We're coming. Go set the table."

"Yes, sir!" She took off, and I smiled down at Faith.

"What's that look?" she asked.

"Just happy. Really damn happy."

She whispered in my ear. "You can show me how happy you are later. I woke up needing you, and the feeling has only grown."

"If the girls weren't waiting for lunch, I'd take you to the bedroom right now. Tonight, you're mine. I don't care if the girls need earplugs, or have to go spend the night somewhere. I want to hear you scream the house down."

Her cheeks flushed as she turned to walk into the house. I had to be the luckiest man on the planet. Walking into the kitchen, I saw the baked chicken, brown rice, and salad on the table... and quickly amended my statement. My evil wife and kids were going to kill me with healthy shit.

Chapter Eleven

Faith

The girls were staying with Spider and Luciana, which meant Bear and I had the night to ourselves. I'd laid out one of my new dresses, and I'd taken a shower. While Bear cleaned up and got ready, I curled my hair and put on a small amount of makeup. It had always bothered me, so I didn't use it often. Thanks to Piper, I had a neutral lip stain I wouldn't have to worry about reapplying. She'd also selected my blush and eyeshadow. I'd drawn the line at mascara because it made my eyes burn.

Once I'd finished dressing, I slipped on the property cut and admired my reflection. Bear placed his hands on my waist, and I thought we looked nice together. He'd put on a dark blue button-down shirt under his cut, and a newer pair of jeans. The soft lavender dress I'd selected made a nice contrast.

"Ready?" he asked.

"This isn't necessary, Charlie. You know that, right? I'd be just as content eating at home."

"The kids aren't home tonight, and soon enough we'll have a baby wakin' us up at all hours. I want to enjoy a night with my beautiful wife and show her off."

"All right. When you put it that way…" I turned around and kissed him before picking up my purse and going out to the truck.

The girls were peering out at us from one of Spider's lower windows, and we waved to them. They'd smiled more since we'd met Bear than they had in the entire past year. I couldn't wait to see them flourish in their new lives. Since the kidnapping, and then our impromptu vacation, we hadn't had a chance to enroll them in school yet. I knew I wasn't smart enough to homeschool them, but I planned to ask one of the other old ladies if they'd be willing to help the girls. Since the school year was close to being over, it would be better for them to take classes online. Then if they needed to work through the summer, they could do it from the house, and I wouldn't have to worry about them being held back a year.

Bear rubbed the spot between my eyes. "Stop frownin'. You'll get wrinkles, then you'll look old like me."

I swatted him on the arm. "You don't look old. You're distinguished, and sexy."

"Long as you find me sexy, that's all that matters. Don't care how anyone else looks at me."

He helped me into the truck and drove us to the restaurant he'd selected. The place had a small courtyard out front, with a fountain and a few benches surrounded by flowering plants. It looked charming and elegant. I also worried it would cost a small fortune.

Bear took my hand and led me inside. After giving his name to the hostess, she seated us at a table near a window. A small candle flickered on the table, and soft music played in the background.

"Do you like it?" he asked.

"It's very romantic." My cheeks flushed as I smiled at him. "Thank you for tonight."

"You may have had a rough time of it before now, but I intend to treat you like a queen. Just remember, your actions also reflect on me. Around the compound, and when you're in public, people will associate your words and behavior with either me or the club."

I bit my lip and watched the candle flame dance

for a moment. "Is this about what I said in regards to the clubhouse?"

"Yes, and backin' up Raven when she demanded a new buildin'. She's the President's old lady, and he didn't take kindly to her voicing her opinion the way she did. The fact all of you chimed in helped a little. But remember in the future to talk to me about that sort of thing in private, and I'll bring it up to the club. I have a duty to protect you and our kids, but I also have to do what's best for the Hades Abyss."

I leaned in and lowered my voice. "Is this your way of scolding me?"

"Things are different with the Hades Abyss than they were with the Raging Demons. I know it will be adjustment. I'm not scoldin' so much as remindin' you of your place. It's by my side, not behind me or under my feet, but as an officer of the club, my old lady needs to be mindful of certain things."

"I understand, Bear. And I'm sorry if I caused any problems. It wasn't my intention."

He reached across the table, and I took his hand. He laced our fingers together, and the warm look he gave me sent butterflies rioting in my stomach. Whatever it took, I'd make sure he was proud of me. I didn't like disappointing him, and I certainly didn't want his club to get angry because of something I said or did. They respected him, and so did I.

"I love you," I said.

"Love you too."

Our server came over and handed us menus, then took our drink order. I didn't see a single price listed, which worried me, but Bear didn't seem bothered by it. I wondered if he'd eaten here before. After ordering, we talked about the girls for a little while.

"Surge is going to set the girls up for online schoolin' to make sure they can move on to the next grade. He's goin' to do the same for Corvin, and Fox gave permission for a tutor to come to the club twice a week in case any of them need extra help. Just have to figure out where they'll meet."

"The girls are still sharing a room right now, and soon we'll need a nursery set up. Otherwise, I'd suggest turning one of the bedrooms into a place where they could study." I thought about the baby growing inside me. "I need to see an OB-GYN too."

"We'll get it handled, and get the girls situated, as well as get the nursery ready. Don't stress over any of that, all right?"

"Time is running out, Bear. This baby will be here before you know it."

"I'm going to clear out the other two bedrooms. Whatever I want to keep, I can store. Get one of those small buildings to stick out back. That way the girls each get a room, and so does the baby. As for where to study, the kitchen is pretty big. With our family expandin', wouldn't hurt to get a larger table."

"Would you be all right with Corvin coming over to study with Piper? Or the tutor using our house for all three kids?" I asked.

"Don't see a problem with it. We'll buy new furniture and get those rooms ready this week." He squeezed my fingers. "Can't let Piper and the baby get all the new stuff. We'll get rid of the bed in Cordy's room and get her somethin' else too."

"You're going to spoil them."

"That's the idea." He winked at me.

The rest of dinner passed without issue, and by the time we got back home, I felt like a young bride on her wedding night. It didn't make sense, since Bear and I had been intimate before. Didn't stop the nervous flutter in my stomach though. I'd even bought a special nightgown for tonight.

"Will you give me a few minutes before you join me in the bedroom?" I asked.

"Whatever you want, Faith. Take your time. I'll make sure the windows and doors are locked."

I hurried to our room, then freshened up a little and brushed my teeth before changing into the silk nightie. It hit me mid-thigh, and the thin straps kept slipping off my shoulders. Staring at my reflection, I wondered if Bear would think I looked sexy. With my baby belly, I felt awkward and not the least bit graceful.

I turned down the bed and spritzed the sheets with some lavender linen spray one of the women had gifted me. The candle Bear had lit before was still in our room, and I searched for a lighter.

"My, my. Are you tryin' to seduce me, wife?" Bear asked as he leaned against the doorframe.

My cheeks flushed, and heat flickered inside me. It seemed he liked the nightgown. The way he watched me, made my nipples harden.

"Maybe."

"Let me take care of the candle. You get on the bed."

I hurried to obey while he lit the wick, then removed his clothes and boots. He pinned me to the bed, his large body looming over me. In the past, such a move might have scared me. With Bear, I knew I was safe, and loved.

"You sure we won't hurt the baby?" he asked. "I know it's not our first time, but your belly seems bigger today."

He wasn't wrong. My baby belly popped almost

overnight. Where I'd had a slight curve before, I now looked like I was carrying an NFL star. Either the baby had nearly doubled in size, or I'd been eating too much.

"It should be fine. Just be gentle." I ran my fingers through his hair. "But then you always are. You treat me like I'm made of glass."

He leaned down to kiss me, his lips brushing against mine. "Because you're more precious than any treasure on earth."

"Make love to me, Charlie." I gave him a slight smile. "In case you hadn't noticed, I'm not wearing panties."

He gave me a soft growl, sounding just like the bear they'd named him for. Heat flared in his eyes as he reached for the straps on my shoulders. He pulled one down, then the other, until the top of the nightie slipped far enough to expose my breasts. The hungry way he stared at them made my pussy slick.

His lips found mine again, and as he drugged me with his kiss, I felt his cock sink into me. I wrapped my legs around him, hooking my heels over his thighs. He barely gave me time to breathe between kisses, and it felt like I was floating. The slow drag of his cock felt incredible, but every deep thrust made him brush against my clit. Little sparks of pleasure shot through me. I came, my pussy squeezing him tight, and still he didn't stop.

Bear took his time, making me come again and again. He stroked in and out of me, slow and deep. My toes curled, and I begged for more. I'd never felt like this. Every time with him seemed better than the one before, if such a thing were even possible.

"Don't stop. Please!" I clung to him, wishing the moment could last forever.

I met his thrusts, chasing another orgasm, and as I came, I felt the hot stickiness of his release. Bear's chest heaved as he tried to catch his breath, and I tugged his beard until he came down for another kiss. He pulled out, then rolled to his side, holding me against him.

"Give me an hour or two and we'll try again. But next time, I'm givin' you three orgasms before I get inside you." He kissed my forehead. "When we aren't able to have sex for a while, I want you to look back and remember this night. Hell, one day, I won't be able to get it up anymore."

"Hush." I placed my finger over his lips. "The sex with you is incredible, Charlie, but there's more to being married than that. Cuddling like this, kissing, and holding hands are all intimate acts as well. There are plenty of ways for us to show our love to one another. If the time comes you aren't able to have sex with me, we'll have all these fond memories."

"You're only in your thirties, Faith. You'll miss sex."

I tugged on his beard. "Until you, sex was miserable and something I endured because I didn't have a choice. Besides, I've heard of men in their eighties still having kids. I'm assuming that means their cocks still work, so there's no reason to think yours will suddenly break in the next few months or years."

"Such a smartass," he muttered.

"I love *you*, Charlie. All of you. Yes, your cock is wonderful, especially the way you make me feel when we have sex. But if something happened and we could no longer have sex starting tomorrow, it wouldn't change how I felt about you. What if the roles were reversed? If I were the one who couldn't have sex, would you go find someone who could?"

"What kind of question is that?" he demanded.

"An honest one. If you wouldn't be disappointed with me, or wish for another woman, why should it matter to me whether or not you can have sex?"

"You're an amazin' woman, Faith. I'm lucky you're mine, and I'll do whatever it takes to make sure you never regret bein' with me."

"You're the amazing one. Now kiss me."

We cuddled in bed another two hours, kissing and holding one another. By the time the sun rose the next day, he'd made me come so many times I was sore. Silly man. Worried about nothing. I'd meant every word I'd told him, and I'd prove it to him every chance I had.

* * *

Bear
Two Months Later

I didn't know how my wife hadn't pulled out her hair yet. Even from outside, I could hear the kids arguing. Not just Piper and Cordelia. Nope, Corvin was here too, and seemed to be pissed as hell about something. The boy had a massive chip on his shoulder. I knew it would take time for him to realize no one here would hurt him, and that he could be a kid. But if he didn't stop yelling at my daughter, I'd have to rethink the violence.

I opened the door and saw Faith lying on the couch, a washcloth over her eyes. She'd been getting a lot of headaches lately, and I knew the little shits in the kitchen weren't helping matters any. I kneeled next to the couch and lifted the rag. She opened her eyes, and I realized how much pain she was in. Her face was paler than usual, and her eyes were much darker.

"How long?" I asked.

"The last hour. Maybe more," she murmured.

"I'll handle it." I kissed her forehead before laying the rag over her eyes again. Then I went to the kitchen, ready to bust some heads.

Cordy stood and ran to me. "Daddy!"

"What's goin' on in here? Your mother has a headache and the three of you are makin' it worse. You should be ashamed of yourselves."

"Piper met a boy in town and had a milkshake with him. Corvin said the kid just wants in her pants. Then they started arguing and haven't stopped since," Cordelia said.

"What boy? When?"

Corvin stopped yelling at Piper and focused on me. "Sorry, Bear. I didn't mean to hurt Faith. Piper let some preppy kid in town buy her a milkshake. The guy grabbed her ass, and she doesn't see a problem with it."

"I'm sorry, could you repeat that?" I asked, shooting my glare from him to Piper and back. What the fuck was going on when I wasn't home?

Corvin said it again, and Piper pouted. Had the girl lost her damn mind recently? Corvin was a good kid. If he thought something was off about the other boy, he was probably right. He'd been protective of my girls, and his little sister, from the very beginning. The second he'd met the three of them, there'd been an instant bond between them.

"It's just a kid from the local school, Dad," Piper said. "You said I needed to make friends."

"Friends, yes. Fuck boys? No."

Piper gaped at me. "I can't believe you just said that."

Corvin grunted. "He's not wrong. That kid is

with a different girl every time I see him. He was toying with you, Piper, and you played right into his hands. And for what? Some ice cream?"

"I happen to like the milkshakes at the diner."

"Then I'll take you to get one whenever you want," he said. "You don't have to accept them from strangers who grab your ass! He's a disrespectful motherfucker, and if I were fully healed, I'd have beaten him into the ground for such insolence."

I liked the kid more and more. "Corvin is right. That boy clearly didn't have any respect for you. Stay away from him, Piper."

"Does Mama really have a headache?" Cordelia asked.

"She does. The noise in here hasn't been helpin' her any. I'm going to tuck her into bed, and I want the three of you to be quieter. Play a game or somethin'. Hell, go outside and get fresh air!"

"What kind of food does she want?" Corvin asked. "We could go pick up dinner, that way she doesn't have to cook."

"Thank you, Corvin. She likes bread and mashed potatoes right now. Just go somewhere to get a bucket of chicken and some sides with a fuck ton of biscuits. She may cry and hug you until you break."

He smiled a little and took Piper's hand. "She can come with me, right? I want to make sure I get the right stuff."

"Yep. All three of you can for all I care, as long as you drive safely." I pulled out my wallet and gave them eighty dollars. "Keep whatever's left to put gas in the car."

The kids left, but on the way out, I nearly laughed. I heard Corvin mumble to Piper, *Your dad is fucking scary*. There were days I saw hatred in his eyes, even if it wasn't toward the club. It made me leery of what he might do in the future. He treated Luciana as if she were a saint and seemed to like Spider as well. And he doted on Marianna already.

I hoped he didn't erupt someday. The kid hadn't had an easy time of it, but then, no one at the Hades Abyss had. We'd all dealt with one type of pain or another. Most didn't have families worth mentioning, except the ones we'd built.

I picked up Faith and carried her to the bedroom. After I eased her onto the mattress, I decided to join her. I pulled her into my arms and held her while she took a nap. The baby wasn't due for another few months, but I'd noticed she'd been getting tired more frequently lately.

According to the doctor, she and the baby were fine. We'd decided to call him Jasper Charles Dupont. Or rather, Cordelia and Piper came up with the name Jasper, and Faith insisted the boy have my name as well. Of course, after I found out they named their little brother after a vampire, I nearly demanded they pick another one. Then I'd realized they might come up with something worse and decided to leave it alone.

"Kids picked up dinner," I said when Faith opened her eyes again. I'd heard them come home about fifteen minutes ago but didn't want to wake up my pregnant wife. "How are you feelin'?"

"Headache is better. I could eat something."

I got up and helped her off the bed. "Corvin may still be here."

"He can stay for dinner." Faith leaned her head against my arm. "I think Cordelia has a crush on him."

"Cordy?" I stared down at her. "Not Piper?"

"Piper is difficult to read. There are times she treats him like a brother, and other times I see her stare at him with longing. I'm not sure she's ready to admit how she feels. Or maybe she hadn't figured it out herself."

"Cordelia isn't allowed to date anytime soon. That girl needs to focus on somethin' else. We should get a puppy."

"Charles Dupont, don't you bring a dog into this house! I'll be changing diapers soon enough. I'm not cleaning up puppy puddles too!"

I smiled and kissed her. "All right. No puppy."

She breathed a sigh of relief and went to the kitchen. I wondered how pissed she'd be when I brought a different sort of pet home. Cordelia needed something to shower with affection, other than boys. Something that could fit into her room would be good. I'd called Doolittle over at the Devil's Fury to get some ideas. If it was furry and cute, I didn't think Faith would be too upset. Especially if it didn't leave puddles on the floor.

"Corvin, can you stay for dinner?" I asked, pulling out Faith's chair.

"I should check with my parents," he said. I noticed the way he hesitated over the word *parents*. He was still adjusting, but he was doing well.

"Go ask. Or use the phone and call them."

Faith stared at the food on the table. "How much did you order?"

"They messed up the first bucket and gave us original instead of crispy, but they let us keep it. So we have thirty-two pieces now," Piper said. "And because the sides and biscuits got cold while we waited on them to fix it, they gave us extra of those too."

"Just ask them and Marianna to join us," Faith suggested.

"Are you up for that?" I asked, placing my hand

on her shoulder.

"I'll be fine." She gave me a tired smile. "This baby is taking a lot out of me, but I'll be fine."

"All right. I'll go talk to Spider. Cordy, set the table."

I paused in the doorway and watched my family for a moment. This is what I'd been missing. I'd enjoyed my life with the Hades Abyss, and I'd liked being the Sergeant-at-Arms, but I hadn't realized how lonely I was. I hadn't touched the club girls in a long while, even before meeting Faith. Now I had a sweet wife, two daughters, and a son on the way. My house was full of laughter and happy memories.

I walked out to get Spider, Luciana, and Marianna. If my wife wanted all of them over for dinner, I'd bring them back with me. Even if it meant I had to threaten Spider to get his ass out of his house.

Epilogue

Bear

Faith gripped my hand so tight I thought she might break my fingers. She'd been in labor for over an hour, and our son still hadn't made an appearance. I could see she was tiring quickly.

"Another push," the doctor said. "The head is nearly out."

She panted and did as he said, pushing with all her might. She tightened her hold on my hand, and I muttered a curse. It would be a miracle if I didn't lose the use of my fingers after this. How the hell had the woman gotten so strong?

"Woman, you're goin' to break my hand."

"Be thankful that's all she's breaking," said one of the nurses. "Delivery earlier today the wife grabbed her husband's crotch. Poor man ended up with a testicular torsion. Now he's down in the ER."

I felt the blood drain from my face, and I swayed on my feet.

"Seriously? That makes you want to pass out? I'm trying to push a giant baby out of a very small opening. Without drugs!" She screamed the last part and I wished I could take her pain away.

"I'm sorry I didn't get you here fast enough." I patted her hand, wanting to keep her calm.

"Bear… shut up. If you value your life, don't say another word." Her jaw tightened and she pushed again.

"The head is out!"

I looked at our child, and immediately looked away. There were some things a man didn't need to see. His wife's pussy stretched around a baby's head being one of them. I couldn't imagine the pain she felt right now. Good thing she wouldn't be having more kids. I didn't think I'd be able to survive another delivery.

"Another push, Faith." The nurse patted her hand. "One good push and you'll be able to greet your son."

She pushed, not stopping until our son came all the way out. Panting for breath, she leaned back against the pillows. I saw her eyes start to droop. She blinked a few times, like she was fighting to stay awake, then her eyes shut, and her hand went limp. An alarm sounded, and both the doctor and nurse froze.

"What's goin' on?" I asked.

"She's passed out." The nurse and the doctor shared a look. "I'm afraid I need you to go to the waiting room, sir. We'll send for you soon."

"What? Why? I'm not leavin' my wife and kid!"

"Bear, your wife is bleeding too much. She could go into shock. We need to treat her, which means we need some room."

It felt like my knees would give out, but I managed to stagger from the room. I found the waiting area and collapsed into a seat. A few of my brothers had come to the hospital. Piper and Cordelia were also here. They all rushed toward me, but Fox held them back.

"Give him a minute. Corvin, take the girls to the cafeteria. I bet Bear could use some coffee."

"We'll be back, Daddy," Cordelia said. I looked up and saw the worry in Piper's eyes and hoped she didn't say anything to her sister.

"What happened?" Fox asked.

"They said she's bleeding too much and told me to leave. I didn't even get to see our son. I have no idea if she's going to be okay, or if Jasper is all right." I put my hands over my face and prayed for the first time in decades.

Please let Faith and Jasper be okay. Please don't take them from me.

It felt like hours passed before a nurse came out to speak with me. She seemed haggard, but she gave me a cautious smile.

"Would you like to visit your son?" she asked.

"Only him?" I asked.

She nodded. "Your wife is being prepped for surgery."

"I don't understand. What's going on?" Fox placed his hand on my shoulder, and Piper came to lean against my side. From the corner of my eye, I saw Luciana put her arm around Cordelia.

"Your wife hemorrhaged after delivery. We tried medication first, but…"

"But what? She's okay, isn't she?" I asked.

"Sir, your wife coded." My knees gave out and I hit the floor. Everything in me went numb at her words. "We were able to get her back, but the doctor suggested a hysterectomy. That's why I said they're prepping her for surgery now."

"She's still alive?" I asked, my voice coming as more of a croak.

"She is. If the surgery is successful, she has a good chance. Recovery will take a while. She's going to need all of you."

"Can our daughters come to see their brother?" I asked.

"They asked me to keep it to one person at a time, and no one under sixteen, but all things considered I'll make an exception. Follow me."

I stood and took my daughters' hands. We peered through the nursery window and found the little bassinet that said Dupont. My son had a head of dark hair and looked much larger than the other babies in the room. I read the little card. 9 pounds 3 ounces, 22 inches.

"There's your brother," I said. "Jasper Charles Dupont. He's a handsome boy, isn't he?"

"Mom's going to be okay, isn't she?" Piper asked.

"She's tough. She'll come through this." I had to believe those words. If I had to raise these kids on my own, I would. But the thought of spending a single day without Faith ripped out my heart.

"Why don't we get something to eat?" Cordy asked. "By the time we're done, maybe they'll have more news on Mama."

"Good idea. You two lead me to the cafeteria."

It took a few hours before someone came to tell us Faith would be all right. By the time I saw her again, it felt like I'd aged another ten years.

I held her hand and kissed her fingers. "I love you, Faith. Don't you ever try to leave me again. I can't live without you."

* * *

Three Weeks Later

I'd propped myself in bed and Faith leaned back against me. She held Jasper in her arms, and I kept my arm around her waist. She still tired easily, and I worried she'd go to sleep and drop him. Once he'd finished feeding, she buttoned the top of her nightgown and I called out for Piper.

"Is Jasper ready for a nap?" she asked.

"Can you put him in his crib? I think your mom is the one needing a nap."

"Sure." Piper came over and picked up Jasper,

then leaned down to kiss her mom's cheek. "Don't worry, Mom. We'll keep him safe while you get your energy back."

Piper shut the door behind her. Faith sighed and laced her fingers with mine.

"I'm not dying, Charlie."

"You *did* die. Your heart fucking stopped! If you don't want me to baby you, and worry, then don't do something stupid like stop breathing."

She smiled a little. "I didn't do it on purpose."

"I know. Scared the shit out of me."

"What am I missing? I feel like all I do is care for Jasper and sleep."

"You go back to the doctor next week. They want to make sure you're doing okay and draw some blood to run a few tests. As for the rest of us, I've taken some time off until you're back on your feet. The club won't come to me unless it's an emergency. The girls started school, and so did Corvin. They seem to like it."

"I didn't get to take them back-to-school shopping." She sighed again, and I knew she'd be asleep soon.

"I gave Piper money. She took Cordelia to the mall. Think Corvin went with them and took Marianna. The kids are fine, sweetheart. You focus on getting better. None of us can survive without you. Especially me."

"I love you, Charlie."

"Love you too." I heard her even breathing and knew she'd gone to sleep. I held her close and placed my hand over her heart. As long as it kept beating, so would mine, because she was everything to me. "I know you think I saved you, but you're wrong, Faith. You and our kids gave me a reason to keep living, so I need you to stay by my side until I draw my last breath. No more dying. I can't handle it."

I heard Jasper fuss and knew the girls would take care of him. I had the most wonderful children. They'd both matured a lot since Faith gave birth and nearly left us. I no longer worried about Piper getting in trouble with the boys at school. If Corvin didn't keep them away from her, she did it herself. Not once had she brought up dating. When I'd asked her about it, she'd informed me there were more important things -- like her family.

I wouldn't let her waste her childhood worrying about the rest of us, but for now, I needed the extra help. Once Faith was back to her usual self, we'd sit Piper down and talk to her about hanging out with kids her age, other than Corvin.

While Faith slept, I hummed to her. *Just the Way You Are* was my go-to when it came to the woman in my arms. I never knew if she heard me, but I hoped she did. I didn't want a day to go by that she didn't know how much I adored her.

"You're my wife, the mother of my children, and my everything, Faith. You're the reason my heart beats." I kissed the top of her head and heard a muffled, *I love you, Charlie.* I smiled and hummed another song for her, and thanked God for answering my prayer. He'd let me keep Faith and Jasper. If my wife had died that day, I'd have followed her to the other side, if for no other reason than to bring her back with me.

Heaven couldn't have *this* angel because she was all mine.

Grimm (Dixie Reapers MC 17)

A Dixie Reapers Bad Boys Romance

Harley Wylde

Oksana -- Growing up in the Bratva wasn't easy, especially for a woman. At twenty, I thought I'd get married soon. Start my own family. All approved by my family, of course. It never occurred to me, my father would implicate me in his shady dealings, or that I'd be punished in the most severe way. So I run, with the help of a friend, and go straight to the Dixie Reapers. I don't know what I expected. Certainly not for a sexy man to make my heart flutter, or make me wish for things I shouldn't. I'm pretty sure I'm falling for him. Grimm will do his best to keep me safe, but who's going to protect my heart?

Grimm -- The Bratva is in my rearview, where I want them to stay. I haven't heard from my last remaining relative in a long, long time. So when Nikolai sends Oksana to me, it's a bit of a shock, to say the least. But the more I get to know her, the more protective I feel. In my gut, I know she's mine. The Bratva can try to take her if they want... anyone who comes for my woman better have their affairs in order. I'll put every last one of them in the ground.

Prologue

Oksana

No matter how scared I felt, I couldn't show it. Growing up in the Bratva, I'd learned early these men fed on fear. The more terrified you were, the more empowered they became. I'd stand here, listen to everything they said, then once I was alone again, I'd throw up and bawl my eyes out.

Nikolai did his best to shield me, but it wasn't enough. Not this time. Feliks may have softened since marrying Raina, but to the rest of us, he remained a monster. And now, he held my life in his hands. Why? Because my father decided to gamble with the Bratva and lost in a big way. Not only had he lost his ranking and had his wealth stripped, but he'd forfeited his family as well.

My sixteen-year-old sister couldn't contain her tears. They ran freely down her cheeks as she sobbed and wrapped her arms around her waist. Feliks seemed unmoved, flipping through the papers on his desk. What would become of us? I'd already heard what happened to our mother. Would our fate be the same?

"Yulia Romanov, you will study at the prestigious girls' academy downtown until your eighteenth birthday, at which time, the Vor will select a husband for you." Feliks didn't look up as my sister cried even harder. "You will leave immediately, and we will provide clothing."

I straightened my spine and waited. At twenty, my options were limited. If he didn't marry me off to someone, then I'd most likely be put to work in the brothels. Neither fate seemed like something I'd survive.

"Oksana Romanov." Feliks lifted his gaze and leaned back in his chair. I flinched slightly, and he smiled. The bastard. "Your father speaks highly of you. According to him, he could have never accomplished so much without the help of his beloved Oksana."

My eyes went wide. What the hell was he saying? I'd never helped my dad!

"Many people were hurt due to your father's actions. He's paid the price for his crimes. Now it's your turn." Feliks motioned to someone behind me. I didn't get a chance to turn around before my wrists were bound at my back. My heart slammed against my ribs, and I fought to stay upright. Black dots swam across my vision, and I sucked in a deep breath. What was going on? "Oksana Romanov, you will be beaten, sold, and used until the day you die. It's no less than you deserve, considering what happened to the women you lured into your father's trap."

No. I hadn't! I'd have never done such a thing. I knew my pleas would fall on deaf ears. Protesting wouldn't do me any good. He'd never believe I was innocent of the crimes he said I'd committed. Yulia started to scream as they dragged me from the room. The men guided me to a car and shoved me into the back seat. The sound of the door slamming shut felt like the end of my short life.

Did Nikolai know what they planned to do? Had he tried to stop them?

The buildings passed in a blur until we reached the warehouse district. The men pulled me from the vehicle and shoved me inside. The air smelled dank and musty. The vast space held only a table, chair, and a ratty-looking mattress. One of the men lifted a hunk of my hair and sniffed it, a lecherous smile curving his lips.

"Are you a virgin, little one?"

I swallowed hard and nodded. Lying wouldn't get me anywhere. But maybe if they knew, they wouldn't rape me. I'd earn a high price if they sold me instead. It didn't mean I'd get away from the beating Feliks said I'd receive.

The second man smacked the other one in the chest. "You know we can't ruin her. Not like that. She's too valuable."

"Only if she retains her teeth and we don't leave many scars."

The man yanked my head back, craning my neck. "There's much we can do and still fetch a decent price for her. Shall we begin?"

I refused to cry. I wouldn't beg. No, I'd remain silent and take whatever they dished out. I'd survive as long as I could. The moment Yulia heard of my death, she'd give up. I couldn't allow that to happen. No matter what it took, I'd keep living. Even when I didn't want to anymore.

The man licked my face, and I inwardly cringed. My outward appearance didn't change. Not so much as a single shift in expression. I'd learned well, and I'd use every skill I had to keep them from knowing how scared I was right now.

"We may not be able to pop your cherry, but we can do anything else," the man said, his voice a low growl in my ear. "Ride your ass. Fuck your throat. By the time we're finished, you'll be broken."

The other man reached for me, gripping the top of my dress, and ripping it down the middle. I'd never been very big up top and hadn't worn a bra. My breasts spilled out, and the bastards groped me, hard enough I knew they'd leave bruises. I bit my tongue until I tasted blood. Whatever they did to me, I'd take it. What other choice did I have?

The lights flickered, then went out. The men started cursing and stumbled around. I heard one of them crash into something, possibly the table. It got quiet. Too quiet. Was it a trap? Or they were really gone? Without either of them holding me, I could flee… if I had any idea of where to go. I couldn't see even an inch in front of my face.

Hands grabbed hold of me, and I tensed until I heard a voice whisper in my ear.

"Follow me, Oksana."

Nikolai! I staggered as he led me through the warehouse. The cool air hit me when we stepped outside. I didn't have the time to be embarrassed over the fact Nikolai would see me half-naked. He cursed when he saw what they'd done and slipped out of his jacket. He untied my wrists and helped me cover myself.

"I'm sorry I was late. Come on. You need to leave town."

"Where will I go?"

"South. Alabama." Nikolai opened a car door, and I got in. He didn't speak again until we'd left the city limits. After another two towns, he pulled over and shut off the engine. "I have a vehicle ready for you. It's nothing fancy, but it will get you where you need to go."

"What's in Alabama?" I asked.

"The Dixie Reapers. More importantly, my cousin is there. Ivan Volkov, but he goes by Grimm."

"You're sending me to your family?"

"You'll be safe, Oksana. He won't let anyone hurt you. I'm going to give you a note. When you see him, make sure he reads it."

"Nikolai, are you going to get into trouble for

this?" I asked.

"Possibly. It depends. I don't think Viktor truly wished to punish you. If your father hadn't said so many lies to Feliks, you'd have never been treated this way."

"What about Yulia?"

He shook his head. "You can't save her. She'll be safe, and I promise I won't let Viktor marry her off to anyone who would harm her. She's used to this way of life. Where you're going, things are less civilized."

I snorted. Right. Because rape, murder, and torture are the building blocks of civilization. Only the Bratva would consider those things to be a normal way of life. They might dress in suits and buy expensive things, but it didn't make them any less monstrous. To the outside, they appeared refined. Rich. Powerful. In reality, they were more dreadful than any horror movie anyone had ever seen. And even worse… they weren't fictional.

Nikolai handed me a set of keys and a sealed envelope. "Take these. The blue car in front of us has a full tank of gas. There's cash hidden under the seat, as well as a fake ID. If anyone asks, you're Oksana Volkov and you're going home to your husband."

My mouth dropped open, and I stared at him. "Are you serious?"

"Grimm can protect you, Oksana. More than I ever could. Please don't decide to start fighting now. If you're going to survive, or have the slightest chance at leading a happy life, then you'll do as I say."

I sagged into the seat, knowing he was right. I couldn't stay. If I did, I'd end up right back in the warehouse. Or worse. I'd never met Nikolai's cousin, and had no idea what he looked like, but if he said I'd be safe, then I'd trust him. He'd never hurt me before and had even come to rescue me.

"All right. I'll go find Grimm. But, Nikolai, please watch over Yulia. Don't let them hurt her in retaliation for me escaping."

He nodded. "You have my word. Go. Be happy. I'll do my best to keep them from searching for you. Just be careful."

I got out of the car and paused, looking down at my ruined dress and his suit jacket. I couldn't travel like this. The moment someone saw me, they'd report it.

Nikolai huffed and removed his shirt, handing it to me. I took it and returned the jacket before slipping the shirt on. I buttoned it, then tied it at my waist. Not exactly stylish, but at least my breasts wouldn't be exposed now.

"Thank you, Nikolai. For everything. Being my friend. Watching out for me. I appreciate it more than you'll ever know."

He gave me a sad smile. "Live a happy life. That's all the repayment I need. Now go. I need to get back before someone comes looking for me."

I got into the little blue car and drove away. I didn't know where life would take me, or if this Grimm person would really help me, but at least the Bratva wouldn't use and abuse me. For the first time in my life, I had a real chance. I might not know the person Nikolai was sending me to, but he couldn't be as bad as the Bratva men I'd known. Nikolai wouldn't send me into a worse situation, would he?

For now, I'd pretend I had a bright future. One of hope and all sorts of possibilities. No one demanding I bend to their will. No men dictating who I'd marry, what I could wear, or what job I'd be permitted to have.

Freedom.

Nikolai had granted me freedom… and I would embrace it fully, no matter the consequences.

Chapter One

Grimm

I couldn't remember the last time I went to a party at the clubhouse. When had I gotten tired of it all? It seemed the parties started earlier and earlier these days. I knew the younger guys were enjoying themselves, and I still went whenever I needed a release, but those days were few and far between lately. My hand got the job done. Less drama. No clingy women wanting to be claimed. As if I'd ever make a club whore my old lady!

I leaned back on the couch and took a swallow of my beer. I had no idea what movie even played. Even though I'd turned on the TV when I got home, I hadn't paid the least bit of attention to it. Something felt off. All day, I'd had this prickle at my nape. I didn't know if it meant good fortune was heading my way, or death and destruction. Around here, it could go either way.

My phone buzzed in my pocket, and I pulled it out.

Problem at the gate.

Great. Guess that answered my question. But why the fuck were they bothering me about it? I might be an officer now for the club, but Tempest was the new Sergeant-at-Arms. Shouldn't they have called him instead?

I set my beer aside and pulled my keys from my pocket. Thankfully, I'd only had the one drink. I went out to my bike and rode over to the front of the compound. Whatever I'd anticipated, it wasn't the tiny woman glaring at the Prospect. With a man's shirt tied off at her waist, she looked like a kid playing dress-up.

"What the hell is going on?" I asked after I shut off the engine.

"Says she needs to see you, Grimm."

I eyed her, admiring her delicate bone structure. Pale blue eyes stared back at me, and her blonde hair seemed nearly white. She looked like an ice queen. Or more like an ice pixie, if such a thing existed. I could probably break her with one hand. I felt the urge to give her a cheeseburger. When had she last eaten?

"Who are you?" I asked.

She reached through the bars of the gate and handed me an envelope. As I tore into it, her voice made me freeze.

"My name is Oksana Romanov, and I need your help."

The slight Russian accent made every muscle in my body lock up. I'd left all that behind me. My parents had died thanks to their ties with the Bratva. I'd joined the military when I turned eighteen, and I'd never once looked back. I'd run across my only living relative by accident when he'd been a kid. I hadn't stuck around, knowing *that* life had never been right for me. So why had this woman come here? How had she found me?

I skimmed the contents of the letter and cursed. My younger cousin, Nikolai, had sent her. Which meant I couldn't in good conscience turn her away. Not without feeling like a complete asshole. Whatever sent her running, it had to be bad. Arranged marriage? Something worse? Only way I'd find out would be to ask, and I wasn't going to do that at the gate.

"Let her in," I said. I backed up my bike and turned it around before eyeing her. "Get in your car and follow me. We'll go to my place and discuss whatever happened for Nikolai to send you to me."

She gave a curt nod and quickly obeyed. I couldn't help but smile a little. Yeah, that woman was

Bratva born and bred. If the women knew how to do anything, it was follow every command given to them without question. She'd jumped to do as I said without a moment's hesitation and hadn't stopped to ask questions. I remembered my mother being the same way. Unfortunately, it meant when my father pissed off the wrong people, my mother got tangled up too.

"Should I notify anyone?" the Prospect asked.

"No. This is personal." I drove to my house, making sure she stayed right behind me the entire way. When I pulled into the garage, she parked on the street. I pointed to the empty space beside me, and she shook her head. So much for obedience. Although, I didn't see even a hint of defiance in her eyes.

She got out of the car, wringing her hands. "I think the car has an oil leak. It will mess up your garage and driveway."

Huh. Most women I'd met wouldn't have thought of such a thing, except maybe Pepper. But then she was different from most women I knew. Oksana followed me into the house, and I pulled out a kitchen chair for her. She sat, and I leaned against the counter. Now that we were under the lights, I could see the shadows under her eyes and the pallor in her cheeks. How long had she been running? For that matter, what was up with her clothing? I didn't think she'd dressed this way on purpose. Had something happened to her clothes?

I noticed her lower lip quivered slightly, and for some reason, I wanted to run my thumb across it. I gave myself a mental slap, needing to focus on the matter at hand. This woman had trouble written all over her. The last thing I needed to do was feel any sort of attraction to her.

"Why don't you start at the beginning," I said.

"No. On second thought, why did Nikolai send you here? What are you to him?"

If she belonged to my cousin, better to know now. She didn't look very old, but if I remembered correctly, Nikolai would be in his mid-twenties or so. I hadn't exactly kept up with my family, especially any with Bratva ties. I preferred the blood to remain inside my body, and if the Bratva came looking for me, there wasn't a guarantee I'd live for much longer. While the sins of my father happened long ago, I knew those men and their offspring had long memories. Still, I'd run across my cousin when he'd been younger. It had been a chance encounter and not the least bit planned.

"Nikolai is my friend. He's tried to watch over me." She placed her hands on the table, fingers laced together. "My father betrayed the wrong people. They tortured and killed him. Put my mother in a brothel. My younger sister fared the best. She's being sent to a girls' academy and will have an arranged marriage when she's of age."

The matter-of-fact way she stated things made me want to tug her into my arms and give her a hug. No one could compartmentalize that shit so well unless they'd had lots of practice. I had a feeling her life had been hell, even long before she'd run.

"And you? How old are you?"

"Twenty. They believed I'd helped my father with his crimes against the Bratva, so my punishment was..." She pressed her lips together. "They were going to beat me. Rape me. Then sell me. Until they discovered I'm a virgin. Although, the men made it clear all the things they could still do to me."

I cursed under my breath and looked away. I knew exactly what they'd have done to her. How had Nikolai gotten her out of there? Was he in trouble now too? Shit. I wasn't about to drag my club into a war with the damn Bratva. If Nikolai had gotten himself into trouble, he'd have to figure it out. I couldn't go after him.

"Before they could follow through on all their threats, Nikolai managed to help me escape. He drove me a few towns away and gave me the car outside, as well as the letter I handed you and instructions to come straight here. I've been driving non-stop with only gas and bathroom breaks. He put cash and a fake ID under the seat of the car."

"That his shirt?" I asked. She nodded. When she paled even further, I knew they'd hurt her in some way. She hadn't gotten out of there completely unscathed. How far had they gone? I didn't see blood, but she'd been on the road a long time. It was doubtful she'd still be bleeding all these hours later. "Is the damage somewhere you can show me?"

She audibly swallowed and her fingers shook as she reached for the buttons on the shirt. I took three long strides to her side and stopped her. No way I'd have her strip in my kitchen. I'd thought maybe she'd show me bruising on her arms or legs. What the hell had those bastards done in the time she'd been with them? How late had Nikolai been when he'd tried to save her?

"Oksana, did they touch you?" She gave a curt nod and dropped her gaze, refusing to look me in the eye. "Are you wearing Nikolai's shirt because they tore your clothes?"

"Yes. I don't have anything else to wear."

Fury burned through me, but I didn't dare show it. Oksana didn't know me, and the last thing I wanted was for her to fear me. I had to keep my cool, no matter how badly I wanted to put my fist through the damn wall.

"What size do you wear?" She stared at the table, not saying a word. Short of undressing her to read the tags in her clothing, I couldn't do anything but sit and wait. It wasn't a difficult question. Or did she worry the clothes would come at a cost? I ran my hand over my beard. "Look, you clearly need help. Nikolai sent you here for a reason. I'm going to assume he didn't even explain everything to you before telling you to come find me. The least I can do is make sure you have something to wear that isn't torn and actually fits."

"A small. I don't need anything fancy." She shifted in her seat. "Maybe some clean panties?"

I looked down at her feet and realized she had on cheap flip-flops. They looked like something she'd have found at a gas station or truck stop. I nudged her foot with my boot. "What size shoe? You can't run around in those all the time."

"Six."

"All right. Do you want something to drink? Are you hungry?"

She hesitated a moment before nodding. I went over to the cabinet by the sink and took out a glass and plate. After getting her some ice water, I took the leftovers out of the fridge and put a decent-sized portion of ham and pierogies on the dish before heating it in the microwave. By the time she was digging in, I'd pulled out my phone to place an order for pickup. I eyed her, trying to figure out what she might like, or what would look nice on her.

Admittedly, I didn't know shit about women's clothes. I added a package of panties to the cart, along with leggings and a few knit shirts. She hadn't mentioned a bra. Since she seemed tiny all over, maybe she didn't wear one often. I picked out a pair of canvas sneakers and some socks. Rubbing the back of my neck, I realized she'd need more than that. I added all the essentials I thought she might require, then checked out and put Owen down as the pickup person.

Oksana finished her food. I refilled her ice water and put the plate into the sink. She looked a little less stressed now that she'd had a hot meal. Despite the rigid way she held herself, I knew she had to be exhausted. I shot off a quick text to Owen to tell him where to go once I received the notice the order was ready.

"Come on. How about a shower and some sleep? We can talk more in the morning."

She stood and pushed the chair in. "I won't be imposing?"

"Oksana, you've told me enough that I know you're in trouble. The Bratva won't let you just run off and never search for you. Especially if they feel you owe them a debt. It's best if you stay hidden at the compound for now while we come up with a plan. In the meantime, I have a guest room you can use, and I'll have some clothing and shoes for you later today."

She looked out the kitchen window. The sun had set, and I wondered how long she'd been on the run. I didn't know where my cousin was at the moment. The Bratva had locations all over the world. Clearly, he was in the US, but I didn't know which city or state.

"How long was your drive?" I asked.

"About seventeen hours," she said. "Maybe a little longer with the stops I made."

"I'll give you a shirt you can sleep in. When your things arrive, I'll set them inside your bedroom door. Sleep as long as you want."

I led her down the hall and showed her the guest bathroom and where she'd be staying for the foreseeable future. Then I got a T-shirt from my room and handed it to her. While she got cleaned up, I decided to make a quick call to Wire. The more I knew, the better prepared I'd be. At the same time, I didn't want to tip off the Bratva. The last thing we needed was for any of them to come to the gates, demanding we hand over Oksana.

She'd claimed they thought she'd helped her father betray them. She might be a stranger, but my gut told me she hadn't done it. The woman seemed too sweet. Too innocent. No, either the father had framed her, hoping to cut a deal, or someone had wanted her out of the way.

I dialed Wire's number and hoped he'd be able to give me more insight. Something told me I needed to prepare myself for a war. I just hoped the club was up for it. Hell, I wasn't sure I was ready. Now I understood why the officers had stepped down. I hadn't been in my current position for long, and already we'd had a lot dropped on us. What the fuck else could go wrong in such a short amount of time?

Chapter Two

Oksana

I'd locked the bathroom door before starting the shower. Even though Nikolai trusted Grimm, I wasn't sure how I felt yet. The man hadn't hurt me. He'd welcomed me into his home, even after hearing about my possible betrayal with the Bratva. I didn't know anything about him. Had he ever been part of the family? How had he become a biker of all things?

My cheeks warmed as I thought about the sexy older man. He had to be nearly twice my age, and yet, I found him rather attractive. I'd never cared for the men in suits surrounding me every day. Most of the men who'd come to our home had been clean-shaven. What would it feel like to kiss a man with a beard?

"Get it together. You're not here for that," I muttered to myself.

I stripped out of my clothes and stood under the hot spray. The bathroom only had generic soap and shampoo, but it would work for now. I'd gladly give up the luxury items I'd once used if it meant I would be free from the Bratva. If they caught me, my virginity wouldn't matter anymore. They'd hurt me. Make an example of me. Then they'd either kill me, or leave me in such a state I'd pray for death.

Whatever Grimm wanted, I'd give him. He'd taken me in, bought me clean clothes, and seemed to want to keep me safe. I owed him my life. Same for Nikolai, and I knew the best way to repay my friend was to trust him. If that meant staying here until Grimm figured out something else for me, then that's what I'd do. It wouldn't be a hardship to remain here for a while. He might not live in a mansion, but he kept his home tidy, and it had a cozy feel to it. Honestly, I liked it far better than the cold place where I'd lived all my life. Those expensive rugs and furniture had come with conditions. I'd had to be perfect at all times, follow every rule, and do whatever was best for my family and the Bratva. It hadn't been a home. Not really. More like a prison. And now I was free for the first time in my life.

By the time I'd finished washing and put on the T-shirt Grimm had left me, I felt a lot better. Exhausted, though. I went across to the bedroom he'd said I could use and pulled back the covers. Even after I laid my head on the pillow, I couldn't sleep. Fear still thrummed in my veins. I'd made it this far, but what if they came for me? Did any of them know about Grimm? Would they think to search for me here?

I didn't think the biker would just hand me over to them, but I couldn't be certain. If it meant keeping his people here safe, what would he do? I wouldn't blame him in the least for protecting his family over the strange woman who'd shown up out of the blue. No, if the Bratva came, I wouldn't put Grimm in that position. I'd either go with them, or I'd run again. I didn't know where I'd go, or how I'd pay for anything, but I'd figure it out.

Maybe I could find a way to earn some money while I stayed here. It wouldn't be a bad idea to build a little nest egg in case I had to leave quickly. If I'd planned for a future outside my family, I might have had a better chance of escaping on my own instead of relying on Nikolai. I didn't want to fall into that same trap again. I'd learned my lesson the hard way.

A light knock sounded at the door, and I sat up. "Yes?"

Grimm stepped into the room, leaving the door open. He didn't come closer, though, and I wondered if he thought I was scared of him. It would be a reasonable conclusion after all I'd been through recently. But he would also be wrong. I didn't fear him. Not even a little. Despite his rough exterior, there was a kindness in his eyes I'd only ever seen on one other man. Nikolai. It must run in the family.

"I ordered stuff without even asking what you wanted. When you get the items, check and see if there's anything I didn't think of. I want to make sure you're comfortable while you're here."

"I don't need much," I said. He huffed and shook his head, but I caught the flash of humor in his eyes. "What?"

"A Bratva lady who doesn't need much? Now I've heard it all. Sorry, Princess. I'm not sure I believe you."

"You've already provided more than I had all day. Safety. A bed to sleep in. A place to wash up. Yesterday, I lived in a mansion, wore designer clothes, and strived for perfection. Not because I wanted to, but because I had to."

He gave a nod. "And now you don't. I get it. I didn't want anything to do with that life. Went into the military as soon as I was eligible, and I never once looked back. I don't regret my decision. But you're different, Oksana. They groomed you all your life to be a wife and mother, to expect fancy things."

"I wouldn't mind being either of those. The difference is I no longer have to marry someone to improve my family's standing with the Bratva."

He leaned his hip against the dresser and folded his arms. "You just gained your freedom, and you'd be willing to get married? Don't you want to experience life a little? Figure out who you are outside the life you've led to this point?"

"You make it sound like I can't do those things if I have a husband. What if he's supportive and wants to stand beside me instead of keeping me in his shadow? Not all men are like the ones I've known so far. You're different. I'm sure other men are too."

He ran his hand over his face. "I'm not quite as different as you think. I may not wear a suit, but I still lead a dangerous life, Oksana. There's a gate for a reason. It keeps the bad people out, in theory, but it doesn't always work. I've got blood on my hands, and I'm sure I will again in the future. Don't make me out to be some sort of saint because I'm far from it."

"I don't understand."

"The heroes you see on TV… they regret killing people. No matter how bad the other guy is, they always wish they could have saved them, or that it hadn't gone down the way it did. I'm not built that way. If I kill someone, I don't regret it later. It meant the asshole needed to be put down. There are some monsters in this world who can't be redeemed. I have no problem taking them out, and I won't lose a bit of sleep over it."

I cocked my head and studied him. Why did he want to push me away? I'd tried to pay him a compliment in my own way and let him know I appreciated what he'd done for me, and instead, he tried to make it sound like he was a jerk.

"If there's a rabid dog, they put it down so it can't hurt people, don't they?" I asked.

"Yeah."

"So, you're essentially doing the same thing. You put down the rabid humans who would try to destroy all the good in the world. Why does that make you a bad person?" I asked.

He smiled softly and shook his head. "You're

something else, Oksana. I've known my share of Bratva women, and I can honestly say you're nothing like them. How did you grow up in that environment without losing yourself completely?"

"I can't be the only one," I said.

"No." He looked away for a moment. "Sarge's woman is Russian. She had Bratva ties as well. I should introduce the two of you."

"Oh, fuck." He groaned. "I'm seeing too many parallels right now. Sarge was in the military and ended up with a Russian wife. I was in the military and now have a Russian woman in my home. If I'm not careful, Wire and Lavender will have us married before either of us blinks."

None of his words made sense. How could someone marry us? Didn't we have to agree to a marriage? There were vows to say. A license to file. We couldn't be married just because someone said so, right?

"I'll explain later," he said. "Although I'm hoping it won't be necessary. If my club starts meddling in your life, you won't be leaving this place. They'll make sure of it. So if you want to taste freedom, to experience life, I'd advise you to hit the road as soon as you have a plan. Otherwise, this will be the end of your journey."

"I didn't understand any of that."

"Get some rest. We'll talk later." With one last lingering look, he left the room, shutting the door behind him.

I felt more confused than ever. Was he warning me? If so, about what? Or was he trying to scare me away? If he didn't want me to stay here, all he had to do was say so. I'd leave, even if I didn't have anywhere else to go. I'd never stay where I wasn't wanted. He'd been nice to me so far, but I refused to take advantage of him.

He was right about one thing, though… we could discuss it tomorrow. I lay down again and closed my eyes, and this time, sleep pulled me under.

* * *

Grimm

I didn't know what to make of Oksana. In a lot of ways, she appeared to be like any good Bratva woman. Quiet. Obedient. Elegant. And yes, despite her somewhat haggard appearance last night, she still had a certain grace about her. Then there were times she surprised me. She had some fight in her. If she didn't, she would have never made it this far. Not even with Nikolai's help. The fact he risked his life to save her spoke volumes. He wouldn't have done that for just anyone. It wouldn't have mattered if he thought of her as a friend or not. For him to put his life on the line, it meant Oksana was different from the others. But how? Sure, I'd seen hints of the woman hiding under the years of discipline, and likely abuse. What would it take to find the real Oksana?

Something told me it would be entertaining as hell to find out.

I hadn't smoked in forever, but I kept a pack on hand and indulged once every blue moon. I pulled them out now and stepped out front to light one. Smoking in the house around Oksana wouldn't be right. Didn't matter if it was my house and she was merely an uninvited guest. I'd treat her with the same respect I'd show my mother, if she were still alive.

I inhaled, held it a moment, then blew out the smoke. My eyes slid shut as the nicotine settled my nerves. Finding the woman at the gate, reading that note… it left me feeling out of sorts. Out of all the members of my club to have some random woman stop by, I'd never thought it would be me. What the hell had Nikolai been thinking? I couldn't remember how many years had passed since the last time I'd seen him, or spoken to him. I'd run across him when he was still a kid. Twenty years ago? Longer? Less? Something had made me give him my contact info, in case he ever needed help. I'd known it was something my mother would have wanted me to do.

It seemed he'd proven me wrong. He did need me, even if it was only as a favor to a friend. For him to send Oksana here, it meant he trusted me with her. As much as I'd love to blame everything on that fact alone, I couldn't. Even if she hadn't been friends with him, I'd have still helped her. I would have been more skeptical, but I wouldn't have left her outside the gates.

My phone buzzed in my pocket, and I pulled it out, swiping to answer when I saw Wire's name on the screen.

"Did you find something already?" I asked.

"You said her name is Oksana Romanov?"

"Yeah, that's what the note said, and it's what she said as well. I don't think my cousin would have lied about something like that. If he did, then he made sure she knew what to say when she got here. Why?"

"Her father betrayed some really bad people and implicated her in his dirty deals. There's a hit out on her. Issued last night. This is some fucked up shit, Grimm. We need to tell Savior and Saint. Hell, Tempest sure the fuck needs to know. What if they trace her here?"

"What about a Nikolai Volkov? Anything on him?"

Wire cleared his throat. "You're related, aren't

you?"

Shit. For him to say it that way made me think something had gone sideways for my little cousin. I couldn't tell Oksana if something bad happened to him. I didn't think she'd be able to handle it right now. Not with everything else she'd had thrown at her in the last day or so.

"Yes. What happened to him?"

"Nothing yet. From what I gathered reading messages between a Feliks Sobol and Viktor Petrov, they believe Nikolai had something to do with Oksana escaping. I'm assuming they're correct."

"They are. Nikolai is a grown man now. He'll have to handle shit on his own. He sent Oksana here for a reason. She's our priority."

"I'd have to agree. If they catch her, it won't be pretty."

He wasn't telling me anything I didn't already know. I didn't need to see the messages between those men to know what the Bratva would do to her. They had already considered her a traitor. Then she'd run. If her fate with them had been bad before, it became a hundred times worse when she escaped to come here.

"Nikolai had a car for her. It's a piece of shit. If you want to check it for trackers or bugs, it's parked on the street in front of my house. Hell, empty it out and dump it for all I care. She's not leaving anytime soon." Fuck. Why had I just said that?

"She's not?" The way Wire asked made me think he had a sly smile on his face. *Motherfucker*. Why did I get the feeling I'd be married by morning?

Then again, the idea of being married to a woman I didn't know should have me running for the hills. So why did the thought of Oksana being tied to me have the opposite effect? I'd found her pretty from the moment I'd first seen her, but looks could fade over time. When I'd been younger, my mother had made me promise if I ever got married, it wouldn't be for something like thinking a woman was beautiful. She'd wanted me to look inside the woman's heart and judge if she was worthy of being mine.

I didn't know Oksana well enough for that. I did like the bits of fire I saw in her, though. How she'd survived the Bratva for so long was a mystery. Women like her had a tendency to be taught their place. Harshly. Or they disappeared. The Romanovs shouldn't have been very high up in the Bratva. From what I remembered, that family had always been in the lower dregs. Had her father gotten greedy? If he'd gone about things the right way, he could have earned a higher spot. Sounded like he'd taken the easy way out and pulled his family down with him.

"What about Oksana's family? She said they put her younger sister into an all girls' academy. They sent her mom to a brothel. The father is dead. Any other blood relatives?" I asked.

"Not that I've seen so far. As for the sister, they've tightened security. Probably think your girl is going to try and get her sister out of their hands."

My girl? I wasn't going to even acknowledge what he'd said. If I did, it would likely backfire on me, anyway. I inhaled another lungful of smoke, wondering if the sister would be okay. With the extra guards, it wouldn't be easy to get her out of there. Not impossible, though.

"What are you contemplating?" Wire asked.

"Wondering if we should send someone after the little sister. If they can't get Oksana back, they may take it out on her. Or worse, pair her with someone who will delight in tormenting her for the rest of her life. However long that might be."

"You going to ask Savior to call Church?"

"Not yet. But I am going to see if he'll put in a request with a few clubs. Surely someone is looking for a little action and wouldn't mind a rescue mission."

"Well, if you need me, let me know." The call ended, and I quickly dialed Savior's number. I knew it was getting late, and he now had a wife and kids to think about, but this couldn't wait. He answered with a mumbled *hello* that had me double-checking the time. Had he been asleep?

"Grimm, what did you need?" he asked, sounding a little more alert.

"It's not the shortest story. You awake enough for it?"

He snorted. "Fell asleep in the recliner. Kids were sick all last night and most of today. Didn't sleep much."

"There's a woman at my house, and she needs our help." I spent the next twenty minutes telling him everything I knew so far and what I wanted to attempt. He could have said *fuck no* and told me to deal with it on my own, but I knew he wouldn't turn away a woman in need. It just wasn't the way our club worked.

"I'll call Charming first. You know he has Bratva ties. He may know someone who can extract her. If he doesn't want to get into this mess, then I'll send out a call to some other clubs. I'm sure someone will be up for it."

"Thanks, Pres."

"Need anything for Oksana?"

"I ordered her a few outfits and a pair of shoes, along with other necessities. They should arrive soon. I sent Owen to pick them up." I heard a door shut softly and wondered if he'd left the house. "She's sleeping right now. After she's had a chance to rest, I'd like to have a doctor come check her out. I think they hurt her, but when I asked to see the damage they'd inflicted, she started to unbutton her shirt. I told her to stop."

"Right. I'll call Dr. Myron and ask him to drop by tomorrow after breakfast."

"Thanks, Pres."

"You keeping her?" he asked.

"Something tells me Wire plans on it. He got that tone. You know the one he gets right before he screws with people's lives? Something tells me I'll be married to her before she even wakes up. Not sure how she'd handle that."

"I'll call him. Maybe I can hold him back, but you know he and Lavender are convinced we all need families to be happy. So far, they haven't been wrong. Makes it hard to argue with them."

I shook my head. "Yeah, I know. The thought of keeping her doesn't send me running, but I hadn't met her before today. She ran from a bad situation. The last thing I want to do is make her feel like I've taken all her choices from her. She's never experienced freedom before."

"Understood. Keep me posted. Once we have more info, I'll call Church so we can update everyone. You need anything in the meantime, just give me a call. Preferably not between the hours of ten at night and eight in the morning."

I could have made a crack about him getting old, but I knew he'd take it as a challenge and do his best to pound me into the ground. So I refrained… barely.

I ended the call, put out my cigarette, and went back inside. I didn't know what the morning would bring, but hopefully, I'd have a clear head to deal with all this shit. It would be great if Wire could find out more on Nikolai as well. I might not really know my cousin, but it didn't mean I wanted him to die. With some luck, he'd get a slap on the wrist, maybe get his rank dropped, and that would be the end of it.

With only two of us left, my bloodline would die out soon. Unless I really did get married and have kids. Hadn't bothered me before. For some reason, it did right now.

Shit. Now Wire had me focused on the wrong damn thing. I didn't need to even think about keeping Oksana and starting a life with her. She deserved the chance to experience new things, travel, or do whatever she wanted without worrying about a spouse or kids.

Realizing my shirt smelled like smoke, I stripped and decided to shower. I'd deal with tomorrow in the morning. My phone buzzed, and I checked it. Owen. Shit. I'd forgotten he was bringing the clothes by.

Left the bags on the porch.

Guess I'd be grabbing everything after I rinsed off. No fucking way I'd be getting them while I was naked.

Chapter Three

Oksana

I hadn't slept well for several nights. Not since they'd picked up my father, then later returned for my mother. The simple fact I'd not woken once all night either told me I'd been exhausted, or I trusted Grimm to keep me safe. It seemed crazy to trust someone I'd just met, but since Nikolai vouched for him, I would put my faith in Grimm. Besides, he seemed like the capable sort.

I stretched and pushed off the covers, tugging down the T-shirt. The sacks on the floor caught my attention, and I went to get them, setting them on the foot of the bed. I pulled out a package of panties, a few plain shirts, and three pairs of black leggings. Another sack contained black canvas tennis shoes, and the third held everything I could possibly need. Hairbrush, toothbrush, hair ties, body soap and lotion, deodorant, and even a tube of mascara, some tinted lip balm, and nail polish.

Staring at the items, I wondered if Grimm had really purchased everything on his own. It didn't seem like the sort of stuff a biker would think of buying. Then again, I didn't know anything about him. He could have a girlfriend. Oh, God. What if he did? Would she be mad I was staying here?

I quickly changed into the clothes he'd provided, then stepped out into the hall. The smell of coffee lured me to the kitchen. Even though I didn't typically drink it, I loved the scent. Grimm sat at the table, a cup in his hands, and his phone on the table in front of him. I padded into the kitchen and stopped, not sure if I should sit down or not. He looked up and gave me a slight smile.

"Morning. Sleep okay?"

"Better than I have in days," I admitted. I shifted from one foot to the other and fought the urge to wring my hands. "Um, do you have a girlfriend?"

He froze, with the coffee cup halfway to his mouth. "What?"

"A girlfriend. Do you have one?"

He took a swallow, holding my gaze over the rim, before setting the cup on the table. "No. Why? Are you volunteering for the position?"

My cheeks heated. How was I supposed to respond to that? Was he teasing me? Being serious? I didn't have a lot of experience with men. I'd only been on a handful of dates, all with men approved by my father. Which meant they weren't the least bit like Grimm.

"Have a seat. Want some juice? Coffee? I'm not sure what you like." He nudged the chair with his foot.

I sat and tried to relax a little. This was the man who'd taken me into his home last night. He'd provided me with food and clothes. So why did I feel so nervous today?

"Juice is fine," I said.

Grimm got up and took down a glass from the cabinet, then poured some orange juice. He set it on the table. When he reclaimed his seat, he watched me. I now knew exactly what prey felt like. Not even with the men who'd hurt me had I felt so vulnerable. What was it about this man's gaze that completely undid me?

"They either outright know Nikolai helped you or at least suspect he did," Grimm said. "I'm having someone keep an eye on the situation, and don't worry, the Bratva will never know. I don't want them to surprise us with a visit, assuming they figure out where you are."

"But Nikolai is okay?"

He nodded. "For now. But you, on the other hand, are in a world of trouble. They've put a hit out on you, Oksana, and added guards to your sister. It's my belief they think you'll try to remove her from the academy."

"They haven't hurt her, have they?" I asked.

"No. And I'm going to make sure they don't. My President has called another club, and he'll call as many as it takes. We'll find someone to extract her. Not sure she'll be able to come here right away. We may need to keep the two of you apart a while longer, to make sure you both stay safe. Can't risk them finding one of you and getting you both. Understood?"

I nodded. I didn't like it, but what he said made sense. I'd do anything to keep my little sister safe. She meant the world to me, and I'd hated to leave her behind. If they hadn't promised she'd be taken care of, I'd have fought harder. It wouldn't have done me any good, but I'd have still tried.

"Should I be worried?" I asked.

"About yourself, Nikolai, or your sister?"

"Yes."

He smiled, shaking his head. "I'll keep you safe. Nikolai can handle himself. And I already told you we'd get your sister out of there. So everything will be fine. If those assholes show up at the gates, we'll send them on their way. Won't be the first time we've dealt with them."

"You fight the Bratva often?" I asked.

"No. And not the men you've been dealing with. However, we've gone up against them in the past. Not to mention, I escaped them when I was eighteen by joining the military. I've never once looked back, and so far they've left me alone."

Except they might come searching for me if they figured out where I'd gone. Then I'd be at fault if something happened to Grimm. I knew Nikolai's aunt and uncle had died. Until this exact moment, I hadn't really thought about the fact they were Grimm's parents.

"Back to the girlfriend thing. Why were you asking?"

"The clothes. They didn't seem like something a man would select. I thought perhaps you had a girlfriend, and she'd helped. Then I got worried she'd be angry I was staying here."

Grimm stared at me for a moment. The silence stretched on, and I started to shift in my seat. Had I offended him? Or did he really have someone special in his life and hadn't thought of how my presence in his home would make them feel? He hadn't seemed like an insensitive asshole, but I could have been wrong.

"No girlfriend," he said. "As for the things I selected, I pay attention. I've helped pick up stuff for the old ladies here, both when I was a Prospect and after I patched into the club. If I got things you actually like, it just means I got lucky."

"You're certain no woman is going to show up, irate that I'm staying here? I don't want to cause problems for you."

He snorted. "Oksana, the sort of trouble you'll cause has nothing to do with another woman. If anything, you may regret coming here when my club brothers decide to meddle in our lives. And trust me, they will. They always do. Worse than a bunch of old women."

"It must be nice to have them in your life. I only

had my sister and parents. Now it's just me and Yulia."

He reached over and placed his hand over mine. "No. It's not just the two of you."

I felt warm all over at his words. I knew Nikolai would do what he could for us. Already had. But this was different. I'd never seen Nikolai as anything but a friend. With Grimm, I felt things I'd never experienced before. I liked having his hand on mine and wondered what it would be like for him to touch me elsewhere. What would kissing him be like? To have him hold me at night?

If I weren't careful, I might act on those thoughts and end up kissing the man. The last thing I needed to do was make him angry and chance losing my safe haven. No, I needed to think of him as an extension of Nikolai and nothing more.

So then, why was he watching me so intently? Was it possible he felt the same way about me? A braver woman might have asked him.

"Finish your juice. When you're done, we're going to take a walk. I'll show you part of the compound, and there's someone I want you to meet. His name is Wire, and he's a hacker. So is his woman, Lavender. They're the ones who got the intel on your sister and Nikolai. They may have a few questions for you."

I nodded. "All right. I'll tell them whatever I can, but I don't know if I'll be of much help."

"You'd be surprised. You probably know more than you realize."

I hoped he was right. I didn't like the idea of having to hide behind him, relying on him for every little thing. If this was the one thing I could do, I'd gladly tell them whatever they wanted. It was the least I could do for all Grimm had offered me so far.

Something told me I wasn't leaving here anytime soon. Not if they'd put a hit out on me. I wouldn't last more than a day on my own.

"Thank you," I said. "For everything you've done, and for risking your life. I know the Bratva won't go easy on anyone hiding me from them. You're a very brave man."

"No. I just know the difference between right and wrong, and I refuse to let those assholes hurt you."

Why couldn't I have met a man like him before now? Even Nikolai wasn't on Grimm's level. Was it wrong I hoped I never had to leave?

* * *

Grimm

Taking Oksana to Wire and Lavender's house probably wasn't the smartest thing to do. Once they got to know her, they'd start meddling, and we'd end up married. So why was I taking her? I rubbed the back of my neck, wondering if I'd lost my damn mind. I didn't know her. Why did the thought of her leaving make me feel… lonely?

Oksana was a tie to my past, one I didn't need any connection to whatsoever. It would be best to clear up her issues and help her get settled elsewhere. She didn't need another overbearing guy in her life. She'd had plenty of those already. But the thought of someone putting their hands on her, getting to hold her while she slept, see her smile in the morning… it pissed me the fuck off.

The moment we stepped outside the front door, a car pulled into the driveway. I'd completely forgotten about the doctor stopping by this morning. Dr. Myron got out of his car and waved at us.

"Morning, Grimm! And this must be Oksana."

He carried his bag over, hand outstretched. I shook it and thought Oksana would do the same. Instead, she stepped behind me. I felt her hands on my back as she gripped my shirt. *What the hell*?

I reached back and placed my hand on her, hoping it would give her reassurance that she was all right. The doctor would never hurt her. He'd treated all the women here, and his partner had helped a time or two as well. Would it make her feel better to know the man was gay? After what she'd suffered, I could understand a strange man making her feel ill at ease.

"Oksana, this is Dr. Myron. He's helped a lot of the women at the Dixie Reapers." I patted her gently. "It's just a check-up. We need to make sure everything is okay, and those men didn't hurt you too badly."

"Is this something you want?" she asked, her accent thicker than usual. Then she started chattering in Russian. "*Eezveeneete*."

"No need to be sorry, Oksana. Let's go inside and you can talk to the doctor. Until you're comfortable, I'll stay with you."

She went back into the house, and I followed, motioning for Dr. Myron to come with us. Oksana went into the living room and curled into the corner of the couch. The doctor remained standing. The moment I sat, Oksana got onto my lap and clung to me. I didn't know where the quiet, brave woman had gone. The one who'd come to the gates and not backed down until she saw me.

"Oksana, what's wrong?" I asked, running my hand up and down her arm in an effort to calm her.

"I'm fine. I don't need a doctor."

The doctor rocked back on his heels and tipped his head toward the door. "I'll just step back outside a moment. I think the two of you should have a quick talk. Let me know if you want me to come back inside."

He let himself out and I held Oksana closer. She cuddled against me, and I wondered what the hell was going through her mind. All her poise and perfection seemed to have flown out the window, leaving her a soft, vulnerable young woman. I rather liked this side of her. Then again, I liked it when she'd been an obedient woman too.

"Talk to me, Oksana. I can't fix this if I don't know what's scaring you."

She squirmed a little. "Not scared."

"Right. You're Bratva born and bred. No fear inside you at all, right?"

She sucked her lips into her mouth and stared at me. Yep. She was scared, even if she wouldn't admit it. Why would the thought of seeing the doctor be so terrifying? Had one hurt her before? Or had something else happened?

"I don't want to take off my clothes for him," she murmured.

"You mean like you'd do for your yearly physical?"

Her cheeks went red, and she turned her face against me. Nope. Not that then. So what had she been through at the hands of a doctor? She'd said she was a virgin, so clearly she hadn't been given to one as payment. Then what?

"What happened, Oksana?" I asked.

"My father had a doctor examine me, to make sure I hadn't given my virginity to anyone. He wanted to use me as a bargaining chip. Offer me up to someone as a bride." Her breath caught, and I noticed her eyes turned glassy with unshed tears. "He stayed in the room. Watched the entire exam. Please don't make me go through that again."

Jesus Fucking Christ! If her father weren't already dead, I'd have beaten the fucker into the ground. Then revived him and done it all over again.

"Oksana, you can go into the bedroom with the doctor on your own. If you have bruising or cuts anywhere, he'll need to see it to make sure you'll be okay. Otherwise, you won't have to take off any clothing. It's a general exam, and he may take some blood."

"Alone?" She trembled.

Apparently, I'd said the wrong thing. If she'd worried about an audience, and didn't want to be alone, I wasn't sure where that left us. It had to be one or the other.

"What do you need from me, Oksana? I want Dr. Myron to check you out and make sure you're all right. What do we need to do for that to happen?"

"Stay with me? Can we do it in here?" she asked.

"Whatever you want, *zaya*."

She put her arms around my neck and hugged me. "You won't leave me? You promise?"

I swallowed hard. What the fuck had her dad been thinking? And how rough had the doctor been during the exam? She shouldn't be this damn terrified.

I lifted her into my arms as I stood and went to the door. I called out for Dr. Myron to enter the house again, then waited for him. When he came back inside, his eyebrows rose. "Are we doing the exam this way?"

"Whatever you can get done while I'm holding her might be best," I said. "But she wants me to stay for the entire thing."

He nodded, a sadness entering his eyes. Yeah, he got it. Oksana hadn't been through the same hell as some of the other ladies at the club, but she'd had a bad time of it. The doctor did what he could before I had no choice but to set Oksana on her feet. I held her hand throughout the process, until he asked about any wounds. I saw her hesitation.

"Oksana, where did they hurt you?" I asked. "You can tell us."

She lightly touched her breasts. "They grabbed me here. It left bruises."

I moved behind her and wrapped my arm around her waist, tugging her back against me. Slowly, I used my other hand to lift her shirt. She tensed before her breasts were bared. I kissed the top of her head and curved my body around hers. She shivered once I exposed her to the doctor's gaze.

Dr. Myron looked at me. His jaw went tight, and his eyes darkened with fury. I looked down and saw the finger-shaped bruises covering both breasts and understood how he felt. I lowered her shirt, and the doctor backed up a few steps to give Oksana some space.

"I'll recommend something for the bruising. It's over the counter, and she'll probably want some pain reliever for it as well. Would it be all right to draw some blood? I'll check for any vitamin deficiencies. Any family illnesses I should be aware of?" Dr. Myron asked.

"I don't know of any," Oksana said. "My parents never shared that information."

He nodded. "All right. At some point, I'd love to get a fasting lab done to check for diabetes. Wouldn't hurt to run an ANA panel too, just to be safe. I'd like to rule out any major illnesses since we're not certain of your family's medical history."

"I'll bring her in. Maybe after she's settled in more." I reached out to shake his hand, and the doctor let himself out. Oksana relaxed the moment the door closed. "That wasn't so bad, was it?"

She shook her head, but when she looked up at me, her cheeks were pink. "You saw, didn't you?"

"Yeah. I saw, *zaya*." I lightly touched her chin. "If I ever see the men who dared to touch you, they won't live to see another day. This I promise."

Seeing her in this light -- vulnerable, soft, sweet -- made me want to wrap her in my arms and never let go. How could anyone have ever hurt her, or dared to think of tossing her into one of the Bratva-owned brothels?

"Would you like me to ask Wire to check into your mother's location? We could try to get her out of there."

She licked her lips, then shook her head. "They'll have broken her. She won't accept. Even if she did, I know she'd end up taking her own life. My mother is a proud woman. She'd rather be dead than have anyone know of her shame."

"You're the eldest, right? And only twenty?"

"Yes. Why?"

"How old is your mother?"

"Thirty-eight. She was seventeen when she married my father, and I arrived shortly after her eighteenth birthday."

My gut clenched. Fuck. I couldn't leave that woman there. If she looked even half as beautiful as her daughter, she'd be used up in no time at all. I'd get Wire to find her location, then I'd ask someone to go after her. Maybe I could convince Stripes to do it. He might not be part of my club, but the man was Russian like me. And single… which meant he didn't have a woman who'd get upset over him going into a brothel to find Oksana's mother. Although his granddaughter wouldn't be too happy about it.

"We'll find her and give her the option of leaving. Will that be all right?"

"Yes. I think she'd like that. Even if she were to die, she'd probably prefer to be free at the time."

"Then I'll take care of it." I smoothed her hair back from her face. "Whatever you need, just tell me. I'll do my best to give you everything, *zaya*."

Oksana put her arms around my waist and buried her face in my chest. We stood in the middle of the living room for the longest time, holding one another. It seemed to be what she needed most, since I got the brightest smile from her when she finally stepped back. The woman had so many sides I wondered if I'd ever discover them all. Oddly, I was looking forward to it.

Chapter Four

Oksana

The way Grimm said he'd give me whatever I wanted or needed made it sound like he wanted to keep me for a while. Or was I reading too much into it? I wasn't sure what I'd expected when he saw my bruises. There'd been a sort of calm acceptance, even though I'd felt him tense for a moment. Had he held back for my sake?

I reached over and took his hand as we walked to Wire and Lavender's house. He curled his fingers around mine without any hesitation. A peace settled over me, one I'd never felt before, and I hoped it was a feeling I could hold onto for a while.

"Will they be upset we're going to drop by unannounced?" I asked, glancing up at him.

"No. It will be fine. Around here, people stop by all the time. We're one big, happy family. For the most part. In some cases, there really are family connections. One of our Prospects is the father of Thunder's woman, and her grandfather is a patched member of the club. Preacher and Torch each have daughters who paired off with men at the Reckless Kings in Tennessee. Venom's two oldest ended up with the Devil's Fury in Georgia. Bull's woman, Darian, is the daughter of a Devil's Boneyard member. He's actually their VP."

"You said someone else here had ties to the Bratva?" I asked.

"Sarge's woman. There's also a Russian who's a member of the Devil's Boneyard. His granddaughter married into the Devil's Fury. And the Devil's Boneyard President also has ties to the Bratva, but his connections are out west. That's the club I'm hopeful will help get your sister out of the academy."

"Will she be safe there?" I asked.

"Definitely. I'd trust them with you or any other woman here." He hesitated. "Although I want to ask Stripes to go get your mom, or at least offer her the chance to leave. He's older than she is, so she might respond well if he speaks to her with authority. They've trained her to answer to orders, right?"

I nodded. "They have. They trained all of us. Those who didn't fall in line paid dire consequences. It's why I can't understand why they punished her. Clearly, she only did what my father told her to do. How is that her fault?"

He squeezed my hand. "I know. We'll get it sorted out and get them both to safety. Whatever it takes, I'll make sure it happens. What they both do with that freedom is up to them. I know your sister is underage, but I don't think it's a good idea to bring her here. Not yet."

"Because if the three of us are in different locations, it would mean Feliks and the others would have to spread out to get to us?"

"Exactly." He smiled down at me. "I know they have plenty of men to call on. Both at their location and others. However, it would take a while for them to organize something like that. If they want to hit quickly, they'll use whoever they have on hand. Which means sending fewer men to each location."

"And each of us will have a better chance at remaining free."

Grimm stopped and pulled me in for a hug. "No one is making you leave. Understood? I won't let them hurt you ever again. Now, smile for me. You're about to meet Wire and Lavender. Can't have her thinking I've upset you. She might drain all my accounts or wipe out my existence entirely."

My eyes went wide. "She can do that?"

"Oh, yeah. She and her husband are two of the best hackers in the world. Or they were. Last I heard, they wanted to recruit some younger people who show a lot of potential. We'll see how that goes."

He led me up to a cute house with toys scattered in the front yard. He didn't even knock before he entered. I could hear a family talking from somewhere inside the home. Grimm seemed to know exactly where they'd be and went straight to the kitchen. A man with ginger hair going silver, and a much younger woman sat at a table with two kids who both looked close to ten years old.

"Morning," Grimm said. "Thought I'd introduce everyone to Oksana."

The little girl jumped up and ran for Grimm, throwing her arms around his waist to hug him. "Uncle Grimm! Is this our new aunt? Mommy said you got us an aunt."

Got them one? I glanced at the woman. She had a smirk on her face, and there was a twinkle in her eyes. I had a feeling the girl's words meant something, even if I didn't understand what.

"I did, huh?" Grimm asked, smiling down at her. "Livvy, this is Oksana."

I held a hand out to the little girl, but she tackled me with a hug. I rocked back on my feet, nearly losing my balance, until Grimm placed his hand on my lower back to hold me steady.

"Would the two of you like some coffee?" Wire asked.

"I'll take a cup. I think Oksana would prefer juice," Grimm said.

The little boy stood up and carried his empty dishes to the sink. "You can have my seat. I'm finished."

Grimm led me over to the chair and sat, then pulled me down onto his lap. The little boy shook his head, a half-smile on his face. "My dad does the same thing with my mom. Guess you really are our aunt now."

"This is Atlas. He's almost twelve… going on twenty," Wire said.

"And I'm almost ten," Livvy said, bouncing on her toes.

"All right. Time for both of you to go get ready." Lavender shooed them from the room. "You're already late this morning."

"We both got tied up looking into stuff for you last night. Didn't realize the kids were awake too. Needless to say, they're late for school," Wire said. "Once they're gone, we'll tell you what we've discovered."

"You aren't taking them?" Grimm asked.

"No. Portia volunteered. I think she's still trying to make up for that big shitstorm she started with Amity. Instead of going away for college, she's taking some classes online and sticking close to home."

"You don't think it has more to do with her crush on Merlin? He didn't just betray us. He probably broke her heart and killed whatever trust she had in men. Well, those she doesn't consider family." Grimm took a cup of coffee from Wire, and the older man set some orange juice in front of me. I didn't know who they were talking about, or what happened, but it didn't sound like a pleasant conversation.

The doorbell rang and I jolted. "I thought you said people just walk in around here?"

"They do, unless they're Portia," Wire said. He yelled out for her to come in, and a girl who looked to be close to my age entered the kitchen. She froze the moment she saw me. "Portia, this is Oksana. She's Grimm's wife."

I hoped the shock of those words didn't show on my face. Wife? What was he talking about? We weren't married. We'd just met! Grimm seemed to take it in stride though and didn't comment or contradict the other man. Unless he knew something I didn't? No. It wasn't possible to marry someone without both parties being present, right?

Portia folded her arms over her chest. "By choice? Or did you and Lavender play God again?"

"If you're asking if I'm upset about it, the answer is no," Grimm said. "As to the other… well, when do these two not meddle?"

Portia's gaze softened and she studied me. "Are you okay with being Grimm's wife? Did you even know?"

I wasn't sure what the correct response would be in this situation, so I remained quiet and just watched her. After a moment, she shook her head, muttered something under her breath that sounded like *perfect for each other* and wandered out of the room. Grimm kissed my shoulder and rubbed his beard against my neck. Heat flared inside me, and I leaned back against him.

Wire rubbed his hands together. "Now that the cat's out of the bag, I might as well tell you both. You're married. If anyone goes looking, they'll find a marriage license on file. But if someone should ask either of you about it, you were married in Oksana's hometown. In secret. Three weeks ago."

Wait. Three weeks? That was long before things blew up at home. Which would have meant I was under Grimm's protection when the Bratva tried to break me. All the pieces started to fall into place inside my head. They hadn't done this as a whim. He and Lavender had put thought into it. If the Bratva came for me, not only would Grimm be able to say I was his wife, but he'd also tell them I'd belonged to him when those men had hurt me. When Feliks had sent me off with the intention of putting me in a brothel… Oh, my. I rather liked these two. I smiled broadly and snuggled into Grimm.

Wire laughed. "I take it the news is all right with both of you. I had a feeling Grimm would be fine with it. But you surprise me, Oksana. Portia was right. You really are perfect for him."

"Guess this means my wife needs a ring," Grimm said.

Lavender came back into the room. "I'll call the jeweler over on Main Street. He can bring a selection to your house. Any idea what size ring you wear, Oksana? Might help him to know that sort of thing ahead of time."

"A five," I said. I'd always had small fingers. Then again, I was rather tiny all over. Even my breasts.

"I'll see that it's handled after the two of you leave," Lavender said.

The front door shut, and I figured that meant the kids and Portia had left. Lavender and Wire took their seats again. This time, she had a laptop in her hands. She opened the lid and typed for a moment before turning the machine so we could all see it.

I pressed my fingers to my lips to hold back my cry. My poor mother! They'd cut her. Burned her. What the hell had happened? I'd thought she was going into the brothels. They wouldn't have ruined her like this if that had been their plan. She wouldn't earn them much looking like this.

"Your mother tried to kill herself after her first night at the brothel," Lavender said. "The Bratva didn't handle it well and decided to teach her a lesson. I'm not going to sugarcoat anything because I think you deserve the full truth. They raped her while she still bled from her wounds. Filmed it. From what I found in their communications, they're going to use it to keep the other women in line. At the moment, she's locked up in the basement of the cheapest brothel they own."

"Stripes and Gator went after her," Wire said. "And I believe Specter is either meeting them there or sending a friend to back them up. They'll get your mom out. I don't doubt it for a moment. Then she'll go to Florida and stay with the Devil's Boneyard for a while. You won't be able to see her until we have everything settled."

"Since she's a widow, we're also going to give her some extra protection," Lavender said.

"Does the poor unsuspecting biker know he's now happily married?" Grimm asked. "Or did you randomly choose someone and not even tell them?"

"Stripes volunteered after seeing the videos," Wire said softly. "I've never heard him that furious before. I'm not sure he'll leave much behind when he goes after her. It's going to be a massacre."

"And my sister?" I asked.

"They showed her the videos. She's... not doing well. The rooms at the academy have cameras installed. I hacked into them. She mostly sits in the corner and rocks. I don't think she's eaten in two days," Lavender said.

"Who's going after her?" Grimm asked.

"Samson and Nitro from the Reckless Kings," Wire said. "But Hades Abyss offered to send backup with them if it's needed."

"So she'll be in Tennessee?" I asked. "With the Reckless Kings?"

Wire smirked. "Looks like Grimm has been telling you quite a bit. Yes, she will. They have a guest house if she wants to be alone, or I'm sure someone will take her in if she'd prefer to be around people."

"When will they be rescued?" I asked.

"Tonight, if possible. If not, then tomorrow. Both clubs will hit the locations at the same time. If they went after one, then the other, it would tip off the Bratva and we'd likely lose either your mom or your sister. Can't have that." Wire leaned back in his chair. "They'll both be safe. I can assure you of that."

I licked my lips and hoped my sister wouldn't hate me for what I was about to ask. "You've already married my mother and Stripes, right?"

Wire and Lavender both nodded.

"Can you do the same for my sister? I know she's only sixteen, but I don't want to leave her vulnerable. It can be a marriage in name only, right? Just a way to keep her safe?"

"There's a Prospect who said he'd keep her safe in whatever way was needed," Lavender said.

"Kye?" Grimm asked.

"Yeah. He's still hurting over the loss of Carina, and he has that little girl to take care of now. The three of them can heal together. And if things don't work out, then they can get a divorce later. I'll mention it to him," Wire said.

Grimm tensed for a moment, and I wondered which part of that bothered him. Was there something they weren't telling me?

"We'll head out so the two of you can work on that. Tell whoever is at the gate to direct the jeweler to my house. Then I'd like some quiet time with Oksana the rest of today. I think we have a lot to discuss," Grimm said. He patted my thigh, and I stood.

It felt like butterflies were swooping through my stomach as he took my hand. A lot to talk about? Did he mean our marriage? What would it be like to be his wife, in truth? Did he want me to move into his room? Did he want a marriage in name only like Yulia would have?

I suddenly felt rather eager to get back to the house and find out.

* * *

Grimm

Did it shock me to discover Wire and Lavender had married us? Nope. I'd honestly been expecting it. The way Oksana took it in stride impressed me. I'd noticed she'd reached for my hand on the way to their house. It gave me hope she wanted this marriage to work. Even if she didn't want me to touch her, I'd still be faithful. I'd never treat her badly. My father had cheated on my mother. In the Bratva, it was normal for the men to seek pleasure with other women. The wives always looked the other way. I'd watched as it slowly destroyed my mother. Even at a young age, I'd known if I ever got married, I wouldn't do that to my wife and kids. I didn't want my son to look at me the way I had my father -- with seething hatred.

Until I'd learned what sort of man he was, I'd looked up to him. Wanted to be like him. But the older I got, the more things I noticed. Like the strained smile my mother wore in his presence. The way he'd come home drunk and smelling like other women. My mother always wore the same scent. To this day, I remembered it. So I could easily detect when my dad smelled like someone else.

I let Oksana into the house and realized I'd need

to have a key made for her. I'd given my spare to the club in case of an emergency. Until now, I'd never needed another one. I pulled out my phone and shot off a quick text to Saint and Savior.

Can someone have an extra key made for my house? I don't want to leave Oksana right now, and it's not safe to take her outside the compound.

Although, technically, it should be perfectly fine. As far as I knew, the Bratva had no idea where she was staying. I didn't think they had hackers. If they did, they could find the marriage certificate, which would lead them to my door. It could either make them back down, or they'd be coming for the both of us. I didn't know if those men still wanted my family's blood or not. It had been so long, it was possible the transgressions of my father were water under the bridge. Then again, Nikolai was in hot water with them, so maybe I wasn't safe, even though no one had come for me in all this time. It could just mean they hadn't been actively looking.

My phone dinged with an incoming message from Saint. *I'll have a Prospect handle it and drop off the spare.*

I knew Lavender would ask the jeweler to bring rings for Oksana, but I hadn't thought to ask for one for myself. Would he think to bring any men's rings? If not, I could always go out and get one. I'd just leave Oksana at home until I'd sorted the mess we found ourselves in.

"Are you really okay with all this?" I asked her. "I'm sure you were blindsided when they said they'd married us."

"You weren't?"

"No. Wire and Lavender have been known to do things like this. Often. And not just with our club. The moment I asked them for help with your situation, I had a feeling they'd end up marrying us."

She moved closer. "You could have asked me to leave. Given me enough money to get a little farther down the road and washed your hands of me. Why take the chance you'd be stuck with me?"

I threaded my fingers through her hair. "Because the moment I saw you and read that note, I knew you'd end up being mine."

Her cheeks flushed a light pink, and she looked away. "I'm nothing special. I'm not beautiful or talented. In case you hadn't noticed, I don't have a lot in the way of curves. My breasts are too small."

"You're perfect the way you are, Oksana. Women come in all shapes and sizes, and I can admit I've been with my fair share of them. Not a single one stands out, though. I can't remember any details of them, or even their names. Why? Because they weren't important. But you *are*."

"I'm really your wife? So that makes me Oksana Volkov for real instead of Romanov?"

"Right. We'll need to get you a new driver's license, a social security card, and figure out what else needs to be done for a name change. I'll have to add you to the bank account as well." I studied her for a moment. "Your fake ID already had my last name on there. I wonder if that was Nikolai's intention all along."

She blinked and stared at me. "You're trusting me with your money? My father had a special account for my mother, and he'd give her an allowance each month."

"You're my wife, Oksana, not my kid. Of course, I'm going to trust you with the money. It belongs to the both of us. Do I want you to drain the account? No. Do

I think you will? Also, no."

"I'm a stranger. How can you be so certain?"

"You haven't taken advantage of me. When I said I'd buy you clothes, you could have demanded high-end items. You could have sneered at the things I picked out. Some women might have been complete bitches about it."

Her brow furrowed. "But you're helping me. Why would I act like that?"

I smiled and tugged her closer, kissing her forehead. "And that's why I'm certain you won't drain my bank account. Whether you want to admit it or not, you're a sweet woman. I can tell you wouldn't do anything to hurt me, financially or otherwise. Am I wrong?"

"About the sweet part, yes."

"We'll see. If you want to meet the club whores, I'll allow it. We can go to a party at the clubhouse anytime you want. Then you can see the sort of catty bitches I deal with on a day-to-day basis."

A fist pounded on my front door, making it rattle on the hinges. Only two men I could think of would do something like that. Tank or Tempest. My money was on the second one. He'd likely heard about my new wife. As the club's Sergeant-at-Arms, I doubted the new addition to our family pleased him, since we hadn't consulted him first. Unless Wire and Lavender had kept him in the loop. But knowing those two, I doubted it.

I didn't get a chance to open the door before whoever was on the other side came barging in. The door slammed into the wall, leaving a hole in the sheetrock. I glared at the damage before narrowing my gaze at Tempest.

"You're fixing the damn wall."

He flipped me off, then stared at Oksana, who remained in my arms. Except now it felt like she was doing her best to glue herself to me. It was understandable. To a small woman like her, Tempest probably looked scary as fuck.

"Why wasn't I informed you had a woman living here?" he asked. "How the fuck am I supposed to protect this club if people don't tell me important shit?"

"My cousin sent Oksana here for protection, and then Wire and Lavender stepped in."

He groaned and tipped his head back. "Fuck! How long have the two of you been married? Did they even wait an hour?"

"They didn't say, but yes, we're married. So be nice." I turned Oksana, so she faced him, even though I could tell she didn't want to. "Oksana, this is Tempest. He helps protect our club and is one of our officers."

"It's nice to meet you, Oksana. I'm sorry if I scared you," Tempest said. At least he was treating her better than he had Amity or Dessa. If he'd been a complete ass, I'd have knocked his teeth down his throat. "If you ever need help and can't find Grimm, you can come to me. Make sure he shows you where I live and gives you my number."

"I was serious about fixing the wall."

"Yeah, yeah. I'll get the shit I need. If your wife wants the walls a different color, now would be a good time to do it."

Oksana shrank against me, shaking her head. "I don't need to change them. It's fine."

Great. Now the timid version of her was coming out again. I wanted to literally kick Tempest's ass right now. I nodded at the door, and he seemed to take the hint, letting himself back out. This time, he used a gentler touch on the door.

"This is your home now," I told her. "Any changes you want to make are fine. If you don't like the colors, the furniture, the dishes… whatever you want done differently, just say the word."

"Your home is all one color," she said.

"No, *our* home is all one color. So tell me what colors you like, and I'll have someone grab paint for us. If you want to help, you can do the trim around the bottom. It will save me from trying to get down that low. You're already close to the floor."

She gasped, and her eyes went wide until she realized I was teasing. Then she lightly smacked me on the arm. "That was mean."

"You're pint-sized, but I like it. I just have to make sure I don't break you."

She looked around the space again. "Can I really change anything at all?"

"Of course. Come on. We can sit down and look through paint colors on my phone. You pick a type and color, and I'll place an order for pickup, along with anything else we might need."

I hadn't realized we'd spend the next three hours not only purchasing paint, rollers, and brushes but also selecting throw pillows, pictures for the walls, and little decorative things to place around the house. But it made my new wife smile, so it was worth it.

Chapter Five

Oksana

The jeweler arrived by the time we'd finished picking out things for the house. Since my family had never permitted me to decorate before, I had more fun than I should have, and I hoped Grimm didn't get angry over how much we'd spent. Although, he hadn't so much as grumbled the entire time.

As I made lunch for us, I kept staring at my ring. I hadn't wanted anything flashy. The wives I'd met in my previous life all wore huge diamonds. I didn't want a reminder of where I'd come from, and Grimm had understood. Instead, I'd tried picking out plain bands. He'd said a big no to each and every one, then selected a pretty platinum band with diamond chips scattered. They were inset so they wouldn't catch on anything, and I had to admit I rather liked it. The stones reminded me of stars in the sky.

He'd selected a black band made out of something the jeweler said was nearly indestructible. Apparently, most of the men at the club wore something similar, or a rubber ring. The fact he'd wanted to wear one at all thrilled me. I'd known a lot of men who refused. Of course, I knew a wedding band wouldn't keep women away. There were plenty who got off being with men who were already taken.

"You know I'd have been happy to cook for us," Grimm said, placing his hands on my hips as I stirred a pot of noodles.

"So you've said, but I want to make a meal for you."

Finding something I could make hadn't been easy. I had limited cooking skills. I'd discovered a bag of frozen shrimp in the freezer, a box of pasta in the cabinet, and he'd had olive oil out on the counter along with a spice rack. The only thing I'd lacked had been walnut chips, but he'd left the house long enough to find some.

I drained the noodles, then tossed them with olive oil and ground black pepper. I mixed in the walnuts and shrimp before fixing our plates. Garlic bread would have been a nice touch, but I hadn't had the necessary supplies for it. Next time. Of course, I'd also need to watch some cooking shows, or order some recipe books. Otherwise, he'd be stuck with boxed dinners for the foreseeable future. I'd learned how to make this after running across it on TikTok several months ago.

We sat down to eat, and I couldn't help but think about what Wire and Lavender had said. How would my mother react when Stripes went to pick her up? Would he scare her? Or would she go with him willingly? I wished there was a way for me to speak with her, to assure her she'd be okay. Then again, she'd tried to end her life. I wasn't convinced she wouldn't do it again.

What about Yulia? She'd never been exposed to men like Grimm before. I hadn't met the two going after her. What were they like? Would they be nice to her? What if she got scared and refused to leave with them?

All the doubts and worries swirling through my head were starting to give me a headache. Grimm set his fork aside and reached for my hand. "They'll be okay, Oksana. I promise."

"Why did all this happen? If my father hadn't gotten greedy, if he hadn't implicated us… could we have led a normal life? Maybe even a happy one?"

"Are you unhappy here?" he asked, his voice

low and deep.

"No. I don't quite feel like this is my home. I'm sure I will someday. Your world is so different from mine. I know your family was once part of the Bratva, but you aren't. You cut ties with them and started over. It's what I need to do, but I feel a little lost. I'm not sure how to move forward."

"We can take things as fast or as slow as you'd like. I'm not going to rush you into anything."

It hadn't even crossed my mind. While I might have just met Grimm, I still knew him well enough to trust him with my body, and even my heart. He hadn't said as much, but I had a feeling marriage to him would be a forever sort of thing. I didn't think we'd be getting a divorce in the future. Wait. I stared at him a moment, holding his gaze.

"If one of those men marries my sister, will she be able to divorce him later?"

He slowly shook his head. "The clubs we sent after your mom and sister work the same as this one, for the most part. Once we marry a woman, or claim her as our old lady, it's forever. I know Wire said it would be possible, and there is a very slight chance due to the circumstances of the marriage and her age, but I won't promise she can get free of him."

"Is that only for... what did you call them? Patched members?" I asked.

"Good point. Since it seems she'll be marrying Kye, and he's only a Prospect right now, I think the club would grant a divorce. Unless he patched in before then."

"And us? We're forever, right?" I asked.

"Yes. I'll never let you go, Oksana. Even if you never want to be intimate with me, I'll still remain married to you."

"Would you be with those women you called club whores?"

"No. I'll be faithful to you, Oksana. Now and always. Doesn't matter if you never want me to touch you."

I stared at our joined hands. Was I brave enough to ask for what I really wanted? I'd always felt like I was on the outside looking in. I'd watched happy couples when I'd go out places, and I wondered if I'd ever have that. Could it happen with Grimm? I'd never had a boyfriend or been kissed. Not really. The few "dates" my father set up would occasionally result in the man slobbering on me, but I'd always kept my lips clamped tight.

"Would you kiss me?" I asked.

"Are you sure?"

I nodded. It was the most certain I'd ever been in my life. Grimm stood and tugged me to my feet. He placed one hand on my waist and the other behind my neck. The moment our lips touched, I gasped. He gave my lower lip a lick before taking advantage and kissing me deeply. My toes curled, and I clung to him. No matter how many times I'd watched people kiss in the movies, I hadn't been prepared for what it would feel like. I never wanted him to stop!

He started to pull away, but I held on tighter, refusing to let him go. I felt a rumble in his chest, and a low growl slipped out of him. Before I knew what was happening, he'd lifted me and set me on the kitchen counter, wedging himself between my thighs. My nipples hardened and my panties dampened. I squirmed as my clit pulsed with need, and I wanted to beg him to keep going.

He lifted his head, his breath sawing in and out of his lungs. His eyes had turned dark, and the bulge in his pants told me just how turned-on he was right now.

"Oksana, we don't have to do this." My fingers trembled as I reached for his hand and placed it over my breast. He sucked in a breath and slid his palm down, then back up. "Are you sure?"

"Yes. Please, Grimm. They said we're married. I want to be your wife in more than name only."

"Ivan. Call me Ivan when it's just us."

"Ivan," I murmured, lifting my chin as I silently begged for another kiss. His lips crashed against mine, and it seemed he'd stopped holding back. He ravaged my mouth and pulled me closer.

The world spun as he lifted me into his arms and carried me to his bedroom. He kicked the door open and took me straight to the bed, easing me down on the mattress. I watched as he stripped out of his clothes. When he kneeled on the bed and reached for my shirt, I lifted my arms. He undressed me quickly, then sat back and stared at my body. I felt a flush cover me from head to toe at his frank appraisal.

"So fucking beautiful," he said.

I shook my head. "My breasts are too small."

"No, they aren't. They're yours, and you're mine… which makes them perfect." He leaned down and took one of my nipples into his mouth. When he sucked on it, pleasure zipped along my nerve endings. I gave myself up to him, letting him do whatever he wanted. He placed one hand over my pussy, lightly grinding the heel against my clit. That was all it took for me to call out his name as stars burst behind my eyelids. I'd never had an orgasm before, and it left me breathless.

"You're mine, Oksana. Now and always."

"Yours. Only yours. Please, Ivan. I need more."

He kissed me again, soft and slow. "As my wife commands."

His words filled me with warmth, and I knew I'd made the right decision. I'd never met anyone like him and knew he was one of a kind. My knight in shining armor. Tender. Protective. I knew it wouldn't be long before he was my everything. For the first time in my life, I felt complete. Like I belonged.

His body settled over mine, and I stared up into his eyes as he pressed his cock into me. Slowly. Rocking his hips so that he slid a little deeper each time. The reverent way he looked at me nearly made me cry. Like I was something precious.

The wall I'd kept around my heart cracked even more. He thrust deep, tearing through my innocence and making me his in all ways. I bit my lip at the sharp bite of pain, but it quickly faded to a mere sting. Then he was moving again, and all I felt was pleasure. With every stroke of his cock, he brushed against my clit.

"Come for me, *zaya*."

My cheeks burned as I reached between us and rubbed the hard little nub. I'd tried touching myself before, but it had never felt this good. It only took a few swipes of my fingers before I was coming.

Grimm growled and took me harder. I felt his cock swell moments before he came, the heat of his release filling me up. My eyes widened when I realized we hadn't used protection. I'd never been with anyone, so I knew I was clean. What about him? And what about children? We hadn't had that conversation.

His lips found mine again, and as he rolled to his side, bringing me with him, all my worries started to fade. We couldn't undo what had already happened. It was something we could discuss later.

I only hoped he wouldn't be angry when I

brought it up.

* * *

Grimm

I jolted awake, not having realized I'd even fallen asleep. Oksana still slept peacefully in my arms. A glance at the clock nearly had me groaning. Three in the morning was too early to be awake. So why was I? Staring up at the ceiling, I realized something in the house felt off. There was a tension in the air. I'd left the bedroom door open and cursed the fact I hadn't turned on any lights. I couldn't see a damn thing.

Not to mention, whoever was lurking in the dark could have already gotten a good look at Oksana. I didn't like the idea of other people seeing her naked body. I yanked the covers over Oksana and slipped out of bed. Since I didn't want to face an intruder with my dick out, I pulled my underwear on, then removed the gun I kept in the bedside table drawer. After making sure I'd taken off the safety, and had a full clip loaded, I cocked it and started checking the house for intruders.

Moving silently down the hall, I carefully cleared the bathroom and spare rooms. I couldn't hear anything. No footsteps or heavy breathing. Whoever was here, they were quiet as fuck. The thought didn't exactly settle my nerves. Had the Bratva sent someone after Oksana? How the hell had they gotten in?

Creeping around the corner, I scanned the living room. Pausing near the front window, I checked outside. No people moving out there, but I saw a car in the driveway. One I didn't recognize. But what the fuck kind of psycho parked in front of the house they were breaking into?

I approached the kitchen and a reflection in the

window over the sink caught my attention. I tensed. Judging by their overall height and build, it was certainly a man. Not one of my brothers, though. I crouched and peered around the corner, nearly cursing aloud when I saw his face.

"What the fuck, Nikolai?" I might not have seen my cousin in a long ass time, but he looked just like his father. I'd only met my aunt and uncle a few times, and briefly, but I still remembered their faces. I stood and set the gun aside, but within reach. I didn't think my cousin would come here to harm me or my wife. However, the man was Bratva through and through. They held his allegiance. Not us.

I flipped on the light, and he winced, shielding his eyes. It only took a second for me to clock all his injuries. It seemed they'd beaten him. Bad enough, I noticed he favored his left side. Probably had bruised or broken ribs. So either he'd come here for help, or to turn in Oksana so they'd go easier on him. Although, since he'd been the one to send her to me, I didn't think that was the case.

"Sit and start talking," I said, pointing to the kitchen table and chairs.

"You aren't going to get dressed first?"

"You broke into my house, fucker. Speaking of, how the hell did you get through the gate?"

He pointed to his face. "The guy at the gate saw me, asked if I was here to cause trouble. I told him I was your cousin, so he checked my ID."

"And he just let you through without calling me first?" Something seemed off. Whoever was on the gate wouldn't have known my real name, so Nikolai Volkov wouldn't have meant shit to them. Only those who'd been here before I patched in knew my real name, or my story. Well, them and Cowboy's family.

I'd told his woman enough, so she'd trust me all those years ago.

"They checked with some guy called Wire. He vouched for me. Of course, they also took my weapons and checked my car."

Wire? Why would they do that? Unless they'd texted a picture of his ID and asked Wire to make sure it was legit. Still, they could have just called and asked if I had a cousin named Nikolai. Unless they were trying not to disturb me. Now that word had spread about Oksana, I knew the club would try giving us time to bond.

"Why are you here, Nikolai? Are they coming for Oksana?" I asked.

"I'm in deep shit, Grimm. They know I helped her escape. No one is listening to me when I tell them she's innocent. Not to mention the damage I did to the warehouse. Feliks isn't a forgiving man. Viktor is currently on vacation with his family, and Maksim is having trouble with one of his daughters. Which means Feliks is temporarily in charge, and he's riding a power high."

"What if you were tailed? Did you even think of the fact you could be leading them right to Oksana? It's most likely the reason they let you go." I folded my arms and fought back the urge to beat on him. Fuck! If those assholes came for my wife, I'd start a war. No -- I'd finish one because there was no way I'd let any of them live.

"I was careful. Do you think I'd risk her life after going to so much trouble to get her out of there?" He looked into the darkened living room. "Where is she?"

"Asleep."

His eyebrows both rose. "Alone or in your bed?"

I couldn't tell by his tone how he meant the

question to come across. Would he be pissed when he discovered we were married? Or had that been his plan all along? Since I didn't know my cousin very well, I couldn't say for certain. Did I really want to know was the true question. If I found out he had feelings for her, I couldn't promise I'd remain civil.

I held up my hand, showing him my ring. "Since she's my wife, yes, she's in my bed. Did you give her our last name on her fake ID because you hoped I'd claim her? Or because you wanted her for yourself?"

So much for possibly not wanting to know. It seemed I didn't have a filter today. Whatever I thought was coming right out.

He shook his head. "Neither. I just hoped it would make her more difficult to find if they went searching for her. I didn't think they'd even think about her using our last name. We were friends, but it wasn't like we'd ever dated. Instead, they put a bounty on her head. I couldn't reach out to you in case they were monitoring my calls. I ditched my phone first chance I had and took my car to a chop shop. I swapped it for the one parked out front."

"Even swap? What piece of shit did they give you?" I asked. I hadn't been able to see much about it in the dark, except it was a BMW, and I didn't know a single person who drove one of those.

"It's actually a nice vehicle, but it's not as flashy as what I had. They'll make a lot more off mine than the one I got. And I'm fine with that."

"I take it you need a place to stay?"

"If you have the space, yeah. If not, I'll find a spot to lie low for a while. At least until Viktor returns and I can plead my case in front of him. I'd thought being married would mellow Feliks. It did for a while. Then Viktor put him in charge, and everything went to shit."

"You can stay in the room Oksana was using. I haven't had a chance to change the sheets or move her things out."

"I don't care about any of that. I'll probably be asleep the second my head hits the pillow. I can't remember the last time I slept well, but I know I'm safe here." He smiled faintly. "How sad is that? We barely know one another, yet I trust you more than the men I've spent every day with for the majority of my life."

"They say blood is thicker than water."

He snorted. "In some cases, yeah. With our family? Hasn't always proven true. Look at your dad and mom. For that matter, my own parents were all kinds of fucked up. Can't say I was sorry to see them go."

I hadn't heard anything about my aunt and uncle, and that was a can of worms I refused to open. From his words, they could have gone on a permanent vacation, gone back to Russia, or they could be dead. My money was on the last option. Which begged the question, what the hell did they do? And why was my family so screwed up?

I stood and motioned for him to follow me. I opened the spare room door and flicked on the light. "It's yours for however long you need it. In the morning, we can figure out your next step, and I'll have Oksana move her things out of here."

"Thanks, Grimm. I knew there was a chance you'd turn me away. We might be family, but..."

"Nothing that happened was ever your fault, Nikolai. You were still a kid the last time I saw you. The fact you trusted me enough to ask for my help means a lot to me." I'd always wondered how it would feel to have him here. Now I knew. He might be my cousin, but it felt like more. I'd never had siblings or been close to anyone in the family other than my mother. Was it just because we shared the same blood? I didn't know if we'd have a chance to get closer over this ordeal or not.

He wandered into the room and sat on the edge of the bed. I left him alone and went back to Oksana. She hadn't even moved. I ran my fingers through her hair, admiring her. She looked like an angel. Then again, I thought the same thing when she was awake. I got back into bed with her, tugging her against me.

I'd have to ask Wire to look into things, if he wasn't already. We needed to know if they were actively searching for Nikolai, and how close they were. Would his disappearance give Oksana a breather? Maybe they'd focus solely on Nikolai for now. I hated to offer him up as bait, though. What the fuck would it take to get the Bratva to back down and leave my family alone?

He'd mentioned Viktor was out of town. I assumed he meant Viktor Petrov. And Maksim had to be Maksim Koslov. From what I'd heard previously, and what Nikolai had implied tonight, those two kept Feliks Sobol in check. I hadn't met the Vor before, but I'd heard a lot about Vadim Ivanov. Some good, some horrifying. But one thing everyone had agreed on was that Vadim was a family man.

I studied Oksana while she slept. We hadn't used protection. Probably should have discussed it with her first. Since she'd been a virgin, I hadn't had any doubts as to her being clean. I'd gotten tested since the last time I was with a woman, so I was too. Birth control was another matter, though. I doubted she was on any.

If I got her pregnant, would her odds of survival increase? Could I play that card with Vadim? And just how pissed would Oksana be when she found out?

Best not to tell her. Not yet.

In the meantime, I'd do my best to knock her up. I hoped Nikolai was a sound sleeper. If not, he'd need noise-canceling headphones.

Chapter Six

Oksana

Waking up with Grimm's arms around me brought a smile to my face. Then my face heated when I remembered what we'd done the night before. I was truly his wife now, and I couldn't even describe the joy I felt. Before coming here, I'd resigned myself to a loveless marriage, much like my parents had. One meant to elevate my family's status, with no care whether or not it made me happy.

I started to cuddle against Grimm when I heard a sound coming from the kitchen. The clank of dishes. Had someone come by after I'd fallen asleep? Or had they let themselves in, like Grimm said his brothers often did? I eased out from under his arm and made a quick run for the bathroom.

As the water warmed, I realized I didn't have my clothes in here yet. I'd left everything in the other bedroom. Of course, I could also use one of Grimm's shirts long enough to retrieve my clothing. The thought of anyone seeing me like that made my stomach knot, but there wasn't much I could do about it, unless I woke up Grimm. He'd been sleeping so soundly I didn't want to wake him if I didn't need to.

Before I could step under the spray, I felt a hand on my hip and squealed. Grimm chuckled as he turned me to face him.

"Expecting someone else?" he asked.

"I heard noises in the house. Someone's here."

He nodded. "They are. It's Nikolai. He showed up early this morning. I'm going to get your things from the other room, then I'll join you. He can fend for himself a little longer."

"But what if he hears us?"

Grimm leaned in and kissed me. "I didn't say anything about us doing more than washing. The fact you brought it up tells me you have naughty thoughts running through your mind."

My cheeks heated more, and I playfully swatted at him. "Stop it! You're trying to embarrass me on purpose."

"I am." He smiled. "Your reactions are cute."

He kissed me again, then left, only to return a few minutes later with an armful of my clothes. He set them on the counter before stripping out of his underwear and getting in the shower with me. I hadn't paid attention to the fact he had any on.

I loved his bathroom, even if it didn't have a tub. The shower took up one entire wall, with multiple showerheads, and a built-in bench along one section. More than enough room for the two of us. Since I hadn't moved my bathroom stuff over yet, Grimm used his own bodywash on me. I didn't mind. The scent would remind me of him all day.

I jumped when I heard someone pounding on the bedroom door. Grimm cast a baleful glare in that direction.

"You need to hurry up," Nikolai shouted. "Wire is here and says he needs to speak with you immediately."

"Fuck," Grimm muttered. "Is it too much to ask that we have some alone time?"

"It seems so. Let's find out what he has to say. We have the rest of our lives together."

"Yeah, we do." He brushed my nose with his before kissing me softly. "But once all this shit is behind us, I'm going to kill the first person who interrupts us. Fuckers need to learn some boundaries."

"Thought the club had an open-door policy?" I

asked.

"Not after this."

I bit my lip so I wouldn't smile and washed in a hurry. By the time we'd dried off and dressed, Grimm was still mumbling under his breath about murdering everyone in sight. It probably should have scared me. Instead, it made me feel warm inside, knowing he wanted to spend time with me without interruptions. Then again, neither of us had led a normal life.

Nikolai and Wire were both in the kitchen, and the hacker had brought his laptop with him. He tapped away at the keys, and Nikolai slid a file folder closer to Grimm. I started to sit, but Grimm shook his head, holding out his hand. I went to him, letting him pull me down onto his lap.

"You don't want her to see that," Wire said, without looking up from his screen. "It's ugly. Even for us."

I felt Grimm hesitate and leaned into him. "I want to know. If it involves me or my family, then I think I have a right to find out what's going on."

"I put in a call to Viktor, Maksim, and even reached out to Vadim. I know I'm going above my rank, and Feliks may damn well gut me over this, but I can't sit back and watch all this unfold. It's wrong." Nikolai shifted in his seat. "Oksana, don't look at the pictures. Understood? You can hear what's in that folder, but you don't want to actually see it."

"All right." My gut churned. If Nikolai said it was that bad, I'd believe him. What the hell had happened in the short time since I'd left? I'd known Wire was going to keep an eye on the situation with my mom and sister, but how did things get screwed up so quickly?

I looked away when Grimm opened the file and

held Nikolai's gaze. I knew him showing up out of the blue probably made Grimm cautious about his cousin, but Nikolai had saved me. Until he proved untrustworthy, I'd put my faith in him. I'd never once thought of him romantically. More like a big brother.

"Holy fuck," Grimm muttered. "When did this happen?"

"Last night," Wire said.

"How close are the men going after them?" Grimm flipped another page. "Did they tighten security on both of them?"

What had those bastards done to my sister and mom? I pressed a hand to my mouth, refusing to look at the file in Grimm's hand. If none of the men wanted me to see the contents, then I wouldn't. But it was damn hard to just sit here.

"No. It's my belief they feel they scared the women into compliance," Wire said. "They pulled off the extra men, and they've placed Mrs. Romanov back into the…"

He trailed off, but I knew what he meant. My mom was back in service at one of the brothels. It broke my heart, knowing what she'd suffered, all because of my asshole father who'd gotten too greedy!

"And Stripes? Where is he right now?" Grimm asked. "Anyone had contact with the team going in to extract her?"

"Melina," I murmured. "Her name is Melina."

Grimm gave me a quick squeeze before flipping through more papers. I shut my eyes, wishing I could close out the ugliness in the world just as easily. Why did evil men have to exist? And how had Feliks gotten away with so much? I knew it had to have been done on his orders.

"Stripes will extract her today." Wire clicked

away on his laptop some more. "And the men going after Yulia should have her any minute. Although she's going to need medical care almost immediately."

Bile rose in my throat, and I couldn't keep silent for another moment. "What did they do to them?"

"You don't want to know, *zaya*." Grimm kissed the top of my head. "Trust me on this. It's better if you don't ask. If and when they want to talk about it, let them. Otherwise, it's best if you don't hear the details."

I couldn't stop the tears that ran down my cheeks. In my heart, I already knew what they'd done to Yulia. There was only one way to break her. Nikolai had saved me, but we'd both thought my little sister would be safe for at least another two years. We'd been wrong, and she'd paid a high price for it. I'd never forgive myself.

"Stop," Nikolai said. I held his gaze. "I know what you're thinking, Oksana. None of this is your fault. We couldn't have known what they'd do. And when Viktor finds out how far Feliks went, it won't be pretty."

"How could he?" I asked, my voice breaking. "He has a wife and child, doesn't he? What kind of monster could do something like that?"

"He didn't do it himself," Nikolai said. "But I don't doubt he sent the men who went to keep her in line. As for the other… when his wife finds out, it's going to destroy her faith in him. If I were Feliks, I'd be more scared of Raina right now than the Vor."

"Yulia…" I turned into Grimm, sobbing harder than ever before. I'd failed my little sister. I didn't care what they said. It still felt like my fault since I'd left her there. I'd put myself first when I'd run without even trying to take her with me. It was something I'd regret the rest of my life.

"Your mom is alive, but she's going to suffer some trauma from this. Both physical and mental," Wire said. "I know Stripes can get her free of the Bratva and have no doubt he'll do whatever it takes to save her in every way possible. He's waited a long time to have a wife, and he'll march straight into hell if needs be to keep her out of their clutches."

"And Yulia… the man who said he'd take care of her?" I sucked in a breath and dried my tears. "Will he still want her?"

"Yes." Wire sounded so certain. "If anything, it will make him even more protective of her. He's just a Prospect right now, but I'm sure he'll patch in sooner or later. Kye is a tough bastard, and he's already been through a lot. He has an adopted daughter. Will that be a problem for Yulia?"

I shook my head. "She likes kids."

"Good. There's not a lot we can do right now. As Nikolai said, he's waiting to hear back from the higher-ups. For now, all we can do is try to keep the both of you out of their hands. Since he ditched his car, it will take them longer to find him. Unless they connect him to Grimm faster than I'm assuming will happen. If they're using hackers, it's not anyone I know. I haven't had any of my traps triggered, so it doesn't seem like anyone is looking into the club right now. If they do, I'll know about it." Wire closed his computer. "I've already made sure he doesn't have anything in his possession they can track. Same for you."

"So we sit and wait?" I asked.

"Pretty much," Grimm said. "I'm sorry, *zaya*. I know that's not the answer you want, but that's the best I can give you. And no matter how much you want to see your mom and sister, we need to give them both time. They'll need to settle into their new lives, and I doubt they'll want you to see them right away. Let them heal a little, all right?"

I nodded. It wouldn't be easy, but I'd do it… for them. "Will someone at least tell us when Yulia and my mom are at their new homes? I need to know they made it out of there."

"They'll contact us," Wire said. "We'll make sure you know, Oksana. I know this is difficult for you."

That was the understatement of the year! But I did feel relieved that Yulia and Mom would be in good hands. If Grimm trusted the men who'd help them, then I would too.

For now, I needed to stay off the Bratva's radar. So did Nikolai.

There was just one thing bothering me… If it was dangerous for me, Mom, and Yulia to be at the same location, why was Nikolai here? Didn't it double the chances of the Bratva finding us? So why had he come here?

Something felt off… and I had a feeling Grimm knew it too.

* * *

Grimm

Seeing the destruction cause by the Bratva sickened me. I wished I'd had the ability to save Yulia and Melina before it had been too late. No matter how much I promised my woman she could see her family later, part of me wondered if they'd ever recover from what they'd suffered. Sure, I'd seen firsthand how women could pull through even when faced with the worst of humanity, but not all of them were strong enough.

I didn't think Stripes would give Melina a chance to give up. The stubborn Russian would do whatever he could to help her through it. As for Kye, he had his little girl to consider. I hoped the two of them would be enough for Yulia, but only time would tell. Sixteen was too young to get married, but I knew Wire would create some sort of magical feat that would guarantee Yulia's safety. No one would be able to contest the marriage. Hackers worldwide considered him the best for a reason.

As much as I wanted to believe everything Nikolai said, I'd watched him carefully, and I knew he was hiding something. I wanted to kick his ass out. Probably would have, except a quick call to Savior had stopped me. The Pres wanted me to keep him close. The thought of him betraying us infuriated me. It felt like I'd let a viper into my home. If he did anything to hurt Oksana, I'd gut him. Didn't matter if we shared the same blood or not.

I'd asked Ares to run out and grab some more clothes for Oksana and sent Prophet with her. The look on her face had been priceless. I knew Prophet was biding his time for her to get older, but that girl was going to give him a run for his money. I didn't know why she had her sights set on someone else. The man had raced to her side the moment he'd heard she'd been hurt.

"I don't need more things right now," Oksana said.

"Yes, you do. I also asked them to get a TV and wall mount for the bedroom. While Nikolai is here, I want you to be able to retreat to the bedroom without being bored."

She leaned into my side. "You don't trust him, do you?"

"I think he's not telling us everything," I hedged. I knew she liked Nikolai, thought of him as a friend. In her defense, he'd saved her by sending her to me. Now I had to wonder if there'd been more at play from the very beginning. The entire thing felt like one great big trap. I just couldn't figure out who was the prey. Me? The club?

"Me too," she murmured.

Great. If my wife could tell he was keeping secrets, then we were screwed. I needed to talk to Nikolai, but I wasn't sure he'd tell me the truth. What if I called the Vor myself? It wouldn't be hard for Wire to get the information for me. Even if I hadn't spoken to Vadim before, he'd recognize my father's name, and possibly mine. It could put a target on my head, but at this point, I was ready to tear the entire fucking organization apart, if that's what it took to keep my family safe.

"Have you ever met Viktor, Maksim, or Vadim?" I asked.

"Maksim. Once. It was a family event, and he had his daughters with him. Why?"

"I'm thinking I need to be proactive and make a few calls. I don't like leaving everything to Nikolai and hoping he doesn't fuck us over."

She went over to the kitchen counter and opened one of the drawers. After taking out paper and a pen, she wrote down a bunch of phone numbers. Why did she have those memorized? She hadn't listed names, so I wasn't entirely certain who they belonged to.

"The first one is Viktor's wife. She's blind, and Viktor is overly protective of her. I don't know if the men will answer your call, but anything going to Cerys' phone will have Viktor answering immediately. An unknown call for his wife? He'll want to know who has her number and what they want."

"Great. Nothing like kicking the hornet's nest," I

muttered. "And the others?"

"Feliks' wife, Raina, is the second number. I doubt she knows what her husband has done. If you place that call while it's on speaker, we can both talk to her, and I'll explain what I can."

"The others?"

She pointed to the third one. "Aleksi Voronin is a byki. He often guards Cerys when Viktor can't be with her. The last one is Vadim Ivanov."

"Why do you have the Vor's number?"

"My mother made me memorize it in case I ever needed help. With everything that's happened, I can't guarantee he isn't already aware of what's going on. It's possible Feliks had his permission all along."

"Right. So we'll start with… Raina? Feliks is the one causing all the trouble, so let's see how his wife feels about it," I said.

I took Oksana's hand and led her to the bedroom. I dialed the number and put the call on speaker like she'd requested. Then we waited. It rang a dozen times before going to voicemail. Oksana reached over to end the call, then immediately dialed it again. This time, the woman answered on the third ring.

"Who is this?" she demanded.

"It's me, Raina, and my husband. We need your help," Oksana said.

"Oksana? What husband? No one said anything about you getting married. Why I wasn't I invited?"

"Raina, where's Feliks right now?" she asked.

"Working." I heard a door shut, then Raina's voice lowered. "What's going on, Oksana? I heard something earlier, before Feliks left. They mentioned your mom's name and Yulia's, and they sounded frantic."

Oksana told her everything from the beginning. I

heard the woman cuss more than once, and she screamed long and loud at the end of the recounting. I didn't blame her. The man she'd married had done something truly horrific, or at least authorized it. If I'd ever done something like that, I'd hope like hell Oksana would try to tear off my balls and feed them to me. We might call our women our property, but the truth was that they made us more human. The old ladies were essential, and each played an important role.

"I'm going to murder him," Raina said. "No. I'll divorce him and take half of everything!"

"Raina, my husband is part of the Dixie Reapers. They're a motorcycle club and have friends in other clubs. My mom and Yulia are okay or will be. Men went to get them. It's probably why Feliks was angry. We stole them out from under his nose." Oksana blew out a breath. "I have another question. Do you know anything about what's going on with Nikolai?"

"He came here yesterday," Raina said. "I couldn't hear his conversation with Feliks, but it sounded like he'd given him a job to do. Why?"

"Because he's here," I said. "My name is Grimm, or that's what I go by now. Nikolai is my cousin. Have you heard anyone talking about Ivan Volkov?"

"You're Ivan?" she asked.

"Yes. Please, Raina. It's important. I already know the Bratva is after Oksana. I need to know if my name is on their list too. Nikolai is here, but I can tell he's hiding something."

"I've heard your name mentioned, but not during Nikolai's visit yesterday. I'm sorry. I wish I could be of more help. Oksana, does anyone else know what my husband is doing?"

"You mean Viktor?" Oksana asked. "I don't

know, but I doubt it. I was going to call Cerys next."

"I'll give you twenty minutes. After that, I'll call and talk to her. I'm so sorry for everything you've suffered. You and your family. I'll do whatever I can, but you know my power is very limited," Raina said. "I'd thought Feliks had changed, that he'd become a better man. It seems I was wrong. I… I can't…"

"It's not your fault, Raina," Oksana said. "I'm sorry we called with such bad news. I know you love him. I can only imagine how much it hurts to hear what he's been up to."

"I need to go, Oksana. I have much to think about. But please call me again so I'll know you're okay."

Oksana agreed, and I ended the call. From what the women discussed, it seemed like Feliks had a dark side before now. His wife might have tempered it for a while, but the beast inside him apparently couldn't be contained forever. I didn't know what it meant for their marriage, or for Feliks himself, for that matter. If he'd done all this unsanctioned, then he could very well lose his life.

"Ready to call Cerys and Viktor?" I asked.

Oksana nodded. "Let's do it. If Raina didn't know what Feliks was doing, I doubt Viktor does. He's always reined him in before. Feliks is known for his temper, and his darker needs. People whisper about him at parties, even in front of the women and children. The fact he's done all this, knowing what it will do to Raina… He may be a lost cause."

"After this, we'll order pizza and spend time in the living room with Nikolai. I don't want him to get suspicious. Until we know what game he's playing, I want to tell him as little as possible."

Oksana took my hand and held it as we made the

next call. I let her do most of the talking, filling in the gaps. To say Viktor was furious would be an understatement. Feliks would be lucky to live until the end of the day. I felt sorry for Raina. What would happen to her if her husband really did lose his life? Then again, even if he didn't, would she be safe with him?

Chapter Seven

Oksana

The waiting would kill me. Or rather, it would have if Grimm didn't insist on distracting me. We'd eaten pizza with Nikolai and watched a movie. When he'd stepped outside to answer a call, Grimm and I had shared a look. What couldn't he say in front of us? Who'd called him? While he'd been outside, someone dropped off my new clothes and our bedroom TV and wall mount. Grimm insisted he needed my help with it, so I'd followed him to our room.

He shifted things in the dresser and made space in the closet for me. I put away my things. He hadn't needed my help with the TV at all, but I'd stayed and kept him company. I'd heard Nikolai come back into the house, then he'd left again almost immediately. We heard his car start up, and I wondered if the club would have someone follow him.

If Nikolai was up to no good, I'd rather find out now than later. I still couldn't believe he'd stab me in the back. Or had he come for Grimm? I knew my husband's parents had been part of the Bratva. Had Nikolai offered up Grimm? I'd never forgive him if he ever did such a thing. Of course, I was assuming they wouldn't snatch me too.

"Are we going to hide in here indefinitely?" I asked.

"We're not hiding," he said, coming over with the remote in his hand. He sank onto the edge of the bed and turned on the TV. I remained quiet while he set everything up. It didn't take long before he put a movie on.

"Still worried about Nikolai?"

"More than ever," he mumbled. "I want to trust

him, but my gut is saying I can't. What the hell did Feliks say to him? What did he promise?"

"I'm more curious if I'm the cost of his salvation, or you are. He has to be here for one of us, right?"

"If he really has turned against us, that means your mom and Yulia could be in danger already. He knows where they were going, and who they're staying with." Grimm ran his hand over his beard. "I hope Wire managed to tap his phone when he wasn't looking. I know it's just a burner, but we need to know everything we can if we're making it out of this."

"At least we have Viktor on our side, and Raina. I'm sure she's going to let Feliks have it."

He reached for my hand, twining our fingers together. "You don't think she'll be in danger? A man like Feliks Sobol won't like a woman mouthing off to him. You don't think he'd hurt her? Or worse, put his own wife into the brothel?"

Out of all the things I knew without a doubt, it was that Feliks would never do that to Raina. Not after all she'd been through. Grimm didn't know her history, and it wasn't my place to tell him. Finding out what her husband had tried to do to me and had done to my mother and sister was a devastating blow for Raina. She didn't have to tell me. I already knew.

"Let's just say Raina's past isn't a pretty one." I leaned my head against his shoulder. "What Feliks did to my family will feel like a betrayal to her. I'm certain she'll tell him as much too."

"Think it will do any good?"

I sighed and shook my head. "Sadly, no. As far gone as Feliks is, I'm not sure he'll even care what Raina thinks anymore. Even their daughter probably can't reach his heart at this point."

Grimm tensed. "Are you telling me that asshole

has a little girl, and he was still able to do that to Yulia?"

"Now you understand. The only way to stop him is for Viktor or someone else of higher rank to interfere."

"I'm going to text Wire. Maybe he can give us some insight into what Nikolai is up to. It's worth a shot anyway." He grabbed his phone and typed out something before hitting send. When the phone chimed, he showed me the reply.

Nikolai is at the coffee shop in town. He called someone named Konstantin.

"He's a good friend of the Vor. If Nikolai is speaking with him, it means one of two things." I looked up at Grimm. "Either Konstantin approved of what Feliks did, or Nikolai's hoping the man will step in and fix things. I don't know why he felt the need to leave the house to speak with him."

"Which means there's a good chance Konstantin already knew what Feliks did. No way for us to know for sure without hearing their conversation. Does that mean the Vor knew as well? If so, we're fucked." He tipped his head back and closed his eyes. "I can't leave you locked up like this. It's not fair."

"I'm not complaining." I'd rather be trapped in our home, than the alternative. Although, someone had let Nikolai into the compound, and he'd gotten into our house. I wasn't sure how safe I was here, or anywhere.

"What if we went somewhere? Leave while Nikolai isn't here. He'd find the house empty. We could leave a note that we've gone on a short honeymoon, and not tell him where." Grimm stared at the TV. "Your sister is at the Reckless Kings. Your mom is going to the Devil's Boneyard. Both places are compromised as of now. Although, Charming is also ex-Bratva and still has connections. I doubt anyone can get to your mother. His family had a much higher rank than mine."

"And Yulia?" I asked.

"As long as Beast knows the Bratva could have been tipped off, he can prepare for them dropping by sometime soon."

"But you don't think we're safe staying here?" I prodded.

"Without knowing Nikolai's involvement in everything, no. We have a rat in the house. But if we leave, we're going to be on the road for a bit."

"Why?" I turned a little to face him more. "Where would we go?"

"Another club. Either Savage Raptors or Broken Bastards. Both have good men. The Wicked Mayhem are closer, but… they're into some shit I'd rather not get involved in. Best to give them a wide berth for now."

"Where are the other two located?"

"Broken Bastards are in New Orleans. Savage Raptors are in Oklahoma. The first one wouldn't give us much wiggle room if we needed to make a quick escape. But Oklahoma? Lots of directions to run if the need arose," he said.

"Are you sure that's what we should do?" It felt cowardly. How could we run and leave so many people behind? If the Bratva did come, they wouldn't spare anyone in their effort to get to us. With Nikolai possibly lying, I'd be worried he'd hurt someone. "What if we confront him?"

"He'd probably lie to us."

"True, but if we run, then he'll suspect we don't trust him. I'm not sure he'll be convinced we went on a honeymoon with everything else going on. Your cousin isn't stupid. He'll likely see right through our plan."

A throat cleared and I jolted, not having realized we weren't alone. Judging from the look on Grimm's face, he hadn't either.

"I guess I've been a bit off with my behavior." Nikolai entered the room. "So I should probably explain, even though I was told to remain silent."

"Told by who?" I asked.

"Konstantin, although he's following the Vor's orders." Nikolai folded his arms. "We can talk here, or over coffee in the kitchen. Which do you prefer?"

"Kitchen," Grimm said. "Although, I can't decide if I'll believe a word you say. You've been lying to me from the start."

"True. I'll tell you everything I know, and then you decide for yourself. Just know, I didn't deceive either of you because I wanted to. There's something much larger going on. Things I can't divulge, not without the risk of it costing me my life. Understood?"

In other words, political crap within the Bratva, and since Grimm wasn't considered part of them anymore, and neither was I, then we were both on a need-to-know basis -- and apparently, Konstantin felt we didn't need to know at all. I didn't want Nikolai to put himself in danger, but I hated being blind to everything going on around me. If Grimm and I were going to survive this, we needed as much information as we could get.

I finally had someone who looked at me like I mattered. While Nikolai had been my friend for a long time, and he'd done his best to save me, it wasn't the same as what I had with Grimm. Never would be. I'd do whatever it took to protect my new family. Grimm, and the rest of his club. What if we had children some day?

I pressed a hand to my belly. For that matter, what if I was pregnant now? We'd had unprotected sex, and I wasn't on birth control. We still hadn't discussed what happened, but as usual, it would have to wait. Other matters were more pressing.

Grimm helped me off the bed, and we followed Nikolai into the kitchen. I brewed a pot of coffee for the men and got a cold bottle of water for myself. I had a feeling this would be a rather lengthy conversation and would possibly only confuse us more. But at least we weren't running, and we'd learn something useful. I hoped.

* * *

Grimm

Nikolai twisted his coffee cup on the table in front of him, appearing to be lost in thought. But I had a feeling he was merely deciding how much to tell us, and in what order. Or weighing his options. If he really could lose his life for telling us anything, then it wouldn't surprise me if he backed out of spilling secrets to us. In his position, I'd probably do the same. He'd gotten caught between blood family and the Bratva, which had to be uncomfortable to say the least.

"The higher-ups have known for a while that your father was into some shady stuff, Oksana. He implied you and your mother helped lure in women, whom he then sold either to private buyers or brothels in multiple countries. Human trafficking isn't exactly an oddity in our world, but he overstepped." Nikolai rubbed at his forehead. "Viktor had a particular plan he wanted to execute for dealing with him, but the Vor stepped in."

"I don't understand," Oksana said.

She might not, but I was starting to. Not only did they want to take out her father, but Feliks had been left in charge for a reason. He'd been tested. I assumed, at any rate. From what I'd heard, the man was a monster. Were they wondering how far he'd be willing to go? Did they want him to do horrific things? My past experience with them told me yes, that's exactly what they'd wanted. Nikolai confirmed it with his next statement.

"Raina smoothed Feliks' rough edges, and made him more human," Nikolai said. "The Vor didn't trust the change would be permanent. He needed to know if the darkness inside Feliks still lingered, for multiple reasons. But first and foremost, he's always done the dirty work."

"What kind?" I asked.

"If someone steps out of line and their wife or daughters are used to drive home the point, then Feliks would be the one to step in. He'd rape them in front of the man who'd stepped out of line. Threaten to put them in the brothels. In some cases, he's tortured them." Nikolai seemed to age before my eyes. "He had to harden his heart. No one could survive doing such things, unless they were truly evil. Then he met Raina. He tried to keep her and go through with a political marriage."

"Until Raina got into trouble?" Oksana asked.

It seemed my wife knew quite a bit about these men. Would they consider her a liability? I worried they'd never leave her alone. I'd fight them all, take down as much of the organization as I could, if it meant keeping her by my side. But I wasn't invincible, and I didn't have nearly enough resources to make a big enough dent that we wouldn't be looking over our shoulders the rest of our lives.

Nikolai nodded. "Correct. He realized he couldn't live without her. Viktor had forbidden him from keeping Raina as his mistress if he followed through with the marriage to another woman. It was a test, but not one the Vor sanctioned. Feliks passed by choosing Raina."

"And then put himself on the Vor's radar when he acted out of character," I surmised. "So Viktor had to leave him in charge to see how he'd handle things in everyone's absence?"

"Essentially, but Viktor didn't want to. He likes the new version of Feliks." Nikolai took a sip of his coffee. "The Vor, however, wants a hellhound he can unleash when necessary. With Raina in the picture, Feliks isn't going to hurt women. Not personally. At least that much didn't change, even when he was placed in charge. He gave the orders but didn't participate."

"Which means the violence doesn't bother him. He cares enough for Raina not to touch another woman," Oksana said. "I'm not sure Raina sees it that way."

"You told her, didn't you?" Nikolai asked, a slight smile curving his lips. "I thought you might. Eventually. I don't know how things will play out. Raina can't leave Feliks. If she tries, it won't be pretty. She'll likely end up in handcuffs, which will make her hate him. Divorce is out of the question."

"And the Vor won't let him back down," Oksana said. "What I don't understand is how cold he appeared when he sentenced me. I didn't even get a chance to defend myself. He just decided I was guilty, and my fate was sealed."

"It wasn't just your father who threw you under

the bus, Oksana. Some of the women who'd been sold also blamed you and your mother. I have no doubt they were bribed in some way, but the result is the same." Nikolai sighed. "I don't see a way out of this for you, in all honesty. The Vor won't leave you running loose. Even if you found proof of your innocence, you've been privy to too much."

"I was worried about that," I admitted. "They won't let her go, and I refuse to let them take her. No matter what happens, we'll end up in a war."

Oksana leaned against me. "You know I can't let the people here die because of me. If the only peaceful way to end this is for me to go back, then that's what I'll do."

"Have you forgotten something?" I asked. "You're my wife, and you could very well be pregnant already. Do you think for one second I'm letting you go back to that hell?"

"Wait." Oksana looked at Nikolai. "You weren't really beaten, were you? Sure, you showed up wounded, but not as bad as you should have been after going up against Feliks. What did he say to you in his office? Raina heard the two of you speaking, but not the actual words."

"Feliks needed it to look like I'd been punished and escaped. I had to keep up the ruse, even with the two of you. As for my call to Konstantin, I had to let him know whether or not Feliks was back to his usual self, or still weak."

"So the two of you faked it?" I asked.

"Sort of. He really did take a few swings at me. He just didn't go all out and try to destroy me." Nikolai pushed his cup aside. "Feliks needs some time. So do Viktor and Maksim. None of them want to go against the Vor, but they need a plan. When Viktor met

Cerys, the Vor was grateful he'd settled down and would start a family. With Feliks, it's different."

"Because he needs an attack dog," I said.

"Right."

"Then give him one." I curled my arm around Oksana. "There have to be men who would be eager for that type of work. Have Feliks choose a successor for the dirty parts of his job, at least where women are concerned. Surely that would be all right with everyone involved."

"I'll bring it up, but I make no promises," Nikolai said. "And don't be surprised if Konstantin or Vadim show up at the gate. They know where you are, that Oksana is with you, and at the very least they'll want to talk."

"Fine. I'll let the club know." I pulled out my phone and shot off a text to Savior, giving him the latest update. It only took a moment for my phone to ping with an incoming text. Except it wasn't one he sent only to me.

Church. Now!

"We're going to the clubhouse," I said, kissing Oksana on the cheek. I placed a quick call to one of the Prospects and had them clear out the club whores and give the place a quick wipe down. Then I asked a few brothers to bring their women. It was time for Oksana to make a few friends and start building a support system. I had a feeling she'd need it in the days to come.

We got ready and headed out. It was the first time for her to ride on the back of my bike, and I had to admit I liked having her there. I placed a hand on her thigh as we rode toward the clubhouse. She clung to me, squealing as we went around every curve, even though I wasn't driving very fast. I couldn't wait to take her out on the open road. Maybe after we knew if she was pregnant. I didn't like the thought of putting her in danger considering how stupid people were. Too many times I'd nearly been sideswiped or run over.

I saw Lavender on the porch, waiting for us. She gave Oksana a wave and a friendly smile.

"You're going to meet a few of the other wives and old ladies. No need to be nervous," I said, taking her hand and leading her inside. I spotted Amity and Dessa's stepdaughter, Ares. If she was here, then she must not have caught whatever Savior's younger kids had. "And it looks like Savior's oldest daughter is here too. You'll like Ares."

"I'll introduce her to everyone. Head into Church," Lavender said. "I'll message Wire on his laptop if we need any assistance."

I gave my wife one last lingering look before I went down the hall and pushed through the doors into Church. Taking my spot at the table, I gave Savior a quick nod and focused on the others coming into the room.

"Who's the new woman?" Prophet asked as he took his seat.

"She's a beauty." Royal smiled. "Since she's hanging with the old ladies, I'm assuming someone has decided to settle down. Are we here to vote her in?"

"No." Savior stood. "That woman is already a part of this club, no questions asked. She's married to Grimm."

I heard a muffled *holy shit* somewhere to my right, but I couldn't tell who'd said it. I knew everyone had questions, and they'd get the answers they sought. Mostly. Since I hadn't had a chance to tell Savior everything, there would be a few things I'd keep to myself right now.

"Her name is Oksana," Savior said. "And she's on the run from the Bratva. They tried to rape her and toss her into a brothel. I know quite a few of you already have women who suffered similar fates, so I'm sure you understand why Grimm didn't hesitate to give her the protection of his name, and our club."

"Are they coming for her?" Tempest asked.

"Probably." I glanced at Savior before addressing the others. "At least one of their members knows where she is. It's all more involved than we first thought, and I'm learning more every day. Nikolai is caught up in all of it. I want to trust him, but I'm not sure how much of what he's said is the truth, and how much he's tossing at me, so I won't ask too many questions."

"And he's here?" Warden tapped his finger on the table. "At the compound?"

"He is. Someone let him in when he showed up at the gate, then he let himself into my house. I woke up to find him in my damn kitchen," I muttered.

"My fault." Wire raised his hand. "In my defense, all I knew was that he'd sent Oksana here for protection. I didn't realize he might be dirty and involved in everything. Nothing I found when I went digging led me to believe he would be a rat."

"Jury is still out on that one," I said. "But he's told me some interesting things. Honestly, it's all so confusing it hurts my brain. Some of what he says seems to contradict other statements he's made. At this point, I think he's building a web of lies that even he can't keep straight. We probably won't know what's true and what isn't until it's too late."

"Wire, do what you can to keep an eye on

Nikolai and the rest of the Bratva involved," Savior said. "Everyone else, be vigilant. I'm going to request no parties until this is handled. I don't like the idea of the gate being open to just anyone. Women have betrayed us before, and other clubs we call family. I don't want to give these fuckers an easy way into the compound."

"Agreed," Tempest said.

"The underground bunker isn't ready. It won't be of much use this time." Savior folded his arms. "I don't like the idea of the women being in the clubhouse either. If shit goes south, we need to keep them safe. But this building is too close to the gate."

"If the Pres is okay with it, when everyone leaves today, I'd like Savior, Wire, and Saint to stay behind. Maybe the four of us can come up with a way to keep the women and children safe. I'm sure Grimm would prefer to be with his new wife." Tempest looked around the table. "Anyone else wants to stay and lend a hand, I won't say no."

"What are some of the half-truths you've been told?" Wire asked.

"The Vor wanted to test Feliks. See if he still had the darker instincts he had before getting married. But too much of what Nikolai said doesn't make any sense. I think he was rambling and hoping to tell me enough I'd need time to wade through it all, or just would give up on figuring all this shit out." I smirked. "He clearly underestimated me. When it comes to Oksana, I'll never give up. She may very well be pregnant already."

"And if she's not, I'm sure you'll do your best to make it happen." Zipper snickered. "Been there and done that. Think a lot of us have."

He wasn't wrong. We'd only been intimate the

one time, but I planned to fix that soon enough. As much as I didn't like being in that vulnerable of a position with Nikolai in the house, I wasn't going to keep my hands off my wife either. Besides, I had hope that if the Bratva found out she was pregnant, they wouldn't hurt her. It would buy us the time we needed. If we couldn't beat them, maybe we could at least negotiate.

"What's that look?" Savior asked pointing at me.

"Just wondering if we could sign a contract of sorts with the Bratva, in exchange for them leaving Oksana alone."

"And offer what? We don't condone the bulk of what they do." Savior shook his head. "Sorry, but I don't see that being a viable option. They hurt women and children. Sell them. Beat them. Rape them. I don't want to get my hands dirty dealing with those monsters, unless it's to put them in the ground."

"Agreed," Tempest said.

"However, we should call Charming and see what his Bratva friends have to say," Wire said. "Maybe they know of something that will make them back off."

"I'll call him tonight," Savior said. "For now, everyone is dismissed. Remember what I said. No one comes in who isn't already a part of this club. No parties. We have too much to lose."

I stood and started to leave, but Savior placed a hand on my shoulder. I hung back, waiting to see what he'd say.

Chapter Eight

Oksana

Having Lavender present made me feel less anxious meeting the other women. I'd never made friends easily, and I wanted them to like me. This would be my home now. My family. It was a fresh start, and I didn't want to screw it up.

Lavender gave me a warm smile as she introduced me to everyone. "Amity is married to Thunder. She's only been with us about seven months. Although the newest woman to join our ranks is Savior's wife, Dessa. She couldn't make it because the little ones weren't feeling well."

"I'm Savior's daughter," a girl said, stepping forward. "Ares."

I shook her hand and wondered how a teenager had gained so much confidence. Would my children grow up to be as strong as her? It seemed the club didn't keep the women under their thumbs like the Bratva did. Grimm might have put me on lockdown, but it was only to keep me safe, which I understood.

"I'm Sofia," said a pretty Hispanic woman. "I'm with Saint, the club's Vice-President."

"And Savior is the President, right?" I asked.

"Yes. Your husband is also an officer." Lavender motioned for me to sit, and I did. "He's the club's Treasurer. You've already met Tempest, or so I've heard. He's the Sergeant-at-Arms. I'm sure you'll get to meet the other officers soon."

"We didn't want to overwhelm you," Amity said. "There's a lot more of us, and a ton of kids. But the first time the club has a big family gathering, you'll have a few friendly faces in the crowd."

"What's it like living here?" I asked. "It seems

different from what I'm used to."

"According to Katya, it's nothing like the Bratva," Lavender said. "I'd hoped she'd be here."

The women at the table with me seemed happy. Sure of their places in this world. I felt like I didn't belong. I wasn't as strong as they were. Or maybe they'd been more sheltered? I'd felt so incredibly weak when those men took me. No, Grimm mentioned others here had been through traumatic events. Would it be rude of me to ask how they came to be part of the club?

"I can see you have questions," Lavender said. "So, I'll kick things off. I met Wire when I came to ask for his help. He'd known my parents when they were all younger. In fact, he'd even dated my mother for a while. My parents were hackers, like Wire and me. They got into something they shouldn't have, and it cost them their lives. When I started having little accidents, a bit too frequently, I knew I couldn't take them down on my own."

I gaped at her. Sure, I'd shown up at the gate asking for help, but it hadn't been anything like that. I'd felt awkward, and worried Grimm would turn me away. But Lavender sounded so bold!

"Thunder rescued me," Amity said. "He found me on a bridge, ready to jump. Brought me to his house, claimed me. And he hunted down all my demons and made them pay."

"My dad adopted me." Ares smiled faintly. "I was in a bad situation. A few clubs rescued me and a bunch of other women and children. We'd gotten caught up in a human trafficking ring. Dad was one of the ones who came busting through the door to save us."

The doors to the clubhouse flew open and I

tensed, until I saw three women coming through. None of them were very tall, even though they were all older than the rest of us. The way they carried themselves, I could almost feel the air of authority around me. Who were they?

"I had a feeling you would show up," Lavender said. "Let's not scare her off, all right?"

The blonde, who seemed to be the ringleader, gave me a wide smile. "I'm Ridley, Venom's woman. Until recently, he was the VP of the club. Now he's at home, under my damn feet all day."

The dark-haired one nudged her. "And you love it. Tell me you don't, and I'll call you a liar."

"That one is Isabella," Lavender said. "Her husband, Torch, was the President, until he handed everything over to Savior. The old officers stepped down within the past year and decided to let the younger ones run things so they could spend time with their families."

The third one waved, a bright smile on her face. "I'm Darian. I'm with Bull, and he wasn't an officer, but he is Ridley's dad."

Wait. What? I looked from one woman to the other. They seemed to be close in age, but they were… "She's your stepdaughter?"

Everyone cracked up, and I wasn't sure if I should run or stay my ground. What had I walked into by coming here? This place was more than a little strange.

"She gave me hell when we first met." Darian pulled up a chair. "I'm younger than her, so she didn't like the idea of her dad being with someone my age. Until he pointed out she was a hypocrite because Venom is two decades older than her. I'm also related to another club. The Devil's Boneyard."

"Her dad is their VP," Ares said.

"For now." Darian shrugged. "Wouldn't surprise me if that club has some changes coming too. I know Cinder already stepped down and put Charming in charge, but my dad isn't exactly a spring chicken."

"He's only in his sixties. He's not dead, Darian." Ridley rolled her eyes. "Did you forget how old my dad is now?"

Darian winced. "Let's keep that between us. I'm not sure my ass can handle another spanking right now."

"TMI!" Ridley put her hands over her ears. I couldn't help but laugh at the two of them. Although, I had to admit, I was curious about the spanking part of the conversation. Darian didn't seem to be abused. I couldn't see any bruises on her. I'd heard some women liked that sort of thing. Being spanked. Maybe she was one of them. My cheeks burned, and I knew I'd never ask!

"So you're running from the Bratva?" Isabella asked.

"Yes. Nikolai sent me here with a note for his cousin. I didn't realize I'd end up married to him, but I'm not complaining. We get along well, and he makes me feel safe."

"I'm guessing you haven't had that in your life before," Ridley said.

"Not really. My father got involved in some bad things and implicated me. Probably as a way to save himself." I twisted my hands in my lap. "Some men were going to hurt me. Nikolai caused a distraction and got me out of there. Gave me money and a car, along with instructions to come here."

"We already told her our stories," Lavender said. "The three of you want to share? I wanted her to know she's not the only one who came seeking help and ended up getting claimed by a hot biker."

"Did you just call Grimm hot?" Ridley asked, arching her eyebrow. "I'm so telling Wire!"

"If you do, I'll empty your bank account, close out all your credit cards, and drop your credit rating to a four hundred." Lavender grinned at her. "Don't try me."

Ridley huffed but didn't say anything else for a moment. Until she decided to share how she came to be here. I'd assumed it was because her father was a Dixie Reaper. I'd sort of been correct.

"My mother and stepfather tried to sell me to someone. I ran and came straight to my daddy. Except I encountered Venom first," Ridley said. "He'd always fascinated me. When he saved me from a mouthy Prospect, I latched on and didn't want to ever let go."

"Who was the Prospect?" Ares asked. "Are they patched in? Or did they not cut it?"

Ridley's eyes flashed with sadness for a moment. "Pete was his name. He did patch in, but he died about a year ago. He went by Coyote. He wasn't always the nicest guy, and he and I went toe to toe a few times over the years. But I knew he'd have Venom's back, or my dad's."

"My dad refused to help the Dixie Reapers until Torch married me," Isabella said. "I was still in high school at the time. He inked me as his property and sent me back to graduate. Then I ran for a few years."

"You ran?" I asked.

She nodded. "Yep. I wasn't ready to settle down. I didn't realize at the time the man had kept tabs on me. I'd thought I was hiding, but really, he let me have that freedom. It made me love him even more when I finally came home."

"Bull saved me," Darian said. "My somewhat boyfriend at the time drugged me and planned to let a bunch of guys rape me. I managed to get away and ran aimlessly. Ended up outside the gates here. Bull found me. Took me into his home."

"And the rest, as they say, is history," Ridley said.

"Does everyone have a story like that?" I asked.

"Pretty much." Sofia shrugged. "Mine is uglier than most. I have two sisters. They're both with the Hades Abyss. Our father used to let his men abuse us however they wanted. We have physical scars, and mental ones. We've been gang-raped, sold as prostitutes, or given to random men as an incentive to do business with our father. We thought the same thing was happening when Isabella's father brought us here. We didn't realize these men would be our saviors."

My heart ached for her. But it gave me hope. It meant my sister and mother might be able to get the care they needed, and the men who would take them in wouldn't see them as dirty because of what they'd suffered.

I might not know if I could still trust Nikolai, but he'd done me a big favor by sending me here. Because of him, I'd found a wonderful man I was quickly falling for, and I knew my sister and mother would be taken care of. I couldn't have asked for more.

"Have you ever been around a motorcycle club before?" Ridley asked.

"No. Never." I eyed the women. "Is there anything in particular I should know?"

"Club whores," Sofia muttered. "I hate those women. I know they're here voluntarily, but they don't care if a man is taken. They'll still try to sink their claws into him."

"Club whores are women who come to party," Ridley said. "They like the bragging rights of having slept with the men here. Some are hoping to hang onto one and get claimed, but these guys would never fall for one of those women."

"It sounds like the men look down on them."

Isabella nodded. "They do. Mostly. The younger ones are eager to be with them and think those women are awesome. But the older they get, and the longer they're around club whores, the newness wears off. I guess when you see dozens of random women come through the doors year after year, they probably come off as desperate. It's a turnoff for the men."

"Whatever you do, don't grab a man's cut," Ridley said. "Unless it's Grimm's. He won't care because you're his."

"Cut?" I wrinkled my nose and tried to figure out what she was talking about.

"The black leather vests are called cuts," Sofia said. "They're considered sacred. I've seen more than one of these men put a woman on her ass for touching his cut without permission."

I'd certainly have to remember that. I looked at each one of them, noticing they all had one too. Isabella noticed my attention on hers and smiled.

"These are property cuts. I'd imagine you'll have one soon enough," she said. Then she stood and showed me the back. Hers said *Property of Torch*. "Yours will say *Property of Grimm*."

"And that's what the club whores want most. A property cut and old lady status. Even if a biker isn't married, he can claim an old lady. For this club, it's pretty much the same thing since it's forever. Some clubs that isn't the case. An old lady can be dumped and a new one selected later." Ridley waved a hand around the room. "But not here. These men play for keeps. There's no such thing as divorce."

"Never interrupt Church," Ares said. "Women aren't allowed."

"Not entirely true," Ridley said. "When Torch was still President, he called me into Church. There are times our presence is requested. But for the most part, she's right. If you haven't been invited, don't go in there, and don't knock on the door unless it's life or death."

I felt like I was on information overload. Still, I was grateful for all they'd shared. It felt nice to have women to talk to like this. In the Bratva, even the women only spoke with you if they had a reason. Either in an attempt to climb the social ladder, or make sure you understood your place -- under their feet.

I had a feeling I'd really like being part of the Dixie Reapers. The more I got to know these people, the more I wanted to stay.

Chapter Nine

Grimm

Savior's words kept playing in my mind. After everyone left, I'd stayed behind to talk with him. I hadn't known what to expect. Him asking my opinion on an officer's position hadn't even been on my radar.

Every club I knew had a Sergeant-at-Arms, Secretary, Treasurer, Road Captain, VP, and President. At one point, instead of SAA, Tank had been our Enforcer. Then his position changed, and no one filled the Enforcer spot. We'd been without one for a long ass time.

So why did Savior want one now? And why had he pulled me aside to speak about it? He should have asked all the officers at the same time. I wondered if he wanted Prophet for the position because of his interest in Savior's daughter, Ares. Either way, I told him he had my support. I didn't have an issue with Prophet, and he would probably do a good job as the club Enforcer.

I didn't think he'd bring it up in Church until everything was settled with the Bratva and Nikolai. But when he did, I'd gladly vote for Prophet to become our Enforcer. I couldn't say how the others would vote.

I shook my head, trying to focus on what mattered right this moment. I owed my brothers, big time. They'd gone above and beyond for me. Even though the compound wouldn't permit outsiders at the moment, they still threw a party at the clubhouse. There just weren't any club whores in attendance. Slayer and Viking both convinced Nikolai to go hang out with the single men and have a few drinks, which meant Oksana and I had the house to ourselves.

I'd quickly rinsed off, and now Oksana was

taking a hot shower. As much as I'd wanted to wash her, I'd decided to do something better. I couldn't even remember where the damn massage oil came from, but I'd been happy to find it earlier. As I stared at the bottle in my hand, my phone buzzed with an incoming text.

Did you find my gift? What the hell was Kayla talking about? Wait. Gift. She couldn't mean the oil, could she?

I took a picture and sent it with a text. *This*?

She sent back a thumbs-up. At least I now knew where it had come from. I saw the dots appear as she typed. *Check the hall closet for something from Delphine.*

I went to do as she said and found three scented candles. I placed them around the bedroom and lit them before flicking off the lights. It looked like the old ladies wanted to help me out. Or at least, make sure my new wife had a nice time tonight. Had they also planned for Viking and Slayer to come get Nikolai?

I sent Delphine a thank you message, and she responded almost immediately. *You're not done yet. Check your fridge. The next item is from Mara.*

How many things had they hidden around my house? I needed to remember to lock my doors in the future. In fact… I went and did exactly that, so I wouldn't have any surprise visitors at an inopportune time. Then I checked the fridge. A container of chocolate-covered strawberries sat on the top shelf. I took them to the bedroom and thanked Mara.

There isn't anything else, is there? I asked in a group text to all three ladies. My phone buzzed with another incoming message. This time from Lavender. When I opened it, I found a link. What the hell had she sent?

I clicked it and a playlist opened on a music app I

didn't remember downloading. Since it came from Lavender, I decided not to ask questions. I synced my phone to the wireless speaker on the dresser, and a romantic song started to play. It seemed they'd thought of everything.

Thank you, Lavender.

She sent back a heart, and that was thankfully the last message I received from any of them. I went to check on Oksana and grabbed a towel for her when she turned off the shower. Holding it open, I wrapped it around her after she stepped out onto the bathmat.

"I'm able to dry myself," she said.

"I'm aware. I want to take care of you tonight." I gently dried her, then led her into the bedroom. I heard her soft gasp before nudging her onto the bed. I picked up one of the strawberries and held it to her lips. She bit into the fruit, moaning as the juice slid down her chin.

I wiped it off and then licked the juice from my thumb. Her cheeks flushed and her lips parted. I fed her more of the berries, kissing her between bites. When she'd had enough, I had her lie on her stomach and I picked up the oil.

"It might be a little chilly, but I'll try to warm it." I poured some into my palm, then rubbed my hands together. When I smoothed it on her back, she tensed for a moment before relaxing once more.

As I worked her stiff muscles, my cock started to rise. I'd have never thought just touching her back would be enough to make me hard. I took my time, worshiping every inch of her, from her neck all the way to her toes. I nudged her, and she rolled over. I noticed her nipples were already hard, and I could see her clit peeking from between the lips of her pussy. It seemed I wasn't the only one getting turned on by the experience.

I slid my hands along her collarbones, and down her arms, then back again. I used long, slow strokes. Oksana panted, eyeing me as if I were a treat she couldn't wait to taste. I kneaded her breasts and rubbed my palms back and forth over her nipples. Her back arched, and she gave a soft cry. Working my way down, I parted her thighs and ran my thumbs up and down the slick lips between her legs. She was so wet I knew I'd slide right in.

I continued massaging her, digging my fingers into her thigh muscles, and going all the way down to her feet. By the time I'd finished, I was so turned on I worried I might come the second I got inside her. I spread her pussy open and rubbed her clit with my thumb. Holding myself over her, I pressed the head of my cock into her, then stopped. My heart hammered in my chest as I fought for control.

"Come for me, Oksana. Show me how much you love this."

She gripped the bedding and thrust her breasts up. Her neck arched and her eyes slid shut. As she sank her teeth into her bottom lip, I felt her pussy clench on me. She let out a little cry as she came, her hips lifting, as if begging me for more. I kept rubbing her clit, trying to wring out every drop of pleasure. She shuddered and her thighs trembled.

When I felt her coming again, I slid in deeper, not stopping until she'd taken all of me. Fast, deep strokes took me right to the edge quicker than ever before. My cheeks warmed in embarrassment as I came, filling her with my cum. I hadn't been that fast with a woman since I'd been a teenager.

"I feel like I need to apologize," I muttered.

"Why?" She reached up and placed her hand on

my cheek. "That was wonderful."

"I came too fast."

Her lips curved in a soft smile. "Ivan, I didn't have any experience before you. What we've shared so far has been amazing. We both experienced pleasure and shared something beautiful. It doesn't matter if it lasted five minutes or three hours. Although I think three hours would possibly kill me."

I leaned down to kiss her, wondering how I'd ended up with such a beautiful, sexy, sweet wife. She really was perfect in every way. I didn't even care about her Bratva connections. The fact she knew Russian and had been exposed to the same world I'd grown up in only made her my perfect match.

"Then I won't say anything next time, but if I ever fail to please you, I need you to say something."

"Promise." She patted the bed. "I'm pretty sure the oil ruined the bedding. Should we shower again, then change the sheets?"

"We'll order new ones tomorrow. Right now, I just want to hold you."

I slid from her body and rolled off her. Oksana immediately curled against my side and placed her head on my chest.

"Do you want a family?" she asked.

"Yes. Don't you?" I'd thought I'd made that clear by taking her more than once without using any protection.

"I do, but I'm also scared. What if they come for me and I'm already pregnant? I don't know what they'd do to our child."

"Nothing. They aren't taking you out of here, Oksana. If they try, I'll destroy them. Including Nikolai, if it came down to it."

"Just don't die." She turned her face against my

skin and kissed my chest. "I don't want to live in this world if you aren't part of it."

"I can't promise to live forever, Oksana, but I'll always do my best to come home to you. The club sometimes gets into dangerous situations. Not as bad as what the Bratva deals with every day, but things do pop up. Like your situation. I'm sure the old ladies you met today told you a little about their pasts. Everyone has brought trouble to the club at one time or another, and we've always dealt with it. Sometimes we lose people. It's part of life."

"Death is part of life?" she asked.

"Yes. I know the Bratva is violent, and so is being part of an MC."

"Well, I prefer you to be among the living, so please be careful. You've already come to mean a lot to me, Ivan."

I kissed the top of her head. "You mean a lot to me too, Oksana."

Hell, I was pretty sure I was halfway in love with her already. Cupid hit me with a damn arrow the moment I saw her at the gate. There would be plenty of time to analyze my feelings for her later. Right now, we needed to take things one day at a time and try to figure out what the fuck Nikolai had dragged us into.

* * *

Oksana

The days were slipping by, and with each one, my unease grew. Nikolai treated me the same as he always had, except there was something in his gaze I hadn't noticed before. A darkness. I knew the men in the Bratva weren't fluffy bunnies, but Nikolai had always been different. Now I wondered when he'd become like all the others. Had it been gradual?

Overnight? Why hadn't I seen the signs?

The more I watched and waited, the more certain I became... Nikolai was telling half-truths. I didn't think he'd become as evil as the others. Not yet. But he wasn't here because he was on the run, either. No, they had sent here him. He'd admitted as much when he'd been caught talking to Konstantin. I wasn't sure he'd have said anything otherwise. For every lie he told, he'd come back with what he claimed was the truth. Then the story would shift again. He was building a house of cards, and sooner or later, it would topple.

I'd never felt like I truly belonged anywhere until now. If Nikolai, or anyone else, tried to harm my new family, I'd do what I could to stop them. The women at the Dixie Reapers had been funny and sweet, and while I could tell they were all strong in different ways, I still wanted to keep them safe. Katya knew what the Bratva was like, but the others... they'd dealt with different sorts of monsters.

I wouldn't sit back and wait for chaos to hit the club. There had to be something I could do, some way to slow down, if not completely stop, the train wreck heading for us. Katya and Pepper sat across from me. I'd stopped by Katya's house, needing advice. It just so happened, her stepdaughter, Pepper, was also there.

"So what you are you planning?" Pepper asked. "Keep in mind, whatever you do, it's going to piss off Grimm."

"Not exactly," Katya said. She nudged Pepper with her elbow. "Our men don't act out when they're angry. But if you scare him, put yourself in danger, then he's going to be livid and you'll be punished."

I swallowed the knot in my throat. Grimm had been so nice to me so far. What would happen if I pushed him too far? Would he beat me? Or worse...

walk away? Katya seemed to read my mind and reached for my hand.

"Stop. Grimm might be part of our old world, but he's nothing like those men. When I say he'll punish you, it's not like what you've experienced in the past. He'll probably put you under house arrest. Track your every move. Maybe give you a spanking."

Pepper grinned. "But that's not really a punishment."

Katya glared at her. "I don't need to hear that. Do you want me to start talking about what your father and I do in the bedroom?"

Pepper held up her hands. "Nope. I'm good. Far as I'm concerned, me and my siblings were all delivered by a stork. No sex involved."

Even now, when things were getting dire, these women could make me smile. I'd never had anything like this before. They'd all welcomed me without question. Hearing their stories made me feel less alone. I didn't like the fact they'd all suffered in various ways. Still, hearing their stories made me realize I wasn't as broken as I'd thought. I refused to let the Bratva best me.

"What contacts do you have with them?" Katya asked.

"Feliks is at the root of everything. His wife, Raina, has always been nice to me. I've already spoken to her once. She didn't know what he'd done to my family."

"Want to call her?" Katya asked. "We can see if anything happened between her and Feliks."

"I think we need to go bigger. Even higher up than Viktor." I chewed on my bottom lip. But how?

"Bigger?" Pepper folded her arms and leaned back in her seat. "What's that mean exactly?"

"Well, I'm sure that's the right word. Feliks isn't as high-ranking as Viktor, but we could ask Raina if anything happened. It still wouldn't tell us what Feliks was really thinking or feeling. Same for the other men. What if they tell their wives one thing, then do another?"

"She's right," Katya said. "Although, the fact they care what their women think is surprising."

"It's because of Viktor. Once he met Cerys, he changed. Now he demands his men remain faithful to their wives." But that didn't do us any good. If the Vor was the one demanding Feliks go back to his old ways, then where did that leave us? And why was he doing it? I'd heard it had delighted him when Viktor found a woman he wanted to marry and refused to cheat on her. Wouldn't he have wanted the same for everyone?

"So unless we get all the men into a room to talk..." Katya sighed. "How are we going to pull that off? We'd need the main players in this mess, the men from our club, and then we'd have to hope they all tell the truth and don't kill each other."

"You said the men are faithful to their wives. I'm assuming they're protective as well, right?" Pepper asked.

"What are you thinking?" Katya focused on her, and I had to admit she had my attention too.

"What if we got their wives to come here? Or all of us met in neutral territory, or at a halfway point? The other clubs are involved to some extent. If not their hackers, then they went after your mom and sister." Pepper smiled. "I think it's time we all banded together and made the men stop acting like boys. They're like bullies on a playground, all fighting for dominance."

"You like it when Flicker gets pissed at you, don't you?" Katya asked. "Besides, we can't all leave.

There are the kids to consider, and Dessa is in a wheelchair. How the hell are we supposed to sneak out with her? She seldom goes anywhere with us that's outside the compound."

"Can she not get into a vehicle?" I asked.

"She can, but it's difficult for her. She has trouble transferring from her chair. She's gotten better the more she's practiced, but it's not something she can do quickly."

"Hades Abyss?" Pepper asked. "We helped Surge not too long ago. I don't see why they wouldn't let us all converge on them and have the Bratva wives meet us. Since Oksana and her family aren't part of that club, it shouldn't be an issue."

"Until our men lose their damn minds and start bashing in heads," Katya muttered.

"Let's call Raina first and see what she says. Maybe she and Cerys will have an idea." I pulled out my phone and dialed her number, then put it on speaker. She answered within a few rings.

"Oksana?" she asked when the call connected.

"It's me. I'm here with two new friends. Katya and Pepper," I said. "We need your help, Raina. This has gone too far, and I don't want anyone to get hurt. Not any of us, or you. None of this makes any sense."

"I spoke with Feliks," she said. "People have been putting pressure on him since we got married. He kept it from me because he didn't want me to worry."

"Pressure?" I asked.

"They want him to hurt people like he did before. He doesn't have an issue spilling blood, but he won't hurt a woman. Not unless she deserves it, but as a means to hurt her husband or other male family members? No. He won't do it."

I mulled over her words. So Nikolai seemed to be

telling the truth about Feliks being tested. But why him specifically? There were plenty of men who didn't mind doing dirty work for the Bratva, especially if it would elevate their status. I felt like we were missing something. I eyed Katya, and she nodded.

"Raina, has anything happened recently?" I asked. "Before they brought in my father?"

She hummed, and I could hear her pacing. "Well, I heard Feliks talking about some girls who'd gone missing. Do you think your father could have been responsible? Were those girls trafficked by him?"

Yes. I had no doubt. So who were they? Why did the Vor care so much? And how did Feliks tie into everything? My head was starting to hurt, and we hadn't gotten any further than when I'd arrived.

"What do those girls have to do with your husband?" Pepper asked. "I can see if they're someone important to the Vor he'd be upset with Oksana's dad. But why Feliks?"

Katya narrowed her eyes. "Do you think they gave your father a chance to change his ways and he failed to do so? Could they have given him a warning he failed to heed?"

"Ah. Now that's a possibility," Raina said. "If the Vor wanted Feliks to hurt Oksana, Melina, or Yulia, and he instead gave a verbal warning to Ruslan Romanov, then I could see why my husband would be punished in this way."

"Can you ask him?" I eyed Pepper and Katya. Right now, we were only speculating. Even if we knew, it wouldn't help us much. We'd know the *why*, but not how to stop them. If this was just as much about Feliks failing to do as he was told, as it was about my father's crimes, then I didn't see a way out of this mess.

"I'll ask and call back later. And, Oksana, please be careful. The men... they're out for blood right now. If they get their hands on you, it won't be pretty."

The call ended, and I felt emotionally and physically drained. Would this nightmare never end?

Chapter Ten

Grimm

I hadn't put a leash on Oksana, even though some of my brothers thought it would be best. Instead, I let her roam the compound and interact with the other old ladies. She was my wife and deserved the same freedoms the others had. The last thing I wanted was to be her jailer. But today made me wonder if my brothers hadn't been right. The glint in her eyes and the furrow of her brow told me she'd been plotting something. What? And with whom?

Most of our old ladies weren't the type to sit at home and let us handle trouble when it came knocking. No, some, like Pepper, wanted to charge headfirst into the fray in an effort to keep everyone safe. Was Oksana the same way? If so, I'd have my hands full.

"Who did you meet today?" I asked, kissing the top of her head as she wrapped her arms around my waist.

"Pepper and Katya."

Yep. Definitely plotting something. If I asked, would she tell me? Or would I only tip my hand? If she didn't realize I knew she'd been scheming, then she wouldn't put her guard up and I'd be able to observe her more openly. While I didn't want to put her on lockdown, I did want to keep her safe. Anyone who'd been part of this club as long as I had knew the compound had weak spots. More accurately, people tended to be let in through the gates when they shouldn't.

"It seems like you're making friends." I hugged her to me. "Are you happy here, Oksana? I know you haven't had a chance to explore the town, and things have been tense with everything going on."

She smiled up at me. "I'm happier than I've ever been. Yes, I'm still scared someone might try to come take me from you, but I've never felt like this before. Like I belong, and I'm wanted."

I leaned down to kiss her. My lips lingered on hers for a moment. Every time I kissed her, I wanted to do so much more. "You're wanted. Never doubt it. I've done my best to prove that to you every night."

Her cheeks warmed, but her eyes lit up. The massage I'd given her several days ago had helped us bond more. I really did owe the old ladies. They'd come through for us in a big way. Since then, I'd made love to Oksana every night -- and yes, I knew that's what I was doing. It wasn't just sex. Not with her. I looked forward to seeing her when I opened my eyes in the morning and fell asleep holding her close to me. Like Oksana, I was happy. It seemed crazy, with everything going on, but it was true.

I wasn't sure what love felt like. I knew I liked Oksana a great deal. Wanted her by my side for the rest of our lives. But was it love? Or simply a connection I'd been lacking all this time? Sure, I'd used the club whores when I'd had an itch to scratch. When I'd been younger, I'd even had a girl or two I'd liked enough to keep around longer than a few nights. None of it compared to how I felt when I was with my wife.

Nikolai entered the house and paused when he saw us. I didn't know where the hell he'd been, and I wasn't going to ask. I knew Wire was keeping tabs on him. As much as I wanted him to be a good man, something told me he was just as rotten as our fathers had been. I had no doubt my uncle's darker tendencies had gotten him into trouble. I'd never heard what happened to him, but I had a feeling the Bratva took him out. It was probably too much to hope Nikolai would be different. Because he'd sent Oksana to me, I'd let him stay at our house. I'd thought I could at least somewhat trust him, but that seemed less and less likely.

"Nice to see the two of you getting along," Nikolai said. "Sending her here was the right thing to do."

"I think it's time you and I had a talk." I released Oksana. "I have some lingering questions."

I'd found it odd the Bratva wanted Oksana so badly, and yet they hadn't come for her. From what the other clubs said, no one had made a move on Melina or Yulia either. I didn't know what to believe right now. Had my cousin really been trying to save Oksana? Or was she just one small part in this mess?

"I'm going to go say hi to Lavender," Oksana said. "Something tells me you'd rather have this talk without me being present in the house."

I nodded. "You're right. I'll text Lavender when I'm done, and you can decide if you're ready to come back or want to visit longer."

She went up on her tiptoes to kiss me, then hurried out the door. I stared at my cousin, who looked like he hadn't a care in the world. He gave me a smile, but I noticed it didn't reach his eyes. Had he been playing me from the very beginning? Counting on the fact we were blood, and lying straight to my face? It pissed me the fuck off. If I found out he'd had anything to do with what happened to Oksana and her family, I'd tear him apart.

He followed me to the kitchen, and I brewed a pot of coffee. Hell, at this point, I should keep the damn thing full all day. I'd had more caffeine since Nikolai showed up than I typically would. Better coffee than alcohol, I supposed. One was bad for my heart, and the other bad for my liver. I poured us each a cup and took a seat. Nikolai claimed the seat across from me and sipped his coffee. Not a single tremor in his hand. No nervous behaviors at all. He was good, I'd give him that.

"How long do you think it will take for you to get your wife pregnant?" Nikolai asked, staring at his cup. "The way you two go at it, it wouldn't surprise me if you'd knocked her up already."

"That's for me and her to think about. Why do you care?"

He glanced up. "We're family. Of course, I care!"

Right. Family. Except when you're Bratva, family doesn't mean quite the same thing. It's all about using them for your gain. Power is all that matters. So what would Nikolai gain if I got Oksana pregnant? Nothing that I could think of. He wanted a kid, he could go have one with someone else. Unless there was a reason the Bratva specifically wanted a child of mine. I couldn't think of a single reason they would, but they didn't always do things that made sense to normal people. My child wouldn't give them power. Wouldn't benefit them in any way that I could think of.

"Too much going on to take her to a doctor right now," I said. "Besides, it's probably too soon to tell."

I wasn't about to admit some of the old ladies had known within a week of being pregnant. Unless Nikolai made it a point to question pregnant women, I doubted he'd know if I was telling the truth or not.

"What did you want to ask me?" Nikolai asked. "If it's about the Bratva's next move, I have no idea. They aren't keeping me in the loop right now. Konstantin is no longer sharing information with me. Only asking lots of questions."

I called bullshit. He left the house every day and stayed gone for hours. I knew he wasn't lurking somewhere in the compound. He drove through the gates and toward town. He had to be meeting someone. While it was possible he was spending time with one of the local women, I doubted it.

"Why did you send Oksana here?" I leaned back in my chair. "She says you saved her. Sent her to me so she'd be safe."

"You don't believe her?"

"I think you've made her trust you unconditionally. Probably took you a while to groom her. Be the knight in shining armor amongst monsters. I don't buy it. You wouldn't have done it without getting something in return. I'm just trying to figure out what."

He smiled faintly. "I see. So I'm nothing like you. I take after my father, and yours. Is that it? I'll only do something if it benefits me, or raises my rank?"

"Sure. Why not?" I watched him. His jaw tensed slightly, but otherwise, he didn't give anything away. "Prove me wrong. Tell me you haven't been cultivating a friendship with Oksana all this time, knowing you might need her at some point."

"Fine. Maybe I did want something from her."

"You wanted to know if she's pregnant. Is it not her, but maybe her child you want?" I asked. I'd assumed this was about *my* child. What if I'd been wrong and it was only about my wife? What if I was the variable he hadn't accounted for? "Or were you hoping she'd get pregnant with your kid?"

"Sending her here was a gamble. I knew you wouldn't turn away a damsel in distress. As sweet as she is, there was a good chance you'd decide to claim her. It's what the Dixie Reapers do, after all. Isn't it?"

He smirked. "You admittedly moved a little faster than I'd thought."

"And her mother? Her little sister? Where do they fit into all this? You left them behind, knowing they could be in danger. On purpose?"

He twisted his cup on the table. "So now I'm a monster who condones the rape and torture of women? Do you think I do those things as well?"

"Other than the fact we share the same DNA, I know nothing about you, Nikolai. It wouldn't surprise me if you got off on that sort of thing. The fact Oksana doesn't see you in that light tells me you've hidden any darker urges you might have."

"Feliks gave those orders. Not me. Or did you forget?" He folded his arms. "I'm a pawn just the same as everyone else."

No, he wasn't. He wanted me to believe he was. Why? Someone framed Oksana, making it seem like she'd been involved in the human trafficking with her father. It wouldn't have saved her father's life. He wouldn't have been the one to implicate her, even if she'd been told otherwise. It wouldn't have served any purpose, and men like Ruslan Romanov only did things that would benefit them. No, it was someone else. Someone close to her. Someone who wanted to gain something through her suffering.

"You needed to be her hero. But she already considered you her friend. Why did you need more from her?"

"It's cute, the way you're trying to figure out things you could never understand." Nikolai stood. "You might have been born into the same world as me, but you left, Ivan. Gave up your name. Your family. Everything."

"No, I didn't. And you don't have permission to

call me that. I'm Grimm as far as you're concerned. I didn't lose anything, Nikolai. That's what you can't grasp. I gained everything. True family. People who don't stab each other in the back and give a shit about one another." Well, mostly. There were still a few who turned on their brothers, but those were few and far between. "Now Oksana has them too, so why does she need you?"

His nostrils flared and his eyes darkened. "Is that so? You don't think she'll need me when they come for her?"

"No, I don't. Because she has *me*. In case you haven't figured it out yet, I'm the better Volkov. No. Not better. I'm the fucking best. Oksana knows it. Soon, your precious superiors will know it too." I placed my hands on the table and stood, leaning forward to glare at him. "The life you've created is going to crash down around you, Nikolai, and I'll be the one ripping down that wall. Brick by fucking brick. You put my wife in danger. Hurt her mother and sister. I may not be able to prove it yet, but I will, and when I do, nothing will stop me from destroying you."

He sneered and started to walk off. I reached out and grabbed his arm. The disrespect from this fucker was really pissing me off. At least, he'd finally shown his true colors. I'd poked at him enough he'd cracked. Only for a moment, but it was enough.

"You're nothing, Nikolai. A sorry excuse for a man. Pitiful. I bet your dick can't even get hard." He tensed and his face flushed. Ah! Now I got it. "That's it, isn't it? You sent her here, hoping I'd take her to my bed. Then you'd convince her to leave with you and raise the child as yours. Were you going to keep Oksana too? Or throw her away once you got what you wanted?"

He started cursing me in Russian before storming from the room. At least I'd finally figured out part of his motivation for the insanity surrounding us right now. I sent a quick message to Wire.

Nikolai is impotent. Find out what caused it. That may be our clue. He's very interested in Oksana and I having a baby.

Even if it didn't crack this thing wide open, it would at least head us in the right direction. Finally. He'd slipped up. How much longer before the rest came spilling out?

* * *

Oksana

Wire entered the room and Lavender stopped mid-sentence to focus on him. The tension in his jaw and the way his lips pressed together said he had bad news. He held out his phone to her and she read it. Her gaze flashed to mine, and I knew whatever it was had to do with me. Would they tell me?

"How well do you know Nikolai?" Lavender asked.

"He's one of my best friends. Why?"

They shared a look, and Wire left, only to return a moment later with his laptop. Lavender remained quiet while Wire tapped away at the keys. We sat in silence for probably thirty minutes before he let out a low growl.

"Is that your *aha* sound, or the one where I need to lend a hand?" Lavender asked.

"Little of both. Found something I don't fucking like, but I need more."

"Oksana, would you do me a huge favor?" Lavender asked. "Raid the kitchen and bring some snacks that aren't messy, and some sodas?"

"Of course." I stood and headed that way while Lavender disappeared farther into the house. I returned to the living room with a bowl of pretzels, as well as some cheese with crackers. Lavender sat next to Wire with her own laptop out. I didn't know if they wanted me to stay or go, so I decided to take a seat. If they wanted me to leave, they'd say something.

It took them another hour or more before Lavender stretched and smiled. During that time, I texted back and forth with Grimm. He'd asked if I wanted to come home, but I needed to find out what was happening. If I stayed, then maybe Lavender or Wire would tell me what they'd found.

"Think I have something," Lavender said.

Wire looked at her screen, then turned his computer toward her. She scanned whatever was on his device and her eyebrows rose.

"Can I ask what's going on? Am I allowed to know?" I asked.

"This isn't technically club business," Wire said. "It involves you. A lot."

"Should we ask Grimm first?" Lavender asked.

"No. But we're not divulging all this to Oksana right here and now. I'm going to ask Savior to call Church. Then the two of you are going with me." Wire pulled out his phone and called the club president. When he'd finished, we went outside to Lavender's vehicle and rode over to the clubhouse. Grimm pulled up on his motorcycle just as I stepped out.

"You know what's going on?" he asked.

"Not exactly. They said it involves me, so Wire brought me along."

Grimm took my hand, and we went inside. The place seemed a lot dirtier than the last time I'd been here, but at least there weren't naked women lounging around. I'd heard that was a possibility if the club whores were here. Since Savior had said they weren't allowed at the compound right now, I hadn't run into any yet.

We entered what the club called Church and Grimm took a seat, pulling me down onto his lap. The men already present eyed me with curiosity. I hadn't had a chance to meet many of them.

Someone closed the doors after every seat had been filled. Lavender stood behind Wire with her hand on his shoulder.

"I understand why Wire brought his woman, since she likely helped find whatever information he has. Why is Grimm's woman here?" The man's cut said *Warden*.

"Because this involves her." Wire shot him a glare. "For those who haven't met her yet, Oksana is a sweetheart, and good friends with Lavender. Anyone says something they shouldn't, Grimm won't have to get up and pound you into the ground. Lavender and I will make you cease to exist. No driver's license. No birth certificate. No social security number. I could go on, but I think you get the picture."

Warden winced and gave a nod. The man at the head of the table banged his fist on the wooden surface twice, and anyone who'd been speaking immediately shut up.

"I'm letting Wire have the floor," the man said.

"That's Savior, our president," Grimm whispered in my ear. "He's Ares' father."

"Grimm asked me to look into something today in regard to Nikolai," Wire said. "What I found only left me with more questions, so Lavender pitched in. Together, I think we've figured out a lot of what's going on. I also sent an email with the information to

Shield and Shade, since Oksana's family is at both clubs."

"Shade emailed back," Lavender said. "Oksana, Shade is with the Devil's Boneyard, where your mother is staying. They haven't been completely honest with us, and neither have the Reckless Kings."

"What the fuck does that mean?" Savior asked.

"While it's true Oksana's mother was put into a brothel, the images we found after Oksana arrived weren't real." Lavender patted Wire, and he picked up where she'd left off.

"When Stripes rescued Melina, she wasn't as banged-up as she'd have been if those images weren't doctored. Someone wanted us, and probably Nikolai, to believe she'd been raped and tortured. She really did suffer at the brothel, and nearly took her life. Stripes will help her heal, but the fact things didn't seem to be adding up made him keep quiet. He worried something was going on that could further harm Melina."

"So my mother is all right?" I asked, then pressed my hand to my lips, knowing I should have remained quiet.

"She will be," Lavender said softly. "She just needs time to heal from what she's endured, but it wasn't as bad as we thought."

"Her sister?" Grimm asked. "Was that a lie too?"

Wire nodded. "Far as I can tell, the Bratva knows the clubs use hackers. I think they planted that evidence, hoping we'd stumble across it."

Lavender nudged him again and Wire shook his head. She narrowed her eyes at him, nodding. They went through a silent battle for a minute or two before she huffed.

"Since he won't tell you, I will!" Lavender kicked

his chair. "Yulia wasn't hurt by those men like you thought. However, she did suffer a mishap at the school. The students are all female. The teachers aren't."

"Are you saying a teacher put his hands on her?" Savior asked.

"Yes. He didn't beat her up, like the pictures showed, but he did rape her. Kye is going to do everything he can to take care of her. She's in good hands."

"And the Reckless Kings didn't say anything to us either." Savior pinched the bridge of his nose. "Did they think we weren't trustworthy?"

"They worried Nikolai wasn't being truthful. Since they didn't trust him, they didn't want to risk anyone realizing the images weren't real. They had no way of knowing for certain who planted them, or why," Lavender said.

"Which brings us to Nikolai Volkov." Wire tapped on his computer before he started speaking again. "Nikolai is impotent."

Snickers erupted around the table, and I pressed my lips together so I wouldn't laugh too. It wasn't really funny. Well, maybe a little. The way Wire just tossed out the information made me want to giggle. Why hadn't Nikolai ever said something to me? We'd met often for lunch and hung out quite a bit. I'd thought we were close friends. For that matter, he'd been my *only* friend. Was he embarrassed? And what did it have to do with any of this?

"He asked me if Oksana was pregnant," Grimm said. "It made me wonder why he was so curious. I got him to admit he was impotent, sort of. More like his reaction gave him away."

"He pretended to befriend Oksana. For one, he

was in league with her father and part of the human trafficking. I don't have solid proof, but I believe he was sampling the merchandise and caught something, which affected his ability to get hard." Wire ran a hand down his beard. "As a way to get back at Ruslan Romanov for bringing in infected women, Nikolai implicated Oksana in the scheme."

I gasped, unable to hold it back. *What*? Nikolai was responsible for what happened to me? How could he do such a thing?

"The Bratva knew she was innocent, and her father denied her involvement. But someone had ratted her out to the higher-ups. They didn't just take the person's word for it. From what we were able to find, it seems like they researched the matter before making any decisions. However, it made them question if there was a traitor in their midst," Lavender said.

"And there was. Nikolai." Wire looked over at me and Grimm, giving us a sympathetic smile. "Sorry, guys. I know it hurts when you're betrayed, even if you halfway expect it to happen."

"What about Feliks?" I asked. "He ordered those men to take me."

"The Vor is pulling the strings on this operation," Wire said. "Feliks sent your sister to the academy, thinking she'd be safe. He didn't get a say in what happened to your mother. Someone else made that call, and he had no choice but to follow orders. They really did believe your mother knew of Ruslan's activities, and possibly helped. Just the same, he didn't ask someone to hurt her more. He figured she'd suffered enough. As for you, I'm afraid you were bait for whomever sold you out. As we now know, it was Nikolai.

"He wasn't informed ahead of time and only

heard what happened to you. At first, it made me curious. If he'd been the one to betray you, what was the point in running in to save you? Apparently, the Bratva felt the same and it raised a few eyebrows. But maybe that was his entire reasoning… he wanted to keep them guessing. Perhaps they thought he'd only relayed information he'd heard secondhand and hadn't witnessed you take part in the trafficking ring. So, the Bratva beat him, and then gave him a way out."

"So he thought," Lavender muttered. "Those Bratva men are sneaky. He likely thought he was in the clear."

"Konstantin is pretending to be on Nikolai's side," Wire said. "They want to see how much he'll fuck up so they can bury his ass."

"No," Grimm said. "He's mine. He put Oksana in danger."

"I don't think they'll give him to you," Wire said. "But you can ask."

"They're coming?" I asked.

"No," Savior said, glancing at the doors and tilting his head a little. "I think they're already here."

And he was right. A moment later, Viktor, Feliks, and the Vor came through the doors. Something told me a Prospect was going to have his ass handed to him later. Savior wouldn't be pleased these fuckers had just strolled inside like they owned the place.

Chapter Eleven

Grimm

I patted Oksana on the thigh, and she stood. Immediately, I put myself between her and the Bratva men. Viktor took note and smiled at me. The bastard. I didn't know why he found this situation the least bit humorous.

The Vor stepped forward. "Ivan Volkov. I remember your parents well."

"I'm nothing like my father," I said.

"No, I should think not. Your mother, however, was a fiercely loyal and very sweet woman. I imagine she influenced your life a great deal. It's a pity your father's crimes cost her so dearly."

"Isn't that the way things work with your organization? A man fucks up and the entire family suffers. Doesn't matter if they were mixed up in it or not. They have to be used as an example of what not to do, right?" I narrowed my eyes at him. "Well, you're not getting your hands on Oksana. She's mine now."

"We came to talk. Not take your woman." Feliks folded his arms and glowered. "I have my own wife. I don't need another one."

Viktor snorted. "You're still upset Raina burst into tears and started yelling at you for betraying her."

"Since no one would let me tell her anything, she believed the worst of me. I can't blame her. I don't have a pristine past, and I've done horrible things. This is exactly why I didn't want any part of it." Feliks looked away, clearly pissed.

"I know you don't owe us an explanation," Savior said, standing up. "But I think everyone here would like one. Oksana is now one of us, and she's been terrified you would come take her away. So, if you wouldn't mind, can you please tell us what's going on?"

The Vor smiled and nodded. "First, my name is Vadim Ivanov. The men with me are Viktor Petrov and Feliks Sobol. Konstantin Bykov is another of our associates who's had a hand in all this. He's Nikolai's puppeteer, and as such, is currently keeping him busy."

Viktor took a step closer, and I reached back to place my hand on Oksana's hip. I felt her trembling against me. He held up his hand and stopped.

"I don't wish to frighten her. I only wanted to apologize. None of us could tell her, or you, what was going on. Not until we had time to figure everything out ourselves." Viktor gave her a sad smile. "I hope you'll forgive us, Miss Romanov."

"It's Mrs. Volkov," I said. "She's my wife. Didn't Nikolai share that information with you?"

If I'd realized he didn't know, I'd have said something before. Would that have fixed anything or made everything worse?

"*Nyet.*" Viktor shrugged. "But I haven't spoken with him in person this entire time. Perhaps he told Konstantin, and the information never made it to me."

Savior glanced at Viking and Slayer. "The two of you bring some chairs in for our guests. If anyone wants a drink, now's the time to get it."

Oksana tugged on my cut. "Do I still get to stay?"

I nodded. Even if Savior didn't want her here, there was no fucking way I'd kick her out when we were finally getting the answers we'd sought. She deserved to hear everything firsthand.

"Feliks should probably explain about his background a little," Viktor said. "It might help you understand why we used him the way we did."

"I'm a *kryshas* for the Bratva, or enforcer. I collect debts, and when people can't pay, then things get messy. Before marrying my wife, Raina, I not only tortured men and their families, I'd also been ordered to rape their wives or daughters in front of them, as a way to keep them in line. I'm not proud of the man I used to be. My sweet Raina gave me a chance to prove I could be different, and for her, I'd do anything. I haven't touched another woman since the first day I met her." Feliks looked around the table and smirked at us. "I see the hatred on your faces. Yes, the old me deserved it. I didn't enjoy doing those things. I simply followed orders."

"Your orders?" Tempest asked the Vor.

The man nodded, and I knew every brother at this table wanted to make him disappear. It wouldn't do any good. Someone else, just as ruthless, would take his place.

"Ruslan Romanov decided to sell women and young girls to earn extra cash. He did it under our noses and might have gotten away with it if he hadn't made a mistake." Vadim's eyes went dark, and he fisted his hand at his side. "He took two girls who are precious to me. By the time we found them, they'd been violated for weeks. Neither one is of sound mind anymore, and possibly never will be again."

"It didn't take terribly long to discover what Romanov was up to," Viktor said. "We weren't sure if he acted alone, or had business partners."

"He had two," Feliks said. "Nikolai Volkov, and an inconsequential person who's already been dealt with. It was during our hunt, we got word Oksana and her mother were involved."

"I'd met Oksana before and didn't believe she

could do such a thing," Vadim said. "She'd been an angel with innocent eyes. We kept digging, and realized we'd been lied to. Nikolai called from a burner phone and tried disguising his voice. He wasn't aware we knew he'd ratted out Oksana and Melina Romanov."

"The fact he didn't say who he was made you suspicious," I said.

Vadim nodded. "If they'd truly been part of it, he'd have wanted credit for turning them in. It could have helped with his status, or at least earned him a reward. He hid his identity."

My brow furrowed. If they'd believed my wife to be innocent, why had her mother been sent to the brothel? Vadim just said he wasn't sure either of them had anything to do with Ruslan's scheme. So why had her mom still been punished in such an awful way?

"The Vor has often teased me that he's lost his best enforcer, saying marriage has made me soft," Feliks said. "Many have heard him make those comments. While I know he says them in jest, others do not. I still have my position and do my job."

"Nikolai is one of the ones who believed the Vor's words," I said. "Which meant you could set up a test for Feliks to prove he was still capable of following your orders, or at least, make Nikolai believe that's what was happening. So Feliks ordered those men to take Oksana. But what the fuck were you doing with her mom? That wasn't all staged. She really went to the brothel."

"Yes to the first part." Vadim stared at Oksana and I held her close to me. "As for Melina, while I don't believe she took part actively, she still knew of her husband's treachery and said nothing. Even if she hadn't told one of us directly, there were ways she could have let us know we needed to take a closer look at her family. A simple slip of the tongue she could have played off as a moment of stupidity."

"Do you know what those men did to Oksana? Because clearly no one told them it wasn't for real. They tore her clothes. Left bruises on her breasts. Threatened to shove their dicks up her ass and down her throat, so they wouldn't take her virginity and devalue her price. They terrified my wife." I was so fucking furious I wanted to kill someone. "You'll have to pardon me if I think your plan was shitty. I don't care who the three of you are. If you're the ones responsible for putting her in that situation, then I'd love nothing more than to tear you apart and feed your remains to the wildlife. And putting her mom in a brothel for not coming to you? What the fuck? If that's how you do business, it's a wonder anyone remains loyal to any of you."

"We'd thought Nikolai would get to her before anything happened," Viktor said. "We're truly sorry she suffered. There are times a sacrifice is needed. This was one of them. No one else was close enough to Nikolai for him to care if they were being hurt. And her mother needed to be taught a lesson. I may not agree with how it was handled, but we never intended to leave her there for long. It never occurred to us she'd try to take her life."

"Jesus fuck," I muttered. "Next time you think my cousin is a piece of shit traitor, just call and tell me. I wouldn't have hesitated to put a bullet in his head if you explained the situation."

"So Nikolai believes everything that happened was a setup for Feliks, but in truth, it was a trap for Nikolai?" Oksana asked. "Why not just take him the moment you knew?"

She brought up a good point. I wondered how they'd respond. But even more than that, I had a question of my own.

"Why the fuck does he want our baby?" I asked. "I know he can't get it up. Still, he's single and I don't imagine he wants a kid because he can't wait to have a family."

The three men shared a look and seemed almost as perplexed as I was. Great. So they either didn't know about Nikolai's condition, or hadn't realized he wanted Oksana's baby. *My* baby. If there even was one...

Oksana pressed a hand to her belly and whimpered. I kissed her temple and wrapped my arm around her waist.

"We aren't sure," Vadim said. "Perhaps he thinks the child could be leverage if we figured out what he'd done. To answer Oksana's question, we needed Nikolai to remain free so we could ensure it was only two of them involved. We've been watching him closely, hoping he'd reach out to someone."

"So he wouldn't gain money, rank, or anything else by having a baby?" I asked. I didn't much care why he was still free at the moment. I needed to know if my kid would be in danger whenever we had one.

Viktor rocked back on his heels. "Hmm. Not exactly. However, the Vor is closer to those who have families. It might have been an attempt to gain power down the line."

"The planted photos and video," Wire said. "Why did you do that?"

"We know of Ivan Volkov's connection to this club, and that your hacker is world renowned. We've also heard other clubs use them. There was no way of knowing what Nikolai had figured out, if anything. We planted those to see what would happen. Nothing more. In the case of Yulia Romanov, we needed her scared. If you were to access the footage at her school and saw her thriving, you'd have never tried to save her, which would have left her in a precarious position. She'd either still be under our thumb, or Nikolai could have tried to get her. We didn't think he'd hurt Oksana, but he cares nothing for her little sister. She'd have been a bargaining chip and could have ended up in the wrong hands."

"I thought you'd sent men to brutalize my sister and mother," Oksana said softly. "It destroyed me, and it was all just a game to you."

"We used you for another reason," Vadim said. "We knew there was a chance Nikolai would send you to his cousin."

I glared at them. "Why the fuck did that matter? I'm a Dixie Reaper. Not Bratva."

"While there are some parts of our organization we can never change, I would like to usher us into a new era," Vadim said. "Part of that is cultivating relationships outside the Bratva. Oksana gives us a tie to your club. Just as Melina and Yulia will give us ones with the two clubs who rescued them."

Sarge growled. "Are you going to use my wife too?"

"Katya Voronin never fell off our radar. We've known where to find her, as well as you and your children."

"Why did you need another tie to us, then?" I asked.

"Need isn't necessarily the word I'd use. But it certainly wouldn't hurt anything." Vadim sighed. "I need monsters in my organization. And yes, they're a necessity. However, it doesn't mean I want all my men to be like that. Those who hold higher ranks, and are closer to me, need to be hard on the outside and soft inside. Like Viktor and now Feliks. For those who can't change, I'd like the chance to get their daughters into better situations."

"Explain," Savior said.

"If we were to pair some of the daughters with men in your club, as well as the other two clubs, it would give those young women a chance at a better life. A happier one. Their fathers wouldn't use them to climb the social ladder, and I wouldn't worry about them being mistreated by their spouses."

"You expect me to believe you give a shit?" I asked.

"Yes. And if my word isn't enough, let me prove it. We mean no harm to any of you."

"Except Nikolai," Viktor said.

"My cousin put my wife in danger. Wanted to take her and our child. That asshole is mine to destroy."

Vadim held out his hands, as if to beg me. "Please, Mr. Volkov. You must understand. We have to bring his crimes to light and make an example of him. I can assure you, he'll suffer far more at our hands than yours. Besides, do you wish to do that to your wife?"

"What the hell does that mean?" Tempest asked.

"If your Grimm were to torture and kill Nikolai, his wife would have that memory forever. But if you let us have him, he still gets punished without getting your hands dirty." Vadim eyed Oksana. "I can assure you, he'll receive the harshest punishments, and in the end, his life will be forfeit."

"Let them take him," Oksana said. "Please. He's right. I don't want to see you and think of all the things you might have done to Nikolai. Even if he did betray me, he was my friend for many years."

"Fine." I didn't like it, but what the fuck ever. If that's what Oksana needed, I'd give it to her.

"Why do you want a connection to our club?" Savior asked. "We aren't going to do any dirty work for you."

"We don't want you to," Feliks said. "What we'd like is an underground railroad of sorts. Instead of tossing women into brothels, or killing them, we'd prefer to secretly send them elsewhere to start their lives over. That's where your club comes in."

"We can't take them all in," Savior said. "No room."

"We'll give you funds to house them, feed them, and clothe them. We aren't asking you to keep them indefinitely. Only help them start new lives far from the Bratva, and make sure they never return. Your hacker can create new identities for them." Vadim glanced at Wire. "You can do that, yes?"

"We can," Wire said, reaching up to take Lavender's hand. "But even if the club can't do what you're asking, we'll still be happy to provide new lives for those women with our computer skills."

"It sounds like we need to set some terms," Savior said. "But if you're planning to involve the Reckless Kings and Devil's Boneyard, we should call them. Might as well get all the cards on the table at once."

Vadim nodded. "I agree. Perhaps Oksana would like to leave now? I'd imagine this has been a lot for her."

"I'm not sending her out there alone while Nikolai is still running around the place," I said.

"We'll take a break. I want all officers back here in thirty minutes. Tempest, find Nikolai. Restrain him and put three guards on him. The Bratva can take him with them once this is finished." Savior looked my way. "Stay at the clubhouse with her until we know Nikolai isn't an issue anymore."

"I know Oksana wants me to hand him over, but… do I at least get to hit him a few times?" I asked.

Savior cracked a smile. "Sure. I doubt they'll mind if you knock some of his teeth out."

"Not at all," Vadim said.

I stood and led Oksana from the room. This hadn't gone the way I'd thought it would, but if it meant Nikolai was no longer a threat, nor the Bratva, then I was all right with that.

* * *

Grimm led me to a table in the main part of the clubhouse. He pulled out a chair, and I sat, still processing what had just happened. The Bratva and the Dixie Reapers were going to work together? Well, in a sense anyway. I liked the thought of those women getting a chance to start over, like I had. If it weren't for Grimm, I didn't know what would have happened to me. He'd also been the reason Yulia and my mother were safe.

He came back with a bottle of water in one hand and a beer in the other. After handing the water to me, he took the seat next to mine. I had so many questions for him. Was Church always like that? How often did they meet? How did he feel about everything we'd learned?

As much as it hurt my heart to hear about Nikolai's betrayal, I wondered how much worse it was for Grimm. Even if they hadn't seen each other in a long time, they were still family. Despite everything I'd been through, the thought of my father being the one to turn me in had hurt the most. Knowing he hadn't had been a relief. I might not have liked him, but I still loved him.

"Are you okay?" I asked.

"Am I…" He snorted. "*Zaya,* you just found out your best friend is evil. You worried for your mother and sister, thinking the worst, because those assholes didn't give a shit. So, no, I'm not okay."

"None of that had anything to do with you. All those things were about me."

He reached over and tugged on a lock of my hair. "Precisely. The most important person in my life… is *you.* So them hurting you means I'm far from fucking okay. I want to pound them all into the ground. They didn't once stop to think how all this affected you."

I reached for his hand and laced our fingers together. "I'm so glad I came here and met you, Grimm. I was only existing before. Now I get a chance to really live."

"We may be here for a little bit. Want anything to eat? I can either make you a hamburger or a sandwich. I'm afraid we don't keep a variety of food here."

"I'm okay."

He tightened his hold on my hand. "About what I said in there…"

"You mean our baby?" I asked.

He nodded. "I know there may not even be one. I'm not sure why Nikolai wants our child. It can't be for anything good, though. And since the Bratva is taking over his punishment, we may never find out. Not unless he tells me everything when I take a few swings at his face."

"Are you really going to hit him?"

"You bet." He winked at me. "I have to get my pound of flesh for everything he did to you. After all, it's my job to protect you."

I bit my lip and wondered if he'd agree to my request. "Can I be there too?"

"You want to watch me punch him?"

"Yes. More than that, I want to talk to him. I need to know why he did this to me. I thought he was my friend. Was it a lie all along?"

He shrugged. "Honestly? I can't say for sure, but I'm thinking the answer is… yes. He's said just enough here and there, plus what the Bratva said, I think we can assume he befriended you on purpose."

Tempest and the others walked through the clubhouse and out the doors. I hoped he found Nikolai quickly. For all we knew, he could have left the compound. What if he'd left town completely? I knew they'd said Konstantin was keeping him occupied, but how? If he became suspicious, would he run? Or stay and cause more trouble? I knew I wouldn't feel safe with him on the loose.

"Back to the baby…" He cleared his throat. "When do you think you'd know?"

My cheeks burned. "Are you asking when my period is due?"

"Yeah, that."

"Now-ish. It's never exactly when it should be. Sometimes I start a few days early, and other times I'm up to four days late. If I haven't started in a week, then we can make an appointment with a doctor. I'll need one anyway. It's not like I can go all the way up north every time I need to see one." The thought of seeing one didn't give me warm fuzzies, but as long as I had Grimm by my side, I knew I could handle anything. He'd been my rock. My savior. My everything.

Someone started shouting outside, then I heard what sounded like gunshots. Grimm moved so fast he was nearly a blur. He pinned me to the floor, putting his body over mine. More gunshots filled the air, until everything went completely silent. Grimm still didn't budge. At first, I worried he'd somehow been hit, until I heard his ragged breathing. I turned my head and my gaze locked with his, and I saw fear.

"I'm okay, Ivan," I said softly, knowing I shouldn't use his real name right now. I hoped he would either get angry with me, or it would assure him I really was fine.

He stood and pulled me into his arms, hugging me so tightly I could barely breathe. I patted him on the back, then clung to him. I didn't know what happened outside, and I was almost too scared to ask him to check. What if it wasn't really over?

Savior and the three men from the Bratva entered the room. They watched us for a moment before going outside. I heard Savior yelling at someone, and when the doors opened again, two men were carried inside, dripping blood on the floor.

"What the fuck happened?" Grimm asked.

"Let's just say Nikolai didn't want to come peacefully." The man's cut said *Prophet*. The doors opened again, and Ares came running inside. I'd expected her to go for her dad. Instead, she skidded to a halt in front of Prophet. He held up his blood-covered hands. "Not mine. I'm okay."

"Who got hurt?" Grimm asked.

"Gears and Warden." Savior's gaze strayed to us again. "Nikolai… He's gone."

I tensed. "He escaped?"

Savior shook his head. "Sorry. He took a bullet. Probably planned it when he opened fire on the club. I'm sure he figured out the Bratva was here to take him back, and he didn't want to go."

"You're kidding, right?" Grimm asked. "I

wanted to ask that fucker some questions before making him bleed."

"I'll keep looking into it," Wire said. "You want to know why he was after your baby, right? I won't stop until I have an answer."

"It may not have anything to do with Nikolai himself," Vadim said. "You'll need to look into anyone close to him. That includes Grimm. It could be something in their past."

"Fine. I'll start there."

"We'll take the body with us," Vadim said. "As for the other, we'll discuss terms later. Take care of your wounded. I'll get something together and send it to you within a few days. Look it over, then get back to me."

Savior shook his hand, then the Bratva men left. "Someone call Dr. Franz."

"Come on, *zaya*. It's time for us to go home."

Grimm led me out to his bike. Once he swung his leg over the seat, he held his hand out to me. He helped me onto the back, and I wrapped my arms around his waist. He drove slowly, probably so I wouldn't fall off. He pulled into the driveway and brought the bike to a stop.

It took me a moment to get off, then I hurried into the house. The first thing I saw was a book Nikolai had been reading. I picked it up and wondered what else was still here. Everything? Deciding to purge our home of Nikolai and his evilness, I grabbed a trash bag and started tossing all his things inside. When I grabbed the car keys, Grimm snatched them from my hand.

"Not that, and no electronics. We can actually get something for them. I'll have Wire wipe his phone and anything else he has. We can sell the car."

"Do we need the money?" I asked.

"No, but I'll put it into a savings account for a baby. We can sign it over to them when they turn eighteen."

It wasn't an awful idea, but I had one even better. "Or we could set the money aside and wait until our baby is here. Whether that's soon or in a few years. Then we can invest the money into an IRA and put them as the beneficiary."

"Smart." He kissed me. "Sexy. Sweet. You just have it all, don't you? I'm the luckiest man on earth."

My cheeks warmed. "Stop teasing and help me finish clearing everything out. I don't want a single reminder of Nikolai in this house."

"Me either."

We worked for another twenty minutes, making sure we'd purged everything, and he called Wire to pick up the keys to the car and anything else he thought might be of value. Then we both collapsed on the couch and didn't move until dinner.

Chapter Twelve

Grimm

If I could bring my cousin back from the dead, just so I could kill him myself, I'd do it. I felt cheated. Even if the Bratva had wanted the kill, they'd given me permission to throw a few punches. Instead, Nikolai had been a chickenshit and taken the easy way out.

Oksana slept soundly at my side. Neither of us had been up for much of anything, so I'd ordered pizza and she hadn't moved from the couch once she'd sat down. Today had to have been emotionally exhausting for her. Not only facing the Bratva but hearing just how much Nikolai betrayed her. Then getting knocked to the floor when I heard gunfire.

I ran my fingers through her hair and marveled at the amazing woman I got to call my wife. She'd been through so much. Anyone else might have been in tears by now, or ready to give up. Not her. I hoped she realized how strong she was. Then again, I wouldn't expect anything less of an old lady with the Dixie Reapers. She fit in perfectly, not only with me but everyone else as well.

Not wanting to wake her, I stood and slowly lifted her into my arms, careful not to jostle her too much. I carried her to our bedroom and eased her down on the mattress. As uncomfortable as she looked in her clothes, I didn't want to risk undressing her and disturbing her sleep. Instead, I toed off my boots, removed my belt and cut, then slid into bed next to her. Tomorrow started the next part of our lives. We wouldn't have to worry about Nikolai or the Bratva anymore.

Oksana murmured something in her sleep, and I strained to hear her. Tugging her to me, I breathed in her scent. A little smile curved her lips and she spoke in her sleep again. This time, I was almost certain she said *I love you*. My heart kicked against my ribs, and I held her closer.

"I love you too, *zaya*."

She snuggled against me, even though she didn't wake. I had to wonder if subconsciously she knew what I'd said. Even though my wife might be sleeping soundly, I didn't think I would be anytime soon. Now that the danger had passed, all I could feel was anticipation. There was so much we'd get to do together. I could show her around town. Take her for a ride on my bike. Ask the club to have a family night where she could mingle with everyone.

My cousin might have been a piece of shit, but he'd done me a favor when he sent Oksana here. I'd have never met her otherwise, and she was perfect for me. Not only did she understand the life I'd left behind, but she wholly embraced my brothers at the Dixie Reapers, and fit in well with the old ladies. Even though she hadn't interacted with them as much as I'd have liked, the times she'd been around them, she hadn't been scared. Considering her past with the Bratva, it was understandable she'd find both men and women threatening. The Bratva wives would have tried to crush her under their feet, and the men were abusive assholes. She'd done her best to make friends. I didn't need to be psychic to know we'd have a happy life. We were like two puzzle pieces that fit together.

Excitement buzzed under my skin.

I picked up my phone and opened one of the apps for a store nearby and started browsing. My wife still didn't have enough clothes or shoes. She'd need purses. Jewelry. Hair things. I knew she'd want to pick out her own stuff, but I wanted to surprise her. Hell, if she was anything like the other women around here, it would take a while before I could convince her to spend my damn money. Why did the women always think we were dead-ass broke? Didn't they know how much our bikes cost? Even a used Harley Davidson didn't come cheap, but they were worth every penny.

Of course, we also had Flicker and Pepper with their Indian motorcycles. I could admit the machines were pretty, but they weren't for me. I loved my Heritage Classic, but now that I had a woman to ride on the back on a regular basis, I was tempted to check out the new Road King Limited bikes. It would be a more comfortable ride for Oksana.

"Shit," I mumbled. A car. I'd asked Wire to get rid of the piece of shit she'd arrived in, which meant she was now without transportation. Since she wouldn't be on lockdown any longer, I needed something safe for her to drive around town. A vehicle with room for a kid or three, if we were ever blessed with any.

I clicked off the app for the store and headed over to one of the local car lots. After browsing their selection, and checking on the safest family vehicles, I opted for a mid-size SUV, and bought the damn thing sight unseen. My woman would get a brand-new GMC Acadia when she woke up. All I had to do was stop by the dealership to sign the papers and pay for it by a certain time of day. They wouldn't hold it more than a few hours after they opened, but that should be plenty of time.

I knew I had enough money to cover the cost, but I wondered what else I could buy for her, or our home. I started to double-check my bank account when I saw a text from Wire.

With permission from the Vor, I drained Nikolai's

accounts and transferred the money to you. It should be available in your account after midnight.

I checked the time and saw it was already that late. Opening my banking app, I stared at the number on the screen. Blinked, and then stared some more. I couldn't remember ever seeing so many zeros. Where the fuck had he gotten all that? From human trafficking? It made me sick to think of profiting off victims of Ruslan Romanov and my cousin. At the same time, if I didn't accept the money, the Bratva would take it. I knew damn well they'd use at least part of it for illegal shit.

I knew we didn't need all that money. Even if we lived two lifetimes, we'd never spend it all. I could buy a new bike for every brother and still not make a dent. So, I messaged Savior.

Wire transferred Nikolai's money to my account. It's more than I could ever spend. I'd like to give some to the club.

I didn't expect an answer, since it was so late. Ever since he married Dessa and brought those kids home, he'd been going to bed earlier than usual. Couldn't blame him. I knew they got him up pretty early in the morning, and the man wasn't getting any younger.

Still… that was a fuckton of money.

I shopped some of the online stores to buy her nicer clothes and shoes, purchased new cookware, and even ordered some picture frames. I'd never had a reason to put pictures up around the house, but I hoped we'd make a lot of memories over the years. By the time I'd finished, the sun was rising.

I got out of bed, still wide-awake, and took a shower. After I put on clean clothes, I went into the kitchen to start a pot of coffee and figure out what I'd make for breakfast. The dealership wouldn't open for a while, but I wanted to get there when they first opened, which meant waking Oksana soon.

I opted for something simple like bacon and eggs with toast. Once everything finished cooking, and I'd plated our food, I went to wake my wife. She curled into me, murmuring in her sleep, and I kissed her brow.

"Time to get up, *zaya*."

She whined. "Want more sleep."

"I have a surprise for you, but it requires us to leave the house. Come eat breakfast. I cooked for you."

Her eyes opened. "You cooked?"

I kissed her. "Yes. Come on. It will get cold if you don't hurry."

I helped her from the bed and watched her stumble into the bathroom. When she came back out, she seemed slightly more alert. I took her hand and led her to the kitchen. It didn't take long for us to eat, and for her to get ready. Before we left, I texted two of the Prospects and asked them to follow us in a club truck. I'd need one of them to come back with my bike, and the other could follow us. I might be buying her an SUV, but I had a feeling we'd need more room than that.

I'd never been one to spend money if it wasn't necessary, but with so much to spare, I felt like splurging. I not only wanted to spoil my wife, but I wanted to get things for my brothers' kids. And in the event we were ever blessed with children, it wouldn't hurt to go ahead and start setting up a nursery. Even if we couldn't have any of our own, we could always adopt later.

Sam and Owen would meet us as the gate. I helped Oksana onto the back of my bike, then we rode through the compound. The truck fell in behind us as we pulled through the gate, and we went straight to the dealership. Oksana's eyes were wide when we parked, and she tugged on my cut.

"What did you do, Ivan?" she whispered.

"Bought you a car. Or at least, put a hold on one. Let's check it out. If you don't like that one, we can pick something else."

She held onto the bottom of my cut and followed behind me like a baby duck. Someone greeted us when we went inside and showed us to the waiting room until a salesman was available. One joined us a few minutes later.

"Mr. Volkov?" he asked, holding out his hand. "My name is Mike. Ready to see the Acadia?"

"We are. And call me Grimm."

He nodded and led the way. The dark red SUV was pretty, and Oksana's jaw dropped. Mike took his time going over the various features and safety options on the vehicle. He let Oksana sit behind the wheel, and we even took it on a test drive. I could tell she liked it, but the way she worried at her bottom lip made me think she was about to say we didn't need it.

I reached over and took her hand as we parked once more. She stared longingly at the dashboard before looking around the inside cabin.

"*Zaya*, I have more than enough to cover the cost of this car. Please let me get it for you. It's the perfect family car, and since it's brand-new you'll have a warranty if anything goes wrong with it."

"It's so expensive," she said.

"It's not as pricey as some of the ones I looked at. I tried to find something I thought you would like and wouldn't cost so much I knew you'd outright refuse to get it."

She ran her hand over the steering wheel. "We can really afford it?"

"Yep. In fact, I'm going to pay for it outright. They may even drop the cost a little since I won't be financing." I reached up to brush the back of my fingers over her cheek. "Do you like it?"

"You know I do."

"Good. Then let's go sign the papers." I got out of the vehicle and asked Sam to drive my bike back to my house. It took a while to finish the paperwork and get the keys. Oksana smiled widely as she got behind the wheel again, this time to drive off the lot in her new car.

I directed her to the mall and made sure Owen followed. He got out and went inside with us but kept a little distance so I could spend time with my wife. For that, I knew I owed him a beer. I hadn't even had to ask him.

"You just bought me a car," Oksana said as I guided her into a department store. "Why are you trying to buy me more things?"

"Because you need them, and because I want to. Now hush, *zaya*. Let me spoil you."

She sighed and nodded. I wasn't sure how much she'd let me get away with, but I'd buy everything she showed even the slightest interest in. At least for today. I had a feeling she'd have fun when it came time to buy stuff for the kids. Even the teenagers, although I'd most likely get them gift cards so they could come shop for whatever they wanted.

We didn't leave the mall until we'd loaded not only the SUV, but also the bed of the truck. When we got back to the compound, I called everyone to the clubhouse, anxious to give out the items we'd purchased. I'd gone a little overboard and bought things for the old ladies and my brothers as well. Today was a day for celebration, and I wanted to spread the joy.

* * *

Oksana

I knew I needed transportation, so the car was understandable. I'd come here without my clothes or anything else from back home, which meant I could willingly accept new clothes and shoes. But why did Grimm insist on buying all this extra stuff? He'd said he wanted to celebrate. I found his word choice to be odd. His cousin had died. While it was true Nikolai ended up being a bad man, didn't it hurt Grimm at all? He'd lost his last remaining blood relative.

We gave out gift cards to the teens. Fast-food places, clothing stores, and the electronics store. All things they could use and enjoy. The younger ones received toys. Then we'd gifted the old ladies with various things, from spa days to books. For his brothers, he'd picked out things he knew they needed. For Viking, he'd bought a new toolset. Tank received two cases of his favorite beer. Grimm bought a nice lighter for Thunder, since he occasionally smoked. He'd taken the time to find the right gift for each of the Dixie Reapers, and his brothers loved their presents.

"What brought this on?" Venom asked.

"I came into some money. Wanted to share the wealth by treating everyone to something nice." Grimm wrapped his arm around my waist. "And yes, I bought a shit ton of stuff for my wife, including a new car."

"I refused to let him buy furniture for a nursery, since we don't even know if I'm pregnant."

"Speaking of that, I think I know why Nikolai

wanted your baby," Wire said. "Did you know the Romanovs and Volkovs had an agreement nearly three decades ago?"

"What are you talking about?" Grimm asked.

"Ruslan Romanov signed a contract with Nikolai's father. If their children were to marry and produce a child, they would receive the deeds to several joint ventures the men had at the time. I don't think Nikolai became aware of this until recently, or he'd have made a move sooner. Out of those businesses, two were run into the ground. Another closed after Grimm's uncle died." Wire folded his arms. "The others are still up for grabs, and one happens to be a casino in Atlantic City that earns around five million per quarter."

"Twenty million in revenue for the year?" Grimm asked.

"Yep. I don't think Nikolai just wanted the baby. He more than likely planned to marry Oksana, even if she wasn't willing, and once the baby was born the contract would be complete. Even though the Bratva took control of any property Romanov owned when he died, they'd have probably honored the contract for the casino and called it a wedding gift." Wire shook his head. "I'm sure they won't be gifting that to you since they let you keep Nikolai's money."

"What?" I looked up at my husband. "What is he talking about?"

"He transferred all Nikolai's funds to me last night. I wasn't exactly poor to begin with, but now I have more money than I know what to do with. I may not like how my cousin earned that money, but I'd rather use it for good things than let the Bratva have control of it." Grimm rubbed the back of his neck. "It's roughly ten million."

"Are you shitting me?" Savior asked. "When you said you wanted to give the club some money, I figured you'd gained a few hundred thousand. Maybe half a million. I'd planned to refuse your offer."

"If I give the club a million, it has to be used for things that benefit the club as a whole. Things everyone uses, including the old ladies and kids. That's my only stipulation," Grimm said.

"I can live with that." Savior grinned. "For one, we can bulk up our security."

"I'll move the money tomorrow," Wire said. "You'll still have plenty, especially if you invest any."

"I wouldn't even know where to start with something like that," Grimm admitted.

"I don't know a lot, but I did pick up a few things," I said. "I can help you set up an IRA that will start paying out within twenty years. If we do have children, we set up one for each of them."

"I like the way your wife thinks. If you invested the max allowed per year, your kids would be set for life even if the rest of your money ran out." Wire nodded. "Great idea, Oksana."

"You know, if we ever have another pandemic, we'll be at a disadvantage again. It wouldn't hurt to use some of the money to make us more self-sufficient," Isabella said. "Get a few cows for milk, chickens for eggs and meat, and plant a vegetable garden. At least we wouldn't starve if the stores all ran out of food."

"We'd need nearly two hundred chickens to have enough eggs for everyone," Tank said. "Kasen did a project on chickens for school several years ago. They said it takes about four to six chickens to provide eggs for a family of four."

"Okay, so maybe instead of one giant chicken

coop, those who want fresh eggs can just keep a coop behind their homes." Isabella shrugged. "I don't know anything about them, but I do love eggs."

"Let's start with the vegetables," Savior said. "We can set up two acres and see how it goes. If we need to expand, we can discuss it later."

"Now that we've given everyone the gifts we bought, I'm taking my wife home," Grimm said. "Unless the sky is falling, don't bother us."

A few men snickered and my cheeks warmed. I knew exactly why he'd said that. I'd been too tired last night to do more than sleep.

Grimm helped me back into my new car, but this time he drove.

Knowing we were free felt exhilarating. I no longer had to hide. I could fully embrace my life with Grimm and the Dixie Reapers. And I wanted to start right now…

I reached over and placed my hand on his thigh. The muscles tensed under my fingers, and I squirmed in my seat. He gave me a wink that I found far too sexy. It emboldened me and I slowly inched my hand between his legs. He spread them wider, a flush tinging his cheeks as I reached for his cock. I'd never done something like this, and my heart raced.

I had a feeling I wasn't the first woman to grab him like this, but the way he reacted made me feel like the most seductive creature ever. I felt the bulge of his cock and rubbed over the hard ridge in his jeans. He shifted and pressed up against my hand. I gave his cock a gentle squeeze. If we hadn't been right in front of our home, I'd have unfastened his pants and taken things a little further.

Grimm let out a soft growl as he parked in the garage next to his bike. We barely cleared the door before he started tugging at my clothes, disrobing me as quickly as possible. He didn't even bother to take off anything, and only unfastened his pants before shoving them down his thighs.

He slid his hand between my legs and rubbed my clit. I was already wet and ready, which he discovered as he slipped a finger inside me, thrusting it in and out a few times.

"Need you right fucking now," he said before removing his fingers and thrusting into me.

I gasped and gripped his shoulders. The intrusion took me by surprise for a moment, but it didn't take long for my body to adjust. Soon, I was moaning and pleading with him.

"Please, Ivan. I need to come."

"Such a naughty girl," he whispered in my ear. It sent a shiver down my spine. Grimm reached between us to rub my clit. A few swipes were all it took before I was coming. I screamed his name and locked my ankles over his ass, pulling him closer. He drove into me again and again, chasing his own orgasm. When I felt the heat of his release inside me, I came a second time, nearly seeing stars.

"We didn't even make it to the bed," I said.

"Did you think this was a one and done sort of thing? Because it's not. Give me a little time to recover and we're going again. I can do this the rest of the day and through the night."

My eyes went wide, and I wondered if I'd be able to walk tomorrow. He lifted me before shuffling his way across the house. His pants had slid farther down and were now around his knees, but he didn't stop to pull them up. We made it to the bedroom, and he tossed me onto the bed before removing his clothes, then he stretched out beside me. He'd said he needed to rest, but apparently, he didn't think I did. Instead, he used his recovery time to play my body like it was his favorite instrument. Between his lips, tongue, and fingers, he drove me wild and made me come so many times I worried I might not survive.

His lips closed over my nipple, and he sucked on it long and hard. I gasped and arched my back, wanting even more. He worked my clit with his thumb while thrusting two fingers in and out of my pussy. Another orgasm was so close yet just out of reach. I wanted to touch him. To put my mouth on him. I slid my hand up the outside of his thigh and rested it on his hip. As badly as I wanted to reach for his cock, I didn't think he'd let me. Not yet.

He rubbed my clit faster and drove his fingers in deeper. On the third stroke, I came, screaming out his name. Something told me I'd be hoarse by morning, but it was so worth it.

"Death by sex… if that's a thing, you just may kill me," I said when he reached for me again.

He chuckled. "Not that I'm aware of, but if you need to rest, we'll stop for now. Can't have you too tired to do this again tomorrow night."

He kissed my shoulder, and I sighed in contentment. Of course, if my pussy hurt in the morning, I'd be banning him from touching me tomorrow. Or I'd try. If he really wanted me, I had a feeling I wouldn't be able to say no. The man's kisses made my toes curl.

"I love you, Ivan," I said softly. "I know it's really soon to be saying that, but after all we went through, I don't want to go another day without telling you."

"I love you too." He kissed me softly. "But for the record, you told me last night. In your sleep."

I gasped. "Are you serious?"

"Yeah." He smiled. "Sweetest words I ever heard."

At least it hadn't sent him running. I knew the L word did funny things to some men. I didn't know how I lucked out with such an amazing husband, but I'd make sure he knew how much I wanted him for the rest of our lives. He meant everything to me. Not only had he saved me from the Bratva -- or would have if they'd actually been the enemy -- but he'd also protected me from Nikolai. I'd never met anyone like him before.

I pressed a hand to my belly, hoping we'd made a baby. I couldn't think of anything I wanted more than to have a family with this incredible man.

"Now… where were we?" he asked. Before I could process what he was doing, he'd lain down on his back and reached for me, dragging me onto his chest. He tapped his lips. "I want your pussy right here."

My cheeks burned. "What? Are you serious?"

He nodded. "Come on. Ride my face and come for me. Be bold, my beautiful wife."

I swallowed hard and did as he said, placing my knees on either side of his head before lowering myself. He licked me and I spread my legs a little more. I had to admit, it felt really good. Grimm placed his hands on my hips, then sucked my clit into his mouth. I squealed and tensed in shock, but it only lasted a moment before I was panting and moving my body as I silently begged for him to make me come.

He moved his hand over my ass and between my legs. As his mouth tormented my clit, he thrust his fingers into my pussy, and I felt his other hand slipping farther back. When he worked his fingers between my ass cheeks and brushed over that forbidden spot, I came instantly. I'd never known such a thing was even possible!

I rode out my orgasm, but he didn't seem to be finished with me. His hold on me tightened, and he made me come three more times before relinquishing me. I toppled to the side, only to have him flip me to my stomach and enter me from behind. Fisting the covers, I became mindless with pleasure as he took me slow and deep.

Yeah, my husband was definitely going to kill me with sex... but I wasn't sure I minded.

Epilogue

Four Months Later
Grimm

"Ivan Volkov, there's much we need to discuss," the Vor said on the other end of the phone.

"One, my name is Grimm. Two, I already said everything I needed to say. Unless you're going to apologize to my wife, her sister, and her mother."

"Your hacker sent us the contract in regard to a Volkov marrying a Romanov." I heard papers shuffling. "We let you have Nikolai's money to repay you for all the trouble we caused for your wife. Are you trying to get more from us?"

"*Nyet*. I don't know why Wire sent that," I said. "I never asked him to."

"So you have no interest in owning the casino?"

"None."

The Vor grunted. "Fine. However, in spite of your uncle's and father-in-law's treachery, I'd like to at least offer you a portion of the quarterly profits for the next ten years. You can do whatever you want with the money. Give it away. Save it for your children."

"Which brings up a good point. The contract said there had to be a kid."

The Vor started laughing and I stared at my phone. What the fuck had I said that was so funny? I started to ask when I looked up and saw the expression on my wife's face. It seemed the conversation I needed to have wasn't with Vadim, but with Oksana. How the fuck had he known before me? Was that in the paperwork Wire sent him? And if so, why did *Wire* know before I did?

"You're pregnant?" I asked Oksana.

She nodded. "I found out yesterday. I wanted to

surprise you. Had it all planned."

"How far along?" I asked, hanging up on Vadim before we'd even finished the call. I no longer cared what he had to say. My entire focus was on my wife. My *pregnant* wife. Holy shit!

"Two months," she said. "The doctor said everything looked good. I want you to go with me next time. I didn't want to get your hopes up only to find out it was nothing. Otherwise, I'd have asked you to come this time."

I wanted to smile even more, hearing she'd gone to the doctor on her own. When she'd first arrived, Dr. Myron terrified her. She couldn't stand for him to look at her or touch her. Now she was making appointments on her own and leaving the compound whenever she pleased. I couldn't have been happier at how much she'd healed since coming here.

My frightened woman now proudly stood tall. She'd come so far. I knew part of it was the way my club accepted her. The ladies here had been wonderful to Oksana, and they'd given her the friendship she so badly needed. She had a support system. A true family, and it seemed soon, the club would be expanding again with the addition of our own little one.

"We need a nursery! See, we should have set one up before."

She rolled her eyes at me. "Ivan, we have time. The baby isn't going to pop out of me tomorrow. Why don't we at least wait until I'm far enough along to find out the sex of the baby?"

"I don't like it, but fine." I pulled her into my arms, being extra careful with her. "You're really pregnant?"

She pulled out a small piece of paper and I

realized it was a sonogram picture. I didn't know what the hell I was looking at, but it didn't matter. Somewhere on that image was our baby! I was going to be a father, and I couldn't have been more excited.

"What did the Bratva want?" she asked.

"How did you know?"

"You looked ready to murder someone. I figured it was them."

She wasn't entirely wrong. They'd called more than once over the last four months, and each and every time, I wanted to throat punch the bastards. I didn't know why they kept bothering us. Their deal wasn't with me, but with Savior.

"Wire sent them the contract about the casino. Vadim asked if I planned to ask for it after they gave us Nikolai's money."

"And you said?"

"No. I told them no." I kissed the top of her head. "He offered me quarterly payments for ten years from the profits, saying we could do whatever we wanted with the money. So, my perfect little wife, what should we do with the extra funds?"

"Well, the Bratva wants us to help rehome women, but they're footing the bill. I think it's great. But it makes me wonder about women who live around here. Do they have a way to start over if they need to escape their lives?"

"You mean like a battered women's shelter or something? I don't know what they're called to be honest." I winced. "But is that what you meant?"

"Yes, that's what I meant. I'd like to either donate money to them, or give them items they may need like clothes, kitchen items, beauty products. I'm sure a lot of them have to leave their homes with nothing but the clothes on their backs, much like I did. Except I didn't run away from home."

"I think some of the other clubs we know have done something similar. We do a toy run every Christmas for the local kids who wouldn't have anything under the tree. It's not enough, though. We should do something year-round."

She went up on her tiptoes to kiss me. "Then let's donate stuff to the women's shelter as well as to underprivileged children."

"I'll talk to the club in case they want to help. If not, we'll handle it ourselves." I cupped her cheek. "You're an incredible woman. Did you know that? So kind. Beautiful. Smart."

She shook her head. "I'm ordinary, Ivan. But it makes me feel all warm and tingly to know you see me that way. You're pretty wonderful too, you know. There's not another man like you anywhere in the world, and I'm the lucky one who's married to you."

I pressed a hand to her belly. "And carrying my kid."

She smiled softly. "Let's go tell everyone."

"Wire knows, so I'm sure the rest of the club does too. We'll just let him spread the word. Right now, I think we should go practice for when it's time to have the next one."

She looped her arms around my neck, and I picked her up. "I like the way you think, Mr. Volkov. Show me how much you love me. Need me. Can't live without me."

"I *can't* live without you. If you were to die tomorrow, I'd follow you to the grave, because a world without you in it… that's not a place where I want to live." I kissed her soft and slow. "It's not until death do us part, *zaya*. I will love you in this world and the next. You're mine for an eternity."

I spent the next hour showing her I meant every word. *Thanks, Nikolai. I know you're roasting in hell, but thank you for my wife. She's the best thing to ever happen to me.*

"There's one thing I'd like, now that everything is officially over," she said.

"And what's that?"

"To see Yulia and my mother." She hugged me tight. "Please, Ivan. I haven't even been able to speak with them. I know they must be scared and worried. Why can't we go visit them? Every time I've asked, you've said no. It's been months!"

"They both have their own issues to deal with, Oksana, and it's not my call. Your mother is Stripes' wife, which makes her property of the Devil's Boneyard. As for your sister, the Reckless Kings took her in. It's up to Beast, and Kye, whether or not anyone goes to see her. I'm not sure either are ready yet."

She worried at her bottom lip, and I tugged it from her teeth before she made herself bleed. "Can I at least call them?"

I sighed and knew I'd have to give in. It didn't mean Stripes or Kye would actually allow her to speak to the women, but she could try. Maybe that would be enough for now. I took out my phone and called Stripes, putting him on speaker.

"What?" Stripes asked instead of a normal greeting when the call connected.

"Hello to you too, fucker. My wife is going nuts wanting to check on her mom. Can she talk to Melina?" I asked.

Stripes sighed. "Am I on speaker?"

"Yep." I winked at my woman. I knew Stripes wouldn't say anything bad with her listening. Technically, he was now her stepfather. Shit. That made him my father-in-law. Sort of. Hmm. Now there was a way to get to the man. "You know, my wife's father was a piece of shit. I'm sure she's also excited about having a new daddy."

Oksana's eyes went wide, and she smiled broadly. "He's right. Do you care if I call you Dad? Or is that too presumptuous?"

And that's when I knew we had him. If there was one thing Stripes had always wanted, it was a family. Finding out he had a granddaughter had been the highlight of his life. Now he had two daughters by marriage. It wasn't like the man was old. He could even still have more kids with Melina, if she were capable of conceiving. I knew a lot of times the Bratva would sterilize the women in their brothels. I hoped like hell she hadn't been through that.

"Oksana, I'd be honored to be your dad, but your mom… she's in a bad place right now. I'll be happy to tell her you called, but I don't think she's ready to speak with you yet. Give her a few more weeks. I promise we'll call you, or even come see you, as soon as she's ready. What they did to her… it's taken a toll. Mentally, emotionally, and physically. You understand?" Stripes asked.

"Yes, Dad. I do. Just tell her I love her, and I can't wait to see her again. I want to introduce her to Grimm." She glanced up at me. "And… when you think she's ready to know, you're going to be grandparents. I found out I'm pregnant."

I'd have sworn I heard the man sniffle. He cleared his throat and I heard how hoarse his voice had become and knew I was right. He was trying not to cry. The big ol' softie!

"That is wonderful news, my new daughter. We'll visit when we can. Until then, make sure Grimm gives you my number. We can talk as much as you want."

We ended the call, and I tried Beast's number. I didn't have Kye's, but knew I needed to at least get an update on Yulia for Oksana's peace of mind. He answered almost immediately.

"Hello," he said.

"Beast, it's Grimm. I don't have Kye's number, but Oksana wanted to check on her sister. Do you know how Yulia is doing?" I asked.

"She's… not doing so great. We're doing the best we can for her, and I hope she'll heal over time. I've already had words with the Bratva about the torture she suffered by seeing that video, and thinking those men would come hurt her, in addition to what she went through with her teacher. They're offering a large amount of money to appease us. It's not nearly enough, but I'm going to put it into an account for her and Kye. They can use it however they see fit, or just let it sit until they know what they want to do with it."

"Can I not speak with her?" Oksana asked.

"No, honey. I'm sorry, but you can't. I'll let Kye know you called to check on her, and I'm sure he'll let her know you love her and hope she'll be okay soon. That's probably the best we can do for the moment."

Oksana sighed and nodded, looking dejected. I knew it wasn't what she'd wanted to hear, but it was no less than I'd expected. But Beast's words made me wonder about Melina. If they'd given money to Yulia, then they surely owed something to Melina as well. I'd send Stripes a text and let him know he needed to pursue that. Maybe it would show Melina the Bratva admitted they'd made a mistake and help with her healing process.

"If Yulia needs anything, please let us know,"

Oksana said. "I miss her."

"I'm sure she misses you too," Beast said. "I'll make sure you're the first person to know when she's ready for visitors."

By the time our calls were done, and I'd messaged Stripes, I knew my sweet wife would be worrying herself to death until she got to see her family with her own eyes. Until then, I'd just have to keep her distracted. Setting up the nursery was an excellent start.

"Come on, *zaya*. Let's take a look at the room we'll use for the nursery and get some ideas. I know you want to wait, but we could at least get the furniture."

She nodded and leaned into me. "All right. We can do that, and then send the pictures to Stripes. I want to include him in everything."

Our lives weren't quite perfect, but close enough. In time, Melina and Yulia would thrive, and Oksana's family would be complete once more. I'd shower her with love and knew my brothers and their women would as well. She'd found a home with us, but more importantly, my house had *become* a home because of her. She was my world, and I'd spend the rest of my life making sure she knew it.

Harley Wylde

Harley Wylde is the International Bestselling Author of the Dixie Reapers MC, Devil's Boneyard MC, and Hades Abyss MC series. When Harley's writing, her motto is the hotter the better -- off-the-charts sex, commanding men, and the women who can't deny them. If you want men who talk dirty, are sexy as hell, and take what they want, then you've come to the right place. She doesn't shy away from the dangers and nastiness in the world, bringing those realities to the pages of her books, but always gives her characters a happily-ever-after and makes sure the bad guys get what they deserve.

The times Harley isn't writing, she's thinking up naughty things to do to her husband, drinking copious amounts of Starbucks, and reading. She loves to read and devours a book a day, sometimes more. She's also fond of TV shows and movies from the 1980s, as well as paranormal shows from the 1990s to today, even though she'd much rather be reading or writing. You can find out more about Harley or enter her monthly giveaway on her website. Be sure to join her newsletter while you're there to learn more about discounts, signing events, and other goodies!

Harley at Changeling: changelingpress.com/harley-wylde-a-196

Changeling Press E-Books

More Sci-Fi, Fantasy, Paranormal, and BDSM adventures available in e-book format for immediate download at ChangelingPress.com -- Werewolves, Vampires, Dragons, Shapeshifters and more -- Erotic Tales from the edge of your imagination.

What are E-Books?

E-books, or electronic books, are books designed to be read in digital format -- on your desktop or laptop computer, notebook, tablet, Smart Phone, or any electronic e-book reader.

Where can I get Changeling Press E-Books?

Changeling Press e-books are available at ChangelingPress.com, Amazon, Apple Books, Barnes & Noble, and Kobo/Walmart.

ChangelingPress.com

Printed in Great Britain
by Amazon